Sarah Pearse lives by the sea in South Devon with her husband and two daughters. She studied English and Creative Writing at the University of Warwick and worked in Brand PR for a variety of household brands. After moving to Switzerland in her twenties, she spent every spare moment exploring the mountains in the Swiss Alpine town of Crans Montana, the dramatic setting that inspired her debut novel, *The Sanatorium*, which was a Reese Witherspoon Book Club pick and became an instant *New York Times* bestseller and a No.1 *Sunday Times* bestseller. *The Retreat* was also a *Sunday Times* bestseller and No.1 Kindle bestseller. *The Wilds* is her third novel.

You can find Sarah on X @SarahVPearse and Instagram / TikTok @sarahpearseauthor

Also by Sarah Pearse

The Sanatorium
The Retreat

SARAH
PEARSE
THE
WILDS

SPHERE

SPHERE

First published in Great Britain in 2024 by Sphere
Simultaneously published in hardcover by Pamela Dorman Books/Viking,
an imprint of Penguin Random House LLC, New York, 2024
This paperback published in 2025 by Sphere

3 5 7 9 10 8 6 4 2

Grateful acknowledgement is made for permission to reprint an excerpt from
'The Cartographer Tries to Map a Way to Zion' by Kei Miller © Kei Miller, 2014, published
by Carcanet, reproduced by kind permission by David Higham Associates.

A CIP catalogue record for this book
is available from the British Library.

ISBN 978-1-4087-2996-0

Typeset in Minion by M Rules
Printed and bound in Great Britain by Clays Ltd, Elcograf S.p.A.

Papers used by Sphere are from well-managed forests
and other responsible sources.

Sphere
An imprint of
Little, Brown Book Group
Carmelite House
50 Victoria Embankment
London EC4Y 0DZ

The authorised representative
in the EEA is
Hachette Ireland
8 Castlecourt Centre
Dublin 15, D15 XTP3, Ireland
(email: info@hbgi.ie)

An Hachette UK Company
www.hachette.co.uk

www.littlebrown.co.uk

To my father, the kindest and bravest person I know

The rastaman thinks, draw me a map of what you see
then I will draw a map of what you never see
and guess me whose map will be bigger than whose?
Guess me whose map will tell the larger truth?
Kei Miller, *The Cartographer Tries to Map a Way to Zion*

Prologue

The van comes to life at night: there's a warmth inside when the lights are on, an intimacy that makes me feel cocooned. It softens the van's hard edges: the blocky, utilitarian shapes of the stove and fridge, the packets of food stacked up by the sink.

But it's also the time of day when I feel most vulnerable.

The van reveals everything when shadows start to creep over the land outside, the lights illuminating exactly who I am, what makes me tick. Not just my possessions – my books and paintings, but my foibles and routine. Every little movement I make.

Although I try not to think about it, it's frightening, imagining what the van looks like from outside, small, isolated, the sole thing lit up among the darkness.

I glance through the window. The park is almost properly dark now; trees nothing more than opaque imprints against the sky. Night seems to creep over the land quicker here, a sudden plunge into gloom.

Even in dusk, this has become my favourite part of this place – this view – the river snaking a line through the valley, the trees behind rising to villages at the foothills of the mountain. Cloud seems to permanently hover above the roofs, as if the houses have taken a breath, collectively exhaled.

I turn back, my gaze pulled to the piece of paper on the table in front of me.

With every line I've drawn, I've left pieces of myself. First kisses. The rooftop hideout. Bonfire fields that turn the sky to glow.

For a moment, I'm transported back to when I first arrived. Sticky spills of warm beer. Laughter.

I smile. It falters.

A noise from outside. Not the usual soundtrack to the national park – birdsong, leaves being dusted down by the wind – but something more deliberate.

Footsteps, scuffing through the dirt.

All at once, the small space inside the van becomes even smaller, walls contracting, closing in. The space no longer seems cosy; but cloistered, airless.

I hold my breath, send another glance through the window.

The darkness outside reveals nothing. Only shifting shapes, the faint outlines of branches reaching out to one another.

But then there's a clang. Metal on metal.

My insides fold, then fold again. I remember what Mum used to call it: *gut origami*.

Standing up, I snatch the piece of paper from the table, frantically looking around.

I need to hide it.

Bending down to the cupboard, I bump into the shelf and knock over the salt grinder. The lid isn't screwed on properly, and salt scatters across the floor.

When I drag my gaze up, there's a face at the window.

My body does a hard stop. Blood, breath, heart – nothing moves.

Despite the shadows, I can see it: anger.

I take a breath but make no move to run. No surprise, more resignation.

Perhaps, deep down, I knew it would end like this.

Maybe, from the very beginning, the narrative was set.

You can't outrun a monster.

I should have known that from the start.

1

Kier

Devon, July 2018

I read the other day that people who like to travel have a certain gene. An actual, bona fide, wanderlust gene.

It's called DRD4 7R and it apparently influences your dopamine levels, your tolerance for risk-taking – basically, the behaviours common in people who love to travel.

Now I'm checking out everyone, no matter what tribe – the luxe travellers, the culture vultures, the vanlife crowd – imagining us all sharing the same piece of rogue DNA.

I told Zeph about it yesterday and he laughed. Said the only thing we all have in common is that we're escaping something. Or someone. It's a Zeph thing to say, to veer into melodrama. It's the chef in him, his friend said. They're *creatives*, thrive on emotion, drama.

His friend's right, I think: Zeph's cooking our breakfast now, all big, bold gestures that leave no room for doubt. Loudly cracking the eggs against the pan, he drops them into the tomato stew to poach.

Huevos rancheros. Our favourite. The best thing to cook in a van. Eggshells tossed in the trash, Zeph rubs his head, palm rasping against his buzz cut. His features soften, he's done the hard work, making the stew itself – frying the onions to translucency, adding peppers, chillies, and garlic, then bay leaves, tomatoes, seasoning. It's now thick, reduced.

Lifting a spoon to his lips, he tastes, smiles. I can't help but smile too. I love watching him cook; it's the only time he isn't fighting a part of himself.

'Nearly there.' Sensing me watching, Zeph reaches for a buckwheat pancake, lightly frying it in the pan on the other hob, already sizzling with fat. 'Hungry?'

'Starving.' I look out to sea. The breeze is tearing navy slashes through the turquoise, ragged lines pulling from left to right.

We designed the van so that the kitchen faces out, to take in views like this. And this view is something special. Although I've travelled all over, this stretch of Devon coastline will always be my favourite – tiny coves of sand and pebble, rust-red cliffs, and trees that creep right down to the water.

I learnt to swim in this water; kissed in this water; washed bloody, rock-grazed knees in it. I feel the rhythm of it inside me even when I'm miles away.

Zeph hums under his breath as he switches off the hob. Eggs done, he takes the pan to the table, balancing the pancakes and a bowl of grated cheddar on his arm.

I follow with the stew, place it on the table, pushing aside the map I'm working on.

Heaping cheese on the pancake, I spoon egg and stew on top, then greedily push it into my mouth. Texture first, the bite of the pancake, soft egg, before flavours hit, little fireworks of taste. 'Amazing.' I wipe my mouth, take another bite.

Zeph smiles, blue eyes creasing at the corners. This is what he does; takes something that could be ordinary and makes

2

it explode in your mouth. He was a chef until a few years ago, ran a successful restaurant in New York. His thing was doing meat and vegan food together way before vegan became fashionable.

Soon, his vegan stuff was all people talked about. For a while, he was *everything*. He was named Best New Chef in *Food & Wine* magazine, did a TEDx Talk, made it into *Forbes'* list of All-Star New York Eateries three years in a row, and was even nominated for Rising Star Chef in America by the James Beard Foundation.

He told me stories of celebrities who'd book out the entire restaurant, all show, and ones who came in incognito, cap pulled down low over their face. I looked him up online and found hundreds of articles – insider and feature pieces, various interviews and reviews on social media.

It became a thing for a while for people to go in, have their photo taken with him. You know the kind of shots – moody-looking chef, over-enthusiastic guest getting a little too close.

And he looked good in these photos; just the right kind of sweaty, one of those ironic nineties bandanna things in a lurid print that popped against his whites.

A stark contrast from when we met, during what he always describes as his 'downwards spiral'. I was in Italy, Liguria, travelling. He was on a break. *Burn out*, he told me, but I later found out he'd been fired.

On the back of three years of rumbling complaints, a sous-chef sued him. After nearly severing his finger with a knife, the sous-chef tried to leave to go to hospital, but Zeph asked him to superglue it together instead. The final straw apparently, after months of warnings from his backers. Bad press. *People want a bad boy, but not too much*. The superglue story went viral, and the tide turned against him. He became a pariah.

Not to me. The night we met he charmed me. Cooked up fat

shrimp on the grill and told me stories that not only made me laugh but stole my heart piece by tiny piece.

'So, I want your thoughts on the map.' I take out the canvas, lay it on the table. I've painted it for my brother, a surprise wedding present for his fiancée.

'Beautiful.' He forks egg into his mouth. 'She definitely doesn't know about it?'

I shake my head. 'She thinks I'm just working on the stationery for the wedding.'

It will be Penn's surprise, but it's no surprise to me that this will be his gift to her. These maps ... they're our thing, me and my brother.

My love of cartography started with my mum's map collection. Her family were nomads, and she told us she hated leaving the places she loved. Places that held memories and places that were memories in themselves. Her way of carrying them with her was to take maps to remember them by.

I spent hours studying them as a kid, rolling the place-names over my tongue, working out their geography in my head, but after a while, I realised that while they told me about the place, they revealed nothing about *her*, what she'd done there, where she ate, danced, who she loved. What set her heart on fire.

So, for Mum's birthday, I decided to paint *our* map of our town: places where we'd left little pieces of our soul.

The landmarks weren't hospitals or garages, but the bakery I went to with Mum while Penn was playing cricket. My grandparents' house, where Christmas came alive in games and laughter. The beach where I learnt to swim, where I'd come to have the last normal conversation with our mother, a place that even now, when I think about it, the words float above my head like stars.

My favourite thing to do with friends is to get them to draw

4

their own map. It reveals so much about who they are, what they value. I've discovered that while most people move somewhere for practical reasons – budget, commuting distance – what ends up on their maps are the places that creep into their souls, places that make them feel alive. Free.

Work rarely features, even with people who say they live for their jobs. Instead, they draw their parents' home, the gym that became their only contact with the outside world after their partner died, or the park where they chew the fat with friends every Friday.

Zeph's still examining the map. 'You're nearly done?'

'Just about, only the last few points. I'm going to show Penn at the weekend, see if there's anything he wants me to add.'

A pause. He pushes his plate aside. 'So now you've finished, are you going to start the artwork for the book?' An edge layers his voice. Zeph's talking about the cookbook. Luxe van food, street food. The kind of thing you can cook on a two-burner. A collaboration: his recipes, my illustration.

'Course.' I tear at the last pancake, dip it in the stew. 'Have you done something different? More garlic, maybe, in the stew?' Dipping my fork in, I make a fuss of tasting it.

It's the knife that forewarns me – the clatter of it against the plate.

I stiffen.

'Different?' He mimics me. 'Have you done something different?' Standing up, he grabs his plate. 'Let me guess, it's not quite right, is it?'

Time slows. I'm suddenly acutely aware of everything; the hot pulse of the blood in my temple, the acute angle of his plate – tipped towards the floor, the watery, rusty rivulets of stew slowly dripping down the china.

I'm conscious of any tiny little movement of my face, as if

somehow the right expression might have an impact on what's to come next.

'If you don't like it, you know what you can do—' He gestures tossing it out of the van, a wonky smile sitting alongside those words, his lips drawn tightly across his teeth, his eyes darting between me and the sea beyond.

I continue to fork and then chew. *Don't make eye contact. Not right now. If you don't say anything, do anything, then nothing can be misinterpreted.*

As he shakes his head, walks away, I remind myself: *This is what you like; people with fire in their belly.*

It's what this is, a result of his passion. Passion that, for now, has nowhere to go.

This idea he has for the book, it's a good one. It will fly. That's the phrase he uses.

We're going to fly, Kier. Our relationship, the book, it's all going to fly.

2

Elin

Parque Nacional, Portugal,
October 2021

'Are we close?' Elin Warner comes to a stop at the crest of the trail, her eyes tracing the narrow route winding up the peak ahead.

'Yeah, you can just about see the Airstreams from here.' Isaac, her brother, raises a hand, points. 'Up there, on the right, above those trees.'

Following his gaze, she squints. For a moment, the Airstreams are hard to distinguish from the hillside, bruised with shadow, but as the light shifts, she glimpses one, sunlight bouncing off its metal flank. 'Let me guess, best view in the house.'

'Top of the world.'

She absorbs it all: seven hundred thousand square metres of Portuguese national park spread over four granite massifs. Huge forests of pine and oak, steep valleys rising to dramatic, rocky peaks. Beautiful, but daunting.

A vast, unconquerable mass. With every step, every turn, the park throws up more – more land, more trees, mountains playing out echoes of themselves. This kind of scale has always terrified her. Places so big that individual detail fades away and all you see is the mass.

Elin thinks about what Isaac told her earlier, about people disappearing here. You could imagine it – being seamlessly absorbed into the depth and breadth of the park.

They keep walking, following the dusty, scrubby path as it winds up the hill.

Striding ahead, Isaac picks up the pace. A few minutes in, the nagging in her rib tips over to a dull throb. 'Hold on, I need a minute.'

Isaac stops, rocking back on his heels. He runs a hand through his dark curls.

The gesture's so familiar, for a moment time slips. They're kids again, all three of them. Everything's right with the world.

Shaking the feeling loose, Elin pulls her water bottle from her pack. She flips the cap, takes a long drink.

'Better?' Isaac's watching her.

'Yeah. Just the rib complaining . . . we've done a lot the past few days.' Too much, she thinks, remembering the doctor's warning. *Take it easy.*

But that's the last thing she's done. Since they arrived at the park yesterday morning, she's thrown herself into it – the first hike to the hut, the longer one today to the Airstreams.

She couldn't help it. Each step she's taken, every hill they've climbed, feels like she's putting distance between her and life back in Devon. The past few months . . . they'd been tough. A challenging case, her first real case as a Detective Sergeant since her career break, the split with her ex, Will.

She *needed* this, wanted to squeeze the most from every moment.

'Sure? We can stop for a bit before we do the last section.' Isaac looks at her, a hesitancy in his eyes. It's been like this since

8

they arrived in the park – not quite treading on eggshells, but an almost formal politeness to their conversations instead of the banter you'd expect between siblings.

But that's natural, she reminds herself. It's still fragile between her and Isaac.

Raw and new. Bar a few phone calls and messages, they'd been pretty much estranged until recently. Four years of minimal contact, awkward conversations. This trip . . . it's a baby step, one she's wary of screwing up.

They had form on that. *Trips gone wrong*. Last year, visiting him in Switzerland, Elin had ended up investigating the murder of Isaac's fiancée, Laure. Hardly the dream reunion.

'Sure.' She's about to put the bottle away when there's a movement in the copse of oak trees a few feet away.

A sudden flash of colour.

Elin slowly exhales as a deer darts across the track, a dark blur against the foliage.

Pulse slowing, she feels relief, yes, but disappointment too; stupid to think she'd outrun it by coming here. These past few months, looking for what's lurking in the shadows has become the default, as automatic as breathing.

'This place keeps catching us out, doesn't it?' Isaac watches as the deer disappears into the woodland, sending a cluster of low-hanging branches shuddering.

'At every turn.' The park was full of tricks like this: abandoned buildings appearing between the trees. Swirling pockets of fog. Roadside shrines with colours that can pull the breath from you.

They start walking again.

'You been doing much of this since you got out of hospital?' Isaac asks.

'A bit . . . gentle stuff. Running's off the cards for the foreseeable, so I've been walking instead.' She looks at him sideways. 'I was about to ask the same question, but looking at you, I reckon I know the answer.'

'Yeah.' He smiles. 'Did a lot over the summer . . . trail running too.' He's playing it down, Elin thinks, examining the lines of muscle in his legs. There's a solidity about him. A new kind of strength. 'It's helped, you know, since Laure.'

'How's it been going?' she asks tentatively. 'I know we've not really talked about it.'

'All right, I'm getting there.' Abruptly, he turns, pointing out a bird swooping low above them. 'Looks like some kind of swift,' he murmurs.

Too much too soon, she thinks, watching him.

She's not going to push it.

Getting to know each other again . . . it doesn't have to be something hurried. Pressured. This is what this trip is about – taking their time, feeling their way. The next few weeks are just about the two of them.

The two of them and *this*, Elin thinks, looking around her.

The track ahead is winding, forking, and then forking again. Branches encroaching over the trail that drew you in while simultaneously pushing you back. An enigma, like every part of this landscape.

A few days in, she had the feeling that, like Isaac, she hasn't even scratched the surface.

3

Kier

Devon, July 2018

'Guessing there's no need to knock.'

Every bit of me lurches. He's stood just outside the open door in high tops, jeans, a threadbare T-shirt, a wide smile on his face.

My twin brother, Penn.

Woody barrels out from between my legs, nearly knocking me flying. Penn bends, scratches his back, screwing up his eyes as the dog lunges up to lick his face.

'What about me?' I don't want just a hug, I want to breathe him in, meld him to me.

Straightening up, he wraps his arms around me. 'Fuck, I've missed you.'

'Same.' I hold him for a minute before we pull back, stare at each other. It's always like this when we've been apart. Intense scrutinisation, trying to work out if we've missed anything new. But apart from a haircut, fair hair cropped a little shorter, he's unchanged.

Penn clears his throat, embarrassed at what I can see are tears in his eyes.

'Softie.' I blink back my own.

'No Zeph?'

'Swim. He'll be back in a bit.'

Penn nods. 'So how is it travelling with someone? I want the inside story, not the PR lines you've been palming me off with so far. Must be hard, seeing as you've only got me to compare with . . . always pretty seamless—'

'Yeah, yeah.' I roll my eyes, but travelling with Penn *is* seamless. The first camping trip I took with him was to Spain, near the cliffs. We arrived after dark, but it was spectacular in the morning, watching the waves crashing to the shore, the blue skies that seemed to go on forever.

Early mornings when you're camping always hold something raw and special. An Earth-fuck, my friend calls it. When you're so at one with nature, it becomes out of body. Transcendental. The world hitting you full in the face, striking the very primal part of you.

You never get it in a house. By the time you've checked your phone, drunk your coffee, it's too late. *Blinkers on.*

'So, do I get a tour?'

'Course. This wood panelling on the ceiling and floors is all new . . . we put the kitchen by the doors so Zeph can see out when he's cooking.' Penn runs his hands over the wooden countertop. 'The kitchen's bespoke.' I point out the cooktop, drawers underneath, the oven below the countertop, the sink and shelves above loaded with oils and spices.

'And sleeping is back here.'

Poking his head into the back, he laughs. 'Let me guess, this was your idea.' He nods at the hollow carved out above for my books.

I point at the driver's area. 'So was this. The front seats swivel round, and you can flip out this desk to create a makeshift office.' I take him through the rest of our hacks. The jet boil. Gel pads so our pots and glasses don't fall when we're moving. Fridge, water heater, cup hooks. The wall library for our books and maps.

I'm talking fast, too fast, because under his gaze, everything seems slightly smaller, shabbier. It's not him. He's not judging – I am. I'm comparing it to their Victorian terrace by the estuary. I want his approval, for him not just to like it, but to feel a flicker of jealousy to verify I made the right choice.

But there isn't a flicker; instead he's kind. *Too* kind, too hearty. It's forced, and that's a bad sign. He's now exclaiming, overemphasising. *Loving* it all. No one could love a gel pad that much, let alone want one for their own house. He even asks me to send him the link.

Beneath that overenthusiasm is pity; he feels sorry for me. Sorry that at thirty-three I can't settle, and he's trying to cover it up.

Straightening, he knocks his head on the plant I have hanging from the ceiling, sending it wildly swinging backwards and forwards. 'This doesn't get claustrophobic at all?'

Finally, a criticism. My shoulders sag in relief.

'Only if you don't get on with each other.' A rasping laugh.

Penn and I turn. Zeph's back, shirtless, a towel wrapped around his waist. Smiling, he stretches out a hand to Penn. 'Nice to finally meet, and sorry for the late arrival, I ...' His words fade as he pauses, looking between us. 'Nonidentical ... I don't know ...'

People often say that. Despite the fact he's almost a foot taller than me and a bloke, Penn and I share something you can't quite grasp in photos. How we smile, eyes creasing up at the corners, the brow furrow when we're concentrating on something. I like to think it's the sheer amount of time we've spent together,

13

subconsciously mirroring each other. Genes, together with the alchemy of time.

'Beer?' I ask, but as I turn, I trip over Zeph's foot. An awkward dance as I try to right myself.

'What were you saying about it not being claustrophobic?' Penn laughs and I notice his eyes tracing Zeph's tattoos.

Zeph tenses. He's not always good at people taking the piss.

'That's only because you're here,' I say quickly. 'Zeph and I on our own. It ... works.'

'Come on, it can't be all hunky-dory.' Penn grins. 'I love Mila, but if we were stuck together twenty-four seven in a place this size, I think we'd both lose the plot.'

I shrug. He doesn't get the mutability of it all; how the van changes when there's more than two of us in it. The space contracts. On our own, Zeph and I have a rhythm, a way of not getting under each other's feet.

'We make it work.' Zeph changes the subject. 'So, how's the wedding planning going? Must be on the home stretch now.'

'Yeah, thank god. No one's getting out alive if it goes on any longer.'

'That bad?' Zeph laughs.

'It's the detail that gets you in the end. When you start having to decide on exactly the number of flowers in each bouquet.' Smiling, Penn looks between us. 'So ... you two next?'

The question lingers before Zeph shakes his head. 'Not there yet. We've only been together' – he looks to me – 'what's it been, nine months? Ten? No time.'

Penn tenses. I can tell the sentiment will piss him off. He hates flakes. Especially male ones. A legacy of a childhood like ours.

There's an awkward silence before Zeph loudly cracks his knuckles. 'Right, I'm going to shower. I'll join you in a bit.' This is a cue; another thing you learn in a van. When to give each other space.

I look at Penn, grab another beer from the fridge. 'Let's go outside.'

We sit on the director's chairs in front of the van, Woody beside us, and contemplate the view. The cove we're parked up in is at the centre of the bay, and it's beautiful – a shimmering curve of water sheltered by tree-covered cliffs still unspoilt by development.

I take a swig of beer. 'So, how's it been down here? Busy?'

'It was. Tourists have thinned out in the past few weeks.'

'In prime season?' I watch the woman running past us. She's making easy work of it as she navigates the rocky path above the beach; an effortless, rhythmic motion, cropped blonde hair shifting about her face with each stride.

'You haven't heard?'

I shake my head, my eyes shifting back out to the beach. Burnt sunbathers. Swimmers. Three sailboats marking a course.

'The boat murders. A couple of girls killed, out at sea. Messed up by the propeller.' His eyes skim over the water. 'One of them was found not too far from here. They reckon it's someone called Hayler.'

I shudder. 'So maybe not the ideal lovers' location.'

Penn catches my eye. 'Is that what you two are, then, *lovers*?'

'You're probing.'

He grins. 'Maybe.'

'Come on, I know you're itching to give your verdict.' I ruffle Woody's ears.

'Hard to tell after a few minutes, but . . .' He exhales. 'Wouldn't really have put you together. He seems a bit . . . stressy.'

A beat passes. 'Honestly, he's good, Penn. We . . . fit.' My voice pitches higher.

Penn looks at me. The air between us is fat and heavy, like a sponge. I want to squeeze it, let the weight fall away.

Beer has pooled on the top of his can. He slurps it away. 'Ignore me. You know what I'm like, K, since Mum, when you meet someone new ... I worry.'

Mum. I swallow hard. 'You can't vet everyone.'

Penn gives me a crooked smile. 'I can try.' He looks back to the sea. 'So, you're coming to ours on Saturday, yeah? Show us the stationery?'

'Yeah. I'm picking up the final designs in town tomorrow. I—' I break off. Zeph's appeared, now dressed, hoody thrown on over his shorts.

'Room for one more?' he says.

'There is, but I'm going to have to be antisocial.' Penn drains his beer, stands up. 'I'd better head. Mila's cooking.'

'Sure?' As I stand up, Zeph winds his hand around my waist, pulls me in close. He does this when we're around other men, stakes his claim. But as his hand comes to rest against my spine, silver rings pressing against my flesh, all I can think is: *This is my brother.*

Penn's face scrunches up like he's seen something bad. 'Right, I'm off.' He loudly crumples the can between his fingers.

Zeph steps forwards. 'I'll take that.'

'Nah, won't trouble you. There's a bin up here. I'll see you Saturday.' Penn smiles, but the rhythm in his speech sounds off. Too slow. Staccato.

The dog lurches after him, but I call him back.

I hear the can unkinking beneath Penn's fingers as he puts distance between us, the metal making loud, random pops as he walks.

4

Elin

'Okay, so you missed this part of the hike out.' Elin falters as the dirt track ahead peters out to a steep drop. Taking a few steps forwards, she peers over the edge and then pulls back, her stomach lurching.

A river.

In any other circumstance, the frothing white water would be the main attraction, but her gaze is now pulled instead to the bridge on their left, a crooked stone arch that looks like it's seen better days.

'Never seen anything built quite like that before.' Moving closer, she examines it, disconcerted. 'Looks like a random pattern.' Stones, rimmed with moss, are haphazardly stacked one on top of another to form the arch. Halfway down, some are bulging, weeds pushing between the cracks.

'Medieval.' Isaac stops at the entrance to the bridge. 'Locals call it the Devil's Bridge. Meant to have been built by the big man himself.'

Elin pulls a face. 'You making this up?'

'Nope. Legend has it the devil built it after a criminal sold his soul for an escape route over the river. Been used for all kinds of things . . . witchcraft rituals, fertility rites.'

This is the Isaac of old, Elin thinks, watching the faint smile playing on his lips. The challenger. Someone who liked pushing people to their limits.

'I'm guessing we need to go across to get to the Airstreams?'

'It's the only route from this direction, so unless you're planning on jumping . . .' Raising an eyebrow, his blue eyes flicker with amusement. 'Scared?'

'Is that a challenge?'

'Could be.'

Slipping past him, Elin starts walking, but a few steps in, she hesitates. From this angle, it's clear that the whole structure is leaning to the right. It feels precarious suddenly. A risk.

'Everything okay?' Isaac calls, concern in his tone.

'Fine.' She keeps moving. Though part of her wants to rush, get it over with, halfway across, she makes herself stop and turn, looking down the winding length of the river to the hill beyond. It's thick with foliage, the bursts of autumnal rusts and reds a sharp contrast to the vivid green of the trees surrounding them.

Absorb it. Be in the moment.

It's something she's been forcing herself to do these past few months. Appreciate what's in front of her instead of constantly looking back.

But it's been hard. The messages that plagued her last case keep playing on her mind – anonymous posts on social media, deriding her, her ability to do the job. She'd have dismissed it as a crank if it wasn't for the message she'd received in hospital after she'd closed the case.

The words are still eating away at her:

Want to know a story about this detective?

A clue: this one doesn't always tell the truth.

If the message wasn't bad enough, they'd attached a photograph of her on the ward.

Seeing the image of herself was like a punch in the gut. It felt personal. Sinister.

Forcing the thought away, Elin extends her hand to the wall of the bridge. As her fingers touch the rough, worn stone, she feels the weight of history almost like a physical presence.

'Not as bad as you thought?' Isaac stops beside her.

Shaking her head, she smiles. 'It's beautiful. Seeing something like this . . . feels like you're stepping back in time.'

'Yeah, I was thinking that. In some places, like this, it feels almost untouched by modern life.'

This is what they've missed, she thinks, watching as he takes a photograph. Moments together, memories shared. The past few days, they'd seen things she knew they'd always treasure. Dilapidated castles high in the hills. The Roman Road.

Sights that would bind them, form part of a new chapter.

'Ready for the last push?' Isaac slips his phone back in his pocket.

'Ready.'

After crossing the final part of the bridge, they walk for another kilometre or so before reaching an intersection. Here, the path splits – left to follow the path that led up towards the Airstreams, or straight on to another plateau.

Elin takes a few steps forwards. Thinning trees reveal a scrubby patch of ground, patchy with moss, flashes of colour between the branches.

A campsite.

Not Airstreams, but camper vans, two next to one another, and two opposite on either side, forming a makeshift semi-circle.

It looks like they've been there a while, dug their heels into the soil. Dust has settled on their surfaces, the bright colours muted and dulled.

'You see that?' she says to Isaac.

No reply.

He's already striding past her, in the direction of the camp.

'Hey, I thought we were going up to the Airstreams?'

Isaac abruptly turns, the movement kicking up a sour puff of dust. 'Not yet.' As he casts a look towards the vans, his expression is grim. 'There's something I need to do.'

5

Kier

Devon, July 2018

'I know what you're going to say. This place feels—' Penn smiles, gesturing us inside.

'Huge,' we say in unison as the dog bundles in, pushing through my legs. It's always the same when you're in a house after travelling in the van. That feeling of space. Permanence.

'Is this what it's like all the time?' Zeph looks at Mila as she comes to greet them in the hall, a broad smile on her face. Curly hair knotted up in a bun, she looks fresh-faced, happy. If she's stressed about the wedding, it isn't showing.

'Yeah,' Mila shakes her head. 'You'd better get used to it. The whole finishing each other's sentences thing ... just the tip of the iceberg.'

Laughing, Zeph reaches up to rub the fuzz on his head, T-shirt rucking up to reveal a line of black hair.

Mila glances down, then away. I can't blame her. Zeph looks good tonight, the dark of his trousers and shirt pulling the blues from his eyes. The shirt isn't tight, but it shows enough of what's beneath. A body that's lean, just the right side of hungry.

A feature piece I once read described him as having the body of a 'junkie rock star coming off tour,' but I know it owes nothing to illegal substances. It's because Zeph's never still. Cooking. Thinking. Living. Feet that never touch the floor.

Mila pounces on the art wallet in my hand, 'Is this—?'

'It is. Final copies of all the stationery. I'll take you through them later. Printing is next week, but the samples are pretty much what you can expect in terms of quality and colour.'

She grins. 'Can't wait. It's starting to feel real now.'

'I bet.' Laughing, Zeph and I follow her down the hall to the open-plan living space at the back of the house. Food covers the length of the table: cooked chicken, griddled courgettes, a rice dish. Fragrant, colourful salads. I absorb the detail – the embroidered tablecloth and vase of wildflowers, touched by the effort they've made.

The thought plagues me again, the devil on my shoulder.

You could do this all the time if you settled here. Live a normal life.

But with a lurch, I remember.

You can't.

6

Elin

*Parque Nacional, Portugal,
October 2021*

'I don't get it,' Elin calls, picking up the pace to catch up with him. 'What's with the whole, *there's something I need to do*?'

Isaac avoids her gaze. 'I promised a mate, Penn, that I'd take a look for his sister while we were out here. Reckons she went missing, here, in the park.'

Falling in step beside him, Elin blinks, discomforted. He hadn't mentioned anything about this before, and looking at his awkward expression, it's clear that was a deliberate decision.

Is this the real reason he suggested coming out here? A favour for a friend? Nothing to do with them spending time together?

'Thought this was meant to be a holiday.' She tries to keep her tone light but it's hard. Isaac knew how much she needed this break. To land this on her now when she's already out here, has no choice . . .

'It is. Don't know what we'll find, if anything. Penn didn't exactly give me much to go on. All he said was that he thinks Kier never left the park.'

Elin nods towards the vans, now properly visible between the trees. 'So what's this place got to do with it?'

'Penn says Kier was last seen here. At this camp. I—' He abruptly stops as a man appears on the trail in front of them.

'Você está hospedado no Airstreams?' The man smiles lazily, looking them up and down. He's in his late thirties, barefoot, bare-chested, sweat drawing lines through the layer of dust on his face.

Isaac's reply is mumbled, faltering. 'Você . . . fala inglês?'

The man switches to English. 'Let me guess, you're staying up at the Airstreams?' The accent is unexpected – American. He's holding a chisel, his forefinger bleeding, and as he puts it to his mouth, sucks, he seems amused as he eyes up their backpacks. Although battered, used, they're clearly not holding up under scrutiny.

'Is it that obvious?' Isaac grins now, all easy, self-deprecating smiles.

He laughs. 'Well, you might as well come and say hey, seeing as we'll be neighbours. I'm Ned.' Sweeping an arm behind him, he gestures for them to come closer. As he turns, Elin glimpses a tattoo at the base of his skull, shadowed by his buzz cut.

'Isaac.' Isaac gestures to her. 'Elin.'

'English?'

Elin smiles.

'If you haven't already worked it out, we're American.' He laughs again. 'Either by birth or sheer sticking power.'

Small talk, batted back and forth as they follow him down the track towards the camp. *Weather. Food. The trip so far.*

After about fifty metres or so, the path breaks open into a space wider than she'd imagined. An encampment. Her first instinct was right; the camp has an air of permanency. People putting down roots. Solar panels. Generators. Tarpaulins set over water butts.

A washing line has been strung across the gap between the white camper vans in the middle, shirts and skirts flapping in the breeze.

Through the open doors of the vans, she examines the framed prints on the walls, the piles of books, herbs in pots trailing down some shelves.

A warm, homely vibe, but something's niggling at her about the scene, something she can't quite get a grasp on. She looks and looks again, but nothing pulls out at her.

Elin casts her gaze away from the vans themselves to a large communal area in the centre. There's a fire pit in the middle, a few faded rugs surrounding it.

A young woman with long, bleach-blonde hair is sat on a bench at the side, the grass beneath it worn to white. The laptop screen in front of her is revealing nothing but a reflection of the sun.

Opposite, there's a slightly older woman with a sharp bob and a heavy fringe holding a squirming toddler of about two on her lap. She coughs as they move closer.

The careless laughter, conversation, comes to an abrupt stop.

Elin feels the hairs on her neck stand to attention as the group turns in a well-oiled unison. Their expressions are friendly, but the defensive body language tells her their arrival is an invasion.

Outsiders.

A dog runs towards them, barking. It's a spaniel, with liver-coloured spots like paint splotches marking his back. Ned gives him a gentle tug on his collar, then gestures to the woman on the end. 'That's Bridie and her kid, Etta.' He smiles at the child, but she doesn't return it, burrowing her head into the crook of her mother's arm. 'And that's Leah.'

He nods at her. The younger woman looks up, her features

shadowed beneath a broad-rimmed sunhat. Late twenties at most, she's painfully thin, her skin pale.

Ned steps back. 'Last but not least, Maggie. The one who holds us all together.'

A woman with curly dark hair, threaded through with grey, appears from the white van in the centre. She's cradling a mug in her hand, broad feet splayed wide in a pair of leather sandals. Though she must be late sixties, early seventies, there's an ease to her movements that belies her age.

Stopping beside them, the mug tips, dark liquid spilling across her linen smock. Loudly cursing, she holds out her hand, the winding scar on her cheek creasing as she smiles. 'Looks like I'm the only one, apart from Ned here, who's going to be polite enough to say a proper hello.' Maggie gestures up the hill. 'You'll love it up at the Airstreams. Everyone who stays there does.'

'She's only saying that because I read out the reviews to her,' Bridie calls. 'It's not like anyone comes back and tells us. One encounter with the great unwashed is enough.' She tails off, openly observing Elin, eyes tracing first her face, then Isaac's.

Elin looks away, discomforted. Despite the warmth of the welcome, she has the sense of something lurking beneath it.

'How long are you planning on staying?' Ned places the chisel on the work bench at the side, raises his finger to his mouth to suck again.

'Rest of the week. Heard there's lots to explore.' Isaac hoists his backpack up his shoulder. 'How about you? A stopover?'

'We're a little more permanent than that.' Ned looks at Maggie. 'Been here, what? Four years or more.'

'I'd say.' She smiles. 'At least that.'

'Fed up with the road,' Bridie adds, teasing a piece of the toddler's hair away from her face. 'For the time being, anyway.'

'And it's just been you guys all that time?' Elin asks.

Ned's eyes drift over her face before settling back to the dog. 'Yeah, just us.'

A silence descends. It's like a cold breeze had swept through the camp.

The atmosphere shifts into something hostile.

Elin feels sweat prick beneath her arms. She looks at Isaac to give him the nod, but as she tries to catch his eye, she notices a shadowy movement through the window of the blue van on the right.

'You didn't get too hot here over summer?' Isaac continues, oblivious. 'We heard about the fires.'

'Didn't reach us, thank god.' Maggie sips her coffee. 'And when it gets hot, there's places to go to cool off, if you know. We can tell you some, if you like, off the beaten track. Not the usual tourist traps.'

'That'd be good.'

Maggie smiles, but it doesn't reach her eyes. Looking away, she picks up a cloth from the bench, starts mopping at the spill on her smock.

'Well, we'll be off, then,' Isaac says, taking the hint. 'See you around, maybe, get those recommendations.'

The group at the bench resume their conversation. Only Ned puts up a hand in farewell as he moves towards the edge of the clearing, quickly consumed by shadow from the trees overhead.

A few metres down the path, Elin turns back, glances towards the blue van again.

This time, the view through the window reveals nothing but the branches of the pine trees behind, shifting in the breeze.

7

Kier

Devon, July 2018

Penn pours the wine. As we eat, conversation drifts to the van; our trip down, the people we met.

'Penn tells me you've done up the van pretty nice since I last saw it.' Mila passes the salad across the table and smiles.

I spoon some onto my plate. 'A labour of love, but it's been worth it.'

She turns to Zeph. 'Is this the first time you've done the whole van thing?'

'Yeah, too busy before. Work was crazy for a while.'

We talk for a bit about Zeph's career, an edited version of how it ended, one I don't contradict. There's no questions from my brother about Zeph, his infamy. Penn isn't interested in celebrity; I doubt he's even looked him up. Food for Penn is a fuel, not an existential pleasure. They won't be connecting on the intricacies of a vegan dish.

Zeph's sneaking glances at Penn, bothered, I can tell, by the fact that he isn't fawning. He'd never admit it – he's anything but showy, demanding attention – but I've come to see over time that because it came, organically, he didn't *have* to demand it.

In the end, it's Mila who obliges. Asks him where he trained, finds his inspiration. Zeph does his usual patter, France, London, Southeast Asia for a time, various restaurants on the East Coast. Rules he broke, people he charmed to get where he did.

Mila's listening intently. 'I've always wanted to go to Asia, but it's never been the right time . . . My friend said it changed his life.'

Zeph looks at her seriously. 'In what way?'

'Spiritually, I suppose. I think he'd been blinkered by Western ideology,' she explains, leaning a little over the table, food abandoned.

As the conversation bats back and forth between her and Zeph, and Mila continues to enthuse, Penn looks at me, raising an eyebrow, but I don't respond. I'm used to it: how people open up around Zeph. How he listens and asks questions. He makes people feel special. Important.

When there's a lull in the chatter, Penn turns to me, changes the subject. 'So, are you going to show us the samples?'

I retrieve my art wallet from the hall, pass the drafts around the table. There's a lot; people are always surprised how much wedding stationery there is past the Save the Dates and the invites themselves. Order of service, place cards, menus, drinks signage. Wedding favours. Thank-you notes. The list is endless and ever-growing thanks to social media.

'I love them,' Mila murmurs. 'Seriously, Kier, they're like nothing I've seen before.'

I smile. 'Thanks. It always means a bit more when you're doing it for someone you know.'

I like to use a rough theme across my stationery, and for their commission, it's the building that Penn and Mila are getting married in – an imposing Victorian mansion by the sea. Until its renovation a few years ago, it had been on the verge of dereliction, nature breaking through holes in the roof, the cracks in the crumbling walls.

I've used the original cornicing as inspiration for the borders of the stationery and subverted it, the building's recent wild past intruding – ivy and wild flowers woven through the delicate pattern. This is all beauty, but in my first draft, one I never shared, nature took over. Consumed the intricate design. A stranglehold.

My initial attempts are always the same. Darker. Uglier. To be palatable to clients, I pare them back. Sanitise.

'Would you ever try doing your own stuff again?' Mila asks.

I shake my head. 'Don't think I could take the pressure.'

'Pressure how?' She's looking at me closely.

'That constant fear of ... judgement, I suppose.' I shrug. 'Gallery owners, critics. The public. This ... it suits me. Regular income, and I can do it from anywhere.'

'I think it's a cop-out,' Zeph says bluntly. 'What she's doing now, it doesn't push her to her limits.' I keep my face neutral. I've heard this before. In his world, not succumbing to your creative calling, in any guise, is akin to failure. 'I think she's scared of what will come out if she lets herself go.'

I swallow, my mouth suddenly dry. He doesn't know how close to the bone he's getting. I'm not just scared of letting go, I'm terrified. Painting as I did as a child, freely, openly, no boundaries ... it frightens me. That kind of art died when Dad did. The only outlet for it now is within my maps, and those are just for Penn and me.

The wedding commissions I take are safe: they have limits.

I flip the conversation. 'So how does it feel? Getting so close ...'

'Exciting, but scary.' There's a catch in Mila's voice. 'Saying that's it, forever. You're the only one.'

'I get that,' Zeph says quietly.

Penn glances at him. 'You ever get close?'

He shrugs. 'Touching distance, maybe.'

My cheeks burn. *Touching distance?* He's always told me that he's never even considered marriage.

My thoughts lurch to her. It has to be her, doesn't it? *Romy.* The woman who haunts not just my thoughts, but Zeph's dreams.

'Why do you find the idea of getting married so scary?' Zeph turns back to Mila.

'The finality of it, I suppose.' She sips her wine. 'I wanted to move away like you have, *do* stuff, and I wonder if, now, it'll ever happen. Marriage, however much you want it, it's like that part of your life, that spontaneous part, is closing.'

'We've talked about this,' Penn says tightly. 'You can do anything you want when we're married. Your choices have nothing to do with me.'

'I know, but it feels like it's the beginning of a cycle of things, that you're on and you can't get off. Kids, all that.' Mila slurs her words, voice loosened from the wine.

Zeph's expression is serious. 'I understand.'

Penn tenses. Just like that, the night has shifted from steady ground to unchartered waters. *It's him*, I think. Zeph. His presence is like throwing a hand grenade into a room. He unsettles people. By being unapologetically himself, not sticking to the rules, it's as if he makes other people realise that they don't have to either.

It's one of the things I love about him the most, but it can frighten people.

They find Zeph too much. Too much energy. Too much thought. Too much life.

I change the subject, ask Penn about the flowers.

Lightly touching my hand, Zeph interrupts. 'Hey, Mila was saying something.' He looks back to her. 'Carry on.'

31

'Zeph.' The sharpness of my tone surprises me. I feel my heart thud.

'What?' His head snaps back. 'You interrupted her midsentence.'

Heat crawls up my neck. I can feel Penn and Mila's eyes on us. I meet his gaze, hold it. 'Don't speak to me like that.'

A stony silence. Penn stands up, starts clearing the plates, gesturing to Mila to help.

Once they're away from the table, Zeph places his foot on mine.

A slow, steady compression.

He's pressing on bone. Agony. I blink back tears.

Zeph looks me right in the eye. 'Fuck you,' he says, so softly I could almost be imagining it.

8

Elin

Parque Nacional, Portugal,
October 2021

'So how long has Kier been missing?' Elin asks, following the track up towards the Airstream. The path is well used, the stony surface only punctuated here or there by patches of scrubby grass.

'That's the thing.' Isaac tugs his water bottle from his pack. 'She's not *actually* missing. Not officially, anyway. As far as the police are concerned, she's still travelling. Bank accounts are active, money going in and out. Penn's had messages from her, saying she wants time out. Police have seen them, say there's no evidence of wrongdoing, but he's not convinced.'

'Was she with anyone when she left? Friends or otherwise?'

Tipping up the water bottle, he takes a long drink. 'No, and Penn said she split with her ex, Zeph, a few months before she went to Portugal.'

Elin raises an eyebrow. 'Was it over over?'

'Penn described it as dead in the water.' Isaac shoves his bottle back in the side pocket of his bag. 'I did some digging, and definitely looks that way. He's a chef, was a bit of a name for a while in the US. From what I could see, after they split, he went back to New York, picked up his old life.'

'Bad breakup?'

'Not really. Sounds like they drifted apart, then Kier pretty much ghosted him. Penn reckons she's done it before. Gets cold feet, doesn't want to commit.'

Elin looks across the valley to the swath of forest tracking up to the peaks behind, thin trails of cloud hovering above. The village, crouched at the foothill of the first mountain, looks impossibly small.

For a moment, she imagines an alternate reality. Her ex, Will, here with them. Every step would bring a photo, ideas about what he could pull into projects at his architecture practice.

Stopping short, she blinks. Will's no longer hers, hasn't been for several months.

The idea stings. It's something she's still struggling with – letting go.

Sometimes she wonders if she's moved on at all, if all she's done is replace Will with the *idea* of Will, using that as much of a reassurance as his presence itself. Thinking about calling him. Imagining the sound of his voice.

Their split had come off the back of her last case. It felt right at the time, but when doubts creep in, like now, all she feels is a crushing sense of loss. Will had been there for so many things, seismic things – the implosion of her career, her crippling panic attacks, her mother's death. He'd always been her anchor, and without him, sometimes it feels like she's floundering.

It's frightening, starting again, when all around her people are moving on. Marriage. Kids. Friends tell her it will work out, that she'll meet someone, but Elin's beginning to question not only whether she even *wants* another relationship, but whether

34

someone will like her for who she really is – especially when sometimes she struggles to answer that herself.

This past year, she's come to realise how much she's always worn a mask, not just with other people, but with herself. Now she's on her own, that mask off, every day she learns something new about who she is as a person.

The path steepens.

They're only a few hundred metres from the top of the hill, the three Airstreams now fully visible, positioned along the ridge.

Elin's eyes lurch behind them, expecting something, but she's not sure what. Some sort of life, maybe, but there's nothing. They'll be alone up there.

She drags her gaze away. 'So has Kier got form for taking off?'

'Apparently so. Family history … it's rough. Both parents dead.' He pauses, thinking. 'Penn said it affected them differently. All he wanted to do was settle down but she had itchy feet, wanted to travel.'

'So why does Penn think anything's happened to her? Sounds more plausible that she's taking time out.'

'From her twin?'

'It's possible. She might have stuff going on she doesn't want him to know about. Sometimes it's hard for people to understand that even when you're close to someone, they don't tell you everything.'

'Maybe.' Isaac shrugs. 'But Penn says they always spoke regularly. It hasn't happened for a while. He's pretty certain that she wouldn't go off-grid.'

'When did Kier first come out here?'

'The end of 2018. Penn said it was pretty weird from the off. The minute she arrived, she seemed … cagey. Didn't share stuff like she normally did.'

'At what point did he start getting worried?'

'About a year after that. He didn't like that she hadn't moved on, never wanted to speak any more, started being vague about what she was up to.'

'But you said she's been in contact in other ways?'

'Yeah, but only messages, and he reckons they don't sound like her. He got one a few weeks ago, supposedly from Italy, but it felt off, like someone else was writing them.' Isaac shrugs. 'I get it. Even now, with you, I'd know how you write. The last time he got a photo was when she was here, in the park.'

'So who saw her at the camp?' They round the bend, the path turning back on itself as they climb the final stretch to the plateau.

'A hiker.' Isaac puts his bottle away. 'Due diligence on Penn's part. Kier doesn't do social media, but when the police here wouldn't play ball, Penn ended up tracking down some hikers via Instagram, different hashtags of the park. It took him a while, but he messaged everyone who'd been in the area when he'd last spoken with her, see if they picked up on anything untoward. Had a few time wasters, then a guy got in touch, said he'd stumbled across a campsite, and something strange happened. He couldn't link it to Kier directly, but he got the impression that the group was hiding something.'

'Like what?'

'He thought the site was public, but when he tried to stop here, he got short shrift. On his way out, one of the group came after him, accused him of invading their privacy. Apparently, they ended up knocking his phone out of the hand.'

She can picture it, Elin thinks, chilled. A group like that, closing ranks, turning sour.

'This guy wasn't even taking a photo, but it made him suspicious, you know? So he finds a spot where he can take one. Sees nothing awry and thinks nothing of it until Penn gets in touch. He sent Penn the photos he took and that's when Penn spotted

Kier's van in the background. He ended up flying out here and going to the camp himself.'

'I'm guessing the welcome he got from the camp was equally warm?' Fine wisps of cloud have appeared, the sky fading to a bluish haze.

'Actually, no. Sounds like he was polite, took it carefully, and they responded in kind. Penn showed them the photograph, asked if they'd seen Kier. They said yes, explained that she'd stayed with them for a few days and then moved on.'

'Did they mention where Kier went after that?'

'They said she talked about Italy, which tied in with the messages Penn got.'

'And there was no sign of her van when he came to look?'

Isaac shakes his head.

'So chances are she did leave. All sounds plausible.'

'It does, but then, a few months ago, he found this photo online. A photo a hiker had tagged of the park.' He tips the screen of his phone. 'It was taken a few months after the first. Her van was still there.'

The hairs on her arms stand to attention. 'Not exactly someone passing through.'

'Yeah, the van was still there, so the whole *few days* line the camp gave—'

'Was a lie.'

9

Kier

Devon, July 2018

'Bloody hell,' Penn says as I show him the map I've made for him and Mila. 'This is why I always got you to paint them.'

I smile, wishing I could see what he could. It's hard to be objective with your own work. Months, even years after I've finished something, I can still pick holes in it. Especially the maps. No matter how much time I work on them, it never seems like I've quite captured the locations as they feel inside me.

'You like it?'

'Love it. It's ... us.' Penn's voice catches as he runs his finger over the canvas, the different locations. The coast path where they hike. Their favourite dive bar and their go-to bookshop.

My maps are a little abstract, impressionistic in feel, but with recognisable elements, and with theirs, I've amplified that. I want Mila to feel an instant sense of coming home. I've tried to capture not just the essence of a place in time, but their bond. Their map is one of the few I've painted here that's all love: light, bright colours, softer shapes and lines. No shadows.

Penn's quiet for a minute, then looks at me. 'Do you ever think about why you're still drawn to doing these?'

'I like travelling, recording places. Sharing them with you.' I gently knock his arm with mine. 'It's our thing.'

'But the fact that you've kept it up all these years. I've always wondered if there's something underlying.' A pause. 'You know, about . . .'

I pretend not to hear him, looking through the window at Mila and Zeph.

They've just reached the river beach. I can see that the Zeph of a few moments ago is gone, so quickly that for a moment it makes me doubt it even happened at all.

He's dipping his fingers in the water, looking up at Mila. I imagine he's asking her which fish you can catch. Telling her how he'd cook them. *Lemongrass. Chilli. Coriander.*

She's nodding, a smile playing on her lips.

I know in this moment that she'll get why I love him. How he can make food from words, conjure it from the very air.

Penn looks at me. 'Quite the charmer, isn't he?'

'He can be.'

'And the rest of the time?'

Shrugging, I pick up the map and put it back in my bag. I walk over to the stack of dirty plates by the sink, pick up the one on top.

'Look,' he says, when I don't reply. 'The last thing I want to do is judge, but how he was back then, is that normal?'

'What do you mean?' I scrape the leftovers into the food recycle bin.

'How he was when we were talking about you?' His mouth makes a funny hard line as he takes the plate from me, puts it into the dishwasher.

'And how was he?' I ask flatly.

'He didn't like it. It made him … uncomfortable. And at the end, when we got up from the table, how he looked at you.'

A bead of sweat trickles down my back. 'He's had a rough ride of it the past few years. Everything that went down with his job, it was hard for him. He's used to … *being* someone, the shining light. Not being that … he's struggling.'

'I get that,' Penn says carefully, 'but you're sure he's right for you?' He smiles, but it's all wide and weird.

'I wouldn't be with him if I didn't think that. He loves me, Penn, absolutely.'

'But what he said, the other day, about not calling it a relationship—'

'He isn't into labels.' I shrug.

'I just think if you have doubts, it's not worth it, not at our stage of life. I want you to find someone you can settle down with.'

'Like you, here?' Smiling, I raise an eyebrow.

'Yes,' he says seriously. 'I'd love you back here, you know that.'

'I can't.' I falter. See the blood again in my mind's eye. Winding a path across the floor.

This is what coming home does: dredges it all to the surface. Everything I've worked so hard to escape.

I've only been back a week and already it feels like I'm on a precipice. I go one way, I get to leave unscathed; the other, and it all comes crashing down.

Counting to ten in my head, I tell myself: *Only a few more weeks. Once the wedding's over, I can go. Run.*

Penn looks at me. 'Think about it, that's all I want, and if you can't settle in place, at least in person. You deserve that.' He pauses. 'I just worry that what happened … it's made you vulnerable.'

'Vulnerable?' I laugh. 'I'd hardly be travelling if I felt *vulnerable*.'

40

'Physically no, but emotionally.' He shrugs. 'Sometimes, I think, K, you can't separate yourself from what Mum did. It's like ...' There's a small silence, as if he's struggling to find the right words. 'Like you've taken it inside you.'

My head is pounding suddenly.

'I could separate myself,' I say finally. 'It was other people who couldn't. Don't you remember what they used to call me?' The next-door neighbour's kids used to shout it from their yard outside our grandparents' house.

The monster's daughter.

Penn's face looks pained as I mimic the words in a singsong voice. I can tell he wants to put his hands over his ears like he did as a kid. Put his hands over his ears and wish it away.

'But I think you believe it too,' he says after a beat. 'That you're tainted somehow by what she did. Not worthy of being loved.' He meets my gaze. 'But you are, Kier.'

Penn's wrong. It goes deeper than that. It's not that I think I'm tainted by what Mum did, it's that part of me wonders if they're right.

If I *am* my mother's daughter, if the monster's there, lurking, after all.

Isn't that anyone's biggest fear? That the dark inside will find its way to the surface.

For most people, it's a hypothetical, but I'd seen it happen. Seen the person I trusted the most become a monster.

There's a lot of reasons I can't settle, but that's the biggest one.

I'm trying to outrun it. Trying to outrun the monster.

10

Elin

Parque Nacional, Portugal,
October 2021

Summiting the hill, for a moment their conversation is forgotten.

They can see two of the Airstreams now, the metal surfaces catching the light, throwing it back to them. The first is clearly visible, the second offset and almost out of sight about a hundred feet away. The third she can't see at all. It must be set back further again, nestled deep between the trees.

'Which one's ours?'

'This one.' Isaac points at the first. 'It's got the best view, right down the valley.'

He's right, she thinks, taking it in; huge gulps of landscape, the hillside dipping to the valley floor before steeply rising to boulder-strewn mountains on the opposite side. Each peak conceals another, concertinaing into the distance until they blur, autumn rusts bleeding into blackened pockets from the forest fires. Interspersed are lush greens, swaths of pine and oak. Beyond, the river cuts a line through it all, fading to a silvery ribbon in the distance.

Elin turns back, studying their Airstream, the small decking area in front, the fire pit. The setup is shouting cosy, but the tall tangle of trees behind says anything but. Her gaze drifts to the other Airstream, the dark voids of the windows. Her eyes roam across it, unsettled. When she'd looked at the photos online, the Airstreams didn't seem so close to one another. 'Anyone staying in the others?'

'Not until next weekend,' he says, examining the wood stack below the fire pit. 'Even if anyone was, I don't think we'd see much of them. There's a path at the back, so they don't have to pass by.'

Elin nods. People wouldn't come here for a communal thing. They want seclusion and, if not total privacy, then the illusion of it.

Reaching for her phone, she takes a photo. She tips the screen towards her and examines it, satisfied. The effect she wanted: Airstream dwarfed not just by the trees, but the sheer face of the peak behind. It captures the essence of the park, the scale and drama.

'Sending a photo?' Isaac's watching as she types.

She nods. 'To my boss, Anna, and Steed.'

'Steed – he's the guy you worked with on the last case?'

'Yeah, we've got close the past few months.'

'Since the breakup?' Isaac raises an eyebrow.

Heat creeps into her cheeks. 'Nothing like that. He's been there when it got tough. He messaged a few days after I'd moved out of Will's flat, must have known from how I replied that I was feeling shitty. Hour or so later, he turned up with a bag of junk food. We spent the evening eating, watching crappy TV.'

'The right kind of mate to have.'

'He is.' Elin glances down at her phone. Steed's already replied. **Enough, spammer. My current view:** beer on the table, a screen showing rugby behind, snail trails of rain crawling down the window on the left.

Isaac's found the lockbox attached to the metal chassis at the rear of the Airstream, is already keying in the code. 'Ready?'

'Yeah. I need a drink, and to get these boots off.' Stepping into the Airstream behind him, she whistles between her teeth. 'Okay . . . the boy did good.'

'Told you.' Isaac grins.

It's bigger than she expected, zoned out to make the most of the small space: kitchen area in front, and on the right, a snug. A wooden countertop stretches the length of the wall on the left towards the bunk beds and bathroom.

Neutrals everywhere; off-white walls; a wooden floor; soft furnishings in olive, ochre, burnished yellows. Framed vistas of the park dot the walls. Waterfalls. The Roman Road. An aerial shot of one of the granite villages.

'It's got everything.' Isaac's poking around, opening cupboards and doors. 'Coffeemaker, fridge, little library . . .' He picks up the map wedged in at the front, turns it over in his hands. 'That was the other thing I meant to tell you – another anomaly Penn picked up on. You know I mentioned that Kier was an illustrator?'

Elin nods.

'Her day job is commissions, for wedding stationery, that kind of thing, but Penn said that she paints these maps, her way of sharing the places she's been.'

'Landmarks?'

Isaac shakes his head. 'More . . . personal than that. Places that really mattered, meant something to her. Everywhere she goes, she sends him one, but Penn never got one from here. He hasn't had one for months.'

'Did he mention it to the police?'

'Yeah, but it sounds like they didn't make much of it.' He looks at her. 'But he's certain it means something, the fact she hasn't sent one. It's not like her.'

Elin mulls it over, making a mental note. Anomalies like that are important. People are generally creatures of habit. Someone deviates from that habit, there's often good reason.

'Snack while we talk?' Isaac's fiddling with the hamper on the counter.

'There's food already in?'

'Yeah. I prebooked. Saves us the hassle. Loads of local stuff. Cornbread, cheese.' Holding up a bottle of wine, he reads the label. 'Vinho Verde.' He opens the fridge. 'We've got trout in here. Local beef. Potatoes.' Reaching back into the hamper, he smiles. 'And the not-so-local. Popcorn. We can do some if you want, over the fire pit. Keep us going.'

Elin smiles. Popcorn was their thing, as kids. With their little brother, Sam. Popcorn and movie night every Friday.

By the time she unpacks and changes, Isaac's already started up the fire pit.

Popping sounds out into the silence like little shots being fired, the smell – honeyed, caramel – already permeating the air.

A few minutes later, the popping becomes intermittent before stopping completely. Taking the pan off the fire pit, Isaac pours the popcorn into a bowl, thrusts it towards her together with a glass of wine.

Leaning back in her chair, Elin grabs a fistful and pushes some into her mouth. The sky is fading, blues tipping to pinks, bruising shadows glancing across the peaks opposite. Lights from the village far below are flickering on, one by one.

Isaac glances at her. 'Beautiful, isn't it?'

'It is, but when you see it like this, en masse, I don't know . . .' She's never been anywhere quite like it. So wild, so completely devoid of human life. Yesterday, they'd walked for miles without seeing another soul. There's freedom in that, but also a kind of fear. 'Not sure I could do it alone.'

Shaking her head, she feels a sudden chill. 'Any idea why Kier chose here?'

'That's the big mystery. Penn says the decision to travel to Portugal came out of the blue. She never mentioned it before.' He frowns. 'I can't wrap my head around it. Lovely, but—'

Elin knows what's behind that kind of rumination – a deeper feeling, something that sprang from having thought it through over and over. 'You're invested, aren't you?'

He shrugs.

They sit in silence for a minute. 'I get Penn's your mate,' she says finally, 'and you want to help, but I thought you'd have had your fair share of trauma.' She runs it all through in her mind: their mother's death a few years before; their younger brother, over a decade ago; Isaac's girlfriend, Laure, earlier this year. She'd have thought that, for Isaac, someone else's load would be too much to bear.

'Because of him,' Isaac says simply. 'He's the first person in I don't know how long who gets it.'

'Gets it?'

'What it's like, to lose someone. With him' – Isaac rubs his eyes – 'it's like finally someone speaks the same language. You must feel it sometimes, when people haven't . . .'

Grieved, she finishes in her head. Yes, she often wonders what she has in common with people when they bang on about stuff that seems irrelevant when you've looked death in the eye. When they stress over money and careers or what someone said about them, and all you can think is: once you've seen behind the curtain, at the end, only a few things remain, and all that stuff – superficial stuff – falls away, forgotten.

'I remember this guy at work getting pissed because I was late getting back to him on something.' Isaac shakes his head. 'For most people, if it isn't happening to them, they don't want to know.' He glances out. 'Penn did. And what gets me, is that even with losing Mum and Sam, Laure, it was horrible, but there was a finality to them. With Kier, the not knowing, that limbo, it must be awful . . .'

Elin nods, about to reply, but instead she sucks in a sudden breath, her words interrupted by the shuffle and scrape of footsteps behind them.

11

Kier

Devon, July 2018

Zeph's himself again as we walk home. He tells me that he'd like to take a fishing trip on the river, cook what we catch on the grill.

'Did Mila show you where you can launch the kayaks from?' I give Woody's lead a tug, pulling him away from a pile of rubbish he's sniffing in the gutter.

'Yeah, she says it's pretty nice. Get all the way down to Bantham on the right tide.'

'What else did you talk about?'

'Penn, mainly. Interesting, hearing about him from someone apart from you.'

I raise an eyebrow. 'You quizzed her?'

Zeph smiles. He does this with normal, happy people. Interrogates them. Brief anthropologic investigations to work out why they're content with what he considers mundanity. Mundanity in Zeph's world describes anyone who doesn't *create*. All his friends, acquaintances, are artists of some description – sculptors, chefs, musicians, dancers.

'And?'

He laughs. 'Actually, she said the same as you. That he makes her feel safe. He's a fixer.'

She's right.

Penn's the kind of person you can call in a crisis, who'll know what to do when the car breaks down or the sink is spouting water or the airline has lost your ticket.

He remains calm. He would be the one to do CPR or the Heimlich manoeuvre, while I would be on the floor in a heap.

I know that because he tried that on my father after my mother stabbed him. Penn was the one who tried to plug his wounds, breathe air into his blood-bubbled mouth.

I did none of that. Instead, I lay down on the floor beside my mother and started screaming.

I didn't stop until long after the ambulance came. Penn said I'd only briefly pause to draw breath before starting again, and all the time my eyes were open.

Our mother killed our father when we were thirteen. Stabbed him thirty-four times from his neck all the way down to his ankles.

People don't think it will happen in a small town like ours. Knives and blood and that kind of anger.

But it did, and in some ways, it wasn't a surprise.

Mum was pushed to her limits. Verbally. Physically.

Month by month, Penn and I saw her get taken apart and attempt to put herself back together again. But each time, the pieces were put back slightly wrong, until one day, she was properly broken, didn't resemble herself at all.

Soon after that was when she did what she did and became the Monster.

That's what they called her, the tabloid press. *The Monster.*

A nickname that had its roots in one of their headlines. Riffing off a line like: *What kind of monster would do something like this?*

It stuck.

My father didn't get a nickname, but then, the narrative was never about him.

It was all about her.

I know why. It was because what my mother did was visible and imaginable. People saw the illustrations of my father's body with the thirty-four stab wounds neatly marked in black pen. The images of the bloodstained floor. Studied the old photo of my mother from one of my father's office parties, grinning at the camera, and came to their own conclusions.

What they didn't see was my mother's multiple bruises, long faded, all the years that had built to that one point, when she snapped. They didn't see the home-fixed fractures that never made it to our local GP or the four chipped teeth that she said were from falling down the stairs.

Those details were mentioned but skimmed over. People didn't want facts. They wanted *a story*. A narrative they could buy into, feel something about. They wanted to pile on, have a vessel in which to pour their pent-up rage about their own lives. To hate and to feel justified in hating.

No one likes an angry woman.

But I came to realise that no one likes any kind of woman.

Whoever she is, she's up for being judged.

Mum became the victim of all that misogyny, internalised and externalised.

She deserved it.

Should have controlled herself.

Were hormones to blame?

Women have a fine act to balance. To be, but not be too much.

What hurt me the most wasn't the strangers' judgements; it was those of the people close to us. They looked at my mother as if all the years before didn't matter. They forgot about their friend who used to run the annual Christmas stall, the woman who swam the bay twenty times for cancer research.

Instead, she became the headline, and they believed it.

The trouble was, the more they believed, the more I believed, too, and I started to struggle to see the other person my mother was.

I shut my eyes, already feeling my heart rate rising. What my mother did and didn't do always sets off a strange roller coaster of emotions inside me.

An up and down of love and fear and hate.

I don't understand what she did, but at the same time I absolutely get it.

How could she, and at the same time, *Why did she wait so long?*

I remember my friend asking me about it, a few years after it happened.

'Do you hate her?'

I replied: I hate her, and I love her.

I hate what she did to our lives, how she exploded it into thousands of tiny pieces, and I love her more than life itself.

Zeph waves a hand in front of my face. 'Penny for them? Isn't that what you Brits say?'

'Nothing.' I give another tug on Woody's collar. 'Just thinking about the wedding.'

As we cross the road towards the beach, I do think about the wedding: how many hours I've got to get through until it happens.

How many hours until I can leave again.

12

Elin

Parque Nacional, Portugal,
October 2021

'Nice spot you got here.' It's Bridie, her daughter clamped to her hip. 'Thought we'd take a little walk and say hi.' She nods at the Airstream, her dark fringe slipping forwards to conceal her eyes. 'Never seen one of these up close.' Lowering Etta to the floor, she watches her toddle around the decking. 'Plus, Etta gets antsy this time of night. Maggie calls it the witching hour. I like to get her away from everyone, calm her down.'

'You've never been up here before?' Isaac's words are light but Elin senses his discomfort, the sudden arrival putting him on edge.

'No, too far when she was smaller, but now she can walk a little of the way.' Bridie crouches. 'You can walk like a big girl now, can't you? You—' She's cut off by Etta's howls. She's tripped up, landed hands down.

As Bridie scoops her up, Etta glances, indignant, at the stones dimpling her palm. 'It hurts.'

Whispering platitudes, Bridie carefully brushes them away,

kissing it better. With an unfamiliar pang in her gut, Elin watches Etta gazing up at Bridie with total trust.

She'd like that one day, she thinks. A different kind of bond.

Bridie turns back. 'Look, I was thinking, what you guys said about dropping by, it's probably best if you give it a miss. Everyone's busy, you know.'

The comment is thrown out there, casually, but it's not. It's a warning. *Stay away*.

Elin looks at Isaac, unsure of how to respond. 'I—'

'Bridie? You there?'

Ned.

His voice, at least. It's the dog that appears first, straining on his leash as he crests the top of the path. 'Thought I heard you.' Ned stops at the edge of the decking, winding the dog's lead a little tighter around his hand, the veins in his forearms bulging as the dog springs towards them. 'Food's ready.'

Bridie smiles. 'Ned's a stickler for the food not getting cold.'

'You camp cook?' Isaac asks.

Ned smiles. 'Something like that. Can knock up a few things when I'm in the mood.'

'Oh, he's being modest.' Bridie winces as Etta reaches up, roughly tugs her fringe. 'He's better than all of us put together.'

'I wouldn't say that . . .'

Elin looks between them. The banter is superficially friendly, but she can't help feeling there's something performative about it. Forced.

Still trying to pull on Bridie's hair, Etta starts grumbling, pointing at something on the floor. 'Look . . . look.'

Meeting Elin's gaze, Bridie smiles. 'Better be off before this one starts. Hope you enjoy the rest of your trip.'

'Should be good weather the next few days.' Ned gestures up

towards the hill behind. 'You'll be able to get some miles under your belt.'

After saying their goodbyes, Ned tugs on the dog's lead to get it moving and they start back down the path.

Elin and Isaac watch them leave, Bridie making easy work of the uneven ground, despite the weight of Etta, still balanced on her hip.

Once they're out of earshot, Isaac turns. 'So, what do you make of that?'

'Pretty much a warning to stay away from the camp.' Elin rubs her eyes, a weariness settling over her. The intrusion and the odd dynamic between Bridie and Ned had darkened her mood.

'But why?' Isaac frowns. 'Ned was the one who invited us into camp earlier.'

'Probably a way of doing introductions on their terms before we found them later.' She shrugs. 'To be fair, it's their home. Must get pissed off with people wandering in.'

'Maybe.' His brow is still furrowed as he picks up his beer.

Elin knows where his mind has gone. *Kier.*

'To be honest,' she says carefully, 'I think we do as they say.'

'Stay away?'

'Yeah, this trip, it was meant to be . . .' She doesn't know what it was meant to be, but after the stress of her last case, the breakup with Will, she knows it isn't this. She wants to get to know Isaac again, not spend time chasing other people's ghosts.

A beat passes.

'Meant to show you this before. Penn sent it.' Isaac pushes his phone into her hands.

A photo.

It's Kier, sat at the top of a hill; her mud-encrusted boot soles tipped up towards the camera. Her dark hair is mussed over her face. Grinning widely, she's looking right into the lens of the camera.

Elin's about to pass the phone back when she pauses.

A little flicker of recognition. Something about her face, her eyes.

Moving the phone closer, she studies the picture more carefully this time, but she still can't place her. Probably looks like someone she knows, she thinks, dismissing it. A resemblance, nothing more.

'Kier's all he has left,' Isaac murmurs, watching her.

'No other family?'

He shakes his head, something passing across his eyes. 'The same as us,' he says quietly. 'Just each other.'

Elin nods, says nothing, but as she passes him back the phone, her hand is trembling, fingers wobbling against the glass.

13

Kier

Devon, July 2018

After spending time with other people, Zeph always finds a way to reclaim me as his own.

Mentally. Physically. Hand on my heart. Hand on my soul.

It's all about us. Just us. Everyone else falls away.

It's been like this from the moment we met; a late summer's evening in Liguria when a friend's parents were hosting a post-beach party, Zeph the designated chef.

The attraction was instant, electric. Zeph was the only thing I saw on the dusty terrace, despite the crowds of people. Shirt off, he was leaning over the grill, sweat trickling down his face, pooling in the divot above his collarbone.

I couldn't take my eyes off him.

He didn't look up as I walked closer, didn't even try to catch my eye. He was preparing food with the care and delicacy of a surgeon – shrimp lightly plucked from its marinade, laid carefully on the grill. Chopped salad. Vegetables.

'Are you watching me?'

His words hit me like a cold splash of water to the face. I flushed, almost dropping the beer in my hand.

I didn't reply. Couldn't reply. My eyes were locked on the angles of his jaw, the lines of his body.

Zeph said, smiling, 'If it's the shrimp you're not keen on, I can always do something else.'

It was then our eyes met. He was looking at me, really looking, with the same, studied absorption he looked at the food. Like I meant something. Like he already cared.

He made me up a plate, and as I ate, it felt like I could already taste him. Shrimp and salt and sea.

We talked while he grilled, late into the night. Later, over beers and rum-soaked fruit, Zeph confided in me what happened with his job, the restaurant. How his life and career had fallen apart.

Voice quiet, he told me how he arrived one morning to find they'd changed the locks on the restaurant doors, how the paparazzi had captured the moment, how the column inches tore his life to pieces.

I saw in him then the same extremes that lived inside me. The lows, the highs, the in-betweens where the only thing you can do to stay afloat is keep moving.

Laying himself bare made me want to do the same. When you know that someone else has touched the bottom, it's easier to tell them what it felt like when you did too.

I told him things that I never told anyone. Mum and Dad. The maps.

I came that night with a group of people, but over the course of a few hours they all fell away. All I saw was him – his eyes, tattoos, the dark fuzz of his buzz cut.

Someone pulled me aside at one point, told me who he was, what he was famous for.

I barely heard them. Already, it was just him and me. Me and him. The two of us, our worlds colliding.

'This was meant to be,' he told me later that night, and I agreed with him. Not because I believed it yet, but because he did. I'd never had that kind of certainty. Someone who looked at me without seeing her.

'I love you, you know that, right?'

Zeph's voice jerks me back into the here and now.

I nod, and he gently pushes me back onto the bed. A familiar dip, low in my gut, as he slides up my top, nudging it over my belly. He splays his hands over my waist, his thumbs making a point at my belly button, lightly pressing until the shape of my ribs is exposed.

He softly kisses each one, his lips dry and cool against my skin. I can smell his skin. Spice and salt. The sea.

The first two kisses I can feel, the rest blur, my stomach hollowing out as he moves his head lower. I close my eyes as he reaches up, grazes my cheek with his finger. Moving up, he kisses me on the lips.

Hard. Hungrily.

Something softens inside me.

All those words that have calcified over the years, become something rigid and ugly.

You're like your mum. A monster. Killer.

I remember the first time he kissed me like this, eyes wide open, watching. No one had ever done that before. Looked at me like I was the answer to their question. It was our second real date, at a climbing wall in Liguria, the first I'd ever tried.

Zeph got me to simply touch the wall at first. Not to look up or down. Just concentrate on the wall ahead, what's right in front of me.

He told me: *It's what I do when I'm cooking. If I thought about*

58

a full night of service, everything that could go wrong ... bad reviews, shitty customers, anaphylactic shock, I'd be paralysed. I just go step by step. One foot in front of another.

I can still feel that rock beneath my hands, warmed from the last rays of the sun, the powdery residue of the chalk on my fingers. I didn't go far, maybe fifteen, twenty feet, but I wasn't scared. He believed in me, so I did too.

After that first climb, Zeph leaned me back against the rocky wall, kissed me like he couldn't stop. He did, frequently, checking in I was okay, and then started again, his mouth on mine, searching for something.

Someone wanted me. Someone wanted me. Despite everything, someone wanted me.

And so I wanted him, I wanted him all.

Afterwards, he falls asleep, but I lay there for a while, my mouth dry, lips bruised.

Disentangling myself from Zeph's arms a few minutes later, I slip out of bed. I've only taken a few steps when I stumble, knocking the shelf above the bed with my arm.

Something falls to the floor with a thud.

Reaching up, I grope for the light, flick the switch. The floor illuminates. One of Zeph's knife sheaths has fallen.

I crouch to pick it up and as I lift it, something slithers out onto the floor.

A necklace. Long, weighty, a gold triple chain, emeralds studded through at intervals. Beautiful, but extra.

Picking it up, I turn it between my fingers. It's broken – not at the clasp, but somewhere in the middle, ends uselessly dangling. Something flickers at the edges of my mind before I remember.

I've seen this necklace before.

My heart thuds. *It's hers.*

Romy's.

As it spools between my fingers, my eyes lock on something on the emerald closest to the clasp.

Marks on the green stone. Tiny, rust-coloured droplets.

14

Elin

Parque Nacional, Portugal,
October 2021

When Elin wakes her head is heavy, muzzy, her heart thumping.

Her sleep was disturbed. Lurid, jumbled dreams: *A shadowy figure in the underbrush. The camp. Kier's face in the photograph.*

It's only as she gets out of bed, pulls her clothes on, that the dream disperses.

Yet one thing lingers: Kier. Elin can't shake it; the sense that she's seen her somewhere before.

It's not the only thing about the image that's worrying her. Kier's smile to the camera ... *too bright.* People say the camera doesn't lie, but she'd bet good money that smile was hiding a multitude of worries.

Cradling the coffee in her hand, Elin goes outside, quietly closing the door of the van behind her. After dragging a chair over to the edge of the decking, she stares out over the valley.

Dawn is opening up the sky – ray by ray peeling back the darkness to a frenzy of pastel. Her breath catches in her chest. Beautiful, too beautiful not to share.

Grabbing her phone, her finger hovers over the FaceTime app. Will's number.

He'll be up, like her, probably making a coffee, checking his phone, eyes sleepy behind his glasses. They were both early birds, but he always took longer to get going, needed the jolt from that extra cup of coffee.

No. She tells herself. *You can't. One call would become another, and —*

Her finger wobbles slightly before she takes a breath, scrolls to Steed's number instead.

'Warner,' he says, a few moments later. His face is swathed in shadow, the room behind him dark. 'You're up with the lark.'

'Don't tell me you were still asleep.' She laughs. 'Standards slipping, because I'm away?'

Steed suppresses a yawn. 'Yeah, yeah, I was just getting up.'

'I wanted to show you this,' she interrupts, flipping the screen so he can see the view. Slowly panning, she lingers on the view of the valley. 'Don't get many of these at home.'

'Beautiful.' He whistles between his teeth. 'Take it you're enjoying, then? Operation R and R all on track?'

Switching the screen back, Elin smiles. 'Not exactly. We've been pretty much full on hiking since we got here and Isaac's trying to rope me into something.' She hesitates. 'His mate's sister's gone missing.'

'Out there?' His brow furrows.

'Yeah.'

'Thought this was meant to be a break.'

'It is. Haven't committed to anything yet.'

A pause. She can tell he wants to say something but thinks better of it, changing the subject. 'How're things going with Isaac?' The question's loaded. He's well aware of what's riding on this trip, her nerves over whether Isaac would still be

62

harboring some lingering resentment over how their estrangement played out.

Elin couldn't blame him if there was. The distance between them was on her. For years, she'd blamed him for the death of their younger brother, Sam, and it had driven them apart. It was only in Switzerland that she'd discovered it wasn't Isaac who'd been there when Sam died, as she'd always believed – it was her. She'd frozen when he'd fallen into the sea and hit his head, and then she'd blocked it out. Projected her guilt onto him.

'Good,' she replies. 'But strange. Sometimes, it's like we've never been apart and then it feels like I'm getting to know him all over again.'

He nods. 'I'm glad, though, you decided to do this. From what you've said, it's important, for you both.'

'It is. He's the only real family I've got left.' She stops, her throat thick, taken aback at how quickly they'd gotten here. Steed . . . he always surprised her like this. Among the banter was someone not just emotionally intuitive, but a real friend, someone who saw beneath the barriers she had in place.

Sensing her discomfort, he changes the subject. 'And how's the rib?'

'A few twinges, but it's bearing up.'

'Don't go pushing it. I've signed us up for a ten K in January.'

She laughs. 'Nice try, but not sure I'm going to be up to it.'

The conversation goes back and forth for a few more minutes. The usual bad jokes, office chat.

As they say goodbye, Elin's overwhelmed by a sense of relief – that it had been him she'd called, and not Will. She'd been close to cracking, but she knew once she breached that barrier, it would be hard to go back.

Her chain of thought is broken by something catching her

eye – a soft toy, wedged between the decking. An ear is flopped over the slats, the bright blue a stark contrast to the silvered wood.

Elin gets up, walks over to it and gently tugs it out.

A rabbit.

It's damp between her fingers, tiny twigs and debris clinging to the fabric. The glassy eyes are misty with dew, and she wipes them away to find them staring balefully at her, the black pupils oversize, engorged.

She thinks about Etta last night, her distraction. *Look . . . look.*

'You're up early.' Isaac appears behind her, barefoot, hair still sleep tousled. 'Don't think I'm going to survive the next few days if you keep going at this rate.'

Elin smiles. 'Couldn't sleep.'

'What's that?' He nods at the toy.

'Found it on the decking. I reckon it's Bridie's kid's. Etta's. She kept looking at the floor.' She turns it between her fingers. 'I'm going to take it down there. Gives them no excuse to come back.'

Elin doesn't voice the other motive: another look at the camp.

Last night, it kept playing on her mind: not just the movement she'd glimpsed through the window of the van, but the niggling feeling that she'd missed something, something lurking at the periphery of her mind, just out of reach.

At first glance, the camp looks deserted. Each van closed, dark. Beer bottles are lying upended beside the bench, the amber glass sticky and shimmering in the light. Elin can picture the scene – the group sat around the bench, talking and drinking late into the night.

Walking forwards a little, she looks around, eyes flitting between the vans. Studying the space, she tries to recapture the feeling she had yesterday, but nothing comes.

Shaking the thought free, she walks over to the bench. The

wooden surface is dirty – grease marks and crumbs, a sticky imprint from the bottom of a glass. Tugging the toy from her bag, she places it on the seat instead. They'll find it easily enough.

'Hey.'

Elin startles.

Ned.

He's stood under one of the trees, the dog at his feet, gnawing on an antler. There's an orange in his hand. Holding a segment up in the air with his thumb, he drops it down into his mouth, slowly chewing.

'I didn't think anyone was up.' Elin gestures to the bench, a flush creeping up her cheeks. *Had he seen her looking at the vans?* 'Bridie's child dropped her toy on the decking. I was returning it.'

'Huh . . .' His smile is amused as he looks at her, eyes lingering on her face. 'Nice of you to drop by this early.'

'Early riser.' Her voice sounds out, unnaturally loud into the still.

Pushing another piece of orange into his mouth with the tip of the knife, Ned nods. 'Best part of the day. It's when I get all my thinking done.'

'The same. My head is clearer first thing, before all the stuff the day brings starts to get in the way.'

This time his smile is warm, genuine. 'Yeah, I—'

He doesn't have a chance to finish his sentence.

Tiny glitter-sparks. The afterburn of a firework, then a dark, mushrooming cloud, erupting from the centre of the van on the right.

Lightning flash then burst and boom. Orange and rust and brown.

Elin feels a strange vacuum in her ears. A soft suck, then silence.

Soaring peaks of light.

Flames.

15

Kier

Devon, July 2018

Zeph told me about Romy a few months after we got together, but truth be told, I'd already googled her.

It's funny what you can find out when someone's a little bit famous. If he'd been a regular person, socials set to private, the most I'd have discovered was either what he'd told me, or the gossip I'd been able to prise from any mutual friends.

As it was, I could find out quite a lot. It was just idle curiosity at first, the whole, borderline insecure *who did he date before me*, because odds suggested that he'd have dated someone with a profile, but it turned out she was more than a little bit famous too.

In fact, a whole lot more famous than him.

I knew *of* her, of course, everyone did, but I'd missed the fact that they were together. I was out of the country when it all played out, and by the time I got back, they'd split, and it was no longer in the news. One of the fallouts of travel. You go away and your cultural references remain fixed at the point you left.

The first time I saw a photo of them together I couldn't wrap my head around it.

Romy.

You know someone's really famous when they only go by their first name. Classically trained in ballet, she'd gone rogue a few years before, Sergei Polunin style – tattoos, temper tantrums, the works.

Persona non grata until she starred in an advert for a perfume brand that went viral. It showed her performing a dance off the top of a building to a haunting song that until that point was fairly unknown.

As she fell, time seemed to slow. She managed to keep dancing, making beautiful shapes in the air, before landing on her feet.

At the beginning, the advert caught some flack. Opinion pieces asking if the dance encouraged the idea that whether under extreme pressure, women are expected to perform, keep dancing. Keyboard warriors got involved – a pile-on.

Yet, after a high-profile interview, the tide turned, a critic commenting that there was strength in the performance, Romy's dance defying not only the laws of gravity, but something more profound – life and death itself.

Was she, in fact, a symbol of *hope*?

Very quickly, Romy became one of those fleeting cultural icons. She was everywhere, in everything. Newspapers, magazines, video clips.

My interest in them as a couple started off with a quick search or two, where I found some paparazzi shots of them.

Photos taken one night in New York, leaving some underground club. Despite the obvious interest in Zeph, my eyes were drawn to *her* – the red dress, battered high-tops, oversize necklaces draped around her neck.

Striding down the steps, dark curls springing across her face, she looked so fucking vital, strong. Like nothing and no one could stand in her way.

Another, taken that same night, suckered me in the gut. A passionate kiss on Zeph's doorstep. I was jealous. Not only of her beauty, but her presence.

It was around then that Zeph's sleep talking started. Romy's name, shouted out, either just as he was drifting off or in the middle of the night. A violent cry that would wake me. Sometimes I'd catch only the end syllable, but it was enough to set my mind spiralling.

Was he still in love with her? Was I enough?

More searches ensued. One image fascinated me – not of the two of them, but a feature showcasing Zeph's flat in an edition of *Architectural Digest.* A headline full of admiration:

Zeph Dosen's brownstone went from unloved to a forever home. A deeply personal twist on old-school style

I pored over the images, an artful blend of antiques, contemporary classics, bespoke shelving for vinyl and books.

The consummate bachelor pad, bar one detail: a necklace on the bedside table.

Romy's. It was a work of art; a triple strand of gold, studded with emeralds. I'm not sure why it captured me like it did – it wasn't the expense, although it was clearly expensive, more how bold it was. I couldn't get over how she'd feel comfortable carrying something like that off. Something that would make people stop, stare.

I became plagued by the thought: *How could he go from someone like that – someone so out there – to me?*

My foray into detective work also pulled up the fact that Romy had gone missing. Another fact that had passed me by while travelling. Well, missing with caveats. Missing from public life, but apparently no ongoing investigation – her apartment, also in Brooklyn, is still being paid for, money going in and out of her accounts.

'Sources' speculated that she'd left town. Rumours abounded that she's holed up in the desert somewhere or that she's still recovering from plastic surgery.

When I asked Zeph about her disappearance, he didn't appear surprised. He described her as 'tortured'. Said she'd struggled with her mental health and had been on a cocktail of meds, rebounded into an unhappy relationship.

'It happens, more than you think,' he said, his expression serious. 'People just . . . go. Put it this way, when she comes back, I'm pretty certain her star won't have waned.'

I'm still holding the broken necklace when Zeph stirs in his sleep.

Clocking me standing there, he smiles, a dopey, sleepy smile that slips away as his eyes drop to my hand.

16

Elin

'It's out. You can stop,' Ned chokes out, tossing the fire extinguisher down. The metal canister bounces against the floor before coming to rest alongside the others on the grass. Discarding hers, Leah stumbles towards them, coughing.

Elin tries to take a breath, but the smoke has made her chest tight, one breath not following the other like it should. She feels the first familiar fingers of panic clutching at her throat.

Fumbling for her inhaler, she takes a long pull, then another. It takes a few moments, but her chest starts to loosen, the brief flicker of fear ebbing away.

'You did good,' Ned says as Leah stops beside him, the sentence ending in a spluttering cough of his own. He bends double, hands on knees, sucking in long, slow breaths.

Leah reaches up, pulling tangled strands of blonde hair away from her face. 'Shit,' she mutters. 'If her van hadn't been set back, all of them might have gone up ...'

Elin surveys the van through the cloud of ash lingering in the air, her pulse still racing.

A smoking, half-molten mess.

The back end is almost completely blown out, metal and plastic curling up like petals.

Objects litter the floor of the communal area. Indistinguishable chunks of metal. Half-burnt clothing, books, some toys. Her gaze locks on the melted remains of a doll, hair reduced to ashes, and she feels a twist in her stomach.

'The van was Bridie's?' she asks softly.

'Yeah.' Maggie stops beside them, holding some bottles of water. Her patterned smock is smudged with black, her sandaled feet too, dirty with soot. She looks her age suddenly, Elin thinks, as if the exertion of putting out the fire has taken it out of her.

'Bridie's going to be devastated.' Passing the bottles around, Maggie's shoulders sag as she inspects the damage. 'Goes for a walk with the kid and comes back to this. Her whole world's in there. The kid's too. The vans might not look much, but they're home. Especially with a little one.'

'Only stuff, at the end of the day, but still, when you don't have a lot, it makes what you do have really fucking precious.' Ned shakes his head. 'I don't know, sometimes it seems like bad shit seems to happen to people who've already had the worst shit.'

A beat passes.

'What do you think happened?' Elin slips her inhaler back in her pocket.

'Not sure . . .' Ned wipes his mouth with the back of his hand, 'but that kind of explosion doesn't happen by accident. My guess is someone's set it off deliberately. Plenty of ways in and out of camp.'

'Who?'

A shrug. 'Lots of people don't like us being here as long as we have. They start talking, getting ideas in their heads. I—' He stops.

Bridie's appeared, at the back of the clearing, Etta strapped to her back. Catching sight of the van, she loudly cries out, a low, guttural moan.

The group move in unison towards her, Leah unfastening Etta, scooping the child into her arms.

Elin instinctively takes a step forwards, but Bridie turns away, putting a hand up to shield her face. 'I'd better go,' Elin says awkwardly, aware she's probably intruding. 'Leave you to it. Hope it all works out okay.'

Ned doesn't reply; he's staring at the dog. It's circling the blackened shell of the van, sniffing in the ashes, tail going ten to the dozen.

Two laps in, he stops, nose down, following a scent out to the communal area.

Elin watches, a chill moving across her as he abruptly stiffens, starts barking uncontrollably.

Ned's face darkens. Quickly walking over, he nudges him away with his knee. 'Hey, none of that.'

The dog ignores him, lurching back to the same spot.

'Hey, I said none of that.'

Elin walks away, Ned's words following her out of camp along with other sounds: Louder barks. Raised voices.

Halfway up the path she sees Isaac coming towards her.

'You okay?' he says quickly. 'I saw smoke.'

'I'm fine.' Nodding at the camp, she nudges his arm, steering him back the way he came. 'I'll explain in a bit.'

Elin snatches a glance back at the clearing. The dog has wrenched himself free from Ned's grasp, made his way back to the same patch of debris. Burrowing his paws into the ground, he scrabbles at the dirt, lets out a low, mournful howl.

17

Kier

Devon, July 2018

'What's that?' Zeph sits up, squinting, and then roughly rubs his eyes. Creases from the pillow mark his face like scars.

'One of your knife things. It came off the shelf. Something fell out of it.'

'Okay.' His face is expressionless, a *yeah, and*. It throws me.

'This necklace.' I hold it up, my heart thudding, the broken strand swinging uselessly in the air. I can still see the faint marks on the stone.

My eyes lock on the pattern. Four dots near the bottom, three above.

Zeph's eyes follow the back and forth of the necklace. 'Yeah, I forgot that was there. It's Romy's.' He looks embarrassed. 'Sounds stupid saying it now, but after we broke up, I wanted something of hers. She'd left it in the apartment, and I kept it.'

In the half dark his face shifts and wobbles.

'I thought—' My voice wavers. It feels like something solid has lodged in my throat.

'Hey,' he says quickly. ' I'm sorry, doesn't mean anything, not any more. If we broke up, I'd do the same. Fucking sentimental, despite telling everyone the contrary.' Zeph scrutinises my face. 'Look, I can throw it. Something I was clinging to for no other good reason than after we split, it was the last thing I had of hers.'

'No, it's fine.' Fingers trembling, I gather up the broken strands, slip the necklace back inside the knife sheath, put it back onto the shelf.

'Sure?' Reaching up, he pulls me back into bed.

I nod. I can't tell him that it's not jealousy that was on my mind when I looked at the necklace. I was thinking about his hissed *fuck you* and the pressure of his foot on mine.

I curl up on my side, and Zeph wraps himself around me, chin resting against the crook of my neck. Within minutes, his breathing slows and softens.

Mine doesn't.

A strange thing happens as I lay there. Zeph's arm, slung over me, something I barely usually register, seems to be getting heavier. So heavy I can feel the precise outline of it weighing against my flesh.

I try to focus my mind on something else, but it feels like he's crushing me.

I'm hot suddenly. Burning hot. I reach my hand up, scrabble around to find a cooler spot on the sheet.

It doesn't work.

In the end, I have to move his arm away, shuffle myself to the edge of the bed. As I settle back, close my eyes, I realise I've been holding my breath, high in my chest. Only now, away from him, does it come out.

One long exhalation.

18

Elin

Parque Nacional, Portugal,
October 2021

'What are you doing?' Isaac mutters as Elin ducks off the path.

'Trying to get a look back at camp.' Weaving through the underbrush, she eases back the branches. 'The dog was going crazy over something in the debris from the blowout. Still is, from the looks of it.'

The dog is clawing at the ground, dust billowing into the air as he digs into the dirt. Elin watches, holding her breath, as Ned drags him by his collar to the bench, tethers him with a rope. He stands for a moment, eyes fixed on the dog, before striding away.

Almost immediately, the dog lurches forwards, rope locking. Elin flinches at the sound but Ned ignores him, stopping beside the group. They've formed a loose circle where the dog was fussing and are talking animatedly.

She strains her ears, Isaac silent beside her, listening too, but they're speaking too quietly to hear. Despite that, something about the conversation, the body language maybe, and *how* they're talking – fast, fevered – makes her uneasy.

A few minutes pass and then Ned steps away, walking towards one of the vans.

When he returns, he's holding a blue canvas bag and a small spade. Absorbed back into the circle, only glimpses of him are visible as he bends at the waist, starts shovelling.

Dull thuds sound out as the shovel hits soil. Elin's skin prickles.

'What do you think they're doing?' Isaac whispers.

'I reckon the dog got a scent of something flung from the van and they're getting rid of it.' Her voice rises higher, louder than she intended, and Ned turns, eyes scouring the foliage.

Elin steps back, gestures to Isaac to do the same, but he stumbles.

Maggie turns now too, her gaze slipping past them, between the trees. She nudges Ned, muttering something inaudible. Still looking in their direction, he strides towards them.

'Get back,' Elin urges.

But before Isaac can make a move, Ned stops in his tracks, Bridie's voice ringing out into the silence.

'Ned, take a look at this.' She gestures towards the ground.

They talk for a minute or so before Ned grabs the neck of the bag. Features tensed, he hauls it down the path leading out of camp, the fabric scraping a rough line through the dirt.

19

Kier

Devon, July 2018

I wake up in the middle of the night, breathing heavily, my skin clammy against the sheet.

I didn't dream of Romy's necklace, as I'd expected, but of balloons, hanging on branches high above my head.

The balloons were a birthday tradition Mum started when we were kids. She'd fill balloons with gifts and then blow them up, hang them from the branches of the cherry blossom tree in the garden.

Wielding knitting needles, Penn and I would thrust our hands above our heads to try to pop them. We'd often miss, balloons bouncing out of reach, and some were empty, but when we found something inside – sweets, a bracelet, a small toy . . . it was total joy.

It's one of my favourite memories. Opening the back door and seeing the balloons bobbing wildly in the wind, our giddy excitement as gifts rained down on the floor and we raced to pick them up.

Mum did a lot of things like this, things that must have taken her a disproportionate amount of time to plan and create versus what must have been only ten minutes at most of actual fun, but she seemed to love it as much as us. Maybe even more so.

I've often wondered if all those good things she did for us, experiencing *our* joy, was her way of counteracting all the bad. Balancing the scales.

The balloon tree became a point of interest on my first map. I painted the tree and balloons as one, the tree itself taking on the bold colours of the balloons. The trunk, branches, all of it, somehow transcend the natural world. They look full of life itself, joy. Love.

Looking back now, I can see that all the places I painted on that first map were places where Mum had done something wonderful for us.

But in last night's dream, the balloons aren't wonderful.

When I pop them, all I get is blood.

20

Elin

Parque Nacional, Portugal,
October 2021

'He's gone.' Isaac's eyes roam down the track and then back again. 'Must be a path between the trees.'

'Probably shot through with trails, if you know where to look.' Elin examines the dense patch of forest on the left. 'Go crashing through that and all we'll do is draw attention to ourselves. That amount of tree cover, anyone could be out there.'

'Yeah.' Isaac reluctantly nods. 'Doesn't make sense, though,' he says as they start back up the path. 'Their first priority after something like that is digging stuff up, getting shot of it.'

'I agree, but chances are it's nothing to do with Kier. They could be up to any—'

She doesn't get a chance to finish her sentence.

'One sec.' Isaac abruptly plunges into a cluster of the trees on their right. Within seconds, he's swallowed by the woodland. 'Here,' he calls, a few moments later. 'Come and take a look at this.'

Elin follows him in, weaving her way between the trees. She's only gone a few metres when the forest splinters open to reveal a large clearing. Her skin prickles. 'What the—'

'My reaction exactly.' Isaac slowly exhales. 'Caught a glimpse of it through the trees.'

Scattered pockets of light are illuminating not only the forest floor, but a large wooden structure shaped like a tepee. It's vast, hundreds of branches bound together to a centre point at least five metres above her head.

An odd, vertiginous sensation grips her as her eyes follow branches up to the middle. The sheer scale, the precision in the construction – it couldn't be a starker contrast to the chaos of the natural world around them.

Steadying herself, she moves closer. The floor, soft with decaying leaf litter, gives a little beneath her feet. Elin looks around it, unsettled. She can't help feeling that there's something primal about the structure. *Ceremonial*, she thinks, trying to find the right word.

Shrugging his rucksack from his shoulders, Isaac walks around the perimeter. 'Some kind of den . . . an Outward Bound shelter, maybe?' He slips between a gap in the branches. 'Look, there's a fire ring in here.'

Elin follows him in, one of the branches catching on her jacket as she squeezes through the gap. 'Darker than I thought it would be.' She turns in a slow circle, taking in the weak slivers of light filtered through the branches, the smoky staleness clinging to the air.

'You did say Ned mentioned that some weird shit happened out here.' Isaac's voice is jokey, but she senses an uneasiness in his features. 'You know, this part of Portugal . . . the Celtic culture's apparently still pretty engrained in some places. Folklore . . . not just the witchcraft stuff, but other rituals too. Animal sacrifices—'

'Let's get back.' Elin pretends she hasn't heard him, pushing her way back out.

The structure was making her uncomfortable – that sense of enclosure, of feeling trapped.

It brought back echoes. Echoes of things she desperately didn't want to remember.

21

Kier

Devon, July 2018

'You look beautiful.' I nearly spill my glass of champagne as Mila emerges from the changing room, gives an awkward turn. She looks at me anxiously, cheeks flushed, as if waiting for a criticism.

There's none to give.

Her wedding dress is stunning. White silk and lace and tiny embroidered flowers. She looks bold and beautiful. It suckers me in the solar plexus.

The cynic in me would say this is a hardwired response, something society and hundreds of films and books have primed in me to find emotional, but it's not. I don't do sentimental. It's something visceral.

Studying her, I realise that it's not the fancy shop and the mood lighting and the dress that I'm reacting to, it's *her*. It's what a thousand mothers and sisters of the brides and everyone else responds to: the look on the bride's face. Not the dress itself. It's how it's making them *feel*.

Radiant. Hopeful. Full of love. Joy.

'Not too much?' Mila toys with the bodice. 'I wasn't sure if this was too fussy compared to the simplicity of the skirt.'

'No. You look stunning.'

Beside us, the assistant smiles, indulgent, used to nerves, self-deprecation. She tops up our glasses as I take too many photos while promising not to send them to Penn.

'So, your turn?' Mila heads back into the changing room.

'The bridesmaid's dress?' I feel my heart jolt.

'Yeah, can't wait to see you in it.'

Flushing, I hesitate, ready to give an excuse, but there's none to give. I'm not travelling, sick, or any of the other reasons I've given before as to why I couldn't try on the dress in person. I've got to go through with it.

'Me either,' I force a smile.

'It's already in the changing room.' The assistant gestures to the one next to Mila's. 'Let me know if you need a hand.'

Steeling myself, I head inside. Every part of me recoils at the sight of the dress against the wall, but I force myself to peel off my clothes, take it from its hanger.

'How is it?' Mila calls anxiously through the curtain. 'I know you haven't been able to make all the fittings, but your measurements should have a good starting point.'

Tugging the zip up at the back, I drag my eyes to the mirror, take a long breath in, and then exhale. The dress itself is nothing groundbreaking – almost nineties in design, spaghetti straps over a loose column of pale-green silk – but for me, it's seismic.

Dresses . . . they're a big thing for me, after that Halloween. I haven't worn one, even tried one on, since that day.

I train my eyes on my reflection.

I almost don't recognise myself. My hair's a mess, straggly at best, but the dress, the cut, the fabric itself, it makes me look . . .

not polished, that cheesy word, just lighter. Like someone's taken a layer off me.

'Kier?'

'Coming.' Taking a breath, I jerk back the changing room curtain, step outside.

'You look so diff—' Mila gives a little gasp before smothering it, hand over mouth, as if aware it might come off as rude. 'It's gorgeous, Kier. I can just see the flowers against it.'

'It's beautiful on you,' the assistant echoes.

'Gives me the inside track on what you'll be like as a bride,' Mila says softly.

I force a smile. 'If it does, I think it'll be you accompanying me down the aisle, not Penn.' Picking up my champagne, I take a sip. 'I don't think he's that keen on Zeph.'

Mila looks conflicted. 'He's overprotective, that's all. I don't think anyone would be good enough. The fact that you're so close . . . makes it hard for him to be objective.' She smiles. 'The most important thing is how you feel about him? Right?'

I hesitate. They're there, on the tip of my tongue. My worries, concerns.

'I love him,' I say finally.

'And that's all Penn needs to know.' Mila catches my eye. 'It's been rough, hasn't it? With you and guys in the past?'

My heart starts to beat a little faster.

This is why I don't come home.

This . . . scrutiny.

'Do you want to grab a coffee by the harbour?' Mila asks as we leave the shop. 'I need to talk bouquets. I think Penn's had it now on the floral front. Looks pained every time I bring them up.'

'Peak flower?'

She grins. 'Peak flower.'

We walk down the narrow steps and onto the high street.

The view of the harbour has been eclipsed by the summer throng, aggrieved locals trying to go about their daily business together with meandering tourists clad in cliché coastal.

Among the crowd, I spot a familiar face: the woman who runs past the van in the morning. She comes past more or less every day, same time, same pace.

This time, though, she's with her boyfriend. They're holding hands, talking animatedly. Despite their carefree laughter, there's a tension to her features and a definite emptiness in her eyes. I recognise it. She's there, but not there, her mind on something else.

I put up my hand to wave, then draw it back, thinking it might be odd. She probably sees lots of people when she is running, no reason to think she'd recognise me.

We walk for a few minutes before stopping outside a café just short of the harbour.

'Want to sit outside?' Picking up a menu, Mila then passes one to me. 'Iced lattes are pretty good here.'

I nod, about to sit down, when my phone buzzes. A message from Zeph.

When are you back?

I tap out a reply. **Not for a bit. We're just stopping for coffee.**

R u sure? Thought we could prep dinner together?

I don't reply.

Taking a seat, I pick up the menu. As the waiter weaves his way towards us, my phone buzzes again.

This time, I don't even look at it. Switching it off, I push the phone deep inside my bag.

22

Elin

Parque Nacional, Portugal,
October 2021

'Coffee?' Isaac's already spooning grounds into the cafetière.

'Yeah, then I need a shower.' Peeling off her coat, Elin discards it on the driver's seat. She grimaces. All she can smell is the bitter, acrid stench of smoke. 'Want to wash all this away, start the holiday proper.'

'Don't reckon it's going to be that easy.' The sentence hangs in the air as Isaac reaches for the mugs.

'What do you mean?'

'Well, we need to work out what it is they're hiding down there—'

Bending to unlace her boots, Elin bites her lip, wary of how he'll take what she's about to say. 'Look, I'm not sure we should be getting involved. Maybe it's best we leave it for Penn for when he comes out.'

'Leave it?' His eyes darken. 'After we saw Ned dragging that bag out of camp?'

'Not *leave* it, but I think we pass over what we've seen to Penn. Let him work out what to do with it.'

Isaac pushes one of the mugs forwards with his finger, his features tightening. 'But Penn can't take any more time off, not for a month or so. Might be too late by the time he gets out here, and even then, it's not going to be something he can do himself. If they recognise him, wonder why he's still asking questions, there's every chance they bolt.'

'Too late for what?'

'Finding out if whatever they pulled out from that explosion is linked to Kier.'

'You really think it is?'

'I don't know, but there's a chance, and I know that if it were you who was missing, I'd want to explore that chance.'

'Okay,' she says slowly. 'But what exactly are you planning to do? He could have taken the bag anywhere.'

'I'm not thinking about the bag. I was wondering if we should try and find the rest of the debris. A blast like that, it'll travel, maybe as far as the trees behind. They were looking out front ... might be something they've missed.'

'But that's their private stuff we'd be rooting around in. Bridie's stuff. We'd be crossing a line—'

'I get that, but the camp's the only lead Penn has. If there *was* anything linked to Kier in that van, I wouldn't forgive myself.'

Forgive myself.

Something else is driving this, Elin thinks, watching him. Not just helping someone out.

'What's this really about?' she says. 'It's not just some favour for a mate, is it?'

A long pause. Isaac fiddles with the handle of the cafetière.

'No. What I said before, it's not the full story.' His voice catches. 'Laure ... the grief, I went to a dark place, Elin. Penn ... he was there for me. Only just met the bloke, but ...'

Heat crawls up her cheeks as she absorbs the implication of his words. 'My fault,' she says eventually, 'for leaving you on your own. I should have made you come back with me and Will.' After Laure died, she'd asked him if he wanted to stay with them for a while, and he'd refused. She should have insisted. Not taken no for an answer.

'You weren't to blame. Even if I had come with you, I don't think I'd have told you. Things were' – Isaac pauses – 'new between us. It was complicated.'

They sit, silent for a minute. Elin can't get his words out of her head. *She had no idea.*

'Exactly how dark did it get?' She asks a few moments later.

'Dark enough for him to have to walk me back from the edge.' His voice wavers. 'If he hadn't . . .'

A few beats pass. Elin looks up, out, to the valley opposite, the hills rising up behind, still in hazy, morning shadow.

'I get it now,' she says finally, 'why you want to help. I was just thinking about what Mum always used to say. Never—'

'Leave a debt unpaid,' Isaac finishes, meeting her gaze. 'That's been playing on my mind a lot, you know, since Penn asked me about coming out here.'

Elin's mind shifts to Steed. His unwavering, unshowy support. Not just during the case, but after. The visits to the hospital, the phone calls, texts. That person who showed up . . . they'll always be special.

'When do you want to go take a look?' she asks.

'Tonight. Once it's dark.'

'What are you doing?' Isaac says later, glancing up from his book.

'Bit of research, on Kier. I've just been reading about what happened with her parents. Pretty bad, isn't it?' One of those cases, as a detective, you'd never forget, Elin thinks, headlines still chasing through her mind.

Frenzied attack. 'The Monster' jailed. Wife stabs 'kind and gentle' husband and tells police 'I did it all'.

'Yeah. Took a while for Penn to open up about it. Can't even imagine, can you? How you'd even go about wrapping your head around something like that?'

'No,' she replies, struggling to absorb what she'd read. Shock value and the obvious complexities of the case aside, it adds weight to what they know about Kier's disappearance. Gives her not only a different insight into Kier and her potential vulnerabilities, but Penn too. His drive to find his sister . . . she understands it, she thinks. She'd be desperate in his shoes.

'What else have you found?'

Isaac's still watching her. 'Not much. I went through her social media, but there was nothing apart from work stuff.' Elin keeps scrolling. 'But I've just found an article about her ex, Zeph. You were right, he's still in New York from the looks of it—' She stops, finger hovering over her touchpad, as she notices something flash up on her phone.

A message from Steed.

Proof. No wriggling out of it. We're doing this together, even if I have to carry you.

He'd screenshotted the entry to the 10k.

Elin knows what kind of face he'd have had when he sent it, the stupid grin he does when he's laughing at one of his own jokes. She smiles.

'What's so funny?'

'Steed . . . dumb joke.' She shakes her head. 'I'm going outside to give him a call. If I don't pay enough homage, I'll be bombarded with more.'

*

'So what do you think?' Steed holds up his tablet. 'Probably can't see the screen, but that's the race entry there ... you're committed.'

'Not sure that's allowed without consulting my doctor.'

He laughs, the phone shaking in his hand. They talk about the race for a few minutes before the tone shifts. 'You know,' Elin starts. 'Isaac and I were chatting earlier, about you ...'

'About *me*?' He raises an eyebrow. 'Sounds ominous.'

'Not really. We were just talking about how few people are really there for you when the chips are down. I told him about everything you've done for me since the breakup.'

Steed gives her a lopsided grin. 'Where's all this coming from? You missing me, Warner? Withdrawals from all my crap jokes?'

'No ... seriously.' Elin hesitates, her mouth dry. 'I just wanted you to know that I appreciate it, that's all.'

He brings his eyes up to meet hers, his expression softening. 'If we've got permission to be soppy, I'm missing you too. Weird, without you here.'

'At work?'

A pause before he replies. 'Yeah ... think I've just had one of those days.'

'Doom day?' They've talked about this a lot. *Doom days*, they call them, random days when normal, everyday life had the capacity to floor you. Elin had never probed, but she got the sense that Steed, like her, had stuff going on that sometimes got the better of him.

'Yeah. Feel better talking to you, though.'

Watching the smile appear on his face, Elin's about to reply, but stops, not sure how his words have made her feel, an unfamiliar sensation. Like she's been taken over by something – something out of her control.

As the conversation winds up, they go back to their usual

banter, but the odd feeling his words have stirred inside her lingers.

Elin puts the phone down, not sure what to make of it, confused.

23

Kier

Devon, July 2018

I'm nearly back at the van when a message comes through from Mila.

She's sent the photo of me in my bridesmaid's dress.

My breath catches in my throat as I stare at it, scrutinising it all, the neckline, how the folds of the fabric fall over my legs.

I still can't process it. The idea of wearing a dress. In some way, becoming her.

My aversion to dresses started with Halloween, when someone dressed as my mother for a party. It was a boy, one of the guys who liked to down kegs of beer and slap his mates on the back between their shoulder blades.

He made a big entrance to the party, all swagger and booming laughter, dressed like Mum, an almost identical daisy print dress to the one she always wore on Fridays with her pale pink lipstick and her open-toed sandals that spread her feet too wide.

There was a knife in his hand, covered in a thick, crimson paint that was meant to look like blood, spatter and spray and everything in between. He'd taken time on it.

When he came into the kitchen and saw me, he snorted with laughter, a weird, ugly snort. He actually called people over to watch me looking at him, said *Look, she's here*, did that snorting laugh again.

I remember everything about that moment, just as I remember everything about the moment I found Dad, there on the floor, half in and out of the utility room, Penn knelt beside him, pumping his chest and blowing into his mouth.

At moments like that, moments that become befores and afters, it's as if your body makes you focus on everything but the really important thing that's happening.

I remember noticing that one of the kitchen cupboards didn't have a handle, and how the beer had left a bitter taste in my mouth. I remember Rach's high-pitched laugh, the laugh she did when she didn't really find something funny, and I remember the shuffle-thud of the boys sliding down the banisters.

I remember thinking that everything was riding on that moment. They were all watching me, mouths slightly open, and it was an effort to stop the smile from melting off my face like butter in a hot pan.

It's only a joke, someone kept saying, and I knew I was meant to laugh along. Meant to find it funny. So I did. I laughed, and then laughed some more until everyone drifted away.

I remember coming home and telling Penn, and what he said to me afterwards. 'You didn't have to laugh. You could have just walked away.' He looked at me then like he didn't get me. He never understood why I tried to fit in with people I didn't really like before what happened with Mum and Dad, let alone afterwards.

But it wasn't about fitting in. It was about proving that I wasn't like Mum.

I wanted people to see nothing of her in me.

Those words. *The monster's daughter.* They'd stuck.

What he didn't get was that those people, the almost-strangers, mattered more than our real friends. My friends already knew who I was, so it was more important to prove it to the people who *didn't* know me.

If I proved it to them, then the voice inside me might go away. The voice that whispered in my ear that I was like her, and one day, I might snap, do something like she did.

Penn didn't get how I had to be aware of every move I made, every gesture that might mark me out as being like her.

I couldn't curse or even laugh too much. Or be too much of anything.

I learnt to meld, to be a paler version of myself, have no hard edges. I was featureless.

Exactly two weeks after that Halloween party, I screwed him.

The boy who dressed up as my mum.

I screwed him in his dirty room with his wrestling and soccer posters on the walls and cereal bowl on the floor and part of his costume still hanging out of the laundry basket.

As he lay on top of me, I kept my eyes fixed on it – the fake Mum dress, the splatter of blood that ran across the waistband.

That moment, in his room, would become one of my unmapped.

One of many.

24

Elin

Parque Nacional, Portugal,
October 2021

'I'm heading down to camp now.'

Elin's eyes snap open. It takes a moment for Isaac to come into focus, already dressed, a thin blue waterproof jacket pulled over jeans.

'What time is it?' Her voice is still thick with sleep.

'Just past one. You can bail if you want.' He smiles, his eyes tired, creased at the corners. 'One of those ideas that sounds okay until you're being forcibly ejected from your bed in the middle of the night.'

Hauling herself upright, she smothers a yawn. 'No, I'm coming ... Need a pick-me-up, though. Any coffee going?'

Isaac smiles and reaches behind him to the counter, pushing a steaming mug into her hand.

'Thanks.' She takes one sip, then another, immediately feeling the welcome jolt from the caffeine.

But as her tiredness starts to dissipate, it's quickly replaced by something else: trepidation.

*

The night swallows them whole as they pick past the camp to the woodland behind. Head torch off, Isaac's nothing more than sounds – the heavy pull of his breath, branches breaking beneath his feet.

By the time they reach the trees, he's already pushing forwards, but Elin's eyes dart to the camp.

It's silent, still, the vans nothing more than outlines. Her gaze moves left to the broken shell of Bridie's van. Smoke, still lacing the air, catches at the back of her throat.

'Elin?' Isaac's voice breaks her train of thought.

'I'm coming.' Flicking on her head torch, she pushes armfuls of foliage away as she follows him through the trees. Thick swaths of night collapse and fold under the beam. The forest floor appears in jerky, lurid bursts: leaf litter and pine needles. Weed and bramble.

'Where do you want to start?' She stops beside him.

'Here. I reckon we work left to right, not much deeper into the forest than this. Can't imagine debris will have gone much further.' Isaac reaches down, picking up a piece of plastic. 'Bits of the van littered all around here.'

Elin focuses her head torch: the angular piece of plastic has been deformed into a molten dome at the end. Unidentifiable.

Metre by metre, they pick their way through the undergrowth. It's heavy going, the light from their torches unreliable, absorbed by the trees, a careless angle of the head.

'Found anything?' Isaac spins around, the light from his head torch momentarily blinding her.

She blinks. 'No, only stuff from the van. Metal, plastic. A few bits of burnt paper, but that's about it. I—' She stops.

A noise.

Not the scuttling and scurrying of animals, something louder, more deliberate. A rustling of branches.

Elin listens. The noise sounds out again. Louder this time.

Her thoughts shift to the scene from earlier.

Ned. The dull thud of the shovel hitting dirt.

Sweat pricking beneath her underarms, Elin forces herself to turn.

The beam from her head torch bounces around the underbrush, conjuring up shapes and shadows.

No one there, nothing she can see, anyway, but still, she *feels* something, that inexplicable sense that eyes are on her.

A sixth sense.

She'd read up on it once, came away disappointed. The research concluded that the feeling that someone's staring at you is just a fail-safe. We're hardwired, as humans, to think someone is looking at us when we can't see them, even with no evidence to back it up.

A safety mechanism. Nothing more.

Still, she finds her voice. 'You hear that?'

'What?' Isaac turns.

'Sounds like we've got company.'

His eyes scour the space around them before he shakes his head. 'Can't see anything . . . this time of night, probably animals.'

Elin hesitates. Silence again. Nothing apart from the sound of Isaac moving next to her, a distant birdcall.

Breathing out, she forces the thought away as they shift right, reaching the next section of ground. Less debris here, which made sense from the position of the van.

A few feet on, something catches her eye; a rough path in the underbrush that's left the surrounding plants and ferns trampled and broken.

She beckons Isaac over. 'Someone's made a track. Nowhere to go from here, is there?'

'Nowhere the proper path wouldn't take you.' He screws up his face as he looks up and down the track. 'Maybe someone prefers a back route out. Doesn't want to be seen leaving camp.'

Elin nods, chilled, not sure why she finds the idea so discomforting. Perhaps because it implies that someone had felt the need to escape, that the hostility she'd felt didn't only extend to strangers, but people inside the camp as well.

The next ten minutes yield nothing except more metal. Part of a child's stripy onesie. Toiletries. Soft furnishings. Kitchenware.

Isaac's movements are getting louder, messier. Frustration setting in.

'Look,' she says, walking over. 'This was a good idea, but we knew it was a long shot. They've probably already got rid of anything obvious.'

'You're right.' He kicks at the dirt. 'I just wanted to feel like I've turned over every stone.'

'And you have. Penn won't expect any more than that.'

Nodding, Isaac looks around him once more. 'Yeah, let's call it a night.'

Head torches off, they skirt the perimeter of the camp, keeping close to the tree line.

They've just gone past the first van when Isaac comes to an abrupt stop a few feet from the rear door.

'Thought we agreed we weren't going to get close?'

'I've seen something.' Dropping to his knees, Isaac flicks his head torch on again. 'Keep an eye out . . .' He peers at something out of her sight line before shuffling forwards, straining up to reach past the wheel of the van.

Elin tenses, her eyes crawling up the side of the van to the blank hole of the window above. *Ned's van?* If Isaac turns suddenly, his head torch will be right on the window.

Several agonisingly slow minutes pass.

Scouring the area around them, Elin is conscious of every

sound he's making, every flicker of the beam. Beyond them, the woodland is an enigma, only the first row of trees visible from the dim light of Isaac's head torch.

Anyone could be out there. Watching.

Another long minute passes. All she can hear now is the thud of the pulse in her ears.

She's about to say something – hurry him up – when there's a loud rustling.

'Found something.' Isaac stands up, holding a clear plastic bag. Steadying the head torch, he trains it on the exterior.

'A hard drive.' Elin shoots another look at the window above. 'Okay, but we can't justify taking random stuff. That could be anything.'

'I'd have said the same if I hadn't seen these.' Pulling out a small cardboard wallet from the bag, Isaac passes it to her, his expression grim. 'There are photographs in here. Photographs of Kier.'

25

Kier

Devon, July 2018

Echoes of that Halloween follow me all the way back to the van.

It's only when I'm inside that it leaves me.

An assault on my senses: Zeph, already cooking, consumed. Pan hissing with fat, knife moving so fast over a red chilli that it's almost a blur.

Neat heaps of finely chopped veg sit on the counter. Sugar snaps and mangetout, some cabbage and cucumber. The bowl on the left is heaped high with grated coconut flesh, a finely sliced mango.

He's making a salsa. One of my favourites.

Zeph told me once where his love of cooking began; with his religious zealot parents, who called him out on just about everything. 'Food was my only way to please them.' I remember he smiled, but his eyes were sad. 'Forgive me my sins if the food is good enough.'

'Was it ever?' I asked.

He shrugged. 'Only sometimes.'

He pauses chopping, looks up. The memory disperses. 'Hey.'

'Hey. Smells amazing.' I set my bag down on the floor, almost over-balanced by Woody throwing himself at me. 'Salsa?'

'Yeah.' Picking up a bunch of coriander, he starts chopping. 'How was the coffee?'

'Good.' I grin. 'Still getting over seeing myself in a dress.'

'So, do I get a look?' Zeph pauses again. 'There's not some weird rule, is there, about seeing a bridesmaid's dress, like there is about seeing a bride?'

'I don't think so.' I find the photograph Mila sent me, pass him the phone.

His pupils widen, eyes slowly moving up and down the screen. Half smiling, I wait for the wolf whistle, the lazy smile, but it doesn't come.

A sudden shift in the atmosphere.

'You chose it?' he says finally, sliding the phone back across the counter. 'Not Mila?'

'We chose it together. Bearing in mind I haven't been in for any fittings, fits pretty well, doesn't it?'

No reply.

Picking the knife back up, he carries on chopping, faster and faster, fingers a blur, the coriander now nothing more than dust. The smell, metallic, soapy, is suddenly overwhelming.

I swallow. The air between us has become something solid, a wall.

'Don't you like it?'

''Course.' His voice is flat. 'You just don't look like you in it, that's all.'

I look at the photograph to try to understand, but all I see is the sparkle of the moment and my embarrassed smile and the half-empty glass of champagne in the assistant's hand. I see my slightly fluffy hair and parts of my body that aren't usually seen in a dress, but I look like me. 'But it's lovely, the material, the cut . . .'

'I know. I'm just saying, I prefer you like' – Zeph waves the knife in the air – 'like this. Like how you always dress. You don't look comfortable in it. It's as if' – he pauses – 'you're trying too hard.'

I feel the sharp sting of tears at the back of my eyes.

Shame.

That's what I feel. It's familiar; it's how my father used to make me feel. Every day, without fail.

In front of the rest of the family: *I wish you'd try a little harder.*

As an aside to his friend when I was sat, just a few feet away: *She's always been like this. Chaotic. Disorganised.*

Out of earshot of my mother: *Kier, your clothes are looking tight.*

I look back at the image. Maybe I *do* look uncomfortable. Does my smile look false?

Zeph's studying me. Dropping the knife, he smiles. 'Hey, I'm just being silly. You look good, of course you do. It's just different, that's all.' Using the back of his hand, he scrapes the coriander into the bowl. Bitty fragments of the herb dot his skin.

I look at the photo again, but his words have tainted it. The moment, there in the shop, the dresses, the heady champagne and the laughter, it's been made dirty somehow.

26

Elin

Parque Nacional, Portugal,
October 2021

Isaac still has his coat on as he flips open his laptop, attaches the hard drive.

'Video clips,' he murmurs as the contents fill the screen.

Elin watches with a sense of disquiet as Isaac opens the first, sets it to play.

A static shot of the interior of a van.

The camera is pointed from somewhere near the driver's area, giving a full view of the kitchen area, seating, the bed behind. No one there, but nevertheless, there is a sense of a scene disturbed. Clothing on the floor. Cafetière. Leaflets strewn across the bed.

Scrutinising the screen, Elin's pulse picks up, the sense of disquiet building to something more acute. Alarm.

'Pause it for a moment.' Picking up one of the photographs of Kier that Isaac found, she holds it up to the screen, eyes flicking between the two. 'The interiors ... they match.'

No doubting it. It's the same van.

'Looks like it was parked up somewhere here.' Isaac points to the back window.

'Yeah, but not at the camp. Wherever this is, it's more open. A different backdrop.'

'I agree, I—' He breaks off. A sudden movement on the screen. A door opening.

A woman enters.

Isaac takes a sharp breath. 'That's her. Kier.'

Elin peers at the screen. Kier is dressed casually, in comfy clothes: joggers tucked into a pair of socks, an oversize white hoodie, one of those faux US college ones, YALE emblazoned across the front in dark letters.

Her gaze moves up to Kier's face, the hairs on the back of her arms rising as she studies her features. The sense of recognition – it's even more acute seeing her in the flesh. Racking her brains, Elin tries to place her, but nothing pulls out at her.

She watches as Kier clambers onto the bed and flops down on her front. Grabbing one of the leaflets, she starts reading, hoodie rucking up to reveal the hem of her underwear.

All at once, the camera zooms in, a sudden, smooth motion. Zooms in until Kier, sprawled on the bed, nearly takes up the whole frame.

Elin's stomach rolls. It feels invasive, makes her want to look away, like she's a voyeur. 'Someone was secretly filming her.' Her voice catches.

It's hard to watch as Isaac methodically clicks from recording to recording. They work their way through entire weeks, skipping over the sections where the van is empty.

They keep scrolling.

Kier stretching, cooking, painting. Kier, damp from the shower, hair wrapped in a turban. Kier reading.

Elin swallows hard. Echoes of the past few months. She

wonders if Kier had felt it, like she had. The heavy, dragging weight of an unwanted, intrusive gaze.

Isaac looks at her a little closer. 'Something wrong?'

'It's just hard to watch, seeing someone invade her privacy like that.'

'Close to home . . .?'

'Yeah. The last case.' She exhales. 'Most of the messages I got were just random stuff, saying I'm not good at my job, that kind of thing, but one . . .' Elin rubs her eyes. 'It was this photo of me in hospital, like they were letting me know they were watching.'

He softens his voice. 'Sounds pretty frightening.'

'It was.' Elin blinks.

Isaac is quiet for a moment. 'Hearing you say that, I feel crap now, asking you to look at this. You need a proper break, and I go and ruin it by dumping this on you.' He pauses. 'We can leave it if you want. I can explain to Penn, ask him to take it from here. He'll understand.'

'No,' she says quickly. 'Seeing this . . . I want to. Knowing she's gone through the same thing . . .'

He nods. 'I get it. Feels personal.'

'Yeah.' It's also something else too, something she isn't quite ready to share.

Recognising Kier but being unable to place her – it has echoes of Sam. Of not remembering. Knowing her mind had blocked the episode out, and her role in it, is terrifying. A fear she's been harbouring ever since: *Could it happen again? If her mind had done it once, was it possible it had before? Were there other things she couldn't remember?*

No matter how hard it feels, she can't leave this here, not with any kind of doubt hanging over her.

'Look.' Isaac's finger jerks to the screen, breaking her reverie. 'A dog.'

It walks away from the camera, from the driver's side, leaping onto the bed. Kier makes a fuss of it, rubbing its belly.

Elin stares, her pulse picking up. 'Is that—?'

'Yeah, it's Ned's dog, I'm pretty sure.'

'Did Penn mention Kier had a dog?'

'I think so.'

'Puts the dog going crazy in camp yesterday in a different light.'

Isaac nods, his face pale.

'If it *is* the same dog,' she says, thinking aloud, 'we can't rule out that there might be a legitimate reason why they've got it. Maybe Kier felt like she couldn't look after it any more.'

'Possible, but it doesn't tally with the idea that she didn't know the camp well or didn't stay there very long. No way you'd entrust your dog to a total stranger.'

'Speaking of strangers,' Elin says, biting down on her lip. 'Have you noticed there's no one else in any of these clips? Strangers or otherwise?'

'Perhaps she didn't like inviting people back. Probably wise, in a place like this, when you're on your own.'

'That makes sense at the beginning, maybe, but what about later on, once she got to know people?'

'Unless we're not seeing everything.' Isaac types something and then scrolls. He nods. 'There are gaps in the footage. Some a day, a few days. Others closer to a week.'

She thinks it over, her pulse now racing. 'Is it possible someone's gone through the footage, deleting stuff?'

'It is, but you'd have to be motivated – something happening that they don't want eyes on.'

'When does the footage stop?'

'Looks like October-time, 2020.'

Without any time line, there's no way of knowing if that's

particularly significant, but the gaps in the footage definitely are. Too much to be an error.

'So what do you want to do?' Isaac looks at her, his features tense. 'We can't speak to the camp about this, but we could mention the dog at least in passing, couldn't we? See their reaction. We don't have to link it to Kier.'

'I'm not sure ... The minute we start asking questions, there's every chance they up and leave. I reckon the best approach for now is to watch and wait, give everything a chance to breathe.' Elin looks back to the screen. 'These recordings give us something to work with in the meantime. The leaflets we saw Kier reading on the bed, my guess is they came from the tourist office.'

'Start there?'

'Yeah. Won't hurt to ask a few questions.' Elin's eyes move back to the image of the dog on the bed. She overlays it in her mind with one of the dog, scrabbling fruitlessly in the soil, his haunting howl echoing into the silence as Ned had dragged him away.

27

Kier

Devon, July 2018

'Sorry for reacting like that about the dress.' Zeph forks a piece of fish into his mouth.. 'Seeing you, looking like that, all my insecurities . . .'

'You've no reason to feel insecure.' I slip the dog a piece of my fish underneath the table. I've barely touched my food, my stomach unsettled ever since I got back to the van.

'I think it's being here, back in Devon.' Zeph slowly chews. 'Since we've arrived, it's like this' – he gropes for the word – '*barrier* has come up between us.' He gives an odd, high-pitched laugh, but it doesn't sound like he finds it funny at all. 'It feels like I don't know you, at least not as well as I thought I did.'

'I could say the same about you.' *Deflection.* Years before, I'd done the same to steer someone away from subjects I find difficult to talk about. Dangerous waters. 'What you said, the other day, at Penn's. You mentioned getting close, touching distance. You've never mentioned that before.'

'Touching distance?' Zeph frowns.

'To marrying.' I feel the pulse of blood in my temple. 'Was it Romy?'

He shifts in his seat. I can almost hear his thoughts ticking over. 'This is to do with what you found, isn't it?' he says finally. 'The necklace?'

I don't reply.

'I told you, it was stupid, keeping it. There's nothing there now, and if I'm being honest, there shouldn't have been from the start.'

'So why were you with her for so long?'

Zeph pushes his plate away. 'You want the truth?'

I nod.

He sighs, running a hand over his face. 'Look, it's not something I wanted to go into before, out of respect for her, but Romy was ... troubled, Kier. Not just drugs, but drink, prescription meds. After the whole advert thing blew up, it got worse. I thought success would bring her some kind of peace, but no.' He shakes his head. 'She was at the peak of her career, and she blew it all up.'

'Is that why you split?'

'Yeah.' Zeph's expression is bleak. 'She was on a downwards spiral, angry at the world. Didn't like me getting home late from work, got jealous if I even so much as spoke to someone else. We'd have these fights ... It brought out the worst in me.' He looks at me. 'You know, until we split, I didn't know how many of her behaviours I'd absorbed, come to see as normal.' I see it in his eyes, what he's referring to, how he's behaved with me at times. 'I want you to know that if sometimes I act like an insecure shit, it's because what we have, it's special. Special because it's different to that, and I'm desperate not to lose it.'

All at once, I find I can breathe normally for the first time since we started eating.

'I remember,' he continues, 'when you showed me your maps. Do you remember what you made me do?'

109

'No.' All I recall is his smile when I showed him. The light in his eyes.

'You made me look at the shapes in between what you'd painted. Told me that they were just as important as the paintings themselves.' Inching his fingers towards me, he laces them in mine. 'I remember thinking that you saw the world like I did, that you were looking for beauty in every little place.' Zeph shakes his head. 'Fuck, I needed beauty then, Kier, after Romy. Anything lovely I could get.'

'I know.' I don't want to tell him that it wasn't beauty I was trying to get him to see, but something else. Something deeper.

I wanted him to look beyond the surface, to what lies beneath those first impressions.

There's beauty there, yes, but a darkness too. In the unknowables. The never knowables. The places undefined.

With Zeph's coaxing, we look at the photos of the dress again. This time, he's all compliments, asking me about my shoes, the flowers. What I'm planning for my hair.

'So what else is left to do for the wedding?' He takes a slug of his beer. 'Is it panic stations or are they set?'

'Not much, actually. We're going to the final look at the venue on Sunday.' I raise an eyebrow. 'The day after the hen and stag.'

'Risky move.'

'Yeah, I said that. Penn's not exactly Mr Rager these days.' I smile. 'But apart from that, I think they're almost good to go. I'm taking Penn for a swim tomorrow, talk logistics.'

'Want company?' He puts his can back on the table.

I shake my head. 'The logistics thing is a bit of a ruse, if I'm being honest. I want to check in with him, how he's feeling, you know, without Mum and Dad being here.'

'Has he been talking about them?'

'No, but I can tell he's thinking about them. We both do, at every milestone.' I shrug. 'It's hard . . . this intense longing to have them there, and then feeling guilty about that at the same time.'

'Because of what happened?'

'Yeah.' I rub the dog's head. 'Despite everything, we miss them. All the time. We take it in turns, you know, to fill in for them, Penn and I. Whoever needs it. We sort of . . .' I screw up my face, trying to work out how best to describe it. 'Imagine what they'd have done at moments like this, try to play the part.'

A silence settles between us. Zeph reaches for my hand. 'Going through all of that, coming out standing . . . people don't know how brave you are.' He swallows. 'Braver than I'll ever be.'

I love him, I think, looking at him.

I love how his love consumes me, fills in all the holes, leaves me full to bursting.

All at once, I find myself questioning the doubts I've had. The hissed words, the foot on mine, the careless statements. I've done similar, haven't I?

Perhaps when I look at him and see bad things, I'm simply seeing a reflection of me.

28

Elin

Parque Nacional, Portugal,
October 2021

'Tourist office is over there,' Isaac points across the street. 'But I need some water before we go in.' Hooking his rucksack off his back, he reaches for his bottle.

'Same.' Taking a long glug from her own bottle, Elin peels her damp top away from her body. Although it's still early, the sun not yet at its peak, she's hot, sweating hard. 'I know it's part of the appeal, being so remote, but being that far from civilisation ... I'm not sure.'

As the crow flies, it didn't look too far to town from the Airstreams, but it had taken well over forty minutes, the terrain rapidly changing from rough, rocky trails to narrow wood-land paths.

'Same. Wouldn't fancy it if the weather came in.' Taking a last swig, Isaac hoists his pack back up onto his shoulder. 'Ready to head?'

Elin nods, already walking across the cobbles to the street opposite.

The tourist office sat halfway down the street is a blocky, modern structure, abutted on one side by a rustic café, a hotel on the other. An outlier among the long stretch of buildings lining the main road that all share a faded elegance, an elegance that's overshadowed by its backdrop – the vast expanse of the hills behind.

Isaac follows her gaze. 'So sedate, civilised, and then you look up there ...' His eyes shift past her to the hillside beyond. 'Wild.'

An understatement, Elin thinks, unable to drag her eyes away.

The immense scale of the land behind imbued the town with a strange sense of claustrophobia, as if the buildings were only a stone's throw from being consumed by the forest bearing down on them.

OBSERVAÇÃO DE FAUNA E FLORA. FESTIVAL GASTRONÓMICO. EXPOSIÇÃO DE ARTE. PASSEIO NOTURNO

WILDLIFE WATCH. FOOD FESTIVAL. ART EXHIBITION. NIGHTTIME WALK.

Images of the park loop on a touchscreen in the centre of the tourist office – just about the only slice of modernity among the battered cabinets and the shelves bowing under enormous piles of leaflets and brochures.

The place is gloomier than it looked from the outside, windows obscured by posters and leaflets haphazardly stuck to the glass.

The middle-aged man sitting behind the desk has a bored, hang-dog expression, only emphasised by a greying ponytail that's elongating his features. He eyes them silently before speaking in fluent English. 'Can I help? A map maybe?'

'Not exactly.' Elin walks up to the desk and stops just in front of it. 'We wanted to ask you about a friend of ours, called Kier.'

'Okay.' He looks at them warily, for the first time properly appraising them, eyes travelling slowly across their faces.

'We think she might be missing, and we know that she came here, at least once. We wondered if you might remember her—'

'Missing?' The man interrupts, gesturing behind him to a jumble of Polaroids tacked to the wall, ponytail swinging. People hiking, biking. Camping. 'We have a lot of people coming by. The chance —' He breaks off, the last words muffled by a loud, hacking cough.

'But just in case . . .' Isaac slides his phone across the desk, points to the screen. 'This is the woman we're looking for.'

The man's face is set as he picks it up with nicotine-stained fingers, the detached smile of someone ready to give an apology, before he slowly nods. 'Sim, I recognise her. She came a few times.'

'Did she say what she was doing here?' Elin asks.

'She told me she was an artist. I assumed she was looking for inspiration in the park. A lot of artists do. She was interested in the gallery in the village.' He points to the watercolour on the wall opposite. 'The woman that owns it, that's one of hers.' Glancing down at the photo of Kier again, he scratches his neck. 'And you say she's missing?'

'We think so. She was last seen here, in the park.'

'Happens too many times.' The man's face tightens. 'But sometimes, you know, I wonder if that's why people come.'

'You think people want to get lost?'

'I don't know . . . my father used to say, unless you're born here, or a tourist, you've come somewhere like this for a reason. Most likely running from someone or something.'

'So do a lot of people go missing here?' Elin looks at him uneasily, discomforted by the resignation in his tone.

He nods. 'A man last year, a tourist. Camping out with his

friend. They were hiking on a trail near one of the falls. There one minute' – he clicks his fingers – 'and gone the next.'

'He was never found?'

'No trace.' The man shrugs. 'But look, there are theories, conspiracies about what happens to people who go missing here, but the reasons are mostly more mundane than you think. People aren't prepared for changes in weather, not enough water in hot weather, not enough layers in the cold. Wrong shoes for the terrain, and they fall.' He glances through the window. 'Even if you're used to a park like this, you can still get disorientated . . .'

Elin follows his gaze, looking out a window at the imposing line of hills beyond.

Given the route they'd just walked, the treacherous paths making up the first half of the trail, she could easily imagine feeling disorientated in the wrong conditions, one set of hills and trees eerily similar to the next.

'But what about the other cases?' Isaac presses. 'The ones that aren't so mundane?'

'Well, there's only so much ground the rangers can cover, and when the fog comes in, criminals take advantage of it. Smuggling. Extortion. People trafficking, drugs. Then of course there's' – an odd, unsettling expression crosses his face – 'suicide or murder. Usually friends or family are responsible, but sometimes it's strangers.'

'Does that happen, then?' Unnerved, Elin tries to read his expression. 'Stranger killings in a place like this? I thought that was more of an urban myth.'

'No, not an urban myth. It happens. I—' Another hacking cough. Reaching over for his glass of water, he takes a long drink. 'I'm sorry.' He starts again. 'Like I said, it happens. There's some odd people about.'

'That's what the camp said.'

'Camp?' the man says quickly.

'On the other side of the hill,' Isaac gestures. 'There was an explosion there earlier, one of the vans went up. They reckoned it might have been deliberate, someone who's taken a dislike to them.'

His face clouds. 'Is everyone okay?'

'They're fine. No one inside when it blew but could have been nasty.' Isaac pauses. 'Do you know them? The camp?'

All at once, the man's face closes: a door slamming shut.

'I do, but we don't have much to do with them. They keep themselves to themselves.' He looks Isaac right in the eye. 'You know, people like that, they don't want bothering.'

Elin senses there's something more behind his words, but before she's able to probe, his computer loudly beeps.

Flashing them an apologetic glance, he gestures to his keyboard. 'Look, I'd better ... I'm sorry, again, about your friend.'

'Of course. Thank you for taking the time. One last thing.' Elin points to the painting on the wall. 'How far is the gallery from here?'

'A few minutes' walk, on the right. Ask for Luísa.' A faint smile flickers across his features. 'Tell her I said hello.'

Closing the door, they make their way onto the street. Elin blinks, the bright sunshine glaring after the dim interior of the tourist office.

Isaac's already started walking, but Elin turns to look back inside. He isn't working as he'd indicated, but talking intently into his phone.

As if sensing Elin's eyes on him, he glances up.

When he meets her gaze, his expression darkens.

29

Kier

Devon, July 2018

'Guess what I had a dream about the other night?'

'Woody's superior swimming skills?' Penn grins as he watches Woody frantically doggy-paddling in the shallows.

'No.' I wriggle out of my shorts, discard them above the water-line. 'About the balloon game.'

'I haven't thought about that in years.' Wading into the sea, his outline is absorbed into the gleaming column of sunlight spilling across the water. 'Remember how competitive it got? Seventh birthday, you knocked me over trying to get in there first.'

Following him in, I smile. 'I was thinking, you know, about how much Mum enjoyed all that stuff. Probably more than us.'

'Like this place.' Penn turns, gestures around him, fingers trailing through the water. 'I knew, when you said you wanted to go to the beach to talk about the wedding, it'd be this one.' His voice wobbles. 'Mum loved it here, didn't she?'

'Yeah.' I slowly lower myself up to my chest, enjoying the cool shock as my body is submerged. 'This was our place.'

This cove was on my very first map, where Mum taught us

both to swim, with infinite patience. I can picture her now, in her green costume, hair wet and slicked back from her face, cheeks flushed with excitement as Penn managed a proper stroke.

Back then, I painted the cove in joyful colours – bold blues and greens, an exaggerated golden curve for the sand, as if it were holding us in an embrace. At the time, it felt like it was – the cove not just a backdrop, a bit part, but a major player itself, willing us on, just like she had.

Plunging in headfirst, Penn comes up whooping, shaking water off his head.

'God, I've missed this. You brought Zeph down here?'

'Not yet.' I dip my toes down to find the rocks lurking beneath the surface. 'But I will.' Planting my feet on the largest boulder, I toss Woody's ball back to shore, watch him swim after it. 'So, how's it all going?'

He pulls a face. 'It's going.'

'That bad?'

'Yeah. Mila's put me in charge of catering, and I think we're both now regretting it. She's started micromanaging.'

'Full Bridezilla?'

Penn nods. 'Keeps waking me up in the night, panicking. Barely got out of bed before she starts writing a new list of stuff I'm meant to be doing. I've told her that the caterer's on top of everything, but apparently I'm meant to be' – he makes quote marks with his fingers – '*managing the process*'. His brow furrows and I get the feeling I'm only hearing the tip of the iceberg.

I haven't seen him like this in a while, I think, watching him. Not just stressed, but anxious.

'You need help?'

'Not with that, but maybe some of the best man stuff. The ring ... logistics.' Penn shakes his head. 'He's about as organised as I am.'

'Want me to check in with him?'

He flashes me a grateful smile. 'Please.'

'And there's nothing else you want to talk about?'

'I know what you're doing.' Penn tips onto his back, looks at me. 'You don't have to fill in for them. Not with something like this. I want you to enjoy the wedding, too, without the weight of that on you.'

'But I want to.' My voice catches. 'I don't want you to have missed out on anything.'

'I haven't.' Putting his fist up, he bumps his knuckles with mine. 'We got this.'

'You're not nervous about how things might change?' I swim forwards, flexing my legs. 'I am.'

'What do you mean?'

I half turn so he can't see my face, the heat creeping up my cheeks. 'I keep wondering if when you get married, we won't be the same.'

Penn grabs my hand under the water, squeezes hard. 'I've told you before, we'll never change, K. What we have, it's beyond anything else.'

I turn back, meet his gaze. I know he means it, but the fear is still there. The irrational voice in my head that says: *He's all I have left and now I'm losing him.*

'You've got to trust sometimes, Kier.'

'Easier said than done.'

'I get it.' He lets go of my hand. 'We've both struggled with it, haven't we? The whole trust thing.'

I know it's not pointed, a generalisation, but it stings to be reminded of it. What I've done in the past. Crossed boundaries where none should be crossed.

I watch Woody paddling back to us, neck held impossibly high. 'I think I'm struggling with it now, with Zeph. Questioning him, us. Yesterday he said that he thought I'd changed, being back here. That I was pulling away.' I'm not sure where the words have come from. Whether it's being back here in the cove, a safe space, or whether I just need to unburden.

'And have you?' Penn's gaze shifts past me, to the shore.

'Maybe.' I pedal my feet beneath the water. 'I was going over what you said at dinner the other night, about feeling tainted by what Mum did. I think you're right. After it happened, I did feel marked, I suppose. Desperate to be this ... perfect person so people wouldn't think I was like her.'

He looks at me sideways. 'And how does your relationship with Zeph fit into that?'

'Too many flaws, maybe. We argue.'

'That's normal.'

'I know.' I bite my lip. 'Sometimes I think I've got Dad in me too. That ability to pick people to pieces, like a vulture.' He'd hone in on the smallest thing, amplify it. Unbrushed hair. Overloud voices. A collar not straight. We were never enough.

'I don't think that's to do with Dad,' Penn says carefully. 'I think it's because of Mum. You trusted her, and by doing what she did, despite all the reasons why, she destroyed that trust. Made you think everyone's got something to hide. But no one's perfect, K. You pull at enough threads, eventually one will make the whole thing unravel.'

I don't reply. What he doesn't understand is that it's not just about Mum. When I'm looking for other people's flaws, I can silence the voice inside my own head.

The monster's daughter.

'You know, maybe part of the trust issue is also to do with what Mum did in prison.' His voice is all thick, like he's underwater. 'Taking her own life. Maybe as kids, we blamed her for that.'

Penn's words are physical somehow, grenades, tossed into

the water. All at once, I feel it coming – the rage. A strange, icy numbness.

He lightly touches my shoulder. 'We've got to talk about it one day, Kier.'

No, I want to say. If we talk about it, it makes it real.

Another reason I don't come back here. Penn pins me down, a butterfly in a cabinet. I can't dance around them. The unmapped. The pictures in my head.

I change the subject. 'I wanted to ask you about the hen and stag. Times, that kind of thing.'

He watches me carefully. 'Seven,' he says finally. 'We're meeting at seven. Bar first, then the club.'

30

Elin

Parque Nacional, Portugal,
October 2021

Passing Isaac's phone back across the desk, Luísa, the gallery owner, breaks into a broad smile. 'Yes, Kier visited us often. It doesn't happen a lot. Most people come for a memento and that's it.' Her hand finds the stack of patterned tiles by the till. 'Tourists think *these* are Portugal. They don't see this.' She turns to the landscape on the wall. 'But Kier did. She understood it.'

Elin studies the painting, the muddy colours pulled into sharp relief by the white of the walls.

It's striking, as if someone's scraped her messy jumble of feelings about the scale and wilderness of the park and made it into something tangible. 'It's beautiful, but dark.'

Luísa nods. 'I think that sometimes, artists inspired by a wilderness like this don't just see the landscape, but themselves, reflected in it.' She looks back to Isaac, her expression worried. 'And you're sure Kier went missing here?'

'It's not certain,' he replies. 'Police believe she's moved on, but her brother isn't convinced. Do you have an idea of where she may have gone while she was here?'

'She asked if there were places off the beaten track where she could walk and swim. I pointed her to a few.' Luísa hesitates. 'She must have found what she was looking for, because some of them are featured here, on her map.'

'*Map?*' Elin glances at Isaac.

Reaching under the desk, Luísa rummages for a moment before withdrawing a canvas. 'She made this map of the park. She left it here, but she never came back for it. If what your friend says is true, now I know why. I'd have liked to display it, but it didn't feel right without her permission, so I've kept it here.' Smiling sadly, she slides it across the table towards them. 'A shame, because something like this, people should see it, no?'

The hairs on Elin's arms stand on end as she stares, transfixed, at the canvas.

Kier *did* make a map of the park.

The first map that never made it back to her brother.

31

Kier

Devon, July 2018

Past midnight and my brain has a pulse of its own, sounding out in time with the throbbing pulse of the music, the lights flickering above.

The club reeks. Booze and sweat, cheap aftershave.

My mouth is dry, my throat tight. My stomach turns.

I shouldn't have had that last shot. Lurid blue and flaming, it was like battery acid at the back of my throat. No one else seemed bothered, Zeph and Penn knocking them back as if they were water.

They're out there on the dance floor now; stags and hens and members of public merging in one big drunken melee, strobes like searchlights, jerkily careering across their sweaty bodies.

I should get back there, in the mix, but something's holding me back. An odd sense of grief, I suppose. No matter how much I try to pretend, tonight doesn't feel like a celebration. Even with Penn's reassurances, weirdly, it feels like I'm on a countdown. That this night, this milestone, is one step closer to losing him.

I shake myself; it's the booze talking. Booze and being back here.

Mum always used to say that places held power, but I never knew how much until I left and came back again.

Each time I return, I think it'll be different, but it never is. Every day I'm here, this place strips a layer off me, taking me one step closer to the past. To all the things I've tried so hard to escape.

I scour the dance floor to find Zeph among the crowd. We'd drifted the past hour or so. I'd started dancing, Zeph absorbed in chatting to Penn's best man.

Circling the dancefloor, I walk around, watch Penn and Mila for a moment, swaying from side to side, arms wrapped around one another, but I can't see him. I give up and walk to the bar, order some tap water. The man gets it begrudgingly, like they always do, tap water a chore as opposed to profit. Half full when it arrives, he slides it roughly over the counter.

I sip it slowly, almost finished, when I glimpse Zeph weaving through the crowd.

Within seconds, I can tell something's wrong. His loose walk. The way his hands are clamped tight around his beer.

'You all right?' He stops beside me.

I train my mouth into a smile. 'Yeah, just too many shots.'

We wedge ourselves in by the bar, a bad place to talk because the man next to us knocks over a drink while he's shouting a big order at the barman. Amber liquid rolls towards us. The yeasty, hoppy smell makes my stomach fold. I swallow.

It's only when the order's taken that Zeph starts talking. 'I saw you with him earlier . . . your ex.' He's speaking like he can't catch his breath, lips pressing together, making the shape of something strange.

'Who?'

'That guy, the one you used to go out with. You were dancing with him.' His hand moves up as he says the word and liquid slops out of his glass, foam trickling down its side.

It feels like he's speaking in code. 'I don't know who you mean.' I've danced with loads of people tonight. Friends of mine, of Penn's and Mila's, total strangers.

'The guy. Your brother's mate. The one you used to go out with.'

I think. 'You mean ... Ben?' I say finally. A month-long relationship when I was seventeen. 'I'd hardly call it a relationship, and we were dancing, but—'

I try to anchor my brain to the moment, thinking about Ben's smiling face, his slack, drunk smile revealing his snaggle tooth as he'd flung me around the dance floor. Halfway through, he'd spun me off into a corner, taken a stranger's hand, done the same to her.

'It was *how* you were dancing, Kier. When you're in a relationship, you shouldn't—'

I frown. 'I wasn't dancing in any *way*. We were having fun.'

Zeph keeps talking, making accusations, and though he isn't shouting, only barely raising his voice, it's like he's screaming. My ears burn.

His hands find mine, and they aren't squeezing, but it's like they're crushing me.

He is crushing me.

As he keeps talking, I start to wonder, *did* I do something strange with Ben?

I must have done something because he wouldn't react like this to nothing.

I replay the moment, slowly this time – our back-to-back move, only the barest of touches. The way Ben had spiralled me round and his funny pissed-up mock sexy hip sway, but none of it is weird, none of it can be misconstrued.

126

'Fuck, Kier.' Zeph slaps the side of his head with his palm. 'You're not even listening, are you?' He looks sad. No, worse than sad. Disappointed.

'Zeph, I—' I start the sentence, but the words won't come out. My hands are sweating so hard I can barely keep hold of the glass.

He shakes his head and starts to walk away. I wait for him to turn back, restart the conversation, but he doesn't. All I can see is the back of his head, shoulders, as he pushes through the crowd.

The absence of him, the void he's left, is even worse than all the emotion.

Once again, I start to freeze over. The numbness descends. I am no longer me.

32

Elin

Parque Nacional, Portugal,
October 2021

Kier's map conjures a new place.

Geography and story melding to create something vivid and vital. So raw, so personal, Elin feels like she's intruding on something, but she can't look away.

The granite peaks dominating the park have become something fluid and animal, a frenzied reaching for the sky. Rivers, bisecting the valley, are nothing more than violent streaks of colour. Layers of thick, textured paint give it a gravitas that belies the levity of the colours.

Kier's done the impossible: made an already vast place bigger, bolder. Infused it with meaning. Elin finds herself blinking back tears. The alchemy of art. Someone else's soul reaching out, finding yours.

'It's got you too.' Watching Elin, Luísa smiles. 'She's managed to capture the very essence of the park even without the detail. This . . . it's a kind of cartographic art. After Kier showed me, I did some research. I read that until cartography became a science, mapmaking and landscape painting were associated activities. You can see that in this, can't you? The places she's chosen, how she's painted them, it tells a story.'

'It does.' She still can't pull her eyes away. 'Do you know where these places are?'

'Most of them.'

'This one.' Elin points. 'It's the river beach, isn't it? I recognise the dam behind.' The hard lines of the dam have been softened by the sinuous markings of the river and beach, the trees encircling it. A fierce sense of movement conjured by just a few small lines.

Luísa nods.

'This tree she's painted, at the edge of the beach, it's made up of letters,' Isaac murmurs. Tiny letters, crisscrossing over one another to form the trunk.

Elin examines it, chilled. There's something frenzied in how she's painted them.

'It's a tradition,' Luísa says, watching her. 'That when a couple first gets together, they carve their initials on the tree.'

Interesting. *Had Kier formed a romantic connection while she was here?*

'And this?' Isaac gestures to one of the granite peaks.

Luísa frowns. 'This one . . . I'm not so sure. I'm guessing it's a viewpoint, but if so, it's not well known like some others.'

Kier painted a small circle a little way out from one of the peaks. Inside the circle is a miniature of the park itself. The circle bothers Elin, not just the outline, overpainted several times in a shade of blue so dark it's almost black, but also the uneasiness of the landscape she's gestured to inside. The colours, perhaps. Light, lighter than the rest of the painting. Lighter than they would be in nature.

'I think you're right,' Isaac murmurs. 'It's a viewpoint.

The circle looks like a lens. Focusing on the land beyond the peak.'

'It's possible.' Luísa's finger hovers above the left-hand side of the canvas.

'And that one?' Elin asks. 'A waterfall?'

She doesn't answer right away.

'Is something wrong?' Isaac looks at Luísa with concern.

'Yes,' Luísa says finally, blinking. 'It's just, seeing this, now I know Kier's missing, it's hard. This waterfall ... years ago, a local boy threw himself off, then others started doing the same. Copycats. In English, they've started calling it Suicide Falls. People travel here, from all over, to—'

They all fall silent, staring at the waterfall Kier has painted. The cascading water – greys, whites, blues – are daubed on in thick, angry brushstrokes. Absolute turbulence.

Clearing her throat, Luísa moves her finger a few inches right. Tall trees circle an empty space. The trees are nothing more than ciphers – smudged browns and blacks, hinting at branches. In the centre of the space is a column of light, soaring upwards.

'There's something almost celestial about how she's painted it,' Elin murmurs.

'I thought the same. It's a clearing, probably part of the forest badly hit in the fires over the years.' Luísa shrugs. 'I don't know what the significance would be for Kier. She never mentioned she'd been there.'

'Did Kier ever speak to you about how she'd painted the map?' Isaac asks.

'Only briefly. She was embarrassed, I think, by the fuss I made.' The tension in Luísa's face gives way to a smile.

Elin nods. 'Are we okay to take a photo?'

'Of course.'

After taking the picture, they talk for a few more minutes, and then Elin reaches for a leaflet on the desk, writing on the back. 'If you think of anything else, here's my number.'

The scent of fried fish and herbs follows them out of town, the cafés on the backstreets thronged with locals enjoying a late breakfast in the sun. Elin's stomach growls.

'Fancy stopping?' Isaac peers through the window of the café on their left.

'Yeah, I'm starving.'

As they settle at a table on the side of the terrace, Isaac takes out his phone. 'Didn't want to say anything while we were in there, but did you notice something about Kier's map?' He presses a finger to the screen. 'This park's a pretty big place, but the points that she's painted circle roughly around one spot.'

'The camp,' Elin says, chilled. 'It all comes back to the camp.'

33

Kier

Devon, July 2018

'Kier.'

I flinch. Zeph's voice is like a sharp scratch down my spine.

'Kier, I—' The rest of his words merge with the muted thuds of music from the club as I stumble out onto the street. This back alley hasn't changed since I was a teenager. Oily smells and oily smiles. Neon lights bleeding into petrol rainbows.

'Kier, please.' This time his hand finds the back of my top.

'Please, Zeph, leave it.' I shrug his hand away. 'This is Penn and Mila's night, don't ruin it. I'll head home and you go back in, make my excuses; say I'm not feeling well.'

'But I don't get why you're leaving.' His eyes, unfocused, travel from me to the ground and then back again, in slow motion.

'What you said to me in there, Zeph, *how* you said it.' My voice cracks.

'Kier, I'm drunk, I don't know what I was saying. I saw you with him and I reacted.' He steps towards me. I feel his breath on my face, inhale the bitter smell of beer.

'But being jealous because I'm *dancing* with someone, that's—'

He clumsily tips my chin, so he can see into my eyes. 'I was being a jealous prick.'

'Well, don't be.'

'Come on, Kier, give me a break. It doesn't mean anything.' He reaches out again.

I shuffle a few feet back.

'Jesus,' he mutters. 'You're acting just like she used to.'

My head snaps up. 'Acting like who?'

Zeph flushes. 'Forget it.'

'You're talking about Romy, aren't you?'

Romy. Romy. Romy.

As I say it in my head, I hear her name not just in my voice, but in his.

How he shouts it at night. Splitting the word, emphasis on the last syllable. Ro-*my.*

'Kier ...' Zeph starts talking but I can't hear him. The lurid neon in the window blurs, and with it, Zeph's face. His mouth is moving and his hands, too, and as he's talking, his features morph.

It's not his face I see, but my father's. I see his beard and his eyes that could turn from warm to stone in a flash. A chill is forming inside me again. Growing and swelling, freezing every part it touches.

Zeph circles me in his arms, pushing me back hard against the wall. His mouth is near mine, the bare skin across my shoulder blades scraping against the rough of the brick, and he's still talking, his hands all over me, but I can't hear him, I can't hear any of it.

I push him, hard in the chest, harder than I mean to, the force enough to reverberate back through my arm, shoulders.

Zeph goes backwards, stumbling, breath pushed out of him in a funny, ugly gasp.

133

I don't reach out to help because I still see *him*.

My father, with his questions and his calm voice that preceded everything dark. The napkin he'd use to wipe his mouth over lunch after saying the ugliest of things.

Zeph is picking himself off the ground, dusting off his palms, trousers. As he gets to standing, a sob chokes his throat. 'Fuck, Kier, I don't know who you are any more.'

I blink.

'Don't ever, ever, do that to me again.' Zeph steps backwards, then again, watching me, before he turns, slowly walks back towards the club.

I stare after him, having to bite my tongue to stop me from bursting into tears.

All at once, I feel lightheaded, an odd, disorientating sensation, as if my brain is lagging two steps behind my head. Bending, I put my head between my knees.

It's a few minutes before it passes. I take a breath, then straighten, standing for a few moments before I stumble towards the lights of the taxi rank at the end of the street.

I've only taken a few steps when I glimpse a familiar face: the woman who runs past the van in the mornings. She's in work-out gear, jogging, but slows to a walk as she crosses the road towards me.

My cheeks burn. *What had she seen? What must I look like?*

When she stops in front of me, her blonde hair is damp with sweat, tendrils curling around her temples. 'Everything okay?' Her voice is soft and kind, and it makes me want to cry.

'Yeah, just an argument with my boyfriend.' The sentence comes out all high and weird.

'I saw.' Her expression is unreadable. 'You're staying at the beach, aren't you? In the van? I saw you the other day with your partner, when I was running.' A pause. Like she wants to say something but can't find the words. 'I'm Elin. Detective Elin Warner.' She gestures down the road. 'Are you getting a taxi home?'

I nod.

'Let me walk you over. We can talk on the way.'

34

Elin

Parque Nacional, Portugal,
October 2021

They're about ten minutes from the Airstream when Elin hears the snapping: twigs, broken underfoot, then a soft, choked sound, as if someone's trying to stop themselves from crying.

'It's Leah,' Isaac says. 'From the camp.'

Despite the tree cover, Elin can see glimpses of her through the branches, crouched on the ground, hands pawing at something in the dirt.

As they get closer, she startles, then straightens, hands reaching up to dust off her clothes. Taking a few steps out, Leah raises a hand in greeting. 'You guys been exploring?' Dull, dishevelled hair hangs limply over her face, and she runs a hand through it before her features relax into an uneasy smile.

Elin nods, noticing that Leah is trembling, her narrow shoulders rising and falling beneath her shirt. Even with the dusting down, her jeans are marked with a fine layer of dirt. Her knees too – the denim dimpled with tiny stones, twigs.

We've intruded on something, she thinks, clocking the blotchy skin around Leah's eyes, her fists, clenched so tight the knuckles are turning white.

'We've been into town, had something to eat.' Elin keeps her voice steady.

'Nice day for it. Bet it was busy.' All at once, Leah loosens her grip, dirt and old leaf matter fluttering to the ground. It's only when her hands are fully open, empty, does she seem to realise she's done it. 'Dropped my bracelet,' she says quickly. 'I was looking for it.'

Elin's gaze moves to her wrist. *No bracelet.*

Leah's eyes track downwards to her wrists, the scars crisscrossing the skin of her wrist. Some redder, pinkish, others silvery in the light.

Sticking her hands in her pockets, Leah opens her mouth, as if about to say something else, and then stops, eyes jumping past them to the woodland behind.

Elin's breath catches in her throat as she follows Leah's gaze.

Recognition dawns: they're only a few feet from the clearing where they'd seen the wooden structure yesterday.

But the structure . . . it's gone.

Elin walks forwards until she's at the edge of the open space, her skin prickling.

A pile of destruction.

The branches, so carefully arranged before, now litter the ground, metres from where the original structure stood. A sour, musty smell is lingering in the air, as if the fallen wood had lifted long-forgotten smells from the ground.

'Weird. Who'd have taken it down?' Isaac says from behind her. Leah hovers a few feet away, watching.

'I don't know,' Elin replies. 'But whoever it was didn't want any of it left.' An eerie silence descends as they study it – the empty space, the floating dance of the dust motes, tiny insects catching the light. 'We saw this when it was up,' she adds, noticing Leah's eyes still on them.

Leah's face is expressionless. 'The pyres, they're pretty hard to miss.'

'Pyres?'

'Yeah. Some people here call them pira. Pira funerária.'

Elin goes cold all over. *Funeral pyres.*

Leah gives a brittle smile, and crouches again, running her finger over one of the pieces of wood. 'People say all kinds of things, but when you see it like this, it's just wood. People conjuring something from nothing.'

'So there are a lot of them?'

She nods. 'They crop up all over the park.'

'Do you know what they're used for?'

Leah's face tightens a fraction. 'There's theories. Kids having fun, maybe? Or . . .'

'Or?' Isaac echoes.

'Rumours are they're used by a cult for some kind of ritual, but I think all that's just hearsay.'

Yet the nonchalance of her words is at odds with the reverence in how she's looking, not just at the discarded branches, but at the space vacated by the structure. Her eyes are drilling into the air as if she, like Elin, can still see the ghost of it.

Eventually, Leah drags her gaze away, looking down at her watch. 'I should be getting back, I've got work. A day like this, you don't want to, but I've been putting it off.'

Elin says, 'We'll walk with you, part of the way at least, if you like.'

'That'd be nice.'

'How have things been since the explosion?' She asks as they start down the track. 'You manage to get everything cleared up?'

'Just about. It helps that we've got Maggie, and as Ned

says' – she puts on an exaggerated drawl – '"*Maggie is nothing if not efficient.*"'

'Ned said he thought someone might have set it off deliberately.'

'It's possible. How we live … it's different, and the one thing I've learnt these past few years is that people don't like different.' She stops, as a noise sounds out. A soft shuffle of branches. Leah's eyes dart to the woodland beyond before she brings her gaze back to them and starts again. 'All of them, no matter how liberal they think they are, like to pass judgement when you choose not to follow the same path as them. Makes me laugh sometimes. People think normal society's the best way to live, but I think it's even wilder than out here. Just has better PR.'

'I get that,' Elin says softly, 'but still, it's brave to take yourself out of the loop. Leave friends and family.'

An expression flashes across her face that she can't read.

'Most of the time it isn't a choice,' Leah says sharply, bristling. Colour rushes to her cheeks. 'You have to do what you have to do.'

Elin pauses, taken aback, unaware she'd crossed a line. 'I'm sorry, I didn't mean—'

Leah studies her for a moment before her face softens. 'It's okay.'

Mentally kicking herself, Elin tries again. 'So you work out here?'

'This and that. Tech stuff mainly. I was in a corporate job before, but this lifestyle suits me better. I like the freedom.'

'I can imagine that's appealing for a lot of people,' Isaac says. 'You ever get anyone wanting to join?'

Leah falters. 'What do you mean, *join*?'

'Other people wanting to join the camp for a while.'

There's a long pause. She seems to be weighing something up. 'We do, but usually not for long.' Once again, her eyes shift to the trees beyond.

Isaac ploughs on. 'You have anyone stay with you recently?'

There's a long pause before Leah nods.

'Probably nice to mix it up a bit,' he continues.

'Yeah, brings a new dimension to the place, and sometimes, you know, you really connect. You know, the last person who stayed—' Breaking off, tears suddenly well in her eyes.

Elin looks at her, taken aback. *They'd struck a nerve.*

Leah starts again. 'The last person—' Her final few words are lost, muffled by another noise.

This time definitive.

Not just the sound of branches, but the trill of a phone, quickly silenced.

Someone's out here with them.

Elin turns, pulse picking up. She shoots a glance backwards, half expecting to see a hiker on the path, but the track is empty.

'Look, I'd better go,' Leah says quickly. 'Why don't you come by tomorrow night? Ned's planning a barbecue, a few drinks, now we've got the place all cleaned up. Raise everyone's spirits.' She pastes on a smile, but her eyes stay glued to the woodland behind.

'If you're sure? We don't want to impose.'

'It'll be fine.' She holds Elin's gaze. 'I'll see you then.'

They watch her leave, moving quickly over the rough terrain.

'Someone's out here,' Elin mutters, slowly looking around her. Though the noise had stopped, she had a horrible feeling that whoever it was, was still there somewhere, lingering among the trees.

Isaac nods, his face sombre. 'Frightened her off.' He lowers his voice. 'But she seemed pretty keen to carry on the conversation.'

'The invite tomorrow?'

'Yeah. I wouldn't be surprised if she pulls us aside.'

As Leah disappears from view at the end of the track, Elin pictures the dirt falling from her hand, the tiny leaves and twigs slowly fluttering to the floor.

35

Kier

Devon, July 2018

Woody starts barking as soon I let myself into the van.

The sound cuts like a razor into my skull.

'Hey, it's only me,' I croon, flicking on the sidelight, holding out the back of my hand for him to sniff. 'Woods, it's me.'

After a minute or so, I get a tail wag, and though the barking quietens, he's subdued, like a part of me is strange to him. I reach for the treat tin, scoop out a handful, tip them into his bowl. He's reluctant at first and then starts loudly crunching.

Pouring a water, I rummage in the cupboard for our medicine box, pop two ibuprofen from their foil. It's as if everything that's happened is pinballing up inside my brain.

Zeph's words about Romy. My hands pushing against his chest.

A beep from my phone. The thoughts disperse. It's a message from the woman I'd met outside the club. Detective Elin Warner.

Detective. I hadn't known what to do with that knowledge, still don't. I'd seen the police through so many lenses after what happened with Mum and Dad.

Protectors. Cowards. Friends. Foes.

I scan the message. **I meant what I said. Call if you need anything, ever want to talk.**

Reading it, I feel unexpectedly warmed. A similar feeling to when I paint another point on a map – the power of making a new connection.

I watch Woody finish eating and then undress and get into bed.

Leaning back, I close my eyes, try and drift off, but as twenty minutes pass, then thirty, I know it's going to be impossible. The urge, it's there. I need to paint. *Have* to paint. It comes on me like this – a sudden, desperate force. An itch I can't scratch.

But this is a particular need to do something I've never felt compelled to do before.

Maybe being back here for so long has stirred up all the memories, brought them to the surface like sediment from the bottom of a river.

The unmapped.

These are the worst of places, places that are indelibly seared on my mind, but ones I've always struggled to commit to paper. They come at me hard and fast.

The house we lived in where we first heard Dad hit Mum. The hospice where my grandmother died. The room where I screwed Halloween boy.

Mixing up the paint, my hands are shaking, my body vibrating with an energy that doesn't come from me but outside of myself. This is always a strange hinterland, the moments *before*, when the images don't even exist as something coherent in my head.

Just outlines. I have a vague sense of colour, but that only solidifies as I mix the paint and the first form knits together. Moving my finger over the canvas, I establish where the first location will roughly be.

Small marks at first. Lighter colours of the underpainting before I add depth and shade.

142

I work in a frenzy, my eyes half closed. Places spill from me; places I didn't even know would be there. I mix new colours, more confident this time with my choices, smearing and smudging them into one another.

When I finish, I'm breathing heavily, beads of sweat trickling down my back.

I step away, spent. A few beats pass before I drag my eyes to the canvas. As I stare, eyes roaming across the images, I have to bite my lip to stop myself from crying out.

It's a wreckage: one of those devastating aftermaths of a car crash where pieces are littered all over the road, but this isn't a car, it's pieces of me. My life. All the feelings those places conjured inside me. Destruction and suffocation smothering the canvas.

Slowly inhaling, I take another look. One location jumps from the canvas: the club from tonight. The building is light, but the figure outside is shrouded in a shadow that's animate, giving the impression that it's overwhelming the figure.

I blink. All at once, I'm back there. Zeph pushing me against the wall. The rough rasp of brickwork on my bare skin. His words in my ear. *You're just like her.* The comparison burns. It proves that she's there on his mind, in his waking hours, as she is at night.

My thoughts spiral, past his words, to the broken necklace, the rusted droplets marking the pristine green of the stone.

Ideas form, my mind working so fast, so frantically, that I'm not even fully aware that I'm doing it – reaching for my laptop, typing their names into the search bar.

Zeph Dosen and Romy Hernandez.

It's only as the results appear that I hesitate. I'd promised myself I wouldn't do this again. I'd been down this road with previous partners. *Just one more search. If I find this one last thing, then I'll be sure.*

But I have reason this time, don't I?

Looking back at the screen, I scour the results. The first few pages reveal nothing bar what I've already read in previous searches. Low-rent gossip pages, articles about the split.

Trying again, I type something more specific: *Romy Hernandez disappearance*.

Different sites this time; not only articles, but links to fan pages on social media. Clicking through, I dismiss some instantaneously. Most started at the height of Romy's fame, photos copied from her official page interspersed with pap shots. All apart from one peter out after a handful of posts; Romy discarded, another celebrity obsession found.

It's the last one that intrigues me. This page is consistent; photos posted every few days since the advert was first released. Again, most of these images look as though they were stolen from her own social media, professional shots interspersed with personal.

Every few posts are videos of her performing. I click on one of my favourites; a clip I'd studied again and again. Romy's in flesh-coloured underwear, enabling you to see every muscle, every sinew, her body stripped of fat. A machine.

It's filmed on a backstreet somewhere in the city. The dance is mesmerising – precise but simultaneously fluid and free.

There's something raw in the performance. Romy's dancing as if her life depends on it. To me, it seems like she's not just looking into the abyss, but already has one foot in it. Seen things no person should ever see.

I recognise that trauma, and I think what captivates me most is that she's *living* it, not pushing it away like I do. It's there, in her face, body, as she dances, as if she's channelling it. Using the emotion to elevate her performance.

The video ends.

I resist the urge to replay it, eyes slipping to the comments below.

This is her at her most captivating. A once in a generation talent.

I read a few more, but it's the final one that stops me in my tracks.

A theory about her disappearance.

One idea I'd like someone to look at is that someone made Romy go missing, and by someone, I mean her ex. Won't name names, but you know who I mean. I lived in her block and the relationship was savage. Fights over his work. Hers. I heard it all: he'd accuse her of cheating. She'd accuse him of messing with her mind. When they split, he started showing up at her apartment. I put it down to one of those toxic, codependent relationships, until the pictures started. He'd stand there, on the corner of our block, photographing her as she left the building. For me, knowing his history, it sets off extremely loud alarm bells. I told the police, and as far as I know, they did nothing. Surely they'd want to follow it up?

Whatever I was expecting, it wasn't this. Numbly, I scroll to the comments below.

Wow . . . I heard the relationship was volatile, but I assumed it was creatives being creatives.

Were you friends with Romy? What was she like?

I'd be careful. This is the kind of shit that ruins reputations (now, I know his is pretty shot already after the finger debacle, but even so . . .) All of what you've said sounds pretty spurious. All couples fight, doesn't mean he'd make her disappear. Do you honestly think the police wouldn't have investigated if they were concerned?

A recent comment, only a week ago.

Are there any updates on this?

The person who posted the comment hasn't replied.

I reread the comment again, looking for something that might hint it was simply someone being malicious, but it has the ring of authenticity. Someone genuinely concerned for their neighbour's welfare.

Despite the ibuprofen, the ache in my head has become an agonising throb. I navigate back to the video of Romy dancing playing on loop.

This time, I can't help but see her performance in a different light.

Perhaps it wasn't about Romy's trauma driving her performance to even greater heights, but about dancing *away* from something. Desperately trying to escape.

36

Elin

The decking is dark, slick with water by the time they get back to the Airstream, the light drizzle becoming a downpour, the clouds above now a solid mass.

'I need a shower.' Shaking water off her hood, Elin shivers. For the first time since they've arrived, there's a proper chill in the air, as if winter's already taken a bite out of it.

'Me too, but we should probably get some food on.' Isaac steps forwards, unlocks the door, but before Elin can follow him inside, she's interrupted by the loud trill of her phone.

A Portuguese number.

'Is this . . . Elin?'

She immediately recognises the voice: Luísa, from the gallery. 'Yes, it is.'

'Apologies if I'm interrupting, but you said to get in touch if I remembered anything about Kier.'

'That's right.' Stepping inside the Airstream, she mouths Luísa's name to Isaac. He raises an eyebrow.

'It's about the last time Kier came to the gallery. I spoke to my colleague, Inês, about Kier, and she said that she went to get a coffee after Kier left, and she saw a man following her. At first, Inês thought it was someone just walking the same way, but when Kier stopped to look in a few of the shops, she noticed that he stopped too.'

Elin's skin prickles. 'Do you know if Kier acknowledged the man in any way?'

'No, I don't think so. That's why Inês was concerned. She was about to approach Kier, but she went into a café, and Inês lost sight of the man.' Luísa hesitates. 'I know it might be nothing, but given what you said, about her being missing . . .'

'No . . . that's really helpful, thank you.' Elin stumbles over her words, thrown a little by the tone of Luísa's voice. A genuine concern. She clears her throat. 'And Kier hadn't mentioned anyone following her to you?'

'No.'

'Did Inês say if she recognised the man?'

'I'm afraid not. He had a cap on and she only saw him from behind.'

'Sounded interesting,' Isaac says as the call wound down.

Elin nods. 'One of Luísa's colleagues thought she saw a man following Kier in the town, after she left the gallery. Luísa sounded worried.'

A note of fear creeps into his voice. 'Same person who set up the camera in her van?'

'It's possible.' Glancing outside, Elin feels cold all over. She doesn't want to voice it, not without definitive proof, but her gut's telling her that Kier never left this park.

37

Kier

Devon, July 2018

The first thing I notice when I open the van door the next morning is Penn's face. Not the crumpled blue shirt, half tucked in, his bloodshot eyes or stubble, all to be expected after his stag, but his expression.

It's set, his shut-down face. His face when he's trying to keep it all in.

His eyes flat, emotionless. It scares me.

Opening the door wider, I gesture him inside, letting in a shot of sea air. It's not cold, but I rub my arms, feeling the raised bumps of gooseflesh.

Woody throws himself at him, but Penn barely responds, hovering in the doorway. I feel my cheeks growing hot, acutely aware of the stale smell of alcohol in the van.

'Zeph here?' Penn says finally, peering in.

'He's still asleep.' I cast a look towards our sleeping area, the curtain still closed.

'You want to go outside and talk so we don't disturb him?'

'Sure.' I grab a cardigan from the side, draping it over my

shoulders. Penn doesn't sit on the chairs, so I don't either, awkwardly hovering in front.

Despite my glasses, the light out here is blinding. I squint, hold my hands to my face.

Already I can feel the headache starting up again: pulses of pain criss-crossing beneath my skull like electrical currents.

'So,' Penn starts and then stops, eyes travelling across my face. 'How do you feel?' No attempt at a joke about alcohol consumption or a hard night – a genuine question.

'Not great. Too much to drink.'

Penn nods. 'Kier,' he starts and then stops again, lip wobbling, like there's a mountain of words inside him that he's struggling to climb. 'Look, there's no point beating around the bush. Last night ... it was ours, mine and Mila's. The argument, fine, I can get past that, especially with drink involved, but what I'm struggling with is what you said to Mila.'

'Mila?' I blink. Flickers of the night appear. I don't want to remember, but I can. Blurred by the alcohol, but it's there. The moments after Zeph left me by the bar. Mila finding me, asking what was wrong. Telling her about the fight and then ...

'Yes.' He takes a breath, as if summoning up the strength to carry on. 'You asked her if she was sure, Kier. Sure about us. Sure if getting married was the right thing.' As he rubs a hand over his face, his expression is pained. 'You know how stressful the wedding planning's been ... everything with the caterer. I don't get why you'd want to add to that by causing conflict.'

I feel my cheeks colour. 'I wasn't thinking straight, Penn. Just shooting my mouth, and I wasn't meaning getting married to you specifically. I meant anyone. Zeph and I, we'd had a fight, and I was thinking about Dad, how men—' I stop, not sure what I'm trying to say.

There's a long pause. 'But I'm not "men,"' Penn says quietly.

'I'm your twin, Kier. You need to get past Dad, everything that happened. I know it's hard, but you need to try, in some way, to move on.'

I'm silent for a minute. He makes it sound so easy. Moving on. 'It was different for you, Penn. After it happened, no one looked at you the way they looked at me.'

'No, they didn't, and do you want to know why? It wasn't because they saw something dark and awful inside you, it was simply the fact you looked like Mum, Kier. That's it. You looked like her, so you were an easy target for a bunch of dumb, spiteful kids. No one's doing it now.'

He's right. No one's doing it now.

But I am. Every day, I'm looking at myself.

Watching. Wondering.

'I just want the lead-up to the wedding to be as smooth as it can be, Kier. No added stress.' Penn jams his hands in his pockets. 'Look, I'd better go and nurse Mila's hangover before this afternoon.' He looks at me with the first hint of a smile. 'You're still coming, right? Last look at the venue before the big day?'

Squeezing my eyes shut, I blink back tears.

A lifeline. It feels like he's throwing me a lifeline.

38

Elin

Parque Nacional, Portugal,
October 2021

A delicious fug of garlic and herbs envelops Elin as she steps out of the shower and towels herself dry.

Isaac is cooking, something he never did when they were growing up. The knowledge stings: she's missed so much since they've been estranged. Important stuff. Details of his life – the day-to-day knowledge that most siblings took for granted.

'What are you making?' she calls, pulling her clothes on. 'Smells amazing.'

'Spaghetti.' His voice stretches thin. 'Laure's favourite.'

Pulling back the curtain around the sleeping area, Elin walks over to the hob. She hesitates for a minute, awkward, then puts her hand on his shoulder. 'Gets you, sometimes, doesn't it? Random moments. I'm the same. With Sam ... Mum.'

Isaac's throat bobs. 'I'll be fine, and then something sets me off ... in the stupidest of places. I was shopping the other day and I picked up some aubergines. It was only at the till I realised

I didn't like them, that I used to buy them for Laure. She liked them grilled—' His shoulders heave.

Looking at the emotion on his face, Elin realises how little they've talked about Laure, his grief. She's taken his lead on that, sensing his awkwardness, but she knew that sometimes you needed to be the one to ask. 'Take it you did most of the cooking, then?'

'Pretty much. Laure liked eating food. Was less fussed about the making of it.'

'Same as me.' Elin laughs. 'With Will, my contribution to meals was drinking wine while he cooked.'

Isaac gives a small smile. 'You know, that's what I miss the most, I think, our evenings. Chewing over the day with a glass of something.'

'It's the little things, isn't it?'

'Yeah.' He blinks back tears, and Elin pretends not to notice as he turns his face to wipe them away. 'Right,' he says, with a forced brightness. 'I need the loo. You okay to take over pasta watch?'

'Course.'

Stirring the sauce, Elin glances outside. It seemed to get dark so early here, shadows rapidly rising from the valley floor, enveloping everything in a murky shroud.

The sauce starts to spit, little flecks dotting the side of the pan, so she lowers the heat. As Elin looks back outside, she catches sight of a light flickering in the distance.

Still stirring, she keeps watch, assuming it's a walker, until the light briefly illuminates something she wasn't expecting – the Airstream closest to them.

Elin leans forwards, squints, her pulse picking up.

Didn't Isaac say that no one was coming until the end of the week?

'Shit—' A sudden burning on the back of her hand. Splatters of sauce coat her skin.

Jerking the pan off the heat, she thrusts her hand under the cold tap, waits until the burning eases. By the time she looks through the window again, the flickering has stopped, the van a dark shell once more.

Elin tries to shake it from her mind. *Just a walker, their head torch illuminating the inside of the Airstream* ... But as the cool water spools over her hand, her mind slips to Leah in the wood, the mobile phone trilling out into the silence.

'What's up?'

Isaac's voice pulls her from her thoughts. 'Burnt myself, with the sauce.' She moves her hand, positioning it directly under the stream of water. 'My fault. Distracted. I thought I saw a light on, over by the other Airstream.' Isaac peers out, nose almost against the glass. 'Can't see anything now.'

'Yeah, probably just some walkers.'

She senses him studying her.

'Look,' he starts. 'I don't want to pry, but I've noticed you've been a bit on edge, since we've got here.' A pause. 'Is it to do with the messages?'

'It's the one I told you about, in the hospital. The photo. It felt like someone was trying to let me know they were there. Could get to me. Ever since then, I've been on' – she gropes for the right words – 'high alert. Someone gets into a lift beside me, or bumps into me at the supermarket, my mind spirals. I think it's them.' Even now, she can still feel the fear: her heart pounding, the tightening in her chest.

Isaac's lip curls. 'It's a shitty thing to put someone through.'

'Yeah, and without Will, it's been rough.'

Reaching for the sieve, he drains the pasta, then pulls out a couple of bowls from the cupboard. 'So, you and Will ... it's over over?'

Elin hesitates. A question she's asked herself many times. 'I'd never say never, but for now, I think so.'

'And you're okay with that?'

'Sometimes, no, but overall, I think it's been the right call. I feel ... freer, I suppose. Not tied to who I felt he wanted me to be. We were in these specific roles, I think, when we first met, and when they changed, the balance between us at the end, it was all wrong.'

Emptying the pasta into bowls, Isaac looks at her curiously. 'Roles?'

'Yeah. I suppose I was the victim, and Will was the strong one. The crutch, propping me up.' Elin flushes, embarrassed by how it sounds. Weak.

'And now you've got to be strong on your own.'

She nods. 'I'm getting there, but sometimes I feel exposed. When you're alone, you're forced to really look at yourself, and that's hard. When Will was around, I could choose *not* to see myself, put a mask on. Can't do that when you're on your own.' Elin shrugs. 'Looking back, I reckon I've always been playing some kind of role. At home, work. It's easy in a job like mine, always so busy throwing yourself into other people's problems you don't have to think about your own. Then I'd go home to Will, be what he wanted me to be. I never left myself the time to get to know myself, not really.' She hesitates. 'To be honest, I was scared to.'

'Why?' Isaac's face is briefly clouded by steam coming off the pasta.

'I don't know. Probably thought I wasn't going to like who I was behind the façade.' Elin bites down on her lip. 'I think I've always been pretty harsh on myself. Maybe a hangover from how I thought Mum and Dad saw me ... the whole thing with Sam.'

'And what do you see now?' Isaac says quietly.

'That's the thing. I'm not sure, not yet. I'm frightened I'll find out, if I am myself, whether people will like me.'

'Well, you've got no worries with me on that score.' Isaac meets her gaze. 'This trip, you and me. I'm glad we're doing it.' His voice is thick. 'Feels like a fresh start.'

She swallows. 'Me too.'

Isaac spoons the steaming sauce onto the pasta, and they carry their plates outside.

Elin lights the candles in the lanterns on the table, and they sit and eat in silence, listening to the sounds of the evening around them – owls hooting, the faint rustling of the trees behind.

They're getting there, she thinks, as Isaac leans over to top up her wine.

Bit by bit, they're finding their way back to each other again. Starting a new chapter.

39

Kier

Devon, July 2018

Penn and Mila's wedding venue is a speck in the distance by the time I stop walking. Leaning against the seawall, sweat is beading on my brow.

I couldn't get out of there fast enough.

Despite the beauty of the building, the wedding planner's enthusiastic chatter about seating plans and logistics, there was an awkwardness among the three of us that I've never felt before. Something strained in the conversation, Mila struggling to meet my eye.

Back at the van, I pause for a moment outside, trying to prepare myself for seeing Zeph for the first time. Last night, as he'd stumbled into bed, I'd pretended to be asleep, delaying the inevitable. As I'd left this morning, he was still in bed and I'd slipped out, unnoticed.

Steeling myself, I push open the door. 'Zeph? You there?'

No reply. No Woody either. All I can see is Zeph's laptop open on the table, a cup of coffee sat beside it, half drunk.

Relief trickles through me, but it doesn't last long. As I walk to the sink to pour a glass of water, I notice something odd on the screen of Zeph's laptop.

A satellite image of a map.

I move closer, focusing on the bubble sitting just above it.

My face is inside.

Peering closer at the screen, I slowly put the two together – my face and the map – and it clicks. I realise what the satellite image represents: an aerial view of Penn and Mila's wedding venue.

I swallow, not quite able to take it in: *Zeph's been tracking me.*

'Hey, you're back.'

I startle, my hand shooting out to snap the screen of the laptop closed.

Slowly, I turn. Zeph's there, in the doorway, a carrier bag in one hand, Woody's lead in the other. Heat crawls up my cheeks. 'Hey,' I say, after a beat. 'Where've you been?'

'Just popped out for some milk, a few other bits. Didn't think you'd be back so soon.'

I shrug. 'I left Penn and Mila to it, wasn't feeling well.'

'I bet ... last night.' His laugh dies in his throat as he clocks the laptop.

Pulling up the screen, I tip it towards him, my heart drumming in my chest. 'I wanted to ask you about this. You—' I stumble over my words. 'You've been tracking my phone.'

Nothing on his face. Not even a flicker. 'So?' Hoisting the carrier bag onto the counter, Zeph starts offloading the contents into the cupboard. A can of butterbeans. Two packets of rice. 'It's what you do, so if something happened, you'd know where each other are.'

I falter at his breezy tone. 'But you never said you'd set it up, and I don't have you tracked on my phone, so I can do the same.'

'Never got round to doing mine, and I did tell you about

tracking yours. Ages ago. You probably weren't really listening because it's about tech.' Zeph smiles, but I can't train my lips to return it. I think for a moment, try to conjure the conversation in my mind.

I can't.

'Okay, but why were you tracking me now? I told you that I was going to the wedding venue with Penn and Mila. Hardly warrants a virtual search party.'

Turning, Zeph looks at me, brow furrowed, as if he's wrestling with what he's about to say. 'You want the truth?' he says finally, his voice soft. 'I'm *worried* about you, Kier. What happened last night, you pushing me.'

Pushing me.

My hands are shaking. 'I pushed you because you slammed me against the wall, Zeph. I was trying to get you away from me. You were *hurting* me.' I blink and I'm back there – the sharp jarring pain as my back hit the wall.

Anger flashes across his face. 'I wasn't trying to hurt you, Kier. I was leaning in to kiss you, wipe away that stupid, drunken argument, but you flipped, started going on about Romy.'

'No.' Panic creeps into my voice. '*You* mentioned Romy, Zeph, not me. You said I was acting like her.'

'That? I wasn't talking about her.' He's speaking slowly, like there's a full stop between each word. It's making me feel strange. Stupid. A child. 'I told you the other day. What I had with her, it doesn't compare to us. She wasn't the kind of person I'd ever want to be with.'

I blink, utterly confused, my heart now thumping in my ears. The conversation is twisting and turning like water in a river, slipping out of my control. I think about what I'd read the other day.

They'd have these fights. She'd accuse him of messing with her mind.

'Hey, let's not argue, not now. All the wedding stress probably doesn't help.' Zeph pulls me towards him, conciliatory. 'I was thinking, I know we were planning on staying for the summer, but maybe it's best we leave after the wedding. Penn and Mila will be on honeymoon anyway.' He murmurs thoughts on where we could go.

Scandinavia. Eastern Europe. France.

He pulls me in closer. His hand works its way beneath my top, his thumb ring digging into the soft skin of my back, and something crystallises in my mind.

A half-formed thought becoming whole.

My pulse catches in my throat as I replay his words in my head, lock on one sentence.

She wasn't the kind of person I'd ever want to be with.

The past tense. Zeph referred to Romy in the past tense.

My mind loops back to another conversation.

It isn't the first time.

40

Elin

Parque Nacional, Portugal,
October 2021

Elin wakes to the muffled sound of Isaac's voice outside. A low murmur.

She looks through the window to see him pacing the decking, phone clamped to his ear.

Behind him, the sunrise is a spectacle, jagged peaks turned the soft yellow of warmed butter, but he's looking the other way, oblivious. Whatever this call is, it's got all his concentration.

Getting dressed, she heads out. 'Coffee?' she mouths, waving a hand, trying to catch the thread of what he's saying, but he's speaking too quietly for her to hear.

Elin moves a little closer, straining her ears. Single words drift her way, *Airstream*, *later*, but nothing that reveals who he's speaking to. She waves again.

'Please,' he finally mouths back, giving her a thumbs-up.

Back inside, Elin flicks on the coffee machine, glancing towards the other Airstream. No signs of any activity, but she's hauled right back to last night, and the odd, flickering light illuminating the shadows of the interior.

It consumed her thoughts as she'd drifted off last night, morphing into a strange, warped hybrid imprinted behind her eyes. Pira on map, map on Airstream. Nonsensical.

By the time Isaac comes back inside, Elin's already poured the coffee. 'Everything okay?' She slides the steaming mug across the counter towards him.

'That was Penn. He's going to try to come out early. Maybe tomorrow, depending on flights.' Isaac shakes his head, his expression worried.

'What's wrong?'

'I don't know. He was rambling a bit when I told him everything, in shock, maybe, about the map. Kept coming back to it.'

'You sent him the photo? The—' She stops, her phone loudly vibrating on the counter.

FaceTime. Steed.

'Give me a minute,' she says to Isaac.

'What's up?' Elin smiles as she answers. 'Got to be bad if you're calling this early.'

Expecting a quick comeback, she's thrown when it doesn't arrive. Steed's face is still. None of the usual animation.

'Just wanted to talk. I've been thinking about what you said the other day, about me being there for you.' He clears his throat. 'I wanted you to know it's been the same for me. Not sure I realised it until now, with you being out there, I mean. Don't reckon you ever know how much you rely on someone until they're not around.'

'So what have I done for you?' Elin laughs, trying to lighten the mood, a little unnerved by his awkwardness. 'Apart from providing you with an endless source of shit jokes and junk food?'

Steed smiles, his eyes roaming her face in a way that's making

162

her feel strange. 'A whole lot,' he says quietly. 'The job we do, it's tough, isn't it? The late nights, the stress, all the stuff we see. Having someone there that you can talk to properly, switch off with, it makes things' – he searches for the right word – 'easier. Puts things in perspective.'

'Need to go away more often if I'm going to get this kind of praise.'

'That's the last thing I want to encourage.' His face turns serious again. 'Not sure if I'd cope without you.'

'Well, you don't need to worry on that score, you're not going to be able to get shot of me.'

Steed laughs, but as her gaze finds his, something shifts, something she can tell neither of them were expecting.

His eyes dart away from the screen as if he's interpreted it with the same weight.

The conversation meanders for a few more minutes, and then they say their goodbyes.

Rather than the easy feeling she's usually left with after speaking with him, Elin's not only feeling confused, but uncomfortable. Like there's something still lingering there, between them, the conversation not quite resolved.

Still mulling it over, she picks up her coffee and takes a seat next to Isaac. 'Sorry to interrupt . . . you were saying about Penn, and the map.'

Isaac nods. 'I don't think he could make sense of it. He kept saying the same thing, over and over. That Kier would never leave one behind, not voluntarily.' He sips his coffee. 'He asked if we'll take another look ourselves, at some of the places she's painted on there.'

'Before he arrives?'

'Yeah.' His brow furrows. 'He sounded desperate, Elin. Really desperate.'

*

'ETA?' Elin stops halfway up the track, leaning against a tree to catch her breath. Her heart is thumping in her chest.

The gentle meandering path up the hillside has rapidly mutated, steepening into severe switchback turns that required every bit of their concentration. All around them, the trees were thinning out, the grass receding to bare ground, mottled granite boulders protruding from the soil.

'Five minutes max. I don't think it's far from here.' Isaac cross-references with the map on his phone. 'Hard to tell as the geography on Kier's map isn't exact, but it's the only place in this area that could work as a viewpoint.' He watches her interlace her fingers, stretch her arms out in front of her. 'Rib playing up again?'

'Yeah, it's not properly sore, but I'm feeling it.'

'We can take a break if you want.' He gestures to a pile of stacked-up logs. 'Sit down for a bit. The sun's pretty strong now we're losing the trees.'

Smiling, Elin shakes her head. 'If I sit, there's every chance I won't get back up again.'

They continue climbing.

On the last few turns, the plateau at the top finally becomes visible, the land flattening out ahead of them.

They take a shortcut, scrambling the last few metres, up and off the path, cutting across a scrubby patch of grass. Walking forwards a few feet, Isaac whistles between his teeth. 'Okay, worth the hike.' He gestures to the large granite boulders sitting in the centre of the plateau. 'They block the view of the other side, but even so.'

Elin joins him, still breathing heavily. He's right. The boulders are vast, obscuring the view on the right, but the vista from this side, right down the valley, is imposing.

Tracks crisscrossing both woodland and open land pull her

gaze forwards to the hazy peaks on the horizon. In the bright light, everything has a fragile, unreal quality. Blink and it would be gone. A mirage, an illusion.

Isaac points. 'You can see the fojo.'

'Fojo?'

'The wolf trap.' He frowns. 'Didn't realise it was quite so close to camp. Just the other side of the hill.'

Elin walks a few steps forwards, follows his gaze.

Two long granite walls draw vertical lines down the folds of the hillside, converging to a large circular pit made from the same stone.

'Hunters used to beat the wolves into the pit to stop them from killing cattle. The men would encircle the top of the pit.' He raises an eyebrow. 'Like a net closing in.'

Elin suppresses a shudder. The perfect analogy for this park, how it could feel sometimes. Despite the space, the open vistas . . . a net, closing in.

'It's impressive, all of it, but what I don't get,' she looks in the other direction, 'is how this relates to what Kier painted on the map.'

'The lens?'

'Yeah.' Elin turns the image over in her mind: the circle of landscape inside the lens, almost artificially bright.

Still mulling it over, she walks across to the other side. Slipping between the two boulders, she's greeted by two more, even larger than the first. The stone is a pale grey, lighter in patches, like it's been bleached by the sun.

'The view from where you are is definitely better,' she says, peering between them. 'Can't see much from here.' Elin stops, taking a sudden, sharp pull of breath. 'Hold that thought. I think the view from this side is a little more interesting.'

41

Kier

Devon, July 2018

Sorry to chase, but you said you'd send through some initial ideas last week. Hope all good with you x P.S. We're so excited to see them!

My stomach pitches as I reread the message, a flush crawling up my cheeks.

I'm behind with work.

Ordinarily, it wouldn't bother me, I'm good at making up time, but this is a personal commission for friends, Ramon and Luis. They're getting married in Catalonia, at a beautiful fifteenth-century medieval castle estate. So much inspires me: the imposing courtyard and historic temple, a sprawling vineyard wrapping the bottom of the land.

I have time and space to work, as Zeph's taken Woody for a walk, but I'm finding it impossible to focus.

I feel restless, rattled, my mind spooling through everything: not just Zeph referring to Romy in the past tense, but the necklace, the social media post. His hissed words: *You're just like her.*

There's a strange sense of momentum building. Impending doom.

It's the same feeling I used to get when something bad was about to happen at home.

Back then, it always started in the same way. A thickening in the air, my father using his low, calm voice to ask my mother why she hadn't done one of the three hundred and forty-two things he'd deemed important that day. Why she hadn't gritted the driveway yet or why the clothes were still hanging on the radiator. Why the roast chicken was cooked all wrong.

It was the voice he used in court. Eminently reasonable and never wrong. A moral high road. A voice that never rose or revealed emotion.

I'd sit there, at the table, next to Penn, panic blocking my throat. Listening as he reasoned it out: *Why hadn't she preheated the oven? Why hadn't she used the technique he'd shown her? Scored the skin? Rubbed salt into it?*

As the minutes passed, he repeated himself. I found myself agreeing with him.

Why hadn't she just done it right the first time? Saved us all this? Daddy did *work hard; it shouldn't be up to him to mop up her messes.*

I'd sit there, conflicted, sure they could hear my heart thudding.

That's what it feels like now: physical and emotional alarm bells sounding. Adrenaline. Cortisol. Racing heart. Clammy hands.

Something's going on with Zeph, I can tell, something rippling beneath the surface.

I need to know what it is.

Leaning over the table, I grab Zeph's laptop, flip it open.

Search history first.

My eyes graze the screen. News sites. Food blogs. Social media.

Food sites. Van life. His own, pretty much defunct, website. Travel: London. Madrid, Portugal. Sicily. Portugal again.

If he's looked Romy up, he either hasn't done it recently or he's deleted the searches.

Photos next.

I hover over the app, mulling over what I'd read online: Zeph apparently stood, lurking, on the corner, taking photographs as Romy left the building.

My pulse is racing as I lower my finger to the touch pad.

Do I really want to know?

I click. Thousands of images appear.

No time to search through them all. I need to narrow it down.

Hand shaking, I type *New York* and then *Brooklyn* into the search function.

The sort takes longer than I expect. Foot tapping the floor, I watch the empty screen with trepidation.

What if he's deleted his photos of her? It's what people do after a breakup. There might be nothing left.

But then, all at once, pictures fill the screen in rapid succession.

I stare, breath pushing out of me in one quick and painful exhalation.

It's like I've been punched in the chest.

Romy, Romy, Romy.

Either alone or the two of them together – selfies in her flat or ones he's taken, Romy smiling up into the camera.

What do people call it? The first flush of love? This is what this literally is, the two of them flushed, glowing with it.

But as I scroll, the images abruptly change.

My hand jumps back from the keypad, knocking my coffee flying. I scramble to right it but make no move to mop the pool of liquid already spreading across the table.

I can't tear my eyes away. The images of love and unity – they've become something altogether … darker.

Hundreds of photographs of Romy leaving the building. Walking down the steps. Stood on the pavement.

These aren't photographs that a boyfriend would take. These are taken from a distance. Paparazzi-style shots.

I don't want to look but I can't stop myself.

Click. Click. Click.

As the months roll by, there's a change in her expression and demeanour. She visibly shrinks. The free and easy confidence is gone.

One image in particular makes me shiver. It shows a sallow-skinned Romy looking directly at the camera. Her stare is hollow, her expression haunted. As if she knows someone's out there. Watching.

I keep scrolling, moving the laptop clear of the coffee now trickling in a steady stream down the table.

My eyes flicker from image to image, analysing the dates. They only confirm what I suspected. Zeph had been photographing Romy for months after they split.

Tears sting my eyes. I try to imagine how he might explain these away. He can't, surely? This is the behaviour of someone obsessed.

The woman living in Romy's block, who'd posted her theory about her disappearance, she was right. Zeph had been photographing Romy for months.

Turning, I grab my own laptop and click into her page. As I work my way through her feed, I'm looking for a chink in her armour, something in her profile that would give me an easy way out. Dismiss her as a loon, a superfan who has taken her conspiracy theories a little too far.

But I come up with nothing.

Janey Elton is in her late twenties at most, cerebral, bookish. Her feed is made up of smiling photographs of her with friends and family. Museums and theatres, cafés and bars.

Her apartment is the backdrop of some of the photographs. It fits with what I'd imagined. Huge windows overlooking the city. Elegant, spacious rooms. While I'm not an expert on New York, I know enough to understand that this would be prohibitively expensive.

It's plausible that it's the same kind of block Romy would be living in.

The concerned-neighbour narrative fits.

I hesitate, my stomach knotting. *Do I really want to do this?*

If I do, I'm crossing a line. If he finds out about this, whatever trust there is between us . . . it's gone.

I sit for a moment, thinking, and then click on the message icon next to her profile, start typing.

42

Elin

Parque Nacional, Portugal,
October 2021

'The camp.' Hand on hips, Isaac surveys the scene in front of them, slowly shaking his head. 'Don't reckon we'd have even clocked it if you hadn't come over this way.'

Elin nods, staring at it – an almost unobstructed view of the site. Too far away to see any real detail, but key elements are visible – the shapes of people moving about, rough outlines of the vans.

Isaac steps forwards, slowly shaking his head. 'If you had binoculars—'

'You'd have a pretty good view.' Skin prickling, Elin imagines Kier standing here. Watching the camp, their movements.

Watching what, exactly? Who?

It puts Kier's painting of the viewpoint in a completely different light. Now she's seen this, she can glimpse a certain power in it: in the extreme focus of the lens, the illumination of the image inside.

Was Kier shining a light on something? The camp? Had

she known she was being watched, decided to turn that gaze back on them?

They stand, side by side for a moment, looking out, watching a bird swoop low above them before plunging down, over the drop.

'Might be coincidence,' Isaac says finally. 'She might never have even realised she could see the camp from here.'

'I don't think so.' Elin's eyes shift to the ground. Between the boulders, it's rocky, but there are patches of scrubby grass and weed, almost worn away to soil. 'Looks like someone's spent a fair bit of time here.'

He nods. 'Probably not a good idea to mention this when we go down to camp tonight.'

A knot of fear tightens in her stomach. She'd seen how quickly the atmosphere had turned before. 'Yeah, I think we're going to need to tread carefully. No mention of the map either.'

'Speaking of that,' Isaac reaches for his phone. 'If you reckon you've got another one in you after this, I was thinking here.' He gestures to the screen. 'The waterfall. It's not far.'

A heavy silence falls between them.

Neither of them wants to voice it – the name Luísa had given it. *Suicide Falls.*

The rocky, downhill stretch towards the falls doesn't last long. Fifteen minutes in, it starts to climb again as they turn right, following the line of another hill.

They've only walked a few minutes when the trail narrows, the path barely more than a few feet wide. Elin tenses, focusing; it's taking all her concentration not to trip on the loose stones, the knotted tree roots jutting across the track.

It's about ten minutes or so before they come to some steps roughly hewn into the hillside.

'Listen,' Isaac tips his head up. 'I reckon we're close. I can hear the falls.'

Elin comes to a halt on the step just below him. 'You're—'

She doesn't get a chance to finish her sentence.

A scream sounds out, echoing against the rock face above them.

43

Kier

Devon, July 2018

My mother used to say that people think they have twenty-twenty vision, but most of the time they're totally blind.

It only made sense when I got older, took the words less literally, that I understood that she didn't mean physically blind. She meant people *choosing* to be blind. Seeing only what they want to see.

Like our next-door neighbour who saw the fingerprint bruises on Mum's neck, but didn't want to rock the boat because my father's firm was sorting through her mother's intestate will. She said to my grandmother afterwards, 'It was complicated. He seemed like a nice man.'

Or the postman who saw my father pushing my mother against the wall through the glass panels of the door, but, when questioned, said he thought it wasn't serious. *Didn't want to get involved. We all have our moments, don't we?*

I can't blame them, not really. I've been blind many times. Blind when I saw my mother crying in the shower. Blind when my father locked her in the downstairs loo.

Blind when we went to collect our clothes from the house after she went to prison, and I saw Penn climb into our mother's wardrobe and bunch the bottoms of her skirts together until they were big and squashy and hug them like he used to hug her.

I could be blind now, I think, staring at the unopened reply from Janey. There's still time to come back from this.

I could delete and block. Pretend yesterday never happened: pretend I hadn't searched his laptop.

Zeph will never know. He wasn't suspicious yesterday, and by the time he gets back from Exeter this afternoon, I can delete all trace of my search.

But as my finger starts to move, an image flickers to life in my mind.

Romy dancing, the raw look in her eyes.

I click it open.

To answer your question, yes, I know Romy. We were neighbours, but also friends. I'm happy to tell you what I know, but I'm always hesitant to put things in writing. Are you ok to call instead? This is my number. Leave a message if you can't get through and I'll call back. I'm around for the next few hours.

Half an hour later, I'm sat at the edge of the beach, staring at the blank face of my phone screen, willing it to come alive.

I've called Janey three times already, and every time, no answer. I look back to the screen, frustrated. I wanted this over with before Zeph gets back. If she calls when we're together . . .

I shift position. Beneath my feet, the sand is hot, the small pebbles burning. Shuffling sideways, I find a patch of shade thrown out by the restaurant on my left. The man on my right gives me a pointed look: I've gotten too close.

It's like this everywhere now: a tension in the air.

His wife is reading the local paper. The headline is a version of the one dominating the local news.

175

WOMAN MISSING. PARENTS FEAR THE WORST
AFTER BOAT KILLER STILL AT LARGE.

Snippets of their conversation drift my way. They're analysing. Dissecting in that sorrowful but also macabre way, a *Poor them* and simultaneously *Glad it isn't me* vibe.

All at once, it's too much. The sun, burning down. The newspaper. The smells.

I stand up, shaking sand, small stones from the folds of my shorts.

Almost as soon as I start walking, my phone trills.

A US number.

Janey.

My heart is leaping.

It's an effort to stop myself from fumbling over my words as we exchange stilted hellos. Awkward stranger small talk – a staccato back-and-forth. We laugh over the phone tag; I apologise for contacting her out of the blue.

Small talk drying up, I explain the situation with Zeph. I've rehearsed this in my head, fleshing out what I'd briefly outlined in my initial message: that we're in a relationship, and I had some questions after seeing her comment on Romy's fan page.

When Janey replies, she sounds embarrassed. 'Look, to caveat, the comment I put up on that post was before I knew the full story. I'm happy to talk about it, but—'

'I understand,' I say quickly, 'but still I'm interested in what you thought might have happened.' A white lie. 'It's the beginning of the relationship. Seeing something like that . . .'

A pause. 'Yeah, I get it. I'd want the full story if I found that kind of post.' She takes a breath. 'Right, I'll start at the beginning, and just to warn you, some of this will sound weird if you don't know the context. I'll probably come across as a mildly psychotic, overinvested neighbour.'

'That's fine. Anything you've done, I can guarantee I've probably done worse.'

Janey gives a muted laugh. 'Like I said in the message, Romy and I lived next door to each other. We were friends, but there was always a ... barrier there. There are a few people like that in our building. Fame, money ... it can change people. Makes them wary about connecting.'

That makes sense, I think, from what Zeph had told me. 'And you obviously knew about her relationship with Zeph?'

There's a longer pause. 'Yes,' she says finally. 'You couldn't miss it. They'd fight ... like nothing else. Not just shouting, but I heard things being thrown around, the works.' She sounds embarrassed. 'Sorry, this must be awkward for you—' The line sounds suddenly muffled. The sound of traffic in the background, the loud wail of a siren.

I press the phone closer to my ear. 'It's fine.' So far, nothing different to what Zeph had already told me. 'Did she ever talk to you about their relationship?'

'Not directly, but I did ask if she was okay. I hoped that subliminally, she'd get what I was implying.'

'And did she?'

There's a short silence. 'It was hard to say,' Janey says finally. 'She told me she was fine. I didn't want to push it, and in any case, I heard after that they'd split. She told me it was a mutual thing, but a few weeks later, I saw Zeph hanging around the apartment building. She told me he was taking the breakup hard. Couldn't let go.'

I inhale, my mouth suddenly dry.

This is where the story diverges. What he told me becoming something new.

'So what made you think he might be involved in her disappearance?'

'His persistence, more than anything. The hanging around . . . it went on for months. Then he started taking photos of her as she left the building. Around then, Romy . . . withdrew. Stopped coming out of the apartment unless she had to for work. I assumed it was because she knew what he was doing.'

I think back to the photos on Zeph's laptop, Romy's haunted expression.

'Plus, I thought I might only be seeing the very surface of what was happening.' Janey exhales. 'A few months after that, she went missing.'

'And you said you went to the police and told them what you'd seen?' Next to me, the woman reading the paper is jabbing one of the images. On my other side, someone's unwrapping an oily paper square. The meaty smell stirs a faint queasiness in my gut.

A small silence. 'Yeah, I did. I felt bad about doing it, invading her privacy, but I couldn't let it lie.' Janey gives a tight laugh. 'They more or less told me to get lost. Said there was nothing to be concerned about. That fans, the media, were blowing it up unnecessarily. That they had it on good authority that she was safe and well.'

I pick over her words. *Safe and well.* 'And you didn't think that was the case?'

'I wasn't sure. Their total lack of concern and what they said about *having it on good authority*, it bothered me. You hear about these things, right? People going missing, and someone *thinking* they saw them, and that gets passed round as gospel. What if it was the same with this? Recycled hearsay? If it had been anyone else, maybe I'd have left it, knowing someone was going to bat for her, but she didn't seem to have any kind of support network.' Janey sighs. 'A few weeks later, I spoke to a friend who came by her apartment to collect something. I asked after Romy, and she told me that she'd been seen in Europe, that the rumours about the retreat cum rehab were true.'

'They knew for certain?' This isn't where I was expecting the conversation to go.

'No. It was a mutual friend who'd told them ... that's what bothered me. I kept thinking, if that were me, I'd want someone to go the extra mile, you know?'

'So what happened next?'

'Well, I had a key to her apartment. We'd swapped keys for lockouts, that kind of thing. A few days after I spoke to her friend, I let myself in, to see if I could find anything that would back up what she'd said.' Janey hesitates. 'And I did. A notebook on her bedside drawer, travel plans to Europe, flight dates, et cetera. All tallied with when she'd supposedly gone missing.'

'You're sure it was her writing?' I raise my voice above the sound of a dog barking a few feet away.

'As much as I could be. She'd cleared some stuff out too. Personal stuff. Cases, jewellery ... it all checked out with what her friend said. I felt bad, then, about what I said to the police about Zeph. Between you and me, in her stuff I saw photos of her with other guys. Situations like this, you always blame the man, but looking back, the shouting, the fighting ... it was her too. My guess is she'll come back to a big fanfare soon enough.'

The dog's barking is louder now. Frenzied. I don't know what to think. I can hear from the tone of her voice that she believes Romy's fine. That the police were right. The embarrassment I'd picked up on isn't because she's talking to me about Zeph, but about the conclusions she'd leapt to.

Beads of sweat form on my back as I think about Penn's words on trust.

Picking people to pieces.

What if I've leapt on one negative thing I'd read and extrapolated from that?

The photographs Zeph had taken of her could simply be the result of someone struggling. Struggling to accept they'd lost someone they loved. Extreme, yes, but I, more than anyone, knew about extreme. What happens when your guard is torn down.

'So you think she's definitely in Europe? The flight tickets were to there?'

'Yeah ... Portugal ... Porto airport. She'd written some places down, in northern Portugal, around the national park. A spa town there.'

An odd, burning sensation in my chest. Not heat this time, the sun bearing down on me, but shock.

Portugal.

'I looked it up,' Janey continues, oblivious. 'There are retreats there, rehab places too.' A pause. 'So yeah, I think your guy, Zeph, he checks out.'

I can't get out the words to reply. I'd think so too if I hadn't seen Zeph's search history just a few days before. Hadn't known where he'd travelled, right before we met.

44

Elin

Parque Nacional, Portugal,
October 2021

'Where do you think the scream came from?'

'Above us.' Isaac is already moving. 'Somewhere in the direction of the waterfall.'

They scramble up the steps towards the falls, the sound of water growing more distinct, from muted at first to a deafening roar.

The higher they climb, the more Elin feels a moisture that's not just lacing the air, but the surface of the steps. They're slick underfoot, water trailing in small rivulets around the edges.

Her chest is heaving as they clamber up the last few steps and burst onto the clearing at the bottom of the falls.

Elin stands for a moment, looking up, taking it in: *Suicide Falls*.

The huge wall of white water is thundering down the granite face in front of them with such force that it's foaming where it hits the huge boulders at the bottom. Frothy backwater is surging out from the centre. Her eyes scour the pool of water at the bottom, the sodden grass in front. No one there, no one she can see anyway, unless they're behind the waterfall, the cliff face itself.

'See anyone?' Isaac asks.

'No . . . maybe they've already gone.' She shoots a look behind her, wondering if they'd misjudged the direction of the sound. 'Could have been kids, messing about.'

But as she looks around her again, a movement suddenly hooks her gaze at the top of the falls.

Two people, silhouetted against the blue of the sky, standing just to the right of where the water is plummeting over the cliff face.

Even from this distance, it's clear they're perilously close to the edge.

Walking forwards a little to get a better look, she stops in her tracks.

Her heart jolts.

Leah and Ned.

'Isaac,' she yells. 'It's Leah and Ned up there!'

He's already running towards the falls.

Elin pounds across the grass, struggling for traction on the moist ground.

By the time they reach the bottom of the cliff, her legs are sore, lungs burning. She looks up the rock face with a growing sense of trepidation. No real path up, clearly not meant to be. No signs, or handholds. The viewing point for the falls is down here, in a position of safety.

'It's not steep, and definitely climbable, I've seen pictures of people doing it, but . . .' Isaac tails off, his throat bobbing as he surveys it.

Elin follows his gaze. There's an obvious route up – natural plateaus in the rock, carved out by the elements, but they're uneven and gleaming with water.

They'll have to go slowly, she thinks, frustrated. Anything could happen by the time they reach the top. 'Don't think we've got any choice. Can't see any other way up.'

The steps had been easy compared to this, she thinks as they start to climb, the rocks slippery not just from the water, but the slick patina worn on the surface from the repeated battering of the falls.

It's like walking on ice.

This was a route you had to be determined to take. Determined or desperate, Elin decides, breathing in the damp air, her eyes swerving left to follow the column of water thundering past her. She wonders how many people started this climb and then turned back, faced with the reality of the falls up close.

It's close to ten minutes before they close in on the top.

Breathing heavily, Elin's stomach dips as she takes it in: Leah facing Ned, her back to the falls. She's shivering, her damp clothes clinging to her body, her hair wet, plastered to her skull.

Her eyes lurch to Ned's hand, clamped so tight around Leah's wrist the tips of his fingers are turning white.

They're barely a metre from the edge. One wrong move ...

Elin's gaze swerves up to Ned's face. She feels a flicker of panic. There's something raw and dark in his expression, an emotion in his eyes that she can't quite interpret.

She glances at Isaac, but his face is grey, his expression frozen.

She's going to have to handle this herself.

'You're pretty close to the edge there.' Elin keeps her voice as level as she can. 'You guys need a hand coming down?'

Ned shakes his head, his eyes fixed on Leah. 'We're just heading back, aren't we, Leah?' His voice is rough, raspy.

Leah doesn't reply, her head dipped.

Elin's gaze slips to her arm, the scars crisscrossing her wrist. Against the pallor of her skin, they're silvery, almost colourless.

Ned turns towards Elin, looking at her properly for the first time.

A chill snakes down her spine.

Only his profile had been visible before, and she hadn't seen the side of his face, the livid scratch running down his right cheek. Fresh blood is seeping through the broken skin and dissolving in the spray, running down his cheek in watery rivulets.

No time to compute what it means, what might have happened; as he too is now trembling, the arm that's holding on to Leah quaking with the effort of holding her upright.

Elin's pulse is thrumming in her throat.

If he lets go of her, if she moves even slightly . . .

Isaac glances at her and she can see her own fear reflected in his features.

'I can come a little higher,' she says evenly. 'If you'd like, I—'

But before she can finish her words, Ned's right hand jerks out.

Elin's heart leaps, but before she can react, he grabs Leah around the waist, pulling her towards him in one smooth motion before he steps them back and away from the edge.

For a moment, no one speaks, all of them briefly united in a sense of tension suddenly released.

'She's freezing.' Ned's voice punctures the silence. 'I'd better get her back to camp.'

Still with his arm around Leah, he leads her another step back, inclining his head towards her. His voice is gentle now, soft. 'Leah, we need to get you back to camp. Go and see Maggie, get you warmed up.'

'Do you want a hand? It's going to be pretty slippery on the way down.'

Ned shakes his head. 'We're not going that way. There's a path from the top. It's a long way round to camp, but we'll take our time.'

'You're sure?' Elin looks at Leah, reluctant to leave it there, but what can they do? All they've seen is him helping her, nothing more.

'We'll be okay.' His eyes send a clear message. *I've got this. Back off.*

It's only as Ned leads her away from them that Leah rouses. As she turns to look at them, her eyes slip past them, unfocused.

'He's right, you know. It should have been me,' she mutters, her eyes glazed, unblinking. 'It should have been me, not her.'

45

Kier

Devon, July 2018

Music is playing as I make my way back to the van. A local band, all drums and twanging guitar, heralding the start of the annual food festival.

Smells are already wafting from the stalls. Onions. Fish. Meat. The nausea that gripped me on the beach has intensified to a deep, unsettling queasiness. I push on, forcing my way through the crowds surging towards the stalls lining the promenade, but I'm caught in the groundswell, fighting against the tide.

The festival has drawn more people than I've seen in days, but there's an odd energy about the crowd. Something frenzied. Tense. Empty beer cans being tossed into the air. Hysterical laughter. Most years it ended in a drunken free-for-all, but I got the feeling that this year would be worse than most.

With one last push, I thread through the last of the crowds and head up onto the path, letting myself back into the van. The quiet is a welcome relief, but I don't give myself the chance to sit or compose myself.

I pour a fresh bowl of water for Woody and start scouring the van for Zeph's laptop.

Eventually, I find it at the end of the bed, snarled up in the duvet. Clambering up and onto the bed, I flip it open, one eye on the door. Zeph said he wouldn't be back from Exeter until later, but I need to be careful.

No messing around this time: I know exactly what I'm looking for – his search history. *Portugal.* Any references to it. I'm close to 100 per cent certain I saw it the last time I looked, but I want to know for sure.

I start to scroll.

Nothing this week, but last week . . . yes, these are tabs I'd seen the first time. Places I hadn't recognised then or thought important: the official tourist office page for the Portuguese National Park, YouTube videos of travellers exploring it. Restaurants. Hotels. Information about the main town. Maps, blogs. The spa town Janey mentioned.

I keep clicking, my heart racing. All the Portuguese hits are clustered around the national park. There's no way this keen interest in the exact location Romy was rumoured to be is a coincidence.

Hot, sour bile rises up at the back of my throat.

Although I knew, deep down, that this was only an exercise in looking more carefully at what I'd already seen, it's still a sucker punch.

Taking a breath, I try to look at it objectively, run through every possibility, but all I'm left with are more questions. Far from being over Romy, as Zeph always reassures me, he's been obsessing over where she might currently be living.

More questions fill my head. *Had he been out there? Looking for her?*

I think back to when we first met, how he told me that he'd just returned from Portugal. No mention of Romy, just references to the food, the places on the south coast that he'd explored. He'd confided that he'd liked it, but wouldn't be in a hurry to go back.

I've got no idea if he met Romy there or not, but either way, he hasn't been honest with me. Hasn't given me the full story.

Despite the sun flooding through the window, I feel cold.

I glance up at the photograph of us on the wall. We're lying on the bed, the back door of the van open. We'd travelled to southern France, spent a month on the beach.

I remember coming to the realisation during that holiday that I loved him more than I'd loved anyone. Loved him with a ferocity that scared me. The map I'd made of those weeks is still one of my favourites. Places we'd found off the beaten track. Restaurants, bars, hidden coves.

In the photo, my face is tan, splattered with freckles, a faint splotch of one of Zeph's sauces below my lower lip. Zeph's hair is longer, the dark grazing of hair making the blue of his eyes pop.

We're doing those wide, unselfconscious smiles you can only do when it's a selfie or you know the person taking the photo well. It was one of those moments of total freedom and joy that you try to capture in an image, but know you'll never quite be able to do justice.

I scrutinise his face.

Could someone else be lurking under there?

I know it's possible. My father was two people our whole lives.

Double-sided, that's what I used to call it. Double-sided, like the tape my teacher used in school.

I was only six years old when I realised that my father had two different faces he showed to the world.

There was the face he showed to my teacher when he'd drop me off at school, all smiles, asking polite questions: *How are you? Do you have any holidays planned?*

188

This was the same face he showed to neighbours when he mowed the lawn or work colleagues when they came to ours for a meal. The same face when he was the dad who showed me how to tie a line on the boat and helped me with my history assignments.

I asked my mother once when she was getting changed for dinner if there were two people inside Daddy.

She couldn't look at me, just stared at the faded flowery bedspread and gave a high-pitched laugh, said: 'No. Only one.'

'So Daddy being mean is the real Daddy?'

'I'm afraid so,' she replied, smiling, and she asked me to leave the room so she could get ready, but I knew something was wrong by how her words wobbled as she spoke.

Outside, I peeked back through the crack between the door and the frame, saw her press her face to the pillow. An ugly noise came out.

It sounded like the scream she made when our father put his hand over her mouth when they fought. Wet and muffled, but at the same time big and bottomless, like the sound didn't just come from her, but hundreds of people.

46

Elin

Parque Nacional, Portugal,
October 2021

It's only when they're out of sight that Elin realises she's holding her breath. She blows out a long, shuddering exhalation. Her mouth is dry, her throat thick.

'You're shivering,' Isaac says, watching her.

Adrenaline ebbing away, the thin layers of clothing are now damp against her skin. 'Yeah, I'm freezing.'

'Let's get back.'

Elin steps forwards, making the mistake of looking at the falls properly this time, not just the water in front of her, but the full column, thundering downwards. A wave of vertigo washes over her, but she can't drag her eyes away, her gaze pulling even lower to the seething mass of water at the base of the falls.

The sound, sight . . . it triggers something.

Blinking, she's back there, after the boat murders, cave water sloshing over her nose, mouth. Hayler's hand on her face.

She feels dizzied, disorientated. She has a sudden urge to get down, away, but as she moves forwards, her foot goes out from under her.

Isaac springs forwards, reaching out a hand to steady her. 'Careful. Let's give it a moment.'

They stand for a minute in silence, and as her breathing settles, he leads her over the plateau, onto the larger grassy plain behind the falls. 'Want to wait a bit, before we get going?'

'Yeah. All the water . . . just hit me suddenly. Took me back.'

'The Hayler case?'

She nods. 'Thought I was past it.'

But as soon as she says the words, she knows that's not strictly the truth.

Part of her knew that the Hayler case – the case that had triggered her career break – will always haunt her.

A case plagued by errors. A case that almost broke her.

'Look,' Isaac says finally, 'something like that, it'll probably always be there, and I think that's . . . okay. People always say you're meant to move on when something traumatic happens, but I reckon it's more of a roller coaster. There'll be times when you don't even think about it, then times when it's still raw.' He pauses. 'Probably didn't help up there, putting all that on you. I froze. When Ned reached out to her like that—' Swallowing hard, he shakes his head. 'And what she said, at the end . . .'

Elin nods, playing out her words again in her mind.

He's right, you know. It should have been me, not her.

What exactly was she referring to?

Isaac's expression is grim. 'Reckon we disturbed something?'

'It's possible, but he did a decent job of making it seem like he was playing hero. He—' She stops, her gaze latching on to something a few feet away, snagged in a patch of tall grass.

Standing up, she reaches over and tugs it loose.

The hairs on the back of her arms stand up.

Pira. The pyre.

An intricate miniature of the wooden structure they'd seen in the clearing, no bigger than a closed fist, tiny branches shaped to the same severe point.

'You reckon one of them dropped it?' Isaac leans over and takes it from her, turning it over in his hands.

'Looks like it. Hardly any dirt on it. If it had been there for a while, there's no way it would look like this.' Glancing at the pira again, her thoughts pull in a different direction.

Isaac's studying her. 'What are you thinking?'

'About Leah in the woods yesterday.' She pictures it: Leah's clenched fists full of dirt, the panicked look on her face as the mobile trilled out into the silence. 'How frightened she was when the phone went off. I'm wondering who might have been out there with us.'

'Ned?'

Elin nods. 'It's plausible, isn't it? It's the timing that's getting me . . . seeing her yesterday, how she'd implied she wanted to talk, and then *this*. If it *was* him out there in the woods yesterday, and he overheard us talking to Leah, what we've just seen up there might have been some kind of warning.' She thinks about the blank look on Leah's face. 'And probably a good one at that.'

47

Kier

Devon, July 2018

'K? You there?'

As Zeph walks in, I snap the laptop closed. He's in a vest and jeans, sunglasses pushed onto the top of his head. He smiles, but it takes me a minute to return it.

It's odd looking at him. Destabilising.

For a moment, I don't see the Zeph I fell in love with, but someone else entirely. It's like when the snow comes down and covers all the familiar things in your garden. All still recognisable, but at the same time, something entirely new.

I ache. I ache for what we had, what we've lost. For something I'm unsure we'll ever get back.

'How was Exeter?' I make my voice light.

'Good. Too hot for shopping, so tempers were fraying, but I managed to avoid most of the aggression.' He gestures to his bag. 'Got some new books.' Looking back at me, Zeph frowns slightly. 'You okay? You look red.'

I hesitate, glancing up at the mirror to the left of the sink.

He's right. My skin is pink, clammy, sweat plastering strands of hair to my forehead.

'I'm fine. Couldn't concentrate, so I went for a walk. Way too hot like you said, and people were talking about those girls killed on the boat.' My voice sounds unnaturally high, but he doesn't seem to notice, coming up behind me, his hands finding the back of my neck. He starts to knead the tight knot of muscle above each shoulder.

'You're stressed,' he murmurs.

I nod, and for a moment I lean back, mould myself against him as he presses harder. Neither knot yields at first, but he's persistent, the warmth from his fingers and the pressure gradually working the muscle loose.

Then I remember, panic surging up inside me.

'I'd better get some work done.' I shrug his arm away.

Zeph nods, oblivious. 'If you get done early, maybe we can brainstorm some ideas for the book. I made some notes on the train on the way back.' Pulling out his phone, he shows me the notes he's made. *Watermelon gazpacho. Grilled artichoke. Green tomato tartare.* He talks about a focus on regional foods, organic, the overarching narrative he wants the book to take.

His words, words I usually love because they are full of his passion for food, are too much. They're weighing heavy, pressing down on me.

The van feels small suddenly, the walls closing in.

I feel like I can't think. Can't breathe.

I need him out, I decide, panicked. Need time and space to see things clearly.

'Look, I wanted to talk about the cookbook.'

Zeph laughs. 'Sounds serious.'

I plough on. 'I'm not sure I should commit . . . I need time to work on my own stuff.'

'But we've been talking about it.'

'I know, but I've been thinking that I need some space to work without any distractions, that maybe we should do our own thing for a bit.'

I hadn't planned these words, or that I'd even say them, but they're out there now.

'*Space?* You should have made that call before you decided we travel together.' He smiles, but it snaps back to nothing likes a piece of elastic. 'Look, if you need more time to work, I can always take Woody for longer walks in the mornings.'

'No.' I can't meet his gaze, the words lumpy in my mouth. 'It's not that, I just think we shouldn't be together, not now, anyway. Coming here, for Penn's wedding, it's meant to be a happy time, but it's been … stressful. I need some time on my own.'

The real reason is there, on the tip of my tongue.

Tell me about Portugal. The photos you took of Romy.

'This isn't about me trying to find you the other day, is it? Or the Romy thing?'

I shake my head. 'No. I've just felt things are different. *We're* different since we've got back here.'

'*We're* not different. *You're* different, Kier. That's what's changed. Being back here, it's triggered something.'

I find myself nodding. He's right. Being back here *does* trigger something. What if how I'm feeling, what I've learnt, *is* because of being here?

Penn's words echo again. *Picking people to pieces.* What if I'm doing that now? Misinterpreting things?

All at once, I hear my father's voice, speaking to Mum, echoing alongside Zeph's.

You've got this wrong, Annie. Why are you making this into something it's not?

Zeph's still talking. 'I know what this is about, we've talked about it, and you know what? I get it. I get what it's like to have your parents let you down. That trust . . . it's gone, and when you look around, instead of seeing the positive, all you see is dirt. But it doesn't have to be like that. We're good, you and me. All good. Look at what we've built. What we're going to build.'

His voice is silken, seductive. Warm honey drizzled on toast.

It's the voice I fell in love with. The voice that can take you on a ride not just from the here and now but to the future, where everything is golden.

I squeeze my eyes shut, and I can see it. I can see our future. New maps.

The trip to the south of France as we'd planned. Ramon and Luis's wedding in Spain. Flea markets in Sicily.

I can even see us driving, that beautiful moment when the silence changes from the light, heady silence when the scenery flashes past so fast, each part of the topography bleeds into the other and neither of us would be anywhere else, to the heavy silence once we're settled into the journey, Woody between our legs, cosying us up like a blanket.

When we're good, we're what I've been craving my whole life.

But as I open my eyes, I don't see it any more.

My mind slips to his hands against my chest, Romy's haunted expression.

'We're not good, Zeph. We haven't been for a while.'

When he looks at me this time, there's something strange in his eyes. 'Don't say shit like that, shit you don't really mean. We've got plans, Kier. You can't just snap your fingers and make all that go *away*.'

'I'm not making any final decisions.' I clear my throat. 'Like I said, I just need space.'

He changes tack. 'But it's not safe, you being here alone. You said you thought someone was watching you, and what about all that stuff, those girls killed out on the water?'

'I'll be fine, really,' I stammer. I make a move to go past him, but he sidesteps with me and then stops, feet firmly planted so I can't get past. 'I've got Penn and Mila.'

Zeph shifts his weight and the floor of the van creaks. In the corner, Woody stiffens, his stubby tail rigid, quivering at the end.

A strange buzzing in my chest. An alarm. I feel my heartbeat rising.

'Tell you what, let's start the conversation again.' His eyes are red, watery. 'You're probably tired.'

He makes a move towards me. A single step. The van floor creaks again.

A cold prickle shoots down my spine.

I open my mouth to reply but no words come out.

More images flash through my mind. Romy dancing in the video, making shapes in the air. The necklace and the tiny, rusted droplets.

Zeph's arm jerks out towards me and I reach up, put up my hand to push it away.

It comes up harder, faster, than I expected, brushing the underside of his jaw. He reels back, grunting, as if my touch were enough to wind him.

We stare at each other, breathing heavily.

He looks down and away, and for a minute I think he's going to cry but he just looks me dead in the eye. 'I thought the other night, outside the club, was a one-off, but no.' His voice is barely more than a whisper. 'This, with me . . . it isn't the first time, is it?'

'I don't know what you're talking about.'

'I saw it, Kier. The painting.'

'The painting?' I croak out the word.

Zeph slowly nods. 'You told Mila you didn't paint for yourself any more, but you lied.'

It's like I'm there and I'm not there. I breathe and breathe but everything's gone blurry, black spots dancing in front of my vision.

He'd found the painting. He'd found the painting.

He'd found the painting, and he knew exactly who I was inside.

48

Elin

Parque Nacional, Portugal,
October 2021

Wisps of fog are drifting by the window as Elin and Isaac settle back in the van. Hazy pockets of it, like breath on a frosty morning.

'Don't know about you, but after that, I need something sweet.' Isaac rummages inside the hamper. 'Sure there was chocolate in here some—' He breaks off as his phone loudly beeps.

Unplugging it from the charger, he stares at the screen, brow furrowed.

'What is it?'

'Penn. He's managed to get a flight today. Should be with us by the evening.' Isaac gestures to the other Airstream. 'He's taking that one for a few nights.' Bringing his hand up to his mouth, he bites down on his nail, eyes shifting past her, through the window.

Elin looks at his expression, discomforted. 'Something wrong?'

'I'm just worried that all this isn't going to be what he hoped. After what we saw at the falls, I can't help feeling he's not going to get his happy ending.' He shakes his head. 'I keep thinking, if Ned *was* trying to shut Leah up, what if whatever it was Leah had stumbled on, Kier stumbled on too?'

'It's possible.'

Another beep sounds out.

'Penn's asked what we're planning on doing tonight. Shall I ask him if he wants to join us for something to eat? I'm guessing the barbecue isn't going to happen—' Isaac stops, peering closer at the screen. 'Shit. The charger's not working, my battery's nearly dead.'

'The cable again?'

'Yeah, I think it's had it. Knew I should have got a new one before we came. Sure you haven't got yours?'

'Certain. I looked again yesterday. Don't think I even packed it in the rush to get out. Maybe there's something in the drawers under the sink? I saw an adapter.'

Sifting through them, Isaac shakes his head. 'Nothing. We're going to have to go into town and get one.' He glances at his watch. 'Could be there and back in a few hours if we're quick.'

'You want to go now?' Elin glances outside. 'Fog looks like it's setting in.'

'Well, we could leave it, assume Penn's going to definitely get here tonight with a charger, but I'm not convinced we want to be reliant on that. Going without one overnight, out here ...' He hesitates, looking at her. 'Don't you fancy coming?'

'Not really.'

Isaac studies her closely this time, sensing something else is bothering her. 'Is the rib playing up?'

Elin nods. Her rib *is* hurting, but that isn't the whole truth.

She's desperate for time on her own, to think, and to process everything. After what they've just witnessed at the falls, it feels like her brain is on fire – thoughts flitting so fast through her

200

head she can't get a handle on them. She has an urgent need to get it all written down – the way she thinks best – before she loses sight of anything.

'If you're sure.' Isaac looks back at his phone. 'I've got about ten per cent charge. Should be enough to get me there and back. You?'

'A quarter. Should be fine.'

When the door closes behind him a few minutes later, Elin watches him stride across the decking towards the path. The fog has dispersed – only tiny wisps now, thin and fragile, like candy floss pulled to nothing between a child's fingers.

Despite the clarity it brought, Elin had an overwhelming sense of the landscape pressing in on her.

As the trees and the valley beyond are gradually revealed, she suddenly feels very small. A speck among the vast expanse of the park surrounding her.

49

Kier

Devon, July 2018

'Just go.' I feel blood rushing in my ears. Hot and violent. Woody moves towards me, whining again. 'Just go,' I repeat, and all the time an alarm in my head is sounding.

He's seen it. He's seen it. He knows who I am. What I'm capable of.

I feel naked, exposed, as if someone's held up a torch in the dark, has been slowly sweeping it around the room, and now it's finally settled on me.

The force of it is blinding.

'Please. Just leave.' I turn around wildly, knocking over a bottle of oil on the counter. The olive oil, a lurid yellow-green, chugs onto the wood.

I bend down to pick it up, but the bottle is broken, a sharp edge slicing the soft skin of my palm. Recoiling, my hand opens. It drops back to the floor with a thud. A thin line of blood snakes down my palm.

'You need to see to that.' Zeph's voice is soft again as he grabs a tissue from the side, passes it to me. He takes a cloth from the counter and picks the bottle up by its end. Carefully depositing it into the bin, he lays the cloth on the pool of oil.

After mopping it up, he straightens, looking at me. 'Kier, I stumbled on the painting when I was trying to find something. I should have mentioned it sooner . . . we could have talked, maybe I could even have taken you to see someone. Got some proper help. I know things aren't right with you at the moment.'

I stare at him, my head spinning. If I stay in the van any longer, I'm going to explode.

Clipping Woody onto his lead, I wrench open the door.

'Kier, where are you going?'

I ignore the question. 'When I get back, I want you gone.' I call. 'Please Zeph, just leave.'

Heading up the path behind the van, I charge up the track towards the clifftops, the breeze stripping my hair away from my face. Running ahead of me, lead pulled taut, Woody's already panting.

When I stop at the top, my breath is coming hard and heavy. The town spreads out beneath me, impossibly small. I take in landmarks that have been imprinted on me since birth: the harbour and clock tower. Our old house. The park.

But the more I look, it's not the happy places I see, it's more of the unmapped.

Places I thought I'd buried for good.

50

Elin

Parque Nacional, Portugal,
October 2021

Sitting at the table in the van, a glass of wine beside her, Elin pores over the notes she's made about Kier's disappearance so far. Scrawled one-word thoughts together with more detailed ideas. After what they've just seen, she's looking for new connections, theories that will start to hold weight.

Starting on a fresh page, she strips everything back to the four core points.

Kier. The camp. The map. The pira.

Elin writes each down, then circles them, leaving space between each to draw connections, annotate.

Flip-flopping for a moment, she decides to start with the easiest in terms of notes – something that's still an enigma – the pira. Reaching over to the counter, she picks up the small pira they'd found at the falls. She holds it up, blowing at the dirt and dust caught between the wood, *really* looking this time, turning the small structure between her fingers. Probing, searching.

Elin stiffens. Details she hadn't noticed before: tiny

pinheads of glue turned cold and hard where the wood met at the tip, the smooth surface of the branches where someone's lightly sanded them. The care taken gives her the overwhelming sense that it really *meant* something to the person who'd created it.

Picturing the pira in the wood, Elin thinks about the dirt on Leah's knees, the almost reverent way she'd looked at the space the pira had vacated.

Could the pira play a part in this? Is the camp involved in making them? Do they link to what they're hiding?

Grabbing her phone, she taps the word *pira* into her search app, then *pira Portugal*, but there are no references to it, local or otherwise.

Etching a tentative line between the pira and the camp, Elin moves on to the camp itself, marking a bold line between the camp and Kier.

Mind racing, she jots everything down: what Penn had told them about the camp, the explosion and subsequent removal of something from the site. As she gets to what she saw at the falls between Ned and Leah, she pauses, disecting the theory that Ned had overheard her and Isaac speaking to Leah in the woods. *Could what they'd witnessed at the falls been a way of warning Leah not to talk?*

It's a theory, but only that. Although what they'd seen *looked* like something sinister, given the evidence of Leah's self-harm, her obvious fragility, they can't discount the possibility that Ned might have been helping her. Talking her down.

Elin's thoughts shift to Leah's words as they'd left the falls. The words still chill her.

He's right, you know. It should have been me, not her.

Was there a chance she was referring to Kier?

She bites her lip, frustrated. It's impossible to know at this point. All she can do is note it down, hope she can make sense of it further down the line.

'That isn't everything,' Elin murmurs aloud, looking over what she's written.

She's still unable to shake the feeling of lingering unease that she'd missed something vital about the vans themselves, her subconscious picking up on something at the camp that her conscious mind hadn't yet got to grips with.

Rolling her shoulders, she loosens her neck, playing images of the camp in her mind, teasing them back and forth, but nothing leaps out at her.

Elin takes a sip of wine and decides to leave it there, moving on to the map. Marking a line from the map to Kier and then to the camp, she notes that while there's nothing on the map that references the camp directly, the points seem to roughly circle it.

Locations next: they'll need to visit more before concluding anything definitive, but both the viewpoint and the darkness pervading the map point to something troubling about Kier's experience in the park as a whole. It bothers her, but there's no way of getting to the root of it at the moment.

Her gaze finally settles on the question she's most daunted by.

Kier. Still so many unanswered questions.

Elin swallows, her eyes travelling along the lines she's made between Kier and the camp. Kier and the map. All they have is what Penn told Isaac: that Kier had travelled to Portugal with no obvious reason *why*. No connection to the place, no friends here.

Sliding her finger along the line she's drawn to the camp, Elin jots down their earlier observations: Penn's evidence of Kier staying at the camp – the photos of her van – as well as the fact that it looks like she's left the dog with them.

Is she missing something about the vans themselves?

Elin pulls up the photo Isaac shared of Kier's van when it was initially sighted at the camp, comparing it with what they've seen since being here. Aside from the obvious difference – Kier's van now gone – it all looks pretty much identical.

Same vans. Same positions. Nothing out of place.

The element that's still eluding them was *why* and *how* Kier joined the camp – whether it was a random invite to join or if she'd known someone there.

From this point, things get even murkier – the camp's lie about Kier staying with them.

Was the lie because the camp was covering something up?

Something that potentially could be linked to the videos they'd found on the hard drive, the person Luísa's colleague thought was following Kier?

It's likely, given where they'd found the hard drive and what was on it, that whoever followed her was from the camp.

But who?

Elin runs over the possibilities in her head: *Maggie. Ned. Bridie. Even Leah.*

Given what they'd witnessed up at the falls, Ned's the most obvious suspect, but she doesn't know enough about any of them yet to rule anyone out.

Her thoughts move to Maggie. She'd *seemed* open enough when they'd initially met, but in truth, they knew next to nothing about her. A total enigma. A strong character, that much is clear – mentally and physically robust enough to be living a life on the road, but what else might that strength be concealing?

At this point, Elin's not confident they'll be able to find out. Something told her that Maggie was very much a closed book and intended to stay that way. There would be no easy in-roads in getting to know her.

It might be possible to get more of a read on Bridie and Leah given what she'd gleaned so far, but there would be no guarantee. They'll have to play it carefully.

That leaves her with *why*.

Why would someone want to secretly film and follow Kier?

For kicks, or a more specific reason: were they suspicious of her? Worried she'd stumbled on something, perhaps the same secret Leah might have been about to share?

What they'd discovered about the viewpoint on the map lends weight to this idea – maybe someone in camp had become aware that Kier was watching them, was worried that she'd discovered exactly what they were hiding.

Her mind shifts to something bothering her ever since they'd first viewed the videos: the gaps in the footage.

Thinking it through again, she still believes their earlier theory holds: that the gaps might be a result of deleted footage that revealed something someone wanted hidden.

The only thing she's missing are the precise dates of that missing footage.

Elin knew roughly when the gaps started – in March 2020, about a month after the clips began – but nothing more. Worth noting, she thinks, as it might correlate with something else down the line.

Stretching across the table for the hard drive, she plugs it into her laptop and scrolls through the clips to where the gaps began. Elin records this first date and starts searching.

It's clear from the off that there's no real pattern to the gaps in either regularity or extent. Some are one day, others longer.

The last gap is one of the longest. Nearly a week.

Scribbling it down, Elin scrolls through the footage before and after the missing days, wondering if there's anything else that might give a clue as to what was happening during that time, but the clips show nothing but Kier in the van. Her usual routine.

Putting her pen down, she's about to close the laptop when a movement on the screen catches her eye.

Kier, coming into the van.

Elin immediately sits up a little straighter, noticing that Kier's not entering in her usual way – dropping her bag, kicking off her shoes – and as she steps inside, she abruptly turns, looking back through the door before coming to stand in the doorway itself.

Her face is mostly out of shot, but she's gesticulating.

Someone's stood outside the van. Kier's talking to someone.

Pulse picking up, Elin's about to wind it on to see if the other person comes inside, when she stops.

Another movement.

Not inside the van itself, but in the mirror on the wall opposite to the door.

She can see the back of Kier in the mirror and someone else too – arms wrapping tightly around her, pulling her into an embrace.

A face becomes visible, resting briefly on Kier's shoulder.

Elin zooms in, then zooms in again, her pulse ratcheting up another notch.

Ned.

Letting the footage run on, she keeps watching, but Ned and Kier soon move out of the camera's view, to the side of the van. She continues to scroll, hoping they might come inside, but the screen remains static, still.

Staring at the screen, Elin pulls in a deep breath, trying to process it: whoever deleted the footage had missed this, and after what she's just witnessed, it's likely that person was Ned.

51

Kier

Devon, July 2018

Over two hours pass before I return to the van. I hover outside for a moment, wary, but as I look around, it's immediately obvious that Zeph's left. Markers of his absence are everywhere – flip-flops gone from outside the door, wet suit removed from the roof where he always slings it to dry.

When I finally push open the door of the van, my hand's trembling. I'm still half expecting Zeph to be in there, ready to talk it out one more time, but everything is quiet. Still.

I stand for a moment in the doorway, thrown by the palpable difference from a few hours ago. Not only the absence of Zeph's physical presence and possessions, but his energy and consciousness, the sheer force it usually exerts inside our tiny space.

I remember the same feeling when Penn and I went to our house after Mum went to prison. Everything *looked* the same, but there was already something missing: the indefinable energy a particular person brings to a place. An odd permanency to it, as if the house itself sensed it was final, had already set about rearranging itself, becoming something new.

I glance around. So many things are gone: his recipes tacked to the wall above the stove. The stack of notes for the cookbook. Photographs. Clothes. Only shared things remain, kitchen stuff that wouldn't make sense to transport. Cooking oils and spices. Pots and jars.

While the van feels oddly empty, my shoulders drop, relax. *Relief.*

It feels like not only can I breathe again, but my thoughts are mine and mine alone. These past few weeks, it's as if there's been interference inside my head, his voice, thoughts, stopping my own from getting through.

But a little voice inside me tells me that the relief is in part due to something else.

That if Zeph's gone, I can get rid of what he's just confronted me with too.

I know that the only way that I'll make it through the next few days, to Penn's wedding, is if the painting's gone from here.

All trace of it removed.

I should have destroyed it at the time, but I could never quite bring myself. Perhaps keeping it was a way of reminding myself who I could be in the wrong circumstances. What happens if what I keep locked inside of me finds its way free.

My hands start to shake again as I tug open the compartment in the floor of the van. Pulling back the lid, I can already see the corner of the canvas, sandwiched between some blank canvases still in their wrap.

Shame – ugly, heavy – overwhelms me like something physical as I withdraw it.

The painting is shattering in its intensity.

It's Halloween boy, bruises melting off the contours of his face and jaw, swelling to become more than him, consuming the rest of the canvas.

211

He is bleeding into the canvas, no delineation between the lines of his face and the background, and in that background, there are echoes of him.

Echoes of expressions and words. The colours of decay and disease. Swampy browns and yellows and greens.

I stop, jerked back to the here and now, the memory overwhelming.

Composing myself, I walk outside, making my way around to the back of the van. I open the storage locker and haul the fire pit out, carrying it over to the side of the van facing the woods.

It takes a few minutes of careful nursing to get a fire properly burning, but once it is, I get the canvas from the van, begin slicing it into strips with my Stanley knife. It's humid outside, the heat from the flames making it even hotter, and within minutes, beads of sweat are forming on my face, neck, but I keep going.

Piece by piece, I watch it burn. Watch the paint crack and blister. Turn black.

With every section that's burnt, I feel a weight coming off me.

It's a while before most of it is burnt, the flames gradually dying to nothing. When it's done, I sit and watch the ashes cool.

I slowly exhale, shoulders dropping. I'm aware that it's only temporary, this feeling of erasure, but the only way I can get through the next few days is by knowing that I've quashed every reminder.

Excised it all. Every dirty, rotten part of it, up in smoke.

52

Elin

Parque Nacional, Portugal,
October 2021

The implication is disturbing: if Ned had invested that amount of effort to delete the footage, it puts Kier's disappearance in a whole new light. It also looks increasingly plausible that the person Luísa's colleague saw following Kier in town was Ned.

Slowly exhaling, Elin mulls over their encounter with Leah in the wood.

Could it be possible that Ned and Kier's relationship was what Leah had wanted to talk to them about before she got scared off?

If so, it gave Ned good reason to try to stop that conversation in its tracks.

Her gaze shifts back to the screen. The *timing* of this footage is also important.

In these clips, Kier's van wasn't yet parked up at the camp, but Ned's presence in the video makes it clear that Kier had got to know Ned *before* she moved her van into camp.

Unless there's another explanation, the thought nudging something loose in her mind, something Isaac had told her about Kier being fiercely private, never joining other groups when she was travelling.

Could she and Ned have been friends or something more beforehand?

Knowing her reticence to become part of a group, it would be the most obvious answer as to why she felt comfortable joining this one. While Penn had told Isaac that he didn't believe Kier knew anyone at camp, there's no way he'd have a perspective on everyone she'd met, especially while travelling.

Given more time and resources, there were routes Elin could take to find a possible link between Kier and Ned, but the easiest by far is social media.

Grabbing her laptop, Elin navigates to Kier's sole account: a work account for her illustration business. She'd taken a cursory glance when she was doing some research on Kier before but hadn't found much.

It had been inactive for several years, around the time she left the UK for Portugal, and it seemed purely business focused – videos of her working process, her illustrations in situ in ballrooms and bars. Marquees and elegantly manicured lawns.

It's possible she missed something, Elin thinks, scrolling again. Now she knows what she's looking for with Ned, it might be an easier task.

Methodically, she works her way through the posts, but it quickly becomes clear that there's no Ned and no one else from the camp in any of the photographs. No reference to them in any of the text below the images either.

The captions are purely professional, impersonal.

Illustrations to celebrate the wedding of Luke and Haleh.
A privilege to work with such a wonderful couple.

Next to nothing about Kier in them. None of the 'meet the maker' posts, videos of her talking to camera, but then, as she scrolls lower, she realises that this isn't strictly true.

Glimpses of Kier in some – a profile among a group, a face in the background, at a distance. One post in particular draws her eye: a little more text below the image than the norm, the content itself more personal.

Thanks to Susie and Leon for an amazing day. A privilege to be a part of this special moment. One highlight among many has to be twins meeting twins . . . (scroll!)

Elin clicks past shots of the happy couple until she finds the image in question – a crowd on a lawn in front of a marquee. Big smiles. Cloudless sky. Confetti littering the grass.

This time, Kier is immediately obvious – in profile, stood opposite a pair of identical twins facing the camera in matching navy suits. Beside Kier is a man, presumably Penn, if her caption is anything to go by.

Twin, meet twins.

Elin looks, looks again, so close to the screen now that she can feel it's warmth.

Her heart lurches against her chest wall. Maybe she's mistaken? It's a profile, after all.

Kier's disappearance, it has nothing to do with her. Nothing to do with anyone close to her. Penn is Isaac's friend.

She steps away, as if the proximity to the screen might have been the trigger.

A weird hallucination. A projection.

But when she looks at the screen again, the image is resolute.

It's him. Her colleague. Confidant. Friend. He's there, in the photograph.

Steed is Penn. Isaac's friend. Kier's twin.

Impossible.

53

Kier

Devon, July 2018

'You've broken up?' Penn asks, a quiet uncertainty in his voice. His eyes scour my face as if looking for a cue, a hint at how I'm feeling so he can gauge the right reaction.

I nod, forking a piece of lime and pistachio cake into my mouth. The cake is delicious, moist and tangy from the drizzle of lime juice, but it's an effort to even chew, let alone swallow it down. 'A few days ago . . . Monday?'

A pause, then he raises an eyebrow. 'That's nearly a week.'

I give a non-answer. 'Honestly, it was in the works for a while. I think we both needed space. The best thing all round, with the wedding coming up. I just want to enjoy it. No drama.'

'So where's he gone?' Penn shovels the last of his pastry into his mouth. Tiny flakes stick to his chin, and I lean over and brush them away.

'Back to the US. He's still got his apartment.' My eyes flicker to the newspaper on the table beside us. The same copy from the other day, blocky headline shouting from the front page: **BOAT KILLER STILL NOT FOUND**.

Penn studies my face again, really looking this time. 'Sure it was nothing to do with the stag? I probably overreacted. Shouldn't have made such a fuss of it. This wedding . . . its put everyone on edge, me especially.' He laughs, but it sounds strained.

'The caterer still not playing ball?'

He nods. 'They're asking for more money.' Another forced laugh. 'One word of advice. If you do ever decide to tie the knot, make sure the budget is locked down at the start. It's been a steady creep-creep upwards ever since we've started digging into the details.' As he looks at me, he tries to smile, but I can tell it's an effort.

He's still going through it. 'You need some help?' I ask. 'Can't promise I'm up to much from a budgeting standpoint, but I make a mean Excel chart . . .'

'Nah, you're fine. I'm getting there and you've done enough, geeing up the best man for me.'

'He told you I called?'

Penn nods. 'Said you'd given him a "polite reminder" on a few things.' Pausing, he studies me again. 'So you think you and Zeph . . . it's properly done?'

I shrug. 'I'm not sure. Maybe if we both get our shit together . . .'

A silence settles between us before he changes the subject. 'You used to come here with Mum on Saturdays, didn't you, when I was at football?'

'Yeah.' I glance around. 'It's changed a bit since then, though.' The bakery has responded to its brief: modern coastal. Gone are the plastic chairs and tables and the white vinyl floor tiles. The aesthetic is all crisp white and wood, pots of social media–friendly herbs and plants trailing down the shelves. Sticky buns and rock cakes have been replaced by a rustic counter displaying rows of homemade glazed doughnuts: Yuzu. Marmalade. Nutella.

But it's still there – the bones of the building, the memories.

Mum sat at the corner table with her book, the little noise of satisfaction she made as she took her first sip of coffee.

I swallow hard. Memories like that, they're good memories, happy memories, but they also hurt. Make me ache for what I've lost. For what I'll never get back.

Penn nods, putting his finger to his plate to collect the crumbs, like he did as a kid. I catch his eyes as they lock on my plate.

I slide it across the table. 'Finish it. I've had enough.'

As he digs his fork into the cake, I sense him scrutinising me again. 'You've hardly eaten anything.'

'Stomach's a mess at the moment.'

'Stress?' He puts the cake into his mouth.

'Probably.' I force a smile. 'A twin thing. Maybe I'm feeling the wedding jitters on your behalf.'

Penn makes a joke about telepathy, but it's lost on me, something out on the street catching my eye.

Someone stood on the opposite pavement, a large camera lens obscuring their face.

Tracing the angle of it, the skin on the back of my neck prickles. The lens isn't focused on the group of people sat outside the café, as I'd first thought. It's on us.

54

Elin

Parque Nacional, Portugal,
October 2021

Elin looks to the screen again, to Steed's half-smiling face, the champagne in his hand, white confetti dotting the shoulders of his suit.

The expression he's wearing is one she knows well. A *fuck, the camera's on me* expression. Trying that little bit too hard to smile.

He did that a lot – a slightly forced jollity. These past few months, she's discovered that beneath his relaxed demeanour is someone who sometimes struggles with social anxiety. They'd chatted about it a lot: about his shyness as a child, his reluctance, even now, to be with people he doesn't know well.

Elin looks again, and although it's clear it's him, her brain's still rejecting it.

Steed . . . he can't be Penn.

The different first name and surname for one, although, given his family history, his parent's crimes, it's very possible he'd have changed them, but more than that, it doesn't work. Can't work.

How could he have spent all that time with her knowing he'd already met Isaac, befriended him?

Her mind flip-flops, desperately trying to find an answer. *Maybe Steed never made the connection? It could be a coincidence. Perhaps he referenced something before about knowing Isaac, and she didn't remember.*

Elin sifts through memories; moments they'd spent at work, her flat. They'd chatted everything through in detail: what happened to Sam, their subsequent estrangement.

No. She's clutching at the flimsiest of straws.

Steed never told her that he knew Isaac, plus it's not just what *she* told him that makes any kind of coincidence unlikely, it's what Isaac would have confided in him, too, things that would undoubtedly echo with what she'd shared.

There's no way Steed wouldn't have made the connection.

Heat rushes up her neck as she thinks back to the conversation she had with Isaac about this holiday. He'd told her that it was Penn who'd suggested they come to Portugal, the national park.

Steed had listened to her talk about this break. About this exact place. She'd been sending him photos these past few days.

She feels herself growing hot all over. *No, there could be no excuses. No case of mistaken identity. Steed knew. He'd encouraged Isaac to come to Portugal and look for Kier, knowing the connection between her and Isaac.*

Her heart is thudding, her palms growing clammy. Not just betrayal now, but a strange, slippery sense of fear as the realisation settles in her chest like a solid mass.

The fact that he never told her the connection, the fact that Isaac isn't aware either, it *means* something. It's been kept from her for a reason, but she doesn't know what that could be.

Her thoughts scramble, trying to get purchase.

Isaac.

She needs to talk to him. Perhaps he knows something that will make this make sense.

The phone rings.

When he picks up, there's noise in the background: laughter, the dull rumble of traffic.

'Isaac, I've just found something out, about Penn.'

A short silence, then: 'Sorry, I can't hear, there's some sort of event going on in the town, it's really loud. I . . . ca . . .' Only syllables are audible now, muffled by the loud toot of a horn.

'Isaac?'

He cuts her off. 'I've gone into a shop so I can hear better, but I'm almost out of battery. I was just about to call . . . in case it cuts out, Penn just messaged. He got an early flight. He's already on his way to the park.'

'But—'

The phone goes dead. 'Isaac?' She raises her voice. 'Isaac?'

Fingers fumbling, Elin dials again.

This time the dull notes of the dial tone buzz out in her ear.

She's about to try again when three soft knocks sound out on the door.

55

Kier

Devon, July 2018

I shift left, to get a better look, but a couple walk past the window, blocking the view out to the street. By the time they've moved on, whoever it was is gone.

Maybe I was imagining it. Perhaps they were just trying to get a shot of the café.

Penn's still scrutinising my face. He looks dissatisfied, as if he's seen something he hasn't really wanted to. 'Maybe you should see a doctor if your stomach thing goes on much longer.'

'I'm fine.'

'Sure?'

The way he's looking at me makes me feel uneasy. 'Well.' I pause. For a moment, I'm tempted to tell him, already sensing the relief it would bring. Unburdening myself.

I could tell him not just about Zeph and Romy, but Halloween boy too. What really happened that day.

But if I had any doubts at all about confiding in him, they're gone when I see the worry settle into the very bones of his face. It reminds me of the weight that would settle on Mum when Dad walked through the door in the evenings. A gravitational force dragging her downwards.

I think about Penn's words at the van the other day. *You know how stressful all the wedding planning's been. I don't get why you'd want to add to that by causing conflict.*

What I'm about to tell him isn't conflict, but it's still drama of a kind. Something else for him to stress about.

No, I can't do this to him. Not this close to the wedding. He's stressed enough as it is.

Penn opens his mouth, as if to ask another question, but stops, distracted by the boy at the next table. He's tearing open sachets of brown sugar, emptying the contents onto the table. The mother whispers warnings through gritted teeth: *Stop it. Not while we're having a lovely hot chocolate.*

The boy isn't listening. Two more sachets get emptied. He lowers a chubby hand, smearing the sugar across the grain of the wood.

'A good boy wouldn't do something like that.' The mother's voice is louder now, clipped. Nothing behind it other than frustration, the pained formal language of a parent trying to discipline their child in public, but it takes me back to what our father used to say to our mother. His favourite rebuke.

A good parent wouldn't do that.

A good parent wouldn't leave things until the last minute.

A good parent would know when to pick their child up on time.

I glance at Penn. His face has paled. I can tell that he's gone there too.

All at once, I'm transported back. Sat at our old dining table while Dad grilled her.

His questioning followed the same pattern, a rhythm, and after a while, the questions, the familiar beat of the syllables would find themselves inside me too.

Why was she so lazy? Why couldn't she just do the stuff he asked?

'Do you ever think about it?' I ask.

'About what?' Penn is still looking at the little boy.

'About how Mum could be ... she could be scatty, couldn't she? Dad would get home after working hard all day and stuff *wasn't* done. If she'd just done what he asked, life might have been easier.' Contempt laces my voice. Disgust. *His* voice, taking over, becoming mine.

This happens sometimes still, just like it did back then, his voice crawling into my headspace when my guard is down. Consuming me. Convincing me.

Penn's head snaps back. He looks at me, uncomprehending, heat crawling up his cheeks. 'Kier. You know *why* he said all that shit about her, don't you? He was trying to make us hate her, turn us against her. That's all that was. He was *using* us.'

His words bounce off me. 'But sometimes, Penn, he was good. Nice. You saw what he was like when we used to go out on the water.' Out at sea, he was the dad who helped me study tide charts and analyse swells. The dad who spoke in a calm, quiet voice. The dad who other people saw.

At those moments, in the boat, the sun laying a warm hand on the back of my neck, it felt golden, like the first time you lay out in the heat in spring after a long and rainy winter. On those days, good days, he'd start sentences using my full name.

He'd say, 'Kier Templer, you have blown all the cobwebs off me today.'

And it was like I had. We'd fly across the water, his face all warm and wide and open, and he looked like someone new.

I'd start thinking that perhaps it *was* Mum. Perhaps it was all her fault.

When we got home it felt like it was. Salty and happy, we'd come through the door and her face would crumple when my

225

father asked: *How bloody hard could it be to have the fucking dinner waiting on the table?*

At moments like that, I got what he was saying, I really understood.

How hard was it for her to just get herself sorted? He was the one who worked hard, and she was at home. All she had to do was get things right.

I can hear him now.

A good parent wouldn't do that. A good parent would be efficient. Organised.

I put my fingers to my temples, press, but I can still hear it. He was right, wasn't he?

A good parent wouldn't kill their husband.

A good parent wouldn't take their own life, leave their children behind to fend for themselves.

'Kier?' Penn's voice drags me back to the here and now. 'The fact that he could be nice, and that we loved him, doesn't take away what he did. When you'd come back in so happy, after being out on the water, he *wanted* her to see that. Wanted to make her feel insecure, question the bond we had with her.'

I nod, but it's confusing. Nothing about this is a straight line in my head. It's all squiggles and tangles. A mess.

Another silence falls before Penn picks up the newspaper on the next table.

'They still haven't caught who's done it.' He scans the text, brow furrowed. 'Sure you don't want to stay at ours, until the wedding? I don't like the idea of you being in the van on your own with this going on.'

'It's fine, really. I know it's crazy for you guys right now.' But as I finish speaking, I can't help glancing outside, to the street.

Someone was out there, I'm sure of it. Watching.

56

Elin

Parque Nacional, Portugal,
October 2021

Elin pulls open the door, her heart thudding out beneath her ribs as she takes him in.

Steed. It's him. Penn is Steed.

Despite this knowledge, every part of her is glad to see him, and Elin smiles, her default reaction, and he starts to smile too, and she thinks: *This is where he tells me. This is where he tells me what all this is about, and it will make sense.*

But the smile slips from his lips, a strange kind of battle being fought out in his face.

Part of him greeting her normally, lips turning upwards in a smile, before he catches it halfway and it dissolves to nothing.

No hello, any kind of verbal greeting.

Silently, Steed steps inside, carefully closing the door of the Airstream behind him. Elin tries to meet his gaze and while his eyes find hers, it's as if he's seeing her and not seeing her all at the same time. Like she's deep underwater and he's at the surface, peering down.

He rubs hard at his neck, leaving a red, angry mark.

Elin clenches her hand to stop it from trembling, feeling a prickle of fear – the strange, itchy feeling some primal part of you sends out before you're even aware of any danger. Standing close to her, he seems bigger than she remembers. Broader.

'Look,' she starts, hearing the alarm in her voice. 'Let's talk. I know about Kier, that she's your sister. We can talk about it, and you can explain.'

Steed sways from side to side as if punch-drunk, the pack on his back half slithering down his shoulder. Elin can smell sweat on him, a stale, sour tang.

Features tightening, he takes an audible breath, the only sound in the silence of the small space, a sound that's quickly overtaken by the thud of her pulse in her ears. Thoughts race through her head.

Why had Isaac gone when he did? If he were here, this would be different ...

Stepping back, Elin knocks a mug on the side. It wobbles and they both stare as it rocks backwards and forwards before coming to a stop.

'I—' Steed starts. 'You—' He raises his hand, suddenly, jerkily.

His palm tips towards her. Elin shrinks backwards. She braces for something, but nothing comes.

Silence, then a strange, guttural noise comes from inside his throat, and he starts to cry.

57

Kier

Devon, July 2018

I'm still feeling queasy when I get back to the van, the fragrant notes of the citrus in the cake cloying in my mouth. It's after five, and I should be working out what to make for dinner, but I can't face even thinking about food.

Kicking off my shoes, I grab a glass of water instead. It's only when I sit down on the bed, start sipping, that I sense it: something awry.

Not Zeph's absence this time; the space feels off-balance. Disturbed. I look around, eyes slowly attuning to my surroundings, trying to establish what it is.

It's as my gaze settles on the table that I realise: my laptop.

It's in a different position than how I left it. No longer open, facing the window, but at an angle, the screen pushed down.

A tiny detail, but it niggles. Woody might have knocked it on the way out, it's plausible, but I remember seeing it open when I left the van.

I pause for a moment, the headline from the newspaper and the camera lens directed at the café playing at the back of my mind.

We're not far from the beach. What if someone's been watching the van? Knows I'm alone? I'd left the side window ajar; someone could have levered it open further.

The thought chills me.

Slowly, I make my way around the van. It doesn't take long. I even check the driver's area. No one there and nothing missing either.

I close my eyes and slowly exhale, burrowing my fingers into Woody's fur, but the feeling persists: that the van isn't quite my own.

My gaze moves to the window, an unwelcome thought slipping into my mind: *Is it possible that the person who was in here is now outside the van, watching me?*

I move from window to window, looking for movement, any sign of a presence. There's no one there, but as I look through the window that faces the cliff, I freeze.

I can smell something.

Smoke, but something else too. Burnt paint. A faint chemical odour.

I know that smell. My eyes lurch right, towards the fire pit.

Right away, it's obvious where the smell has come from.

Someone's disturbed the ashes.

I look again, correcting myself: no, not just disturbed them, the ashes are gone.

The fire pit has been scraped almost completely clean.

I swallow hard, the gravity of the complete removal glaringly apparent: with the ashes gone, for the odour to still be strong enough to smell from the van, it must have been done only recently.

As I turn away, I realise I'm still holding the glass of water, gripping it so tight my fingers are starting to feel numb. Putting it down on the table, I make my way outside to the fire pit.

I stop beside it, stare into the now empty metal bowl, thinking it through.

It *is* possible that the breeze may have caught the ashes, but even as I toy with the idea, I realise how unlikely it is.

If that were the case, there would be a thin film of ash, perhaps across the van and the ground, a pattern built up against the edges of the fire pit itself as the wind gusted. Not to mention the larger pieces of the canvas, some of which would be heavy enough to stay put.

There's nothing.

But why? I try and think of benign explanations but there are none.

An odd daze settles over me as I churn it over in my mind. Someone would only do this if they knew what the painting was of, what it meant to me.

There's only one person who did, as far as I'm aware, and that's Zeph.

Yet the more I mull it over, the more it doesn't make sense. I'd seen photos of him, back in New York.

But what if those photos were old ones, posted to simply *look* like he'd gone back?

What if he never left at all?

Thinking for a minute, I decide the quickest way to get a definitive answer is to find out if someone's seen him in New York. I know right away who to call: *Clio*. Zeph's neighbour, fellow chef and closest friend. His first port of call when he's gone back to the city.

We've travelled together a few times since Zeph and I met, and she's become a friend of mine too. She's fiery and opinionated, but the kind of person who gives it to you straight. More importantly, I trust her.

Back inside the van, I sit for a minute to compose myself and then dial her number.

Clio's happy to hear from me, I can tell, asks about the wedding, about Penn. *How is it being home after all this time? Where are they going on honeymoon?*

Small talk, back and forth for a few minutes, before I pivot the conversation to Zeph, ask if she's heard from him.

A pause.

'He's back in the city, isn't he?' I ask.

'He is. I saw him a few days ago, but he looked pretty fucking downbeat.' Another pause. 'I'm guessing—?'

'Yeah, we broke up.' It's an effort to keep my voice neutral while my head is whirling. I feel the thud of my pulse in my ears.

Zeph's in New York. That means whoever's done this, been in my van, it isn't him.

'Shit, I'm sorry, I thought you two …'

I swallow. 'I know. Me too.' My voice is shaky.

I'm quiet for a minute and Clio misinterprets my hesitation for something else: 'Kier, look, I don't want to pry, but the breakup – is it to do with anyone else?'

I know what she's implying. Another woman. Zeph's reputation precedes him.

'Something like that. Romy—' I hadn't planned to mention her, even refer to it, but it's out before I can stop it.

'*Romy?* That's dead in the water, K. Zeph wouldn't go back there, even if she was around, which she's not.' Clio exhales. 'Look, I don't like speaking ill of people, and we were friends, I suppose, when they were together, but Romy … she was messed up. Messed Zeph up too. You know, I've always thought that what went wrong with the restaurant was down to her.'

'You're saying Romy told Zeph to ask the chef to glue his finger back together?' My tone is light, but I don't like what she's implying. Absolving him of any responsibility.

'No, but Romy *thrived* on drama, wasn't happy unless there

was some conflict. Zeph seemed to, I don't know, absorb her behaviour, started acting out, like she did.'

I try to calm the tremor in my throat as I wind the conversation down.

This isn't what I was expecting to hear, doesn't fit the narrative I've been constructing in my head.

Zeph's the bad one, the issue in that relationship, not Romy.

This doesn't make sense.

Saying goodbye, I put my fingers to my temples. The momentary clarity I had with Zeph leaving is gone. Everything's muddled again. Knots and tangles inside my head.

My throat tightens, stomach surging.

I run to the bathroom, start retching violently into the toilet.

58

Elin

Parque Nacional, Portugal,
October 2021

Elin watches as Steed rubs a hand across his face before dragging his gaze up to meet hers.

'Kier,' he starts, nodding. 'Kier's my sister, my twin.'

The words sit there, loaded, in the space between them, and Elin senses that he expects her to do something with them, but she doesn't know what. 'I know she is.' Her heart is drumming inside her chest. 'I saw a photo of you with her, but I don't understand.'

'She came to you, needing help, and I thought, I thought—' He breaks off, tears welling up again, at the back of his eyes.

Absorbing his words, Elin's hit by a sharp sting of realisation. *This* is where their stories collide. Hers, Kier's.

That flicker of recognition she felt, it had roots. Roots in something concrete.

But in what? Replaying his words: *She came to you, needing help*, she racks her brains again, but still nothing comes.

'Look,' she starts. 'When Isaac showed me a photograph of Kier,

I thought maybe I recognised her, but I don't remember how.'

'You don't remember speaking to her?' Steed interrupts, searching her face.

Elin senses something desperate in his gaze that makes her want to say: *Yes, I know her, and I get this, and I can explain, and we can fix whatever this is.*

This was exactly what she feared when she'd looked at Kier's photograph, had that first stirring of recognition – that she'd done it again, that her mind had blocked something out. Missed something vital.

'No, I don't, I'm sorry.' Elin swallows, her mouth dry. 'But we deal with so many people in the job, don't we? There's no way we're going to remember them all.'

Steed pulls out his phone, holds it up. A photo of Kier fills the screen. 'Look. You used to run past her van near the beach, you used to talk to her.'

He keeps scrolling. Images flicker across the screen.

Kier. The van. More Kier.

Photographs Isaac had shown her before.

Elin stares, willing that flicker of recognition she'd felt to develop, but still, nothing comes. 'No, I'm sorry, I can't place her, not properly.'

'Her hair might have been different, she's always changing it, but her face is the same. Her smile.'

Elin takes the phone from his hands, aware she needs to close this down. How he's speaking – so fast – the odd look in his eye, she doesn't like it.

Scrolling through the images, she overlays them with his words: Van. Beach. A different haircut perhaps.

This time, as she focuses on Kier's face, the vague outline of a memory pulls clear.

Someone parked up near the beach, a dog . . .

Elin tries to follow the thought process through, but the memory disperses.

It isn't a surprise. She's dealt with all kinds of issues with vans over the years, campsite disturbances, problems with parking illegally near the beach.

How is she meant to remember this one person?

Steed's staring at her intently. A creeping sense of panic sets in.

'Look, I need more detail so I can understand what exactly it is you're trying to ask.'

'Kier thought someone was following her.' His voice is flat. 'Watching her. It escalated. The van got broken into, she was frightened. She came to you, wanted to report it, for something to happen, but nothing did. You messaged, arranged to meet, but never showed. Kier kept trying to get hold of you, but you didn't get back to her.' He's speaking so fast now the words are running into one another. 'And I kept thinking, you can't do that in our job, you can't make that kind of mistake. The stakes are so high, aren't they? You miss a callback, you're late to something, and it could be the difference between . . .' He tails off, breathless.

Elin picks over his words. Though she can't even grasp a thread of what he's saying, guilt, hot and rancid, sits at the back of her throat. She, more than anyone, knew what it was like to feel on the brink. That there's nowhere left to turn.

Steed's voice splinters. 'I kept thinking, you know, about *why* she left, if it's because she didn't feel safe. And I tried to work out if she hadn't left, whether she'd have ended up here.'

'When was this?'

'July 2018.'

Elin falters, everything pulling into clarity with an abrupt, sickening focus.

'But that . . . that was when everything started falling apart. The Hayler case, my mum . . . I was hanging on by a thread.' Not even a thread, she thinks, remembering the raw, awful pain of it. The desperation. Fear.

Looking back now, it's hard to fathom how far she'd sunk below the surface. She remembers numbness and tears. That strange, dragging feeling, as if someone had her by the ankles and was pulling her under.

Memories are hazy, and some aren't even there at all. Whole days, gone, just lying on the bed, not even looking for a way out because she didn't possess the ability to look.

Her world became distilled to only the immediate; the things around her. Coffee and crinkled bedsheets. Books.

All she can really remember in any detail is a sense of things unravelling faster than she could try to haul them back in. She tried to hold on, but sometimes it felt like she had the loosest grip on the world. Barely a fingertip.

Elin's voice fractures. 'That time, I wasn't there for anyone. I'm sorry that I didn't get back to her, if I missed something.' She'd dropped the ball during that period, and many times. It's why she'd taken the career break. It's highly plausible that Kier had slipped through the net.

Pulling her gaze up to meet Steed's, she's taken aback as his expression shifts, his eyes softening. Heat, flaring in ragged patches up his neck.

'I know,' he says finally. 'What happened with Hayler. How it affected you. Once we started working together, I got it.' The heat is spreading now, reaching his cheeks. Livid, blotchy patches.

Working together. Something doesn't make sense.

Why hadn't he talked to her about Kier when he first started on the team?

He must have known the connection then.

'Why didn't you tell me any of this before? We could have talked it through.'

Steed glances away, a pulse ticking in his jaw. 'Because I,' he says finally, 'I wanted you to know what it felt like' – his face crumples – 'to have someone watching you, like they were watching her.'

Elin recoils, his words like a punch to the chest.

It was him. All this time.

The tweets. The troll.

It was Steed.

59

Kier

Devon, July 2018

Three days since Zeph left and someone's out there, watching me.

It's worse, in a way, knowing that it can't be Zeph. It means that whoever it is ... is an unknown. A stranger.

Every time I go outside, I sense eyes on me: as I walk Woody to the shops, the beach.

Even here, inside the van, I feel it. It's worse at this time of night, just before dusk, when the shadows start to appear, pockets of darkness that my imagination fills with lurid pictures of its own.

I've been trying to take my mind off it with working on Ramon and Luis's commission, but my concentration's shot. I alternate between telling myself that I'm stressed, to overthinking it, to picturing the worst. Imagining someone letting themselves in when I'm out or asleep.

Woody's no comfort. He'd be more likely to smother an intruder in kisses than protect me. I look at him, lying on the bed, legs akimbo, and can't help but smile.

My gaze inches upwards, to the window looking out over the fire pit. The patch of grass it's sitting on is empty, but it's hard to see beyond that, the cliff face casting whole swathes of ground into shadow.

It's enough to send my thoughts spiralling. *Someone could be there, right now, looking in at me. They'd done it before. Who's to say it won't happen again?*

Breathing slowly in and out, I distract myself by pulling Woody's food from the cupboard, emptying some into his bowl. The stale, meaty smell turns my stomach, and I reach over to open one of the windows. It gets rid of the odour, but it also means that I can hear every sound outside.

The wind. Waves crashing to shore. Music ebbing and flowing in the distance.

I clamber onto the bed, pick up my sketchpad again, but a few minutes in, there's a shout from outside, the smash of a bottle breaking.

I stiffen.

When you're with someone in a van, you barely notice those kinds of noises, but now, alone at night, even without the suspicion that someone's watching, I feel vulnerable.

I grab my phone and scroll, my finger hovering over Penn's number. His offer to stay there is playing on my mind, but I can't quite bring myself to broach the subject.

He's consumed by the wedding, hasn't even responded to my last few messages. It would be easy enough to go over to theirs, ask him in person, but I know just what impact that will have. A dampening effect on what should be the happiest few weeks of their lives.

Only four days until the wedding, that's the mantra I keep repeating to myself.

But right now, four days seems an interminably long

240

amount of time to be alone, holding all these thoughts in my head.

Thoughts in my head.

The phrase stirs something, something my father used to say about my mother.

She gets these thoughts in her head.

A memory surfaces.

The night when the policeman came to the door, after one of their arguments. A big one, one that Mum turned into a migraine afterwards, her go-to excuse for taking to her bed the following day.

I remember the policeman craning his head through the gap in the door, his voice soft, insistent. *I was wondering if everything was okay.*

My father listened, nodding in that way he did, head slightly inclined to one side, then saying seriously: *Just an argument. My wife, she gets these thoughts in her head. You know how it is, I'm sure. When she gets like that, I need to talk her down, but sometimes, it can get heated.*

I remember standing behind my father, staring hard at the policeman's face, trying to tell him with my eyes that he needed to come in and talk to Mum herself.

That if he did, he might hear a different story, a story where my father, after complaining that the plate she'd given him was dirty, made her get down on her knees and lick the plate clean like a dog, while he called her *a filthy fucking whore. A filthy fucking whore who can never get anything right.*

But it didn't work.

The policeman didn't pick up on what I was trying to tell him, and after listening to my father, said something like *well, I'll be on my way then,* and as he said goodbye, he smiled at me, but it was sad at the edges.

Shaking the thought free, I get ready for bed.

It takes a while to drift off, tossing and turning for what seems like hours. I don't know how long I'm asleep for before my eyes snap open, a gust of wind shaking the van. Rattling against the windows, doors.

As the gust subsides, I stiffen. I can hear it: the slightest of movements on the door handle, a barely perceptible jiggle of metal.

Woody whimpers.

Flicking on the side light, I sit up, the bed frame loudly creaking with the sudden motion. But before I can even swing my legs out of bed, I see a movement at the opposite window. As my eyes adjust, the shadowy shape becomes more distinct.

A face. Someone out there, looking in at the van.

I freeze. Woody's whimper ratchets up an octave.

The light I've got on is casting a reflection of the van back at me in the glass so I can't see any features, but my mind jumps to fill in the blanks.

It can't be. It can't be.

I close my eyes, count to twenty in my head.

When I look up, the face is gone.

Though the wind has dropped, the van feels like it's moving. I clutch on to the duvet, to Woody, like I'm on a boat in a storm, clinging to the rails.

Thoughts are flashing through my mind so fast, I can't get a grip on them.

I take a deep, slow breath. It doesn't help. It feels like my mind isn't my own, that I'm teetering precariously on the brink of something.

I can't do this any more. Not alone. I need help. If not from Penn, then someone else.

As my pulse slows, I remember a calm voice, kind eyes.

Someone reaching out, offering help.

Picking up my phone, I search for the contact.

Elin Warner.

I quickly tap out a message. **Is it ok if I give you a call tomorrow? There's something I need your advice on.**

60

Elin

Parque Nacional, Portugal,
October 2021

Elin looks at Steed, dizzy, disorientated, the gravity of it all hitting her full in the chest, pulling the breath from her.

It was him.

The odd, insidious creepy messages that have tripped her up, made her question herself, came from him – someone she'd believed was a friend.

Neither of them speaks. He looks at her, blinking rapidly.

'But you can't have,' she says finally, then stops, the sentence becoming garbled.

Steed's face is grey. 'I did. I'm sorry. I kept telling myself that if you'd done your job properly, hadn't lied, saying you'd help her, then Kier wouldn't have come here, gone missing. There was talk, you know, about Hayler, how you went in without any backup. All the mistakes you made. I put that with this and it ... spiralled.' He swallows. 'I built this *picture* of you in my head. Someone out of control. Negligent.'

Elin squeezes her eyes shut, struggling to process what he's saying.

He thought Kier coming out here, going missing was her fault . . . because of her mistake in not getting back to Kier.

'Now I can see it wasn't just that. My marriage had broken down off the back of Kier leaving. My whole world was crumbling, and I needed someone to blame. You became this' – he makes a noise in his throat – 'person to pin everything on.'

Elin opens her eyes, still struggling to wrap her head around what he's saying. *Blame. Marriage.*

Breathing out, he keeps his eyes fixed on the floor. 'I started, I suppose, to fixate on you.' His voice cracks. 'The same thing happened after my parents died. I obsessed.'

Thoughts crowd her head, moving through her mind so fast she can't get a grip on them. It's as if he's walked into the van with a wrecking ball, everything that was safe and certain between them now smashed to pieces.

'But we've been *working* together for months.' Elin can barely get out the words. 'I don't get it. Surely you wouldn't want to work with someone . . .' But as she says the words, the realisation hits her. She recoils, stepping back, away, his face telling her all she needs to know. 'Working together . . . that wasn't a coincidence, was it? You *planned* it.'

'Elin, all I wanted was to get to know you, try to under-stand why you—'

'Understand *what*? You don't inveigle your way onto some-one's team to *understand* them. You were . . .' She's unable to say it aloud, thinking about the message he sent her in hospital, the implicit threat lacing those words. 'You were planning to do something, weren't you? Get me back in some way for not helping Kier?'

'I don't know.' He blinks.

More questions fill her head. 'You changed your name.'

'I had to.' He stutters. 'I couldn't have the past hanging over me. Not with the job we do.'

'And you meeting Isaac in Switzerland, after Laure died. Was that *orchestrated*?'

A shock wave travels across Steed's face. 'Look, I was just trying to find out more about you, work out if what I thought about you was true.'

His words don't make sense. Her head hurts from trying to understand it.

Find out more about her. Work out if what he thought about her was true.

'That's a lie, isn't it? Like working with me, befriending Isaac. It was all part of some *plan* you had, wasn't it? Payback for what you thought I'd done to Kier. It has to be, because I'm struggling, really bloody struggling, to see why you'd go to all the trouble of getting to know Isaac, to work with me, simply to *find out more about me*.'

His eyes dart across her face. 'One thing led to another—'

Elin cuts him off. 'And what about dragging us out here, to the park? What exactly was the idea behind *that*?'

Steed starts rubbing at an invisible spot on his hand. 'I just wanted your help, to find Kier.' He's rubbing so hard now the skin around it is turning red. 'I couldn't look into it on my own because the camp knows I'm Kier's brother. If I turned up again, asking more questions, I thought I wouldn't get anything out of them.'

'So you thought of me,' Elin says dully. 'Despite all the shit you had in your head about me, you wanted me to help.'

'But these past few months, I've come to realise that everything I thought about you – it's not true. You're a brilliant detective, Elin, the only person I'd trust with finding Kier. Any other

246

circumstance, I'd have just asked for your help, but I only found out a few months ago that I should seriously start looking for her here. I'd already told Isaac about Kier going missing by then. There was no way of knowing how much he'd told you about her already, if you'd make the connection. I knew once you did, you'd realise I was lying. Want nothing to do with me.'

'But it's all come out *here*, the whole story. You knew it had to from the minute I saw you. All you were doing was delaying the inevitable.' Her voice is hot, tight. 'Or did you think that pulling us out here and then dropping a bomb like that was somehow *better*? We'd have no choice but to help you because we were already out here? *Invested?*'

Steed's face has drained of colour. 'I don't know. I just hoped you'd understand, that if I explained, apologised, we could then work together in some way, to find her—' His voice splinters, a pleading note creeping in. 'I just wanted it to be like it was, in the summer, you and me. We made a good team, didn't we?'

Work together.

Was that really what this was about, or did he have another motivation?

Had he planned to get her out here, in the middle of nowhere, to exert whatever kind of revenge he'd cooked up, and then got cold feet? And now he's expecting her to believe this half-baked apology? Manipulate her again so she'll forgive him, help him find Kier?

'I'm sorry, Elin. So sorry.'

Elin doesn't reply, now dissecting the timeline, trying to understand how it works with what he's told her. 'But one thing still isn't clear. The messages, the trolling, it *carried on*. All through the case, after you'd got to know me, when you said you realised what you thought about me wasn't true.'

'I know.' He swallows. 'I kept sending them, because as long as I could hold on to the idea that it was your fault, I could keep up the pretence that it wasn't mine.'

'*Your* fault?' Elin shakes her head, uncomprehending.

Steed nods, chest heaving. 'It was my fault Kier left the UK, Elin. Not yours. She left because of me.'

61

Kier

Devon, July 2018

I wake to a light rapping on the door.

Reaching for my phone, I glance down at the screen. It says *8.53 a.m.*

The next knock comes in unison with a voice.

'Kier?'

Penn.

'One sec.' I haul myself out of bed, pull a hoodie over my T-shirt. I glance in the mirror. I look awful. Dry, sallow skin. Shadows beneath my eyes.

When I open the door, Penn smiles. 'Did I get you up?'

'Yeah. Bit of a late one.'

He nods, smile fading slightly as he looks me up and down, as if he's really taking me in for the first time. 'You missed the meal last night, Mila's family.'

I curse. 'Shit, I forgot. Should have put a reminder on my phone.'

'It's fine,' he says, but his voice is tight, and I can tell from the flinty look in his eyes that it isn't. 'Mila's brother didn't show

249

anyway. Think everyone will be fed up to the back teeth with family get-togethers by the time all this is over.' His laugh is strained, and as I look at him, I can see for the first time that the stress of the wedding is not just mentally having an effect, but physically too. Fatigue, settled into his face, lines etched deeper around his eyes.

Penn makes no move to come in, so I step outside. It's bright, the sun barely touched by fine wisps of cloud.

A wave of dizziness overwhelms me, an insistent rolling sensation. As I ride it out, it's hard to even focus on his face.

'But still, you probably wanted someone from—' I say finally.

'*My* side of the family there?' Penn cuts across me, shaking his head. 'Ever since all the wedding stuff started, I never knew there was so much bloody significance between *her* side and mine. I've spent the whole time feeling wholly inadequate on that front, so don't worry about one night.' An attempt at a joke, but I can tell he's having to force it.

'But last night, it went okay?'

'Yeah.' He shoves his hands in his pockets, watching Woody roll on the grass in front of the van, legs in the air. 'And what about you? Everything alright?'

'So-so, but I think that's expected after a breakup.' I look out at the water. In the shallows a family are teaching a child to skim stones, but his attempts aren't even reaching the water.

'Yeah, probably is.' Penn kicks at a piece of dirt with his trainer. 'Sorry I haven't been in touch. I saw your messages, but it's been crazy, we've only just locked down the budget with the caterer, and I thought you could do with time to process everything.'

His words sound contrite, but I notice that he can't quite meet my gaze. An echo of the awkwardness I felt at their wedding venue. It's as if a fault line has opened between us, a gap I'm struggling to breach.

'It's been fine.'

'Sure?'

I nod, about to reassure him, but I can't. I'm not sure if it's utter exhaustion, or fear still lingering from last night, but as I look at him, something else comes out: 'Actually,' I gabble, 'it's been a bit weird since Zeph's left. I'm probably just being paranoid, but it feels like someone's watching me. I—'

I don't get to finish my sentence.

There's a loud shout from behind us, and Penn abruptly turns. He takes a few steps forwards, before coming back, gesturing to the beach. 'Group of kids jumping off the jetty.'

For a moment I'm not sure if he didn't hear what I said, until his eyes come back to find mine.

There's something odd in them – anger and something else too. Guilt.

It's not that he *didn't* hear me, I think, panic rising in my chest, he's choosing *not to hear me*.

The wedding, and now my feelings – are too much for him. He can't cope.

We talk for a few more minutes, making arrangements to meet tomorrow, but the rest of the conversation feels odd, off-kilter.

Watching him walk away, I wait for him to turn, to wave, but he doesn't.

I swallow down a lump in my throat as the realisation hits me: I've never been in such close proximity to Penn and simultaneously felt so alone.

Back inside the van, I check my phone. Elin still hasn't replied to my message. I debate sending another one, wondering if it will seem weird.

But as I watch Penn through the window, receding to a speck in the distance, I realise that here, at least, she's all I have at the moment. The only sounding board.

251

I message her again.

This time, Elin replies almost instantly.

No problem. Could do this evening, after I finish work? Say 8pm, by the beach cafe?

Tapping out a reply, I already feel a little less alone. Just reaching out to someone, connecting, makes the prospect of the next few days more bearable.

62

Elin

Parque Nacional, Portugal,
October 2021

'I fucked up, Elin. I wasn't there for her because I was absorbed in a bloody wedding. I had to hear everything she was going through from a friend. You know, just before the wedding, Kier tried to tell me something was wrong, and I brushed her away.' Steed's eyes are glassy as they roam her face, seeking a reaction. 'I'd had enough. All I wanted was to get married. For all of us, Kier too, to enjoy it—'

He keeps talking, as if he can explain his way out of it, thinking they can have some kind of rational conversation, completely unaware of the devastation he's wreaked.

Elin listens, unmoved. How can he tell her that *his* guilt was a reason to put her through what he had?

'Enough,' she interrupts, unable to listen to any more. 'I don't want to know.'

'I'm trying to explain. I made a mistake. A stupid fucking mistake, and I want to say sorry.' Steed reaches out a hand as if to try to touch her. 'These past few months, I've been seeing a therapist, and she's made me understand that the messages I sent to you were a way of me projecting. Projecting my guilt onto you instead of processing it, even when I knew you weren't what I thought you were.'

Turning her face away, she motions for him to stop coming closer. 'Don't.'

'Elin, please. I'm still me. We're still friends.'

'No, we're not.' She looks back at him, balling her hand into a fist to stop it from shaking. '*Friends* don't do what you've done to me this past year. All these apologies, this *realisation* you've come to about why you did what you did, doesn't make any difference. Did you honestly think bringing me here, telling me this, that I'd want to *help* you? I don't want you anywhere *near* me.'

'I get it.' Steed looks at her helplessly, his eyes now red-rimmed and swollen. 'Part of me knew that in telling you, that you'd probably walk away, but it was my last throw of the dice. Kier—' his voice breaks at the word, 'she's all I've got. I had nowhere else to turn. You're the only person I can trust.'

His emotions are too much against the clamouring of thoughts inside her own head. Not only processing what he's telling her, but the motivation behind it.

Is he telling her the truth or is he trying to manipulate her? What if deep down he does still blame her for Kier's disappearance? How will that play out?

He's clearly unstable, not in his right mind. She's got no idea what he's capable of.

'You need to go,' she says. 'Please. Just go.'

Elin watches him gather up his bag in silence, frozen in position. Although everything about him is familiar: every gesture, every microexpression, it feels like she's looking at someone completely alien. A stranger.

The door clicks as he closes it behind him, but she doesn't move until she hears the sound of his footsteps on the decking growing fainter before fading away entirely.

Elin gives it another minute and then peers through the window.

He's gone, but the fog is back, blowing a filmy gauze over the familiar vista.

Pressing a hand to the door to make sure it's fully closed, she locks it and turns around. She slides to the ground, her back against the door, and sits hard against it, pulling her legs up to her chest. Adrenaline fading away, her body doesn't quite feel like her own. She's cold, shaky.

Elin sits for a while, trying to absorb everything that's happened, let her mind settle, but it doesn't happen.

Part of her had believed it would be better with Steed gone, but it's worse.

Without his sheer physical presence, the shock of him being there in her space, the thoughts that had simply been flitting through her head now come fully formed, crashing in all at once.

How could she not have realised?

How could she have got it so wrong?

Elin pushes her fingers to her temples.

The narrow space is only emphasising the claustrophobic feeling inside her head, the weight of her own thoughts coming in on her.

Out, she thinks.

She needs to get out of the van.

63

Kier

Devon, July 2018

I glance down at my phone. *A quarter past seven.*

Elin's fifteen minutes late. No call, no message to say that she isn't coming.

This is the third time we've arranged to meet, and she's been a no-show every time.

Excuses about work, not feeling well.

The beach café is busy, and as a sunburnt group of teenagers jostle past me to get to the door, I tug on Woody's lead, move us to a quieter spot at the side of the terrace, and send another message:

Hi, I'm waiting outside the cafe. No worries if you can't make it. Just let me know.

Another ten minutes pass.

Shifting from foot to foot, I check my phone again, tears springing to my eyes. I blink them back, not sure why I'm taking it so personally. She was probably just being nice, throwing the contact out there, never actually expecting me to get in touch.

I tell myself I'll give it five more minutes and then head back.

The prospect of another night alone in the van doesn't fill me with joy, but I'm not sure being out here is any better.

The boat murders are still dominating both the news and people's conversation. A group of men clustered by the restaurant door are dissecting the story now: *Another girl's missing in Brixham. They reckon he might have taken her.*

I listen for a moment and then turn away. One last check of my phone.

Still no reply.

Crouching down, I pet Woody and then start for home.

I'm about a third of the way along the beach when my phone rings.

Not the ringtone for a call. FaceTime.

Pulling my phone from my pocket, I slowly tip the screen, delaying the moment.

I already know who it is: the only person who ever FaceTimes me.

Zeph.

My heart plummets, a fiery, prickly heat climbs up my neck. I stare at the screen for a moment, his flashing name, internally debating. Part of me knows I shouldn't go there, shouldn't even consider it, but a bigger part of me is craving the connection. A familiar face.

I hit answer.

'Kier?'

He says my name and every other sound drops away – the waves, the dull buzz of conversation, even the toddler screaming from the buggy – as my eyes meet his.

I slowly exhale, feeling suddenly warm, steady. It's how I imagine an addict feels when they get a hit: dopamine rushing through my veins, a sweet sense of calm despite the fact that my heart is racing.

'Shit.' He swallows hard, his voice croaky. 'I had this all planned out and now seeing you ...'

I slowly nod, unable to take my eyes off his face, feeling an odd sense of seeing him anew.

Zeph starts again, peering closer at the screen. 'You're at the beach?'

I clear my throat. 'Yeah, I'm walking Woody.'

'Woods ... Woods?'

I lower the phone to Woody, who comes up to the screen and sniffs it. 'I reckon he can hear you.' I bring the phone back up to face height. 'But can't see you, so now he's trying to sniff you out.'

Zeph pulls a face. 'What are you trying to say?'

I laugh, and then stop abruptly, not quite sure of what the protocol is here, exes speaking to one another. All I know it's not this – acting like we were when we were together.

'Look,' Zeph says, clearly noticing my awkwardness, 'I just wanted to see how you are, and to apologise.' He clears his throat. 'How I reacted to you saying you wanted space, it was wrong. What I said about you needing help. And bringing up the painting.'

At the mention of the painting, my lip starts to tremble, and I bite down on it, hard.

'I don't want to go over it again, but the painting, it was private, I see that now. It wasn't up to me to delve into what it means, and I want you to know that whatever it's about, for whatever reason you did it, I don't give a shit. All I'm worried about is you and me. The love I have for you ...' He tails off.

I squeeze my eyes tight shut against the tears that are welling hot behind them. I don't want to cry, but it's not just his apology that's throwing me off-kilter, it's what he's saying beneath that. That he loves me whoever I am. Loves all of me.

'K?' Zeph moves his face closer to the phone screen. 'You okay?'

'I'm fine,' I say quickly, wiping the tears away with the back of my hand. I try to take control of the conversation, ask him about being back in New York, the cookbook.

He talks fast, with energy, about a new neighbour, a recipe he's trying out, and I wrap myself up in the sound of his voice. He's more American over the phone. Louder. More intense. Everything around me feels drab compared to what's coming down the phone line. I've missed this, I think. Missed how alive he makes me feel.

He tells me that he's going out tonight with friends.

'Clio?'

'Nah, people from work, restaurant before last. Bishop, Lacey.'

'Lacey?' Her name sloshes over me like acid. 'Lacey, who you used to date?'

'Yeah,' Zeph says quickly. 'But it's nothing like that, you know we're just friends.'

I nod, reprimanding myself. Even if it was, I have no room to talk. A strange recalibration is happening in my head: *I'm no longer his girlfriend. I have no claim on him.*

We carry on talking, and seamlessly, without me even really noticing, we slip back into our usual banter. Stupid jokes, anecdotes.

I feel calmer than I have in days, and I realise that I don't feel how I expected to, speaking to him. That burning anger I felt last week isn't there any more.

A little seed of doubt settles into me.

Whereas a few days ago the picture was clear, told a coherent story, now it seems loose, none of the pieces fitting together quite like they should.

Did I call this wrong, in the heat of the moment? What if Clio was right? Those photographs of Romy were just that, photographs?

Someone passionate, who didn't want to believe the relationship was over?

Then, as I look at him again, reality hits – a slap in the face.

Images flicker through my mind: *The necklace. The photos of Romy. His foot on mine.*

'You okay?' Zeph says, watching me. 'You look a bit pale still.'

'Stomach's still a mess ... haven't really felt like eating. I was saying to Penn the other day, I think it's a twin thing, feeling the wedding jitters on his behalf.'

Zeph smiles, but it falters. 'You're not ...' His voice is shaky.

'Not what?'

He takes a breath, still not meeting my gaze. 'You don't think there's a chance you could be—'

Realisation finally dawns as his eyes pull up to meet mine.

'*Pregnant?*' I laugh automatically.

Zeph nods, brow furrowed. 'I was thinking about it the other day, before I left, when you said you weren't feeling well.'

I don't reply, my heart pumping as I absorb the implication.

It's not something that I'd vaguely considered. We've always been careful.

But as the thought takes root, I mull over the tiredness I've felt these past few weeks, the queasiness that has steadily built. *Could I ... ?*

'Just imagine.' Zeph's voice is quiet, shaky, and although he's trying to smother it, there's a faint smile playing on his lips.

'I ... can't even ...'

He blinks, closing and then opening his mouth before closing it again.

We're both silent for a moment. Though we've talked about having children in passing, the idea has never stuck. In my mind, at least, you don't consider bringing new life into a life already so uncertain.

Zeph's eyes roam my face. 'I shouldn't have brought it up. Probably reading into things.' He looks nervous suddenly. 'Look, I'll leave you to it, maybe we can talk tomorrow.'

'Okay.'

On the way back to the van, I think it all through, dizzied by the enormity of what he's suggested. It takes until I reach the van for my heart to stop racing and the idea to properly take hold.

Inside, I unclip Woody's lead and sit down at the table, my thoughts whirling. Pushing the nail of my thumb between the gap in my teeth, I pull it backwards and forwards, looking through the window.

This time, I don't see anyone else out there.

Just my own reflection. My own eyes, looking back at me.

64

Elin

Parque Nacional, Portugal,
October 2021

Elin dives into the tree line, the breeze catching at her hair, pulling it away from her face.

With every step she takes, a new thought skitters through her mind.

What exactly had Steed been planning? How close had he got to doing something worse than the messages, the photographs?

No matter what he said about not having a plan, how can befriending Isaac, working on her team, be read as anything other than intentionally malevolent?

Elin's mind flashes backwards to the first time they met in the office. Steed's easy smile, the effortless banter, how he'd asked if he could join her for lunch. That shared lunch became an almost daily occurrence, then drinks after work in the pub. Slowly, carefully, he'd got past the barriers she'd put in place by listening. Advising. Pretending to care.

In turn, she'd not only let him past those barriers, she'd *invited* him in. Wanted it, encouraged it. Relished the idea that they had some kind of bond, that she had someone to confide in.

Steed had gone on to support her when she received those first messages. Supported her while knowing that he'd been the one to send them.

What kind of person could do that?

She'd trusted him. Thought they'd built a bond. Even thought . . . her mind lurches back to the last call they'd shared, heat flooding her cheeks. She'd believed that his hesitancy, his out-of-character behaviour, was because—

You actually believed that there might be something more, between you, more than friends.

Her own idiocy, her naivety taunts her.

More memories: their runs together. Watching crappy movies at her flat.

Only now, with those memories in tatters, does she realise how much that meant to her, how much *he'd* meant to her. Exactly how much she's come to rely on him, despite telling herself otherwise.

Had she learnt nothing these past few months?

What she's feeling now – it shouldn't be happening. No one should have this power to destabilise her. She was meant to be past that.

Elin's mind rolls back to calling him the other day, when they'd first arrived at the Airstream, how afterwards, she'd slapped herself on the back for contacting him instead of Will.

A false victory.

Steed had been fulfilling the same purpose as Will, she just hadn't realised it until now. All this time, she thought she'd moved on, was coping on her own, when all she'd done was replace one crutch with another. Relied on someone else to prop her up, make her happy.

As she walks, more moments are thrown into question. She feels a horrible sense of instability, now acutely aware that it's not only all the times she was *with* him that are in doubt, but other moments too.

Instances when she'd felt that ominous chill down her spine – that sense something was odd, awry. Eyes on her as she'd left the office, went running at night.

She thinks about the hand in the small of her back in the spa in Switzerland. *Had he been there at the hotel, at Isaac's engagement party? Did he befriend Isaac after that?*

Elin's thoughts swirl in circles before they finally bleed themselves out.

It's only then that she stops, breathless, looking around her.

An uneasy feeling creeps up her shoulders as she takes in the now hazy outline of the path ahead. It's narrower than she expected, overgrown, leggy ash trees on either side creating an almost living barrier, fine branches crisscrossing over one another.

This doesn't feel right. Has she taken a wrong turn? Gone in a different direction entirely? There should be a proper trail here, surely?

How long had she been going? Ten minutes. Fifteen?

She should be at least halfway to the camp, a path she knows fairly well by now, but there's nothing familiar about this at all.

But then, taking in the changing scene around her, Elin isn't sure she'd recognise it even if there was. Without her realising, the fog has thickened, fine wisps turning into something denser, more impenetrable.

People describe fog as a blanket, but that's a lazy description, she decides, watching it spooling between the trees. A blanket has soft, comforting undertones. Something static. Cosy.

This is anything but.

It's alive and moving, forming shapes that quickly dissolve, morph into something else.

Don't panic, she tells herself, moving forwards, eyes scouring the forest for something familiar, but a landscape usually so complex is rapidly becoming a blank.

A vast desert of grey nothingness.

Up ahead, she can't see more than a few metres in front, the ash trees in front of her now nothing more than blurred outlines.

Anyone could be out there, she thinks, her pulse picking up.

He could be out there now. Steed.

Watching her, like he's been watching her all these months.

All at once, there's a pressure in her chest. A feeling of impending doom.

Her fingertips start to tingle.

A panic attack.

She hasn't had one in a long time. A flicker of it when the van exploded at the camp, and she couldn't catch her breath, but this is something different. Had already set in without her realising, gone too far for her to easily pull it back.

Elin tries to take a deep breath, but she can't. It's as if a weight has been placed across her chest, is bearing down on her.

Her heart starts to thud, pounding out against her rib cage and she thrusts her hand into her pocket for her inhaler.

Stop, she tells herself. *Nothing serious is going on. This is temporary. Your body reacting to a fear inside your mind. A physiological response, nothing more.*

You know what you need to do.

Breathe in for four and out for seven. Repeat.

Using all her concentration, Elin forces herself to slowly inhale, exhale.

Bit by bit, her breathing starts to come under control.

As her pulse begins to settle, she decides the only thing she can do now is keep moving. Maybe she's closer to the camp than she thought, has come at it from a different angle. The fog might not be so dense further on, she might be able to orientate herself—

Her train of thought is broken by a loud rustling behind her. Elin spins around as a voice sounds out.

'I'd stop right there if I were you.'

65

Kier

Devon, July 2018

Two days to go until the wedding and finally I'm working again.

It's like the haze has started to clear in my head, the soupy mess of thoughts still circling, but no longer stuck on the same loop: worrying over who might be watching me. Churning over the situation with Zeph. Romy.

I'm sat outside, Woody at my feet, sketching out ideas for Ramon and Luis's commission. It's taken a few days, but I've finally gotten beneath the skin of the brief, found something that strikes at the heart of who they are as a couple: the vineyards at their venue.

My research has thrown up intoxicating images; intricate grapevine motifs sculpted and painted on tomb walls in Greek and Roman times, the vines winding over ceilings and walls, laden with fruit.

Grapes were taken as an offering on the journey to the underworld, symbolising abundance and prosperity. New life after death. Despite the macabre undertone, there's hope in the images. Growth.

It's perfect: a way of celebrating their love of wine without resorting to clichéd bottle motifs or toasting glasses.

Making sure Woody's settled with a new bone, I start working through my first idea – to not only have the vines as a border decoration but winding through the text itself.

Within minutes, I'm consumed, sounds, sights, drifting away.

It's only Woody, barking, that breaks the reverie. I soon see what's caught his eye: a movement past the side of the van. Flickers of colour – clothing, people.

My head jerks up, but as the shapes become clearer, my shoulders drop, relax.

A mother and daughter, towels in hand, on their way to the beach.

The initial surge of adrenaline quickly dies away. The fear that gripped me a few days ago, it's not so acute. I still feel like someone's out there, watching, but it seems less immediate; a distant threat as opposed to something looming.

Something else is now consuming my thoughts, distracting me.

Zeph's words: *You don't think there's a chance you could be?*

My eyes slip towards the unopened pregnancy test in my bag.

I know I have to do it, be certain, but I haven't been able to bring myself to. Not yet.

The idea feels precious – a bubble I don't want to pop by probing too hard – but every conversation I have with Zeph is shaped around it. Despite the distance between us, it feels like it's joining us together. A tether, a tie, stretching across the Atlantic.

The questions I have about him – they're still there, but they're fading, like pieces of clothing left out too long in the sun to dry.

I stand up, look out to sea. The air is sticky-still, the water glassy. It's beautiful. Reminds me of when I loved living here. Of when I drew that first map.

Somehow, I've lost sight of that since I've been back. The unmapped have become bigger than all those happy times.

But these past few days, it's as if I can see them again. It makes me think about the new maps we could create. Zeph and I, as a family.

I place my hand on my stomach, let it rest there.

Even though the idea isn't yet substantiated, it already feels oddly weighty. Solid. Solid enough perhaps, to do what nothing else has before – supplant the monster inside me.

If it does, maybe I can rest a while. Stop running. Just be.

66

Elin

Parque Nacional, Portugal,
October 2021

'Don't go any further forwards. You're right by the pit.'

Bridie's voice.

It takes a moment for Elin to process the words.

The pit. The wolf trap.

'You need to move back. Two big steps, and you'll be clear.'

Elin holds her breath, Bridie's words almost eclipsed by the sound of the rushing blood in her ears.

A bead of sweat trickles past her eye, stirring her into motion.

Legs shaking, she takes one step, then another, before a hand roughly clasps her jacket, tugs her further up the hill.

Elin turns to see Bridie looking at her, her face pale. Hoisting a sleeping Etta higher up her back, she whistles through her teeth. 'Caught a glimpse of you ... looked like you were about to walk right over. There's a wall around the pit, but it's not high. Catch it at a bad angle ...'

'Took the wrong direction somewhere.' She can barely get

out the words. 'Couldn't see anything. Thought I was still in the woods.'

'The fog can just roll in like that here. One minute fine, and then' – Bridie clicks her fingers – 'the whole park, just gone. Sometimes it's like that for days. Always feel sorry for the tourists who come here this time of year for the views and get this.'

She gives a faint smile, but Elin struggles to return it. She's shaking, from cold or shock, she's not sure.

Bridie's brow furrows as she looks at her. 'Let's get you sat down.' Looping her arm in Elin's, she leads them slowly up the hill.

It's a few minutes before they push through a line of trees onto a rough dirt track. 'Here,' Bridie gestures to a granite slab a few feet away. 'Not the comfiest of seats, but it'll do.' Untying her fleece from around her waist, she passes it to her. 'Probably best, you know,' she says lightly. 'To take a pack with you when you go for a hike. Get lost out here without any layers or supplies . . .'

Elin sits down, tugs the fleece over her head. 'Yeah, stupid move. Left the van pretty quickly.'

A beat passes.

'Something happen?' Bridie says softly, brushing her fringe away from her eyes.

Elin nods. 'Found out that someone wasn't who I thought they were. Caught me by surprise.' The words escape before she can haul them back in. It's not something she usually does – confide in someone who is essentially a stranger – but she doesn't feel any sense of crossing a line, just relief that the words are out. No longer trapped inside her head.

'I know what that feels like.' Bridie inclines her head a little, checking on Etta. 'Rough, isn't it?'

'Yeah.'

Bridie doesn't probe any further, and they sit for a while,

271

looking out. Below them, the fog is breaking up a little, fragmented glimpses of the valley appearing before quickly becoming smothered again. Pulling a bag of jelly beans from her waist belt, Bridie passes her a handful. 'Anyone asks, these are Etta's.'

'I won't say a word.' Smiling, Elin slips a few into her mouth.

'Not a great few days for you guys,' Bridie says after a beat. 'Probably not the break you were imagining.' She pauses. 'You were up at the falls, weren't you? With Ned and Leah? Must have been a shock.' Though she doesn't say any more, something in her face tells Elin that her and Isaac's presence there had been discussed.

Slowly chewing, Elin mulls over how best to respond, what the motive is, if any, behind her question. 'Yeah, it was. Leah ... She looked in a bad way.'

Bridie's quiet for a moment. 'You know, with Leah, it's always been complicated.'

'Personal stuff?'

She hesitates for a moment, then nods. 'Leah's had issues over the years, and recently she's started fixating on her ex. She had it in her head, you know, that he was the one who blew up the van, was stressing about it, but we never thought she was in a place where she'd—' Bridie shakes her head. 'Maggie was keeping an eye on her, but she can't be with her all the time.'

'That's a lot of responsibility.'

'It is, but Leah's like a daughter to her.' A look flits across her face that Elin can't get a read on. 'All of us are. Takes it personally—' Bridie stops, the words drying up in her mouth.

A few beats pass. 'So you really think Leah was planning to ...?'

'Hard to say if she'd have gone that far, but Ned said it looked that way.' Her voice catches. 'Thank god he noticed she was gone. If we'd left it any longer ...'

There's no doubt in her mind, Elin thinks, watching her. *She believes Leah went up there of her own volition. That Ned talked her down.*

Bridie bites down on her lip. 'Something like that happens, makes you realise how much you come to rely on someone.'

'I can imagine. Must be tight, especially in a community like yours.'

'Yeah, we're like family. Leah, especially. She's the one who really understands, gets what it was like to—' Breaking off, she fiddles with the bag of sweets on her lap.

Elin doesn't fill in the silence. She's learnt that sometimes it's best to let the other person's thoughts have a chance to breathe.

Bridie starts again. 'Leah helped me out a lot when Etta was little. Still does.'

Noticing the little line of dribble forming at the corner of Etta's mouth, Elin smiles. 'Guess you guys have a lot in common. A similar age.'

'Yeah, same interests too. We both like the arts, the same books, theatre.'

'So Leah's creative, then?' Elin thinks about Kier, her work, wondering if perhaps that's where a connection might have formed.

'She is, but with that comes a fragility. Leah sees the world in a kind of . . .' – she pauses – '*heightened* way, that's probably how best to describe it. A layer deeper than anyone else. Makes me frightened for her, how much she absorbs as her own, but I thought she was getting there. Yesterday, up at the clearing, it seemed like she'd turned a page—' Abruptly, she stops, as if she's said something she shouldn't. A flush creeps up her cheeks before she changes the subject.

'So you don't know what triggered Leah going up to the falls?'

'No, but I suppose you never know what's going on in someone else's head, do you? No matter how close you think you are.'

No, she says to herself, thinking about Steed. *You don't.* You can spend almost every day with someone, and they still have the ability to pull the wool over your eyes.

'It's just—' Elin hesitates, trying to work out how to best say it. 'Isaac and I, we saw Leah in the woods the other day, by the remains of this wooden' – she gropes for the right word – 'structure that she called a pira. We got the feeling it meant something to her.'

Bridie doesn't let her finish her question. All at once, she stands up, face tightening, looking down towards the valley. 'Looks like the fog's clearing.'

Elin nods, stung by the sudden dismissal. Two steps forwards and two steps back, she thinks. What momentary opening there had been was now firmly closed, but her reaction has revealed something: the piras, whatever they are, mean something to the group. To Bridie as well as Leah.

'Give it a few more minutes and I reckon we can head off.' Bridie turns back.

She's right, Elin thinks, taking in the scene around her. The swathe of grey that looked fairly set in a few moments before seemed lighter at the edges, whole pockets of land now revealed.

Tipping her head towards a still-sleeping Etta, Bridie looks at her watch. 'It's nearly six. This one's going to need something to eat pretty soon, but I can walk you back if you like?'

'It's fine. Once the fog's gone, I know my way back from here. I don't want you to have to walk back to camp in the dark.'

Reluctantly, Bridie nods. 'Better swap numbers, just in case.'

'I don't have my phone on me.' Elin flushes, acutely aware of how unprepared she really was. 'Left it in the Airstream.'

'In that case, I'm definitely walking you back. At least to camp.' Bridie bends down, fiddling with her laces, making a joke about waking Etta, who has tipped forwards in the carrier, her nose now nestled in Bridie's hair. She starts to say something else about Etta, but her words don't even register.

Elin's eyes are locked on Bridie's hiking boots.

The soles are dirty, as expected – dust, little bits of soil – but the fabric itself, the creases around the laces, hold something unexpected.

Ash.

Something slowly turns over in her head.

Still looking at it, she thinks about the clearing painted on Kier's map, the heat that had flooded Bridie's cheeks just a few moments ago.

67

Kier

Devon, July 2018

Three facts about my mother:

1. She used to stand on one leg while she was brushing her teeth because she'd read somewhere that it would help her live a longer and happier life.
2. She pretended to like coffee cake. Penn and I made it once at school and were so pleased by her rapturous reception that we made it every year for her birthday. It was only when we saw her shovelling it into the bin that we realised she was just humouring us.
3. She gave Dad multiple chances. These weren't fake-it-until-you-make-it shots, they were the real deal. She wanted to believe in the dream. Wanted us to be a family.

This last fact is weighing on my mind. Every time I speak to Zeph or message him, it's all I can think about: if Mum gave Dad multiple chances, even after what he'd done, then surely I can give Zeph one too?

Last night, when we were talking, he asked if we could meet up. Skimming over the question, I didn't give a proper reply, but deep down I know what the answer should be.

What we have, what we've built, *could* build – I can't leave it unexplored, not while I'm still unsure about things.

But first, I need to scratch an itch:

Romy.

There's no way of us moving on until I pull that thorn from my side.

After the wedding, I'm going to Portugal to try to find her. Once I know she's okay, properly understand what happened between them, then Zeph and I can move on.

He said it again to me last night: *We're going to fly, Kier. You and me, we're going to fly.*

I lay a hand on my stomach.

I want to believe it this time. More than anything, I want it to be true.

68

Elin

Parque Nacional, Portugal,
October 2021

Isaac's outside when she arrives back at the Airstream, sitting by the fire pit, staring at his phone clasped in his hand.

'Nearly about to call a search party,' he jokes as she crosses the decking, but his smile fades as he takes in her expression. 'What's wrong?'

'Something's happened,' Elin says heavily, casting a look towards the other Airstream, just visible between the trees. 'Probably best we go inside.'

Isaac's features are stiff, tight, as if he can't quite take in what she's told him. 'I don't know what to say.'

Elin nods, trying to hold her emotion in, but she feels her lip trembling.

Leaning over, Isaac pulls her towards him for a hug. 'If it makes you feel any better, he got me too. I genuinely thought we were mates.'

Hearing the pain in his voice, for the first time, it properly hits her that it's not just one deception, but two. Steed had betrayed both of them. She feels another hot surge of anger: Steed knew Isaac was vulnerable after what happened to Laure. Knew that and did it anyway.

'He's lied to both of us,' Elin replies as they pull apart.

There's a sombre feeling as they talk it over again, in detail, Isaac asking the same questions she's tormented herself with and more of his own.

How long do you think he'd been planning it? What exactly did he want by bringing them out here?

As the conversation eventually exhausts itself, they slip into an uneasy silence.

'So where do we go from here?' Isaac says finally. 'With Steed, I mean? You going to tell anyone?'

'I don't know ... haven't really got that far.' Deciding whether to report him or not was something she hadn't even begun to grapple with. It would be career defining for Steed in every sense of the word, and she's not sure she's ready to make that call. 'It's going to be something I need to think about properly.'

'And Kier, how are you feeling about that?'

Elin knew the conversation was going to come around to this point, and she's still feeling her way around an answer. 'I'm not sure.' She glances out through the window to see that the light in the other Airstream is on, the dim outline of a figure moving around inside. 'What do you think?'

Isaac hesitates, frowning slightly, the lines deepening around his eyes.

'To be honest,' he says, 'I don't know if it's going to be something anyone else can decide for you. Sometimes I reckon it's better not to think about how you'd feel about *doing* something, but to work out how you'd feel if you didn't. Hard as it is to go there, you need to work out whether you'd be happy

279

leaving it here, after everything we've found out about Kier, the camp...'

Elin sits for a minute, thinking over what he's said, the raw reality of it.

Walking away now. Leaving Kier's story without any real resolution.

Isaac lightly places a hand on her arm. 'It's not a question you've got to answer now. I don't think either of us can. Probably best we sleep on it and then—'

'Not sure I need to,' she interrupts. 'I'm pretty certain I'm going to feel exactly the same tomorrow. Part of me wants to get the hell out of here, but how can I leave it like this, when I might be part of why Kier came here? Why something's happened to her? What Steed said was exaggerated, yes, but there's truth in it. I didn't get back to her when I should have.' Her voice pitches higher. 'I missed something.'

'Hold on,' Isaac says slowly. 'That's because you weren't well, and Steed said himself he didn't think that's the reason Kier came out here. He reckons that's because of him.'

'But's that's the whole point. I *wasn't well* so I shouldn't have been working, should have held up the white flag, taken the career break sooner.' It was a decision she always feared would one day come back to haunt her.

'So at the time, you knew you weren't yourself?'

'Yeah ... but I carried on. It was pride, that *drive* I've always congratulated myself on, that made me keep going. I didn't want to admit to myself I was out of control.'

'I don't think many people can. You want to believe you've got it altogether.'

'But for most people, it doesn't have consequences. In the job I do, you have a responsibility.' Elin shakes her head. 'You know, before this, I thought I was making progress with the whole getting to know myself thing, but this proves the opposite. Not just this, but leaning on Steed like I did, when he was thinking god knows what behind my back.' She blinks. 'What kind of an idiot doesn't see what's staring her right in the face?'

'A human one,' Isaac says softly. 'And you *are* making progress. What you just said, acknowledging you should have taken the career break sooner, that's brave. Admitting your flaws.' He shrugs. 'Just because something's hard to do, doesn't mean it isn't progress.'

Elin's quiet for a minute, mulling over what he's said. Catching his gaze, she gives him a half smile. 'Getting wise in your old age.'

'Maybe.' Isaac's eyes shift past her, towards the trees. 'Look, I've been thinking as we've been talking. I want to go and speak to Penn.' Grimacing, he corrects himself. 'Steed. There are things, from my side, that I want to ask him before we can make any kind of decision about where we go from here. I need to be sure he's not going to cause us—'

Isaac doesn't finish his sentence but Elin knows where he was going with it, the real reason he wants to talk to Steed.

He wants to be sure he's not going to cause them any problems. That Steed meant what he said about exactly why he brought them out here.

Isaac rubs a hand over the back of his head. 'Before I go, just so I'm clear, the one thing I think we're both agreed on is that if we do decide to continue with this, there's no way Steed can be a part of it, is there?'

'No.' She swallows hard. 'There's no way we can police what he does, whether he's planning to stick around or not, but I don't want anything to do with him.'

Her mind is still churning it over as Isaac gets ready to leave.

Elin knows she should do as he says – sleep on it – before she makes a final decision, but she can't stop thinking about Bridie flushing as she mentioned the clearing, and the fine coating of ash caught in the fabric of her boot.

69

Elin

Parque Nacional, Portugal,
October 2021

Worry is etched in Isaac's eyes as he zips up his pack the next morning. 'You're sure about this? Carrying on? We've still got time to think about it.'

'I'm sure.' Elin bends down to lace up her boots. 'If you reckon what Steed said last night, about keeping his distance, was genuine.'

She doesn't know the nitty-gritty of what happened when Isaac had gone to speak with Steed, but he'd returned flushed and ruffled. From the brief snapshots of the discussion that he'd shared, she'd sensed it had been a tough conversation in every sense of the word.

'I do.' He lifts his pack up onto his back. 'He's not going to be a problem.'

'Then I'm good.' Her words are shot through with more positivity than she feels.

How is it really going to work with him being so close by? There's no way she can *make* him leave, but his presence is going to be an uneasy one.

'So,' Isaac pulls open the Airstream door. 'Ready to test your theory on the clearing?'

'Yeah. I keep thinking about Bridie's reaction, after she mentioned it . . . there's got to be something to it.'

After pulling up Kier's map on his phone, Isaac zooms in on the clearing. 'What do you reckon?' He tips the screen towards her. 'Hard to say from this exactly how long it's going to take, but I reckon it's a good thirty-minute hike.'

In the end, the thirty minutes became forty, the route up to the clearing a tougher task than they'd initially thought – not just the dried leaves and exposed roots snaking across the forest floor, but the dim light cast by the tree canopy. It's disorientating, green bleeding into green. Trees for miles, wildly overgrown. A mixture of ash and oak and yew.

By the time they reach the edge of the clearing, the sun is high, bright in the sky.

'It's hotter than I thought it would be.' Elin peels off her fleece as they push through the final line of trees. 'Should have—' She stops, lost for words, taking in the scene around her.

'Kier painted it well, didn't she?' Isaac's eyes are roaming the space. 'The trees, I mean.'

Elin nods, absorbing it. Apart from the breeze ruffling the trees, it's deafeningly quiet. Where they're stood, at the tree line, the forest fires had eaten away any green at floor level, leaving it sooty and blackened. The oaks above have been stripped of their leaves, the trunks black, even white in places, from the extremes of heat.

It's stark. Not faded, ashen sepia tones; this is harsh blacks and whites.

There's something ghoulish about the whole setting, she thinks, chilled. Graveyard feels, the inherent wildness of the park giving way to something still and sombre.

Her gaze slides upwards to the centre of the clearing, where the burnt ground gradually gave way to a grassy open space in the middle, patchy with a mix of scrubby grass and flower.

Elin studies it, confused. The green broke up the bleak monotony of the scene, but none of it tallied with what Kier painted on the map. The skeletal outline of the trees echoes the painting, but she can't see any of the light, the almost celestial atmosphere Kier conjured.

No story to tell here but one of destruction. Nature giving way to a stronger force.

What are they missing?

As her eyes travel right, Elin notices the remains of a wooden structure at the corner of the clearing, almost burnt to the ground. Only a small section of the building is still standing, the wood smoke-damaged and sagging, part of the roof precariously balanced on what's left of the side wall. A gaping hole indicates where a window once was.

Walking over, Elin peers through the void. Huge pockets of ash are sitting inside, studded with glass and broken bits of wood. Outside too, where the remaining section of roof was protecting the ash from the elements. It's littered with a mess of footprints.

'The ash I saw on Bridie's boots, it's deep enough here to explain it.'

'Looks like it.' Moving around the side, Isaac crouches to examine what's left of the structure. 'What do you reckon it was?'

'Some kind of hikers' hut or shelter. Hard to say,' Elin says, unnerved as she pictures it, someone staying in this shell of a building, so close to where the forest fires had so violently taken hold. 'I'm going to keep looking around.'

Skirting the edge of the tree line, her eyes scour the ground around her. No green here; the earth is grey, soot and ashes trampled to form a thick blanket that's more or less smothered

285

any wildlife. All fairly monotonous, until she reaches a cluster of boulders at the edge of the grass.

Elin's gaze catches on something half concealed behind the lichen-covered surface of the largest stone.

A scorched circle of earth.

Its shape and colour is a stark contrast to the uniformity of the ground around it.

There are obvious signs of a fire, an intense one at that, the remains of whatever's been burnt reduced to nothing more than powder in the centre.

More ash has been blown around, blurring the edges of where the fire took place, but it's clear that it had gone up hard and fast. The strong chemical odour of an accelerant is lingering in the air.

An unpleasant sensation creeps through her as she absorbs the implication – not only of the fact it had taken place recently, but that someone had taken the effort to make sure there wasn't anything left. The perfect place to light something up, she thinks, the ground already scorched from the forest fires. Given a few more weeks, the right conditions – heavy rain, wind – it would all have blurred into one.

'Isaac,' Elin beckons him over. 'Take a look at this.'

As he stops beside her, he takes a sharp pull of breath. 'Recent.'

'That's what I thought.'

He bends a little to examine it. 'Everything's burnt up pretty good,' he says, 'but there's something here.' Gesturing towards a patch on the periphery, he points. 'Looks like clothes.'

Elin crouches, careful not to disturb anything with her feet. At first glance, all she can see is ashes, but when she moves forwards, her eyes hook on a piece of blue material. The edges are blackened, curled up from the heat. Her stomach dips. 'Some kind of blue canvas.'

The same as the bag Ned pulled out of camp after the explosion.

'You reckon it's . . . ?' Isaac's face darkens.

Swallowing hard, Elin reaches for a stick, scrapes away some of the surrounding ashes.

It's then she notices it: another scrap of blackened fabric.

Not the thick canvas of the bag, but a jersey material. Most of it is burnt up, but the middle section is more or less clear, so she can see its original colour: white.

Elin flips it over with the stick and uses the end to hook it up, shake some of the ashes loose. As ash flutters to the ground, something becomes visible in the centre of the fabric.

Dark lettering printed on the material.

An *A* and part of an *L*.

'Do you recognise that?' Her voice wavers.

'Yeah,' Isaac says heavily. 'I do.'

70

Elin

Parque Nacional, Portugal,
October 2021

'It's the hoodie Kier was wearing in some of the videos. The lettering's the same, isn't it?'

Briefly closing her eyes, Elin pictures it again – the white hooded sweatshirt, knockoff YALE logo daubed across the front.

'Explains why the dog was barking its head off down there.' Isaac's voice is shaky. 'It was Kier's stuff they were digging up after the explosion, putting into that bag.'

'And then brought up here to—' Blinking, Elin imagines it: the dancing light of the fire, the bag curling up in the flames. As she turns away, another image arrives – Bridie stood here, part of this, watching Kier's clothes reducing to ashes.

'What are you thinking?' Isaac's watching her.

'About Bridie. No proof the ash on her boots is from the fire, but I reckon it's more likely she got it from here than from the cabin.'

'Not looking good, is it?' he says, his expression grim. 'Burning up her stuff.'

'No.' Seeing the remains of her sweatshirt there, among the ashes, makes her blood run cold.

Isaac's right. Why go to the effort of burning something unless you had good reason?

'Elin, there's something else. Over here.' She turns to see Isaac a few feet away, gesturing at something. 'A ring. Reckon it's been blown out from the force of the fire.'

Elin walks over and Isaac points to a patch of faded grass at the edge of the clearing. 'There, in that patch of grass.'

She leans a little closer so she can see what he's pointing at. A ring is sitting on a thin cluster of grass that's interspersed with weeds.

The silver is dulled, tarnished from the fire, but she can make out interlocking loops of silver forming the band. There's a distinctive green stone in the centre, marbled with blues and greys.

'Definitely too big to be Kier's,' Elin says slowly. 'That's a man's ring. Maybe the bag wasn't just Kier's stuff.'

Isaac nods, his eyes glassy. 'Perhaps the camp's got form in getting rid of other people's stuff.' His voice is strained, a note of fear creeping in. 'Remember what the guy from the tourist office said about the man who went missing a few months ago?'

Elin thinks about his words, gooseflesh rising on her arms.

A tourist. Camping out with his friend. They were hiking on a trail near one of the falls. There one minute and gone the next.

Could the camp have been involved in the tourist's disappearance too?

The thought wears a groove in her mind as they search through the rest of the ashes, taking photographs as they work. *We know nothing about them*, she thinks. *Nothing at all.*

They find more fragments of clothing littered among the

remains of the fire, but it's impossible to tell what's Kier's and what might belong to someone else.

'We done?' Isaac asks a few minutes later. Standing up, he dusts down his trousers. 'Don't reckon there's much left we haven't gone through.'

'Nearly. If you're all right to do a last check by the fire, I'll take another look around.' Easing past him, Elin walks forwards until she's in the centre of the clearing.

Slowly turning, she soaks it all in, immediately struck by the shift in atmosphere from where she'd just been standing. A completely different feeling: no smell of smoke or accelerant, no violence of the fire still lingering in the air.

Here, there's a sense of calm, the trees around her forming an almost perfect embrace. A cocoon.

Stepping forwards a few paces, her gaze drops to the floor, and her eyes travel forwards a few feet and then back.

All at once, something stirs inside her. A sudden sharpening of her senses.

It wasn't visible from the edge of the clearing, but here, the earth, the grass looks different. Patchier than she'd thought ... it looks like some kind of pattern.

Elin walks across to the corner and looks again, but as the cloud shifts, dulling both sky and ground, the effect is lost.

Is she imagining it?

'What do you think about heading off soon?' Isaac's voice disturbs her train of thought as he comes towards her. 'Probably best we don't hang around. We're not that far from camp. If anyone's about ...'

'You're right.' Elin's still distracted by what she's seen.

'Hard to know what to do about this,' Isaac gestures in the direction of the fire. 'Not enough, is it, to take to the police?'

'Not sure. With the video footage we have of Kier in the

hoodie, there might be, but I don't know if getting them involved at this stage is the right call. If the camp get wind of it there's every chance they'll bolt. We need them here. Place this size, the chance of us finding anything concrete without them is going to be impossible. I think we do everything we can to keep them close, see if they let anything slip.'

'Yeah, good shout. Maybe we try to build on what you've started with Bridie ...' Isaac tails off as her phone loudly beeps.

'Looks like we're going to have the ideal opportunity to do just that,' she says slowly, taken aback by the message that's appeared on her screen. 'I've had a message from her. Inviting us to the camp tonight, for drinks.'

71

Elin

It's Maggie they see first when they arrive at the camp, dressed in a bright batik print smock, dark hair tumbling loose around her shoulders.

Stepping out of her van, she's balancing a tray full of plastic glasses in one hand, but raises the other, smiling.

Returning the greeting, Elin glances about, taking in the scene around her. It's warm, inviting, a green gingham cloth laid across the table where Bridie and Leah are sitting, two tall candles flickering in the centre.

Festoon bulbs strung between the trees and the light spilling from the windows of the vans give the camp a cosy, convivial ambience. It's a jarring contrast to everything they'd discovered about them and Elin blinks, discomforted.

'Good to see you both,' Maggie says as they reach the table. 'Hope your walk down wasn't as eventful as yesterday.'

'I take it you heard about the fog?'

'I did.' A frown briefly flickers across her face. 'It can take you by surprise if you're not used to it.'

Elin nods. 'I was lucky Bridie was there.'

Looking up, Bridie smiles and then glances at Leah, something unreadable in her expression. 'Glad you've both come by. We've been looking forward to tonight, haven't we, Leah?'

'Yeah.' Abruptly standing up, Leah gestures towards her van. 'Give me a sec, I need to grab the wine.' Her blonde hair is pulled back into a messy bun, her face makeup free, relaxed. No hint of what had happened up at the falls, but as Elin meets her gaze, she picks up on a glimmer of emotion in her eyes, quickly smothered. 'Bridie forgot to bring it down.'

Bridie pulls a face. 'Wouldn't say *forgot*. Probably buried under a pile of Etta's clothes.'

Elin laughs, her gaze drifting past Leah to the vans themselves, peering past the jumble of washing strung up on the line. As her gaze moves between them, the feeling stirs again in her gut.

Something's not quite right.

Trying to focus, she scrutinises the vans again, even more slowly this time, absorbing it all, but still nothing obvious strikes her. Isaac raises an eyebrow but she looks away, not wanting to draw attention.

'Leah's better now.' Placing the glasses on the table, Maggie misinterprets the direction of her gaze. 'Sorry you had to see that, up at the falls. Ned said it was pretty frightening.'

'It's fine.' Elin takes a seat beside Bridie, Isaac settling next to her. 'We're just glad she's okay.'

'Not okay yet, but better. She's getting there, isn't she, Bridie?'

'Just about.' Bridie's gaze slips between Elin and Isaac. 'But probably best we don't bring it up. Like I said the other day, she's still pretty fragile.'

'Of course.'

293

'Help yourself.' Bridie slides a small bowl of nuts across the table. 'If you don't, I'll have finished them by the time Leah gets back.'

'Thanks.' Elin watches Isaac grab a handful of the nuts, start chewing. 'And for the invite.' Turning, she holds her hands out towards the crackling fire pit, enjoying the warmth. There's a definite chill to the air once the sun goes down, the contrast to the warm daytime temperature something she still hasn't really got used to.

'No problem,' Bridie replies easily. 'Glad we could actually do something this time. The barbecue yesterday was a bit of a nonstarter.'

'That's understandable. Guessing you probably didn't want people about after what happened.'

She nods. 'Ned was pretty shaken.'

'Speaking of Ned,' Isaac looks around. 'Where is he?'

'In town.' Scooping out a few nuts, Bridie holds up her hand, pouring them into her mouth. 'A few errands to run. Also a chance to escape all the women.'

'Yeah.' Coming up behind them, Leah puts a bottle of red wine down on the table with a thud. 'He likes to do that every now and again. *Headspace*, he calls it.'

They laugh, and as Maggie and Leah start talking to Isaac, Bridie turns to her, lowering her voice a notch. 'So how's everything going?'

'Fine.' Elin smiles. 'Thanks again for the rescue.'

'My pleasure.' Unscrewing the wine, Bridie starts to pour. 'Not every day I get to play hero.'

Elin sips the wine, savouring the fruity, slightly spicy notes on her tongue. A welcome warmth settles through her. For a minute, *why* she's really here slips away, and she's just enjoying the moment – the low hum of conversation around her, the crackle of the fire.

'Nice, isn't it?' Bridie says, watching her. 'This is my favourite time of day. Fire on, everyone together, putting the world to rights.' She glances back to the vans. 'Is it wrong to say that when it's also the time Etta's in bed?'

'I don't think so.' Smiling, Elin meets her gaze. 'So how long have you been doing this? The whole van thing?'

'Awhile.' Bridie sloshes some wine into her own glass. 'I'd had enough of the real world, all its associated bullshit. You've got—' – she pauses, as if trying to find the right words – 'absolute autonomy out here. Control over what you do and who you spend your time with.'

'You don't miss your old life?'

'Parts of it, but I never really settled. Kept flitting from one thing to another.'

'Work-wise?'

Bridie nods, lost in thought for a moment, something playing out behind her eyes.

'What did you do?'

'A law degree back in the day. Had a mind I was going to change the world, but in the firm I was working for, it was clear it was never going to happen as fast as I wanted it to, and even if it did, it would be a drop in the ocean.' Bridie looks at Elin. 'Before you say anything, I know that's not the politically correct answer, but it's the truth. I found it hard, not knowing that what I was doing was really worth it.'

Elin holds up her hand. 'No judgement here.' She pauses. 'What about family? Must be tough being away from them when you're on the road?'

Bridie pushes her fringe out of her eyes with the tips of her fingers. 'Yeah, that's the hard bit. Missing people.' Elin can hear the regret in her voice. 'But you have to decide sometimes, to put yourself first.' Her sentence is punctuated by a bird shrieking in the trees opposite. As Elin startles, Bridie looks at her, a smile playing on her lips. 'Still not used to it?'

'No. That's the only thing I think I'd struggle with, living out here. I'm a wimp with wildlife. You never get frightened?'

'God no.' Bridie shakes her head. 'I once worked in a bar back in Kentucky, pretty rough place. Soon learnt that it's people you need to be scared of, not places. Only things out here that can scare you are your own ghosts.'

'Really?'

'Yeah. You know, sometimes people see a place like they do a person, and this park, it's a tough nut to crack. Aloof, unwelcoming. But I always say it's just shy. You need time, patience, to get to know it, and then it starts to reveal itself.'

Elin nods. 'I can see that. What's your favourite place here?'

'The river beach.'

The river beach. Giving Isaac a sideways glance, she can tell his thoughts have gone to the same place: the river beach Kier had painted on the map.

Bridie nudges Leah. 'Leah's probably the best person to describe it. You discovered it, didn't you?'

There's something forced in Bridie's tone. *That's not the real reason she's asking Leah to tell them about it. She's trying to distract her,* Elin thinks, noticing Leah's gaze locked on the trees behind.

It's obvious that the relaxed demeanour she'd projected when they first arrived was just that – a projection. Watching her eyes flit backwards and forwards, it reminds her of the Leah they'd encountered in the woods that day, her panic as the mobile phone rang out.

Her thoughts shift to Bridie's words about Leah's ex.

She had it in her head that he was the one who blew up the van.

'Leah?' Bridie prompts again, nudging her.

'It's the perfect beach, but only sometimes.' Leah smiles, but

296

it's as if she's having to make a concerted effort to focus on them. 'The river's part of the park's hydroelectric system. Water flows to the lower lakes to generate power, then it's pumped back when there's an excess. In winter, when the river is full, the beach disappears.' She shrugs. 'Knowing it's not there all the time makes it even more special when it is.'

'We'll put it on the list,' Isaac says lightly. 'We heard there was a river beach with a tree that people carve their initials in. Is it the same one?'

Giving an uneasy smile, Maggie fiddles with the stem of her wineglass. 'It is, but I wouldn't say that's the main attraction.'

They talk for a few more minutes before Elin looks between them. 'Am I okay to use someone's bathroom?' She says, standing up. 'Not sure I'm up for the full wild experience just yet.'

'Use mine,' Leah volunteers. 'Etta's asleep, but she won't wake. You'll have to excuse the mess though.' Glancing at Bridie, she smiles. 'Now Bridie and Etta have moved in, they've taken over.'

'Promise I won't judge.' Elin laughs, easing out past the fire pit.

She's only a few feet from the door when a voice sounds out. 'Not that van. That one's mine.'

Elin turns. Maggie's right behind her.

'Normally you'd be welcome.' Maggie smiles. 'But my plumbing's all gone to shit. One of the reason's Ned's gone into town. Spare parts.'

'Sorry, got confused.' Looking between the two vans, Elin can see where she made the mistake. As it's dark, the interiors, brightly lit, are more visible than usual and she can see detail inside Maggie's van that hadn't been obvious before. It's more modern than she'd imagined. White walls, pale floor. A space she'd assumed was more Leah's vibe.

Silence falls between them, a silence that extends into

awkwardness.

Why is Maggie lingering? She'd made it clear which was the right van.

'So I'll use this one?' Elin says finally, pointing at Leah's van.

'Yeah. Bathroom's on the right.'

Slipping past Maggie, she steps inside Leah's van. It's as chaotic inside as Bridie had warned – clothes and toys piled high on every surface.

Inching forwards, she makes her way through the narrow space towards the bathroom, careful not to disturb a sleeping Etta, whose cot bed has been set over the bench on the back wall.

She's nearly reached the bathroom when there's a dull thud.

Elin flinches, quickly looking down. She's knocked something off the side.

A cardboard folder is now lying on the floor, splayed open. The word BILLS is scrawled on the front in black Sharpie.

Bending to pick it up, she's about to shove it back on the pile when her eyes alight on a name at the top of the first piece of paper.

Not Bridie's name, or Leah's. Something completely different. *April Blake.*

72

Elin

Parque Nacional, Portugal,
October 2021

Elin waits until they're out of sight of the camp and then pulls out her phone, taps the name *April Blake* into her search, her palm clammy against the handset. Adrenalin is still coursing through her.

'Didn't think any of their names were genuine to begin with, but this is as good a confirmation as any.' No guarantee that April Blake was an alias for either Leah or Bridie, but the fact that the bill was in a folder with a pile of others under the same name doesn't fill her with confidence that either of them are who they say they are.

Isaac's already scrolling. His phone screen is glowing bright in the darkness, the only illumination apart from the moon, bright above them.

As the results appear, Elin frowns, frustrated. A mixed bag, and one that'll take hours to sift through. Social media handles for a variety of April Blakes.

LinkedIn profiles, Facebook pages. Instagram.

'Take it you've got the same,' Isaac mutters. 'Looks like April Blake is a pretty common name.'

'We need to narrow it down.' Elin thinks for a minute, then quickly types in *April Blake* again together with the words: *criminal charges.*

This time, an immediate hit: a condensed version of news article with the link to the full article directly below. Elin scans the truncated text:

James Debray of the Kirkwall County Sheriff's Office identified the suspect on Friday morning as April Blake, 24, of Sandhold. She was charged with multiple counts of digital extortion. Detectives, acting on digital intelligence, interviewed Blake at her home and she, together with her partner, Raymond Kenney, admitted to committing extortion over a period of two and a half years.

Elin's gaze slips lower to the four photographs sitting in a quadrant below the text, her pulse thudding in her ears. One is immediately recognisable.

'You got something?'

'Yeah.' She passes the phone to Isaac. 'Just found this. Looks like Leah is April Blake, not Bridie ... Might explain where they're getting the money from to live out here.'

'Extortion.' He whistles through his teeth. 'Puts working from home in a whole new light.'

It certainly does, Elin thinks, replaying the conversation with Leah in the woods, her vagueness when they'd asked her what she did for work: *This and that. Tech stuff mainly.*

Every day seemed to bring something new to this camp, she thinks, chilled.

Another layer revealed.

*

April Blake dominates the conversation as they hike back to the Airstream. It's slow going in the dark, giving them time to pick it apart, the conversation going back and forth as they tease out different scenarios.

'Might be motive for wanting Kier out of the picture?' Isaac says as they reach the Airstream. 'If that's how the group's making their money and she found out somehow?'

'It's possible.' As she follows him inside, Elin picks over Leah's words at the falls: *It should have been me, not her,* working out how they'd fit with that theory. *Guilt talking?* 'I just—' She doesn't get a chance to finish her sentence.

There's a deafening bang, the sound of a door slamming. A sudden rush of cold air.

Elin jerks her head up to the rear door careering backwards and forwards on its hinge.

'Did you go out that way earlier?' Isaac asks uneasily. 'Doesn't look like it's been shut properly.'

'No.' She turns in a slow circle, her pulse picking up again. 'But someone else has. Someone's been in here, and recently too.' No visible sign of their presence, but a scent is still lingering in the room: sweat. Aftershave.

Whoever it was, they've not been gone long.

Her first thought: *Steed.*

Elin shudders. The idea of him in here alone, in their private space, makes her skin crawl.

'Don't reckon they've gone far. I'm going to take a look.'

Slipping past him, she pushes through the open door. It's dark, but the sky is still cloudless, the moon bright and full, and with the light from the Airstream, it's enough to dimly illuminate the shadowy forms of the trees around her.

No one there, no one she can see, anyway, so Elin slips between them and out onto the track leading down towards the other Airstream.

Her eyes sweep left to right before settling directly down the path.

There's a figure in the distance: a man, running in the opposite direction, his feet thudding out into the silence.

Elin starts down the trail, but a few metres on, he darts right, heading towards the trees.

For a moment, it looks as if he's about to disappear out of sight, but then he does something unexpected: he turns to look directly at her, his face expressionless.

Her stomach contracts.

Not Steed at all, but Ned.

73

Elin

Parque Nacional, Portugal,
October 2021

'It was odd, the way he turned to look at me,' Elin says, catching sight of her warped reflection in the windows of the van, the shock still etched into her expression.

'Deliberate?' Isaac is looking through the window, his eyes drilling into the darkness outside.

'Must have been.' There's no reason, as far as she can work out, for Ned to look her way as he'd run off. He'd made a conscious decision to. 'Maybe I'm reading into it, but it felt like some kind of warning. That he wanted me to know he can get to us.'

'Either way, it means that the invite tonight—'

'Was a ruse.' Elin swallows. 'The whole *thought you could both do with letting off steam* was a way of getting us away from the Airstream.'

And they'd fallen for it, she thinks. *She'd taken Bridie at her word.*

'You definitely reckon Bridie and everyone knew? It wasn't Ned playing lone ranger?'

'They knew,' she says heavily, thinking it over, about Maggie stopping her from going into her van. 'They were jumpy, all of them. I put it down to them walking on eggshells around Leah, but it was this.'

'We've got them rattled somehow, haven't we? No way they'd come and do this otherwise. They think we're onto something.'

'Yeah, and that means we need to keep digging, but we're going to have to be careful.' If Ned had intended his presence at the clearing to be some kind of warning, it had the opposite effect. All it had done was galvanise her. Cement her feeling that they're going in the right direction.

'The map?'

Elin nods, her thoughts shifting not just to the river beach, but to the clearing.

It's bothering her.

The discovery of Kier's clothing up there and the ring are important, but neither explain *why* she'd painted the clearing on the map, or the pattern Elin had glimpsed in the grass.

She needs to take another look. They've missed something up there, she's certain of it. Missed something vital.

74

Elin

Parque Nacional, Portugal,
October 2021

It's just after dawn the next morning when Elin leaves for the clearing. A pang of guilt strikes her as she closes the door, thinking about Isaac waking up, finding her note, his worry.

But as she walks across the decking, she pushes the thought aside, knowing she needs to do this alone. Give it her full concentration.

Elin follows the route she and Isaac took the day before. Easier work, navigation-wise, having already done it, but not in terms of effort. By the time she gets to the top, walking out and onto the grass, she's breathing heavily, sweat sticking to her T-shirt.

Stripping off her fleece and tying it around her waist, she looks around her. A seed of doubt creeps in as the clearing stares back at her blankly, the blackened trees a lifeless backdrop behind. *Has her mind conjured something from nothing? The shock of what she'd discovered about Steed?*

But when she moves a little further in, she catches sight of it again: a pattern.

Walking to the centre of the clearing, she slowly turns in a circle. A breeze peels over the ground, picking up a cloud of dirt and ash. Elin closes her eyes against it, but as she opens them again, a fuller pattern is revealed.

Something only hinted at yesterday with the dense cloud cover.

Her skin prickles: *patches in the grass.*

It looks as if it's been worn away from repeated use – someone following the same path over and over again – similar to what you'd see on sports fields and tennis courts by the end of the season.

But this . . . it's a pattern she hasn't seen before.

A rough figure of eight, with smaller circles in between.

What could have created it?

Playing out scenarios in her mind, Elin traces the pattern with her footsteps, trying to find the link to the image Kier painted of the clearing on her map, but nothing pulls clear.

It's possible it *doesn't* link to the map, but either way, she thinks, it puts someone here, in the clearing, for significant amounts of time. Given the proximity to the camp, there's a good chance it's one of them.

Elin takes some photos and after flicking through them, she slips her phone back in her pocket.

She's about to head back when she feels a hand clamp heavily on her shoulder. Fingers pinching the fabric of her shirt.

75

Elin

Parque Nacional, Portugal,
October 2021

Elin swings around, freezes.

Steed.

How long had he been there? Watching?

'Christ, you scared me …' She quickly moves back, putting some space between them.

'Didn't mean to startle you.' An odd, lopsided smile is fixed on his face. 'Called your name a few times, but you were in a world of your own.'

Elin watches as his eyes travel across her face, the hairs on the back of her neck standing up on end. The same sharp prickle of fear she felt when he'd come into the Airstream.

He hasn't slept, she thinks, taking in his red-rimmed eyes, the crumpled clothes.

There's an emptiness in him that she's never seen before. He looks hollowed out, a shadow of the person she knew.

As he takes a step towards her, dirty boots sending a cloud of ash up into the air, her mind starts to spiral.

He's followed her up here. An isolated spot. She was right. This is what this whole thing was about. A game. Toying with her. Bringing her out here and then trying to get her alone.

The wind whistles past them, shaking the trees. Training kicking in, Elin backs away again.

Steed holds up his hand. 'Don't be frightened. I'm just trying to find out what's going on.' He's trying to sound calm, but his eyes, darting around the clearing, are telling her anything but. 'This is one of the places on Kier's map, isn't it?'

Elin doesn't reply, her mind still trying to process his presence, how he's here at the same time as her. 'How did you know I was up here?' Her voice is shaky.

'I saw you leave the van. Just wanted to know where you were going.'

'Have you been *watching* us? Watching what we've been doing?'

Panic flickers across his face. 'Not watching. Just wondered where you were heading.'

Anger washes over her.

How does he think she'll interpret that, after everything he's done this past year?

He's arrived here, confessed he'd been the one watching her, sending her those messages, and now he's done the same thing *again*?

'Can't you see that following me here—' She stops, lost for words. For a moment, she's not angry, just sad.

How has it come to this? One of her closest friends ...

Steed's face twitches. 'I didn't think, I'm sorry. It's just hard, Elin. This *waiting*. I know how you want to play this, but surely what we've found about the camp already is enough to do something? Confront them? They've got my sister embroiled in whatever twisted shit they're up to out here. My *sister.*' The word hangs in the air and as he looks at her, his face flushes an angry red.

Elin takes another slow step back. She doesn't like this. He looks if not on the brink, then pretty close to it.

'You've found something, haven't you?' Steed demands when she doesn't answer. 'I saw you looking at something. That's why you've come here, isn't it?'

Watching his eyes skitter across the space, Elin's thoughts lurch to the fire.

If he sees the remains of Kier's clothes while he's in this state, he'll assume the worst: that she's dead. If that happens, there's every chance he'll storm down to camp and blow the whole thing up.

Keep it together, she tells herself, keeping her gaze away from the site of the fire. *Don't look at it. Don't give him any reason to think something's up.*

Her pulse ticks in her throat as his gaze flickers back and forth across the grass.

An uneasy silence settles between them.

'Look,' she says finally. 'What you're doing, following me here, it isn't part of the deal.' Her voice holds a steel that she doesn't feel. 'Isaac told you that, didn't he? If you want our help, you have to do this our way. When we find something we can work with, we'll let you know.'

'It's just knowing the camp are down there, that they probably know what happened to her. I want to *do* something.'

'You can't.' Elin keeps her face set. 'We go crashing in there without anything concrete, they'll bolt. Any hope we have of getting answers . . . it's gone.'

'I get it.' Steed's shoulders slump. 'Just feels like I'm living some kind of nightmare. It's not only this, but what's happened between us. It's like I've lost both of you at once. Knowing I can't make it better – I hate it. Hate that I can't even talk to you.' His eyes are drilling into her face, something hungry, desperate in them, and she knows what he's looking for: forgiveness.

But she can't give it. Not yet. Not on his timings. Maybe not ever.

As he continues to look at her, Elin picks over his words, anger coursing through her again: *what's happened between us.* There was no *us.* It was all on him. How can she even contemplate reconciling when he hasn't grasped the enormity of all this, his culpability?

'Look, I should get back.' Elin takes a long, slow breath. 'You should too.'

Steed opens his mouth as if to protest and then closes it again, his face going slack.

He no longer looks on the brink, she thinks, but already broken.

She's seen it too many times in the job she does. People who've got nothing left to lose – they're unpredictable, dangerous.

Watching his face twitch, fear consumes her again.

Biting down on her lip, she strides away, but it's an effort to keep her gait steady. She can feel his eyes on her with every step she takes.

76

Elin

Parque Nacional, Portugal,
October 2021

'He *what*?' Isaac puts his plate down with a clatter, the half-eaten remains of a pastry slipping off the side. 'I told him that kind of stuff wasn't part of the deal.'

Elin rubs her eyes, a wave of exhaustion washing over her. Still morning, but it feels like she's already put a full day behind her. 'I don't think he's even aware of what the deal is.' Tugging off her jacket, she takes a seat beside him. 'He's not in a good place. I'm not sure whether him sticking around was the right call.' She pictures his jerky, erratic motions, the bloodshot eyes.

Another sharp pang of sadness that it's come to this – a gulf between her and someone she thought she'd be friends with forever.

Isaac clears his throat. 'Look, I don't reckon anything we say will have any sway over whether he leaves or not, so I think we need to try to work out if it is the right call for *us* to stay. I get why you think you owe Kier and what this means to you, but it's risky, Elin. Not just Steed, but Ned. We don't know, not yet, what we're getting ourselves into with the camp.'

Elin listens, but part of her knows she can't even consider what he's suggesting: stopping now.

'I get what you're saying, but I don't think we can leave this here,' she says finally. 'I think I owe it to Kier to carry on, especially now we're so close to answers. We just need time, don't we? To piece everything together.'

Isaac frowns, looking as if he's about to protest before he slowly exhales. 'Okay,' he says heavily. 'So what do you want to do next?'

'The river beach. The last place on the map.'

77

Elin

Parque Nacional, Portugal,
October 2021

The signpost indicating the way to the river beach is rustic – a sawn-off plank tacked to a post, just above one for the town, pointing in the opposite direction.

'The town's only five miles from here,' Elin says, glancing around her. 'Didn't realise we were so close.'

Isaac looks back and forth, down the gravelled trail. 'Must be a road somewhere, running through the forest.'

Following the sign, they move right, threading their way through a dense copse of pines. The ground is thick with a mat of dead pine needles, their footsteps muffled.

A few minutes later, Isaac stops. 'Guessing this is one of those times when there's no beach.'

Elin slows, mesmerised by the vista that's opened up in front of them. The trees have abruptly given way to a huge expanse of water reaching right up to the roughly hewn stone wall a few feet away. It's a dark, limpid green, an almost perfect reflection of the colour of the trees on the hills opposite.

An easy swim across to the other side of the river, maybe a hundred metres or so, but nowhere to go from there, Elin thinks, looking up. The land rises steeply from a tiny semicircle of beach to a small peak blanketed with trees. Only a few small houses are visible, nestled high in the hills, their terracotta roofs standing out among the greenery.

'Guessing that's the tree on the map,' Isaac says, pointing.

Her eyes flick up, following his gaze. Fifty metres or so to their right is a large oak tree slightly set apart from the others. Bent over by the wind, the tips of some of the longer branches are trailing in the water.

'Looks like it.' She starts walking, but when they get within a few metres of the tree, she falters, her heart beating a little faster.

Moving closer, Elin catches Isaac's eye, appalled. She's not sure what she was expecting, but it wasn't *this*.

There are pairs of initials carved into the tree, yes, but it's not just that.

Initials scratched away, scraped, burnt, and everything in between.

A brutal erasure of love.

'Surprised the tree's survived, looking at this.' Isaac runs a hand over the trunk, his fingers pressing into the shapes and grooves in the wood. 'Luísa didn't tell us about this part of the story.'

'No, she didn't.' Elin can see why. It's not only chilling but desperately sad. She tries to imagine the state of mind of someone taking the time to come here and violently remove what was once a symbol of their love.

'So what do you think this means? For what Kier's painted on the map?'

'That's a good question,' she replies, still studying it. While Kier's painting captures the tree perfectly, what it means for her time in the park, she isn't so sure. But then, nothing about the images Kier has painted on the map is straightforward, she thinks, frustrated. The viewpoint, the falls, the clearing. They all hold glimmers of answers, but nothing concrete, nothing tying them together to form a coherent narrative.

'No hope of finding Kier's or anyone else's initials on there, is there?'

Following more pairs of initials swarming up the trunk, Elin shakes her head. Only the outlines remained of some. Fragments of letters. Nothing to put Kier definitively here.

But as she keeps scrutinising it, the outline of an idea starts to pull together. 'I'm wondering if maybe Kier saw an echo of something in this. Related to it in some way.'

'A failed relationship?'

Elin nods, and as Isaac meets her gaze, she knows he's thinking the same thing she is.

Ned.

The embrace they'd witnessed in the hard-drive footage.

If Kier's painting of the river beach and this tree on the map *was* related to Ned, something told her that *how* she'd painted it – the heightened way she'd depicted the letters – meant that whatever went on between them hadn't been the positive encounter she'd glimpsed on the video from Kier's van.

'Want to stop off in town?' Isaac asks as they tramp back down the trail, leaving the swollen river behind them. 'It's not much of a detour from here. We can take the path out the other side to get back to the Airstream.'

'Good shout. I'm going to need to sit down soon.' A wave of fatigue crashes over her. It's not just the hike down to the river that's taken it out of her, but what they'd seen on the tree, the violence in the markings still playing on her mind.

Once they reach the outer edges of town, the red-roofed houses giving way to shops and cafés, Isaac stops, looking around. 'Want to try the café there?' He nods towards the building opposite, its small terrace thronged with people. Tourists mainly, judging from the backpacks strewn across the floor. 'Saves us having to go into the centre.'

'Sounds good,' Elin's already easing her bag from her shoulders. Exhaustion was really setting in now, her pack like a lead weight against her back.

But before they cross the road, Isaac hesitates, glancing to his right. 'Try not to be obvious,' he murmurs. 'But look who's over there.'

Following his gaze, Elin glimpses a familiar face outside another café a few doors down, stood between a group of middle-aged tourists laden down with backpacks.

'It's Maggie.' She lowers her voice.

'Yeah, and she's with Ned.'

They're talking to someone working in the café. Elin can see right away that this is no normal conversation; they're stood face-to-face, only a few steps apart, speaking quickly, urgently, Ned gesticulating.

The conversation continues for a few more minutes before the man looks around him and then presses an envelope into Maggie's hand.

Elin's thoughts immediately shift to what she'd learnt about April Blake and her partner – the extortion charges.

Could the café worker be paying them off?

Silently, they watch as the man walks quickly into the café, not looking back.

Isaac shoots a glance her way, but Elin keeps her eyes locked on Maggie and Ned as they slip through a gap in the buildings ahead. Something about Maggie's rapid pace, her tight-lipped, slightly masked expression, hints at someone struggling to hold in their emotions.

'Let's follow for a bit,' Elin says, starting to walk. 'See where they go.'

78

Elin

Parque Nacional, Portugal,
October 2021

Keeping well back, Elin and Isaac trail behind them, following until the cobbled street peters out to a rough track and the outer edges of the forest behind.

Maggie and Ned walk parallel to the woodland for a couple of minutes before coming to a stop at a trail marker at the edge of the tree line.

Elin hesitates, trying to get her bearings. 'That track's leading right. That wouldn't lead you back to camp, would it?'

'Not unless you wanted to take a detour.' Isaac squints upwards. 'Hard to see because of the trees, but looks like the trail goes up, and then right. Might switchback on itself.'

They follow as Maggie and Ned turn onto the trail, keeping a good distance behind.

The path is well-trodden for the first few hundred metres, trail markers placed at regular intervals. After a kilometre or so, it takes a sharp right, but Maggie and Ned turn left, plunging into what looks like dense forest.

Trampling through the underbrush behind them, Elin and Isaac force their way through the thick foliage, feet scattering piles of dead leaves and branches.

'Sure you want to keep following?' Isaac winces as a branch scrapes his cheek. 'We're making a racket getting through this.'

'If we keep back, we'll be fine. They'll only be making the same noises as us,' she replies, picking up the pace. She feels invigorated suddenly, her earlier exhaustion now replaced by pure adrenalin.

After about five minutes walking, the forest thins a little. This part of the track has clearly been used before – shrubbery beaten back just enough to be manageable, scuffs and marks in the ground cover.

Elin wonders how many times they've done this. At the rate they're moving, it looks like the route is familiar to them.

Another half a kilometre on, Maggie and Ned come to a stop in a sudden break in the trees, where some felled oaks have created a narrow clearing.

She puts a finger to her lips. 'Get down,' she says quickly, crouching.

They watch as Maggie walks forwards a few feet, pushing an armful of the tree canopy to one side. The action reveals a sudden flicker of colour: a shiny, artificial white among the muddy greens and browns of the forest. Barely visible, due to the trees, but acutely out of place among the sprawling underbrush.

Easing past her, Ned comes to help, forcing enough of the branches away for the flash of white to fully reveal itself.

The dull glint of light on paintwork.

Elin pulls in her breath.

A van.

Even from this distance, it's clear that it's been there a while, a thin skin of green speckling the surface along with a scattering of leaves and forest debris.

Her stomach drops. 'That's not Kier's?'

'Don't think so. Different colour, isn't it? Kier's is blue.'

Maggie fiddles with the lock on the door before disappearing inside. For a moment, it looks like Ned's going to follow, but he settles himself in the doorway, leaning back against the frame. Lighting a cigarette, he takes a long drag and then slowly exhales. Despite the relaxed stance, there's a tension etched into the lines of his face as his eyes shift among the trees.

'Looks like he's playing guard,' Isaac murmurs.

If so, it's not clear why. Only glimpses through the door of Maggie moving around. Small thudding sounds cutting through the silence.

A few minutes later, she emerges clutching a small bag. Closing the door behind her, the sunlight spilling across her face reveals the silvery markings of the scar on her cheek. She pushes the bag from the van into her own satchel and steps in their direction.

'Let's move,' Elin says quickly, but her fears are unfounded: Maggie abruptly turns, leading Ned around the side of the van.

'Must be a way out at the back,' Isaac whispers.

They let a few minutes pass and then pick their way towards the van.

Up close, Elin instinctively recoils, an uneasy feeling creeping up her neck. The van is dirtier than it looked from a distance – ivy chasing up the rear wheel, ghostly remnants of long dead leaves imprinted on the windscreen.

She tries the handle. 'Locked,' she says, moving to the front. 'And no plates, back or front.' Crouching, she examines the tyres. 'Tyres pretty much flat, but doesn't look like there's much damage.'

Isaac runs a hand across the side door. 'Paintwork's in okay condition. Bit of rust, some chips. Definitely been here a while, but we're not talking decades.'

Elin nods, peering through the windows, but the curtains, a pale-blue gingham, have been tightly drawn.

'Bloody odd,' Isaac mutters. 'Reckon it's one of theirs?'

'Almost certainly.' Elin's still trying to look inside. 'Maggie seemed to know her way around it. Closer to camp and I'd say it might be used for storage of some kind, but not this far out.' Giving up, she turns away. 'I'm going to take a look around the other side.'

Forcing her way between the pushed-back branches, she rounds the rear of the van. The clearing extended to a bigger section in this direction, the denser forest not starting for another hundred metres or so.

As her eyes adjust to the landscape, she notices a rough track snaking between the trees.

'That's the way they went out, then.' Isaac comes up behind her. 'Guessing there's a road not too far off.' He's already walking down the track, eyes scouring the foliage around him. 'Can't be far. The van had to have got here somehow.'

Elin keeps looking around, growing more uneasy, not just about the van itself, but its position.

Why so far from camp?

'Found the road,' Isaac calls, walking back. 'About a quarter of a mile up there. Ground looks patchy leading this way. Probably been disturbed by the van whenever it made its way in.' As he reaches her, he bends to examine the bonnet again. Cupping a hand, he scoops away some of the leaves and branches. 'Scratches, some damage to the front, but you'd expect more if it had come off the road at enough speed to push it in this far.' He squints, looking behind him. 'Bit of a slope, but not enough to propel it in this deep without it getting stuck on something on the way in. My guess is it's been driven in, pushed beneath the tree.'

'Perfect cover if you're trying to hide it. Start of the track from town is pretty dodgy, people wouldn't be stumbling on it by chance.' She glances up at the window again, and this time, she notices something: a small gap between the fabric of the curtains, the only set, as far as she can see, that haven't been so tightly drawn.

Leaning in, she can see glimpses of the interior. 'Here,' she gestures. 'Got a view inside.' Shuffling closer, Elin moves forwards until her nose is almost against the glass. With the other curtains closed, the interior is gloomy, but it's obvious that the space is more or less empty. 'Can't see much apart from the main bits of furniture. No personal items.'

'All been cleared out?' Isaac peers over her shoulder.

'Yeah.' Elin's about to step away when her gaze is pulled higher, to something daubed on the wall above the bench.

Her breath catches in her throat.

'You won't believe this.' Her voice wobbles. 'There's something painted on the wall.'

79

Elin

Parque Nacional, Portugal,
October 2021

'A pira,' Isaac says, his features tight. 'Exactly the same shape . . . '

Elin nods, the blood pounding in her head with a dull roar. Her thoughts swarm: their theory was right. These piras, whatever they are, link in some way to the camp.

'If this van *is* the camp's, you think they could be the ones building them?' Isaac moves closer, tilting his head to examine it.

'Definitely looking more likely,' she replies, still studying it. The pira is about a foot high, painted in a brown so dark that it's almost black in the dim light. No detail, none of the intricacy the branches lend the structure in real life, but the shape is clear. 'I want to get inside, take a closer look.'

'Break in?'

'Yeah. The lock on the front door looked fairly standard.'

He casts his eyes towards the woodland surrounding them. 'You sure? If the camp's rattled already and they get wind of this . . .'

'Sure. They had no qualms about letting themselves into the

Airstream.' No qualms at all, she thinks, picturing Ned's odd, blank expression as he'd turned to look at her.

'Got it.' Tugging open the padlock, Elin leaves it hanging from the door. 'Any questions on my lock-picking abilities should now be firmly quashed.'

'Never doubted you.' Isaac smiles, but there's a waver in his voice as she opens the door and walks inside.

'Want me to keep an eye out?' He lingers in the doorway,

'Please.' Elin steps a little further in, looking around, but the interior is as dim as it looked from the outside, and it takes a few moments for her eyes to adjust.

Vision settling, the first thing she notices is detail. Detail that hadn't been visible through the window – pale-blue walls, hand-painted with bohemian, folksy borders, the same touches on the shelves above the kitchen area. The homely touch felt at odds with the total dearth of possessions.

Everything used to make the space habitable had gone. No appliances – fridge or stove. But while it felt empty, a little unloved, it wasn't dirty. Dust mainly, some spiderwebs hanging in the corners. The smell was musty, but not overwhelmingly so.

There's more to see, but Elin makes straight for the pira, desperate to observe it up close. Leaning in, she absorbs it all, then lets her gaze slowly travel across it in sections.

She stares at it, transfixed, immediately struck by the visible brushstrokes, each one made with definite strength and purpose. Whoever painted this had approached it with the same care and precision as the person who'd created the piras themselves.

'What do you make of this?' Elin says, beckoning Isaac over. 'Dominates the space, doesn't it?'

'Yeah, it does. Seeing it like this, it looks more like some kind of symbol for something, doesn't it?'

Elin nods. 'I searched online, couldn't find anything, local or otherwise.' She shakes her head, frustrated. She's not sure what she'd imagined coming in here, but the pira and what it means remain as elusive as before.

'So what are you thinking now about this and the camp?'

'Even more convinced that it's one of theirs, put to pasture.' She opens the small cupboard above the sink. Empty bar a few glasses on the shelf, gathering dust. 'Everything's dusty but it doesn't smell too bad. You can tell people are coming in and out fairly regularly.'

'Must be a reason why, though.' Isaac peers into the side locker. 'Certainly not being used for storage. There's not much in here, just some T-shirts, old blankets.'

'No sign of the envelope?'

He shakes his head. 'If it *was* money the guy in the café was passing over, I'm guessing they wouldn't leave it here.' Putting a hand to his mouth, he loudly sneezes. 'Looks like all the dust settled in here.'

Elin fights the urge to clamp her hand over her mouth as he tugs one of the blankets out, more dust motes flying up, hovering in the air. 'Nice to see they cleaned things before they're put away.' Coughing, she gestures to a blackish stain spreading outwards from the centre.

Isaac grimaces, laying it on the side before lifting out another.

A cardigan.

More dust billows out as he unfolds it. Elin stares, frowning. The batik pattern and style ... it's familiar.

Her thoughts move to Maggie. The style and shape is like something she'd wear. In fact, she thinks, her skin prickling, this whole van looks like Maggie's vibe – the colours, the folksy pattern painted on the wall.

'There's more clothes.' Isaac's still rooting through the locker. 'Looks like they've seen better days.'

Elin combs through them. A mixture of cardigans, trousers, vests. None of them fit Leah's or Bridie's look; they're all similar to the styles she's seen Maggie wearing.

Maggie's clothes. Maggie's stuff.

Looking between them, her thoughts start ticking over.

One thought, then another – both coming to settle on one moment: last night at camp, Maggie's shout for her not to go inside her van.

Elin reflects on how she'd mistaken Maggie's van for Leah's, and the reason why – the surprising décor inside. Décor that looked nothing like this, she thinks, scrutinising the space again. Maggie's van at the camp looked modern, sterile – a stark contrast to this.

'Have you got the photo Steed sent you?' she says quickly. 'Of when Kier's van was first sighted at camp?'

'Yeah, give me a minute.' Pulling out his phone, Isaac scrolls and then passes it to her. 'This is it.'

Her pulse picks up. 'I need to check something,' she says, heading outside.

Standing in front of the van for a moment, she then walks backwards, away from it, until she can see the exterior in full.

Zooming in on the image of Maggie's van in the photo, her gaze flits between that and the van in front of her.

Same colour. Same make.

But that could be explained, surely? There must be thousands of these vans around.

She needs something definitive to link them.

Elin slowly walks around the front of the van. All at once, her gaze locks on a large gouge above the wheel arch, deep enough to have pulled off some of the paint.

Pinching the phone screen, she zooms in on Maggie's van in the photo again.

The same mark.

Her pulse is racing now.

'What are you doing?' Isaac calls from the doorway of the van.

'I reckon this used to be Maggie's van. It's identical to the one in the picture.' Elin shows him the photograph, pointing out the gouge above the wheel arch.

'Looks the same. But why dump it out here?'

'Upgrade? Maggie fancied a newer model?'

'But it's in fairly good nick, so why not scrap it? Sell it on?' He doesn't look convinced. 'Like you said, storage doesn't make sense, this far out from the camp.'

Elin looks around uneasily, thinking about Kier's van, still unaccounted for, and how it could play into this.

It can't.

While it's the same model as both of Maggie's vans, it's a completely different color and the interiors don't tally. The outside of the van doesn't match either – the bumper and alloys. None of it ties up.

'It doesn't, and I reckon there's a chance not everyone in camp knows this is here.'

'Maybe Ned and Maggie have got good reason for wanting somewhere quiet to stash stuff.'

'Yeah. Let's keep looking inside the van,' she says, still mulling it over. 'Make sure we've searched everywhere.'

'Only thing left is a backpack, buried between these blankets,' Isaac says a few minutes later, elbow deep in the locker.

Curiosity piqued, Elin watches as he digs through the main section. 'Looks pretty empty.' He plunges his hand into the front pocket, rummaging. 'Hold on, there's something in here.' He withdraws his hand. 'It's a passport . . .' Flipping it open, his face drains of colour.

'Whose is it?'

'Zeph's.'

80

Elin

Parque Nacional, Portugal,
October 2021

'*Zeph*?' Elin's thoughts scramble, trying to place the name as she runs over their earlier conversation about Kier.

'The guy she broke up with before Steed's wedding. The chef.'

'But that was dead in the water, wasn't it? You saw the photo of him in New York. I did too. That was months after Kier came to the park.'

'It was. I took a good look at him, I told you. He was definitely back in New York after she came out here. He'd posted stuff about his life. Friends, other women. Nothing about Kier.' Isaac shakes his head. 'Steed said it ended pretty cleanly.'

Her mind is buzzing. Given what they knew, they hadn't put much credence on the idea that Kier's past relationships might be significant to her disappearance, but this completely turns that on its head.

Elin studies Zeph's photograph. A typical passport photo – unsmiling, a slightly greyish pallor due to the harsh lighting.

He's an attractive man, but the look in his eye tells her that he's well aware of it.

Leafing through the passport, she stops on the stamped pages. 'Some of these are a bit faded, but it looks like he came and went a few times.'

'Visiting Kier?'

'Seems like it.'

'When was the last one?'

'September 2020. Nothing since.'

Isaac's brow furrows. 'I don't get why the camp would have his passport.'

She nods. There *are* explanations as to why Zeph's passport might be here – he could simply have lost it. But *where* they've found it, in what is most likely the camp's van, stashed away in a side locker, troubles her.

'There are only a few ways of looking at it,' Elin's throat tightens. 'Either Zeph's still out here, in the park somewhere, has lost it, or there's a reason he's not come looking for it. Unless he's in the business of having multiple passports, which is pretty unlikely, it looks like this is where his journey stopped. No way he could travel back to the US without it. Europe, maybe, but—'

Isaac's mouth twists as if he's tasted something sour. 'What if Zeph came out here looking for Kier, like we have, found something, and the camp then decided they wanted rid of him—'

'It's possible,' Elin says heavily.

Swallowing hard, Isaac looks at her. 'This … it changes everything, doesn't it?'

'Yeah.' It's not just what it represented – a certainty that the camp is embroiled in Kier's life – but what they thought they knew about her disappearance. Knowing Zeph has been out here, probably several times, not only changes *why* Kier might have come in the first place, but *what* might have happened while she was here.

It unlocks new possibilities on not only who might have been following her, but on the video footage of her van: Kier's embrace with Ned. If Kier *was* involved with Ned and Zeph had followed her out here, it opens up a whole raft of theories about what might have gone down.

They stand for a moment, neither of them saying anything, the shadows across the floor of the van drifting as the breeze ruffles the branches of the trees.

'I know you're not keen on involving him,' Isaac says finally, 'but once we're back at the Airstream, I think we need to speak to Steed. Find out what else he knows about Zeph and how the relationship ended.'

Elin pictures Steed up at the clearing, the wild look in his eyes. 'But the state he's in, if he gets wind we've got a theory …'

'I'll keep it broad strokes. Maybe say we're just double-checking everything we have so far. Consolidating notes.' Isaac meets her gaze. 'I'm guessing you don't want to see him?'

She shakes her head. 'I need to do some digging about Zeph Dosen.'

81

Elin

Parque Nacional, Portugal,
October 2021

Isaac's earlier description was right, Elin thinks, scrolling. For a while, Zeph Dosen was a *name*. Nothing so obvious as a celebrity chef, touting for publicity on talk shows, social media – but a name, nonetheless.

There are hundreds of reviews of the restaurants he's worked at, feature pieces, blogs when blogs were a thing. Gossip about who he was and wasn't dating.

Elin keeps searching, clicking now and then to scan the full articles, but it's hard to get a proper read on him. Most of the articles are top line, vanilla, analysis of his 'fiery' personality, mostly paying lip service to the same story over and over – the sous-chef and his finger, the subsequent restaurant closure.

Nothing that gave a real insight into the person behind the headlines.

She flicks through photos, and most back up her earlier assumption: attractive, but fully aware of his appeal. Elin hovers over a photo of him outside his restaurant. No bandanna, like in most of the photographs, so she can see his entire face.

A new perspective.

Examining it, something catches at the very edge of her mind, an outline of an image. A voice. A face.

Still studying the photo, she tries to hold on to it, but it's already evaporating.

She continues searching, hoping that the thread of the thought might come back, but only a lingering feeling remains, a frustrating sensation of having let something slip through her fingers.

Scrolling, she finds another series of photographs. Shots from a food festival, with a group of other chefs. Informal shots interspersed with close-ups.

Her gaze alights on an image of him posing in front of a studio kitchen.

Zeph's arm is casually slung around another chef, his hand loosely sitting on his shoulder. Rings cover his fingers – thumb, forefinger, index – but one in particular draws her gaze.

A silver ring with a bold green stone.

Elin's pulse quickens as she zooms in, takes in the intricate marbled pattern.

It's the ring they'd found near the fire at the clearing, a few feet away from Kier's clothes.

82

Elin

Parque Nacional, Portugal,
October 2021

'Okay, so that was interesting,' Isaac says, walking back into the van. 'I knocked on the door, but Steed didn't want me to go in. Had the whole conversation outside.'

When she doesn't reply, he glances first at her, then her laptop. 'Is something wrong?'

Elin takes a breath, still struggling to process it herself, let alone articulate it to someone else. 'I was looking up some stuff about Zeph and saw this.' Her voice wavers as she beckons him over. 'That's Zeph.' She points to the screen. 'On his hand, there.'

'It's the ring from the fire.' Isaac's face pales.

'Yeah. I'd like to say there's a possibility of a coincidence, but it's fairly distinctive.'

'And that puts him pretty definitively here, tells us he knew the camp.'

'I'm guessing that doesn't tally with what Steed told you?'

'No.' Running a hand through his hair, Isaac slowly exhales. 'Where to start. Okay, background first. Steed says the split with

Zeph came a little while before Kier came out to Portugal. Zeph then apparently moved back to the US after the breakup.'

'And didn't come back?'

'No. It was done and dusted as far as he knew. Steed said he thought it was a shame, reckoned it might have had legs.'

'So I take it he and Steed got on?'

'Actually, no, not at first, anyway. Zeph's got a bit of an ego – the whole celebrity chef thing. First meeting, Steed said he wasn't sure, but Zeph grew on him. They became friends from the sound of it, not buddy-buddy but close enough to stay in touch. Steed hadn't heard from him for a while, but Zeph's checked in with him a few times since Kier's gone missing.'

'Did he go into any more detail on why they split?'

'Yeah, Steed said that's the messy bit. Apparently, Kier told him it was a mutual thing, they'd drifted apart, but reading between the lines, he thought there was a different story.' Isaac hesitates. 'Turns out, there was. Zeph came to Steed before the wedding, worried about her. Said Kier had lashed out.'

'Lashed out?' Elin looks at him, surprised. It's the first time she's heard anything even vaguely controversial about Kier.

Why hadn't Steed mentioned this before?

'Got physical, according to Zeph. Pushing him, that kind of thing, smashed up some of his stuff. Zeph was pretty shaken, but he put it down to do with Kier being back in Devon. Everything that happened with her parents.'

'Triggering?'

'Yeah. It's one of the reasons she never liked going home.' Isaac pauses. 'Steed said Zeph tried to talk to her about it, get her to see a therapist, but Kier wasn't having any of it. Ghosted him.'

Elin absorbs this new information. 'And what did he say about the idea of Zeph coming out here?'

'Steed reckons he mentioned the national park to him, but Zeph never said he was planning on coming to look for Kier.'

'And did Steed talk about the camp to him at all? His suspicions?'

'He can't remember.'

'But it's not implausible to think that Zeph might have found them for himself,' Elin thinks aloud. 'The park's the biggest one in Portugal. He could have asked someone about the camp, followed the same process we have to get here.'

'I reckon it's possible.'

'And Steed says Zeph definitely hasn't been in contact recently?'

'No. He tried ringing him a while back, but it went straight to voicemail. Zeph never got back to him.'

'I don't like it.' Elin blinks. 'Not that Steed hasn't heard from him, that makes sense, you lose touch with people, but the fact Zeph wouldn't have told him, about coming out here, finding the camp.'

'Then there's the ring and the passport.'

'What if . . .' Elin falters. 'What if we're looking at a situation where neither Zeph nor Kier left the park?'

A heavy silence falls, as if neither of them want to articulate what might have happened.

'I reckon the only easy way we're going to get to the bottom of this is to find out if anyone's seen Zeph recently,' she says eventually.

'I thought about that. Steed gave me the number for someone called Clio. Lives near Zeph in New York. A friend of Kier's too, apparently. Steed spoke to her after he thought Kier was missing.'

'He didn't get suspicious about why you were asking?'

'I don't know. Hard to tell if he bought it, but he seemed happy enough to share the number.'

Elin nods uneasily. *Happy enough.* That didn't fit with the Steed she'd seen at the clearing. Didn't fit at all.

83

Elin

Parque Nacional, Portugal,
October 2021

It's a few hours before Clio calls them back. By the time she does, they're both decompressing – Elin sat outside, making notes, the remains of her lunch beside her, Isaac taking a shower.

The start of the conversation is more awkward than she'd expected. Clio sounds guarded, an emotion in her voice that she can't quite get a read on.

'I'll try to help,' she starts, 'but honestly, I think I've said all I can about Kier.' There's a noticeable edge to her voice as she says Kier's name.

'It's actually not about Kier,' Elin replies, her gaze catching on the branches on the trees a few feet away. They're swaying in the breeze, casting dappled light across the decking. 'Not directly. Penn mentioned that you're close to her ex-boyfriend, Zeph. We're in Portugal at the moment, where Kier was last seen, and we've found something of his.'

An intake of breath. 'You think Zeph's been in Portugal? With Kier?' Clio's voice is tight, clipped.

'Yes, at the national park. We wondered whether he mentioned he was going.'

'No, but I haven't seen Zeph in a long time. No one has.'

Elin's pulse quickens. 'When exactly did you last see him?'

'I don't know an exact date, but it's been a while. Over a year.' A small silence. 'I've had messages saying he's travelling, but that's it.'

'That's not normal for him?'

'I wouldn't say *normal*, but he's done it a few times before. Zeph's one of those people who throws himself into something. A new venture, restaurant. Gets consumed.'

'And no one's thought that this time was out of the norm?'

'I have, but I don't think anyone else is particularly concerned.' Clio sounds resigned. 'That's the way it is with our crowd. Out of sight, out of mind. Relationships you think are deep and meaningful turn out to be anything but.'

'But *you've* been worried?' Elin asks the question, but she can already tell from the tone of Clio's voice that she's been thinking about it.

'To a degree, by how long it's been since he's been in touch, but look, it's happened before. People ghosting me. I get it. I just thought he'd moved on.' Clio pauses. 'But yeah, there's always been this doubt in my mind, whether he'd just leave without saying goodbye.'

'What about family?'

'His parents actually got in touch a few months ago to see if I'd heard anything from him. I told them what I'm telling you. They didn't seem bothered.'

'So they hadn't heard from him?'

'Nothing bar a few messages, but I didn't read too much into that. Their relationship – it isn't exactly what you'd call close. They've been more or less estranged for years.'

'And the messages he's sent you, it's been just that? No video calls?' Elin tries to keep her voice steady, but it's hard as she thinks about Zeph's ring and passport, Isaac's words.

Maybe this is where his journey stopped.

'Yes, no video calls.'

Same modus operandi as Kier, Elin thinks, chilled. In both cases, the messages could easily be from someone else to divert suspicion.

There's a small silence. 'You really think Zeph's gone looking for Kier?'

Elin senses not just worry in Clio's voice now, but fear. 'You don't think he would?'

'Look, I don't know what you've heard, but Zeph and Kier's relationship . . . it wasn't what I thought it was.'

Zipping up her fleece as the sun disappears behind a cloud, Elin feels a flicker of disquiet. 'In what sense?'

'Well, at the beginning, I thought they were well suited. Kier seemed calmer than his previous girlfriends. More . . . stable.' She pauses. 'Zeph's always been attracted to – I don't know how best to say this – women he needs to fix. Women with . . . issues. I genuinely thought it was different with Kier.' Her voice grows quiet. 'Turns out, it wasn't. Kier called me a few days after they split, asking after him. At first, I thought she was just checking in, but then she said something about Romy, Zeph's ex. Sort of implied that Romy was involved in why they split. That's when I started thinking something might be off.'

'Didn't ring true?'

'No. As far I knew, Zeph hadn't been in contact with Romy for months.' Clio hesitates. 'A few weeks later, Zeph told me the real story, and Kier's call, it made sense. He said Kier had developed some kind of obsession with Romy, had in her head that Zeph still loved her. He tried to explain it wasn't true, but Kier didn't believe him. Apparently, they started arguing and it got physical. Started with her pushing him, that kind of thing, then escalated. She hit him. Pretty bad from the sounds of it.'

There's a pause. Elin doesn't know what to say. Steed had mentioned to Isaac that Kier lashed out, but nothing of this magnitude.

'Kier never mentioned any of this to you? Their arguments?'

'No, but Zeph said she couldn't even really acknowledge it to herself, let alone anyone else. Afterwards, she used to blame him.' She stops. 'I'm sorry. I feel out of my depth here.'

'It's okay, take your time.'

'All of what I've told you,' Clio says finally. 'It's against the backdrop of some disturbing things Kier told Zeph about her parents. Not just her feelings about what they'd done, but worries about herself. Kier told Zeph that she thought she might be capable of doing something like they'd done. That she'd have these thoughts. Bad thoughts—' Clio breaks off. 'Sorry, I'm not describing this very well.'

'You're doing fine.' A cold bead of dread settles inside her. *Had Kier been keeping all this from Steed deliberately?* Or had Steed chosen not to tell them? 'Did you ever witness anything violent between them?'

'No, but he showed me some of the messages she'd sent him. Awful stuff.'

The hairs on the back of her arm stand up. 'What kind of messages?'

'They were abusive, threatening, what she'd do to him if he told anyone, that kind of thing.'

Listening to her, Elin's having to wrestle against the mental picture she's already built of Kier. Having gone so far down one path in her thinking, hearing this … She feels disorientated. Confused. 'So the abuse – was that the trigger for their breakup?'

'Not exactly. Zeph found something that really frightened him.' Clio takes a shaky breath. 'Before they broke up, he discovered a painting Kier had done of some guy she'd gone out with. It was … dark. Showed his face beaten, bloodied. He thought that maybe she'd done to this guy what she'd been doing to him.'

A pit opens up in her stomach as Elin lays this information up against the fact that Zeph – as far as they knew – was missing.

'So it doesn't make sense to you that he'd come out here looking for her?'

'Yes and no. Zeph – he's a nice guy. Too nice, and like I said, he's a fixer.' There's a heavy pause. 'And you're sure, about everything?' she says falteringly. 'That what you found is his?'

'As sure as I can be. It was his passport.'

'Shit.' The long silence that follows tells her more than any words could.

As they say goodbye, all Elin can think is: *What if they've read this wrong?*

What if Kier wasn't a victim at all but had made herself disappear?

Wasn't lost, but running.

84

Elin

Parque Nacional, Portugal,
October 2021

With her mind still churning over her conversation with Clio, Elin goes back to the search she'd started on Zeph, looking for something, anything, that might either back up or disprove what they'd discussed.

But all she finds are variations of the same stories: the closure of his restaurant, the injuries to his chef.

It's only on the third page of results that a headline piques her interest.

Have they called it quits?

The subheader is equally intriguing.

Has dancer Romy Hernandez called it quits with her relationship with fiery chef Zephyr Dosen?

Romy.

Clicking into the article, Elin scans the text.

Last night, Romy Hernandez was seen walking arm in arm with fellow dancer Stefan Elder looking very cosy. Does Zeph Dosen know what his girlfriend is doing in her downtime, or has he already shown her the door?

Her gaze drops lower, to the photograph.

A man and woman both in sweats and high-tops, walking down a street, arms loosely threaded together. The man is bending his head slightly towards the woman, smiling as if he's found something she's said funny.

It's hard to get a read on either of their faces – the man's is in profile, and Romy is holding her arm up, shielding her face from the camera, but what Elin can see of it – the eyes, part of the mouth – looks familiar.

Elin keeps scrutinising the image, and while she still can't place her, the uncomfortable feeling lingers that she's seen her somewhere before.

She needs to find another picture.

But as she types Romy's name into the search bar, hundreds of photos appear. Daunted by the sheer number, Elin clicks on the first that clearly shows her face – a close-up of Romy sat outside a café – and peers a little closer.

A sudden jolt.

For a moment, Elin thinks the physical similarities are nothing more than superficial – her brain glitching, desperately seeking a connection – but as she takes in the bones of her face, there's no doubting it.

It's her.

85

Elin

It's Bridie.

Elin's breath catches in her throat as she examines the image again. The photo is a little blurry, and her hair is different in it – longer, slightly curly, concealing some of her face – but there's no mistaking her features and expression.

This . . . it's something solid linking Kier to the camp, surely?

Gives her a plausible reason for coming out here?

Her thoughts lurch to what Clio said about Kier's obsession with Romy.

Did she come out here to watch her? Confront her? Ask her if anything was still going on with Zeph?

Clicking out of the photos, Elin goes back to the main search, looking for more information.

A few results down, she finds a brief biography. It details Romy's backstory: she was a dancer. A childhood prodigy, Romy had briefly pursued a career in law before returning to her first love: ballet. She ended up going to ballet school but dropped out, her star only soaring after appearing in an advert that went viral, in which she played the role of a woman dancing off a building.

After that, it says she worked intensively. Dance, and philanthropic work.

Elin scans some of the charities she's involved with, but it's the advert that most intrigues her.

Opening another window, she searches for the video.

As it starts to play, Elin stares, mesmerised.

She can't pretend to be an expert on the technicalities of dance, but the performance is breathtaking. Not just Romy's sheer physical prowess, but the emotions the dance evoked.

Power, she thinks. That's what she feels from watching her. Someone totally in control. Owning the space.

She keeps watching, studying the shapes Romy's body is making.

Her thoughts start to cycle faster, others now entering her head: Bridie's elegant, loose-limbed walk. The patches on the clearing, worn away to soil. The flush that had crept onto her cheeks when she'd mentioned the clearing, a flush Elin had assumed was to do solely with the fire.

Her nerves tingle, a bolt of electrical charge.

It was Bridie who'd made the patterns on the grass at the clearing. The marks are from her dancing.

Elin thinks about Kier's map, how she'd painted the clearing. The beautiful light, transcendence, joy.

It fits.

But as quickly as the idea takes hold, her thoughts flip-flop.

None of this works with the idea that Kier had some kind of obsession with Romy. How Kier painted it implied that she'd been there when Romy danced. Enjoyed it.

You wouldn't do that, surely, if you had some kind of malign obsession?

Still chewing it over, Elin realises she's missed something key in her thought process: Romy's journey to this point. How she went from a flourishing career in New York to being out here, with the camp.

Moving her finger over the touchpad, she starts scrolling again.

A few pages down, she finds an article about Romy going off-grid. Rumours that she's in a retreat, rehab.

Perhaps it's as simple as Romy wanting an escape. Burnout? That kind of sudden fame, it probably took it out of people.

But as she thinks it over, Elin's left with a lingering sense of unease at the idea of *both* Kier and Romy wanting to stick it out somewhere like this. Especially Romy, after that kind of success. She'd have left a whole career behind.

What are the chances of them both coming out here, taking themselves off-grid?

She walks through different scenarios – Kier arriving at the park, tracking Romy down. Perhaps somehow, they became friends, and then along the way, Zeph appeared found the camp too, possibly looking for Kier. It's plausible, from what Clio told her.

Elin's mind worries at it, a knot she can't loosen.

While the story makes sense on one level, on another, it seems a stretch – exes cosying up, then the partner they had in common coming out to join them?

Then what?

Pulling her notebook from her bag, she picks up her pen, ready to brainstorm, when Isaac walks towards her from the van. He looks flushed, breathless.

'I've just found something.' Hand shaking, he passes her a piece of paper. 'I took another look at Zeph's passport and this fell out.'

86

Elin

Parque Nacional, Portugal,
October 2021

Elin places the piece of paper on the table, smoothing out the creases with her fingertips. 'Some kind of leaflet,' she murmurs. The paper is shaped like a bookmark, the name of the tourist office in the middle. It's similar to the leaflets they'd seen there, but something about it feels off. Amateur in comparison.

'Logo looks grainy.' Sitting beside her, Isaac runs his finger over it. 'And the print quality's not great.'

The paper too. Matte, not the gloss finish you'd expect on a leaflet.

Intrigued, she flips it over. Her breath catches in her throat.

'My thought exactly,' Isaac says, watching.

This isn't what she was expecting. Having seen the name of the tourist office, she'd assumed the back of the leaflet would detail some kind of attraction at the park, but no.

A pira.

A chill moves down her spine. No doubting what it is, but it's nothing like the iterations they'd seen before – either the physical creation hewn from wood or the one daubed on the van wall in the forest.

This has a looser colour palette and style. Sweeping, fluid brushstrokes.

'Do you notice something about *how* it's been painted?' There's an edge to his voice.

Elin studies it again, this time picking up on the inference of his words.

She'd been so focused on the idea of the pira itself, what it told them, that she hadn't even considered who might have created it. 'It looks like Kier's work.'

Isaac nods, pointing to the words written below. 'And see what you make of this.'

Para mais informações, consulte Posto de Turismo,
Peça para falar com a Maggie.
For more information, go to the tourist office. Ask for Maggie.

Elin reads and rereads, the blood pounding in her ears.

If any doubts remained over whether the camp and the pira are linked, they're gone. Whatever these piras represent, it's clear that they're significant to the camp, and to Kier too.

'No way we can approach Maggie directly about this, but we can go to the tourist office. See what they know.'

Isaac looks doubtful. 'Not sure we'll get much joy. He wasn't exactly keen on talking the last time.'

'No, but I think it's going to be pretty hard to deny all knowledge' – Elin puts a hand on the leaflet – 'when the name of the tourist office is slapped across the front of this.'

87

Elin

In the tourist office the man they spoke to before is alone behind the desk, eyes locked on the screen in front of him. Although he smiles as they approach – a fixed, professional smile – Elin senses a wariness behind it.

'Hello, again.' The smile slips a little, one eye still on the computer. 'I'm afraid if you have more questions about your friend, I don't have any more information than I did before.'

'No, it's not about that.' Elin steps a little closer to the desk. 'We wondered if you knew something about this?' Withdrawing the leaflet from her bag, she lays it in front of him. 'It has details about contacting the tourist office, and here, on the front—' Flipping it over, she gestures to the pira. 'We recognised this symbol as Kier's work, the woman we're looking for. We thought it might help us understand a little more what she was doing here.'

The man stares at the leaflet for a moment before looking back at them, his cheeks colouring. 'I—' Clearing his throat, he starts again. 'Where did you get this?'

Elin exchanges a glance with Isaac. 'We found it.'

'*Found* it?'

'Yes, and we're wondering if you know what it's about.' She gestures to the pira again. 'What this symbol means?'

The man's head moves a little – a tiny, involuntary movement – before he visibly swallows, as if trying to compose himself.

Elin senses that she's going to have to be the one to lead the conversation. 'We know that this' – she points to the pira – 'is linked to the piras that appear across the park.'

He frowns. '*Piras*?'

'Yes, the structures made of branches, shaped like a tepee.'

A look of recognition dawns before his face closes over, his eyes cast down towards the desk.

'It's complicated,' he says finally. 'All I can tell you is that the tourist office is a neutral place for people to come for more information.'

'From Maggie?' Turning the leaflet over, Isaac runs his finger over the words below the pira. 'That's what it says here. *Ask for Maggie.* Do you know her?'

'I'm sorry,' the man says, a tremor in his voice. 'I really can't give you any more information than that.'

'But why Maggie?' Isaac pushes, frustration creeping into his tone. 'What does she have to do with it?'

'My advice would be to speak to her.'

'We can't. Things are awkward, with the group.' Elin changes tack. 'Please, we just need to know what the leaflet is about. Kier's brother is out of his mind with worry, and it could be important in helping us find out what's happened.'

The man's face softens. 'Look, all I can say is that Kier isn't involved in something bad. In fact, it's the opposite.' He places his palm flat on the image of the pira. 'This symbol, it's a way of communicating to people. People who need it the most.' Flustered, he casts a look towards the door. 'I'm afraid it's not my place to say any more. Like I said, you should speak to Maggie.' Abruptly, he dips his head, looking back at his computer. 'I need to get back to work. I'm sorry I can't help any further.'

Back outside, they stand in silence for a moment, both wrapped in their own thoughts.

'That raises a whole lot of other questions, doesn't it?' Isaac says. 'I wasn't expecting any of that—'.

Elin nods, playing the conversation back in her mind.

People who need it the most.

Somewhere, deep inside her head, connections are starting to form. Thoughts and moments that had seemed entirely innocuous until this point are pulling together, forming fragile links and ties.

'Coffee?' Isaac gestures to the café a few doors down. 'I think we need some help unpacking all that.'

Elin registers his voice, but it's nothing more than background noise as she runs the past few days over in her head, tipping what she'd learnt first one way and then the next.

'You all right?' Isaac waves a hand in front of her face. 'You look out of it.'

'Yeah, just thinking.'

'You need a minute?' He stops outside the café. 'I can order for us.'

'Please. Just a coffee for me.' At the table in the corner of the terrace, a baby is shrieking, throwing small pieces of biscuit over the side of its highchair, but the sound is nothing compared to the rattling of the thoughts inside her head.

Kier's map. The camp's fiercely guarded secrecy. Leah's scar. Maggie's. Leah's fears about her ex being in the park, the one who blew up the van. Bridie dancing at the clearing. Romy's philanthropic work. The scratched-out initials on the tree at the river beach.

Fragments of sentences:

We're like family. Leah, especially. She's the one who really understands, gets what it's like to . . . Leah's like a daughter to her. All of them are . . .

Leah.

More thoughts start to build. Leah, genuinely frightened in the woods. Frightened enough to believe that her ex-partner blew up the van.

Could he have . . .

Theories racing through her mind, she chews over the newspaper article she'd read about Leah. There was a mention of her ex there, how both of them had been charged with extortion. She'd taken it at face value, but . . .

Reaching for her phone, Elin navigates to the article again. Once she confirms his name, Raymond Kenney, she taps it into her search, sifting through the results to find ones relevant to the area where Leah lived before.

Raymond Kenney is mentioned in several news articles. A few are various sites reporting the extortion charge, but the others focus on a completely different crime.

Elin reads and rereads the first article that details it, growing hot all over as Leah's words up at the falls echo in her mind.

It should have been me, not her.

Surely that has to refer to this?

Her hands are trembling as she puts the phone down on the table.

As she thinks it through – what it means for Kier's disappearance – the flicker of the thought she'd had earlier sparks into life.

Elin closes her eyes, focuses, tries to let the memory build. More appears: a van door, near the beach. A male voice, shouting.

The idea grows, and it's as if that thought – now loose – sets another one free. She can see it – in an odd, heightened detail – the nightclub near the harbour. The same face, the same anger. Pushing someone up against the wall.

Eyes still shut, she tries to recapture it. Fragments appear, distilled into individual moments. Not just what she saw, but heard, felt.

Sweat cooling on her skin, a woman's cry. *Fear.*

The thought attaches to another and another and another inside her mind, and as the links between them get stronger she wonders how she didn't see it before.

Elin's skin prickles.

Laying the leaflet on the table, she runs her finger over the pira Kier had painted, testing the idea for strength in her mind. Probing it for flaws.

But there's nothing. Only more thoughts gathering, thoughts that add weight to the idea.

'Sorry about the wait.' Isaac's voice startles her as he places the coffees down on the table. 'Busier than I thought.' He stops, eyes roaming across her face. 'You feeling ok? You still don't look right.'

'No, I'm fine,' Elin says slowly. 'I've been going over what the man said. I think we've been looking at this the wrong way round. Completely the wrong way round.'

88

Elin

Parque Nacional, Portugal,
October 2021

'You're going to have to backtrack a little here.' Isaac pulls his coffee towards him. 'Tell me where you're coming from.'

'I think we started this the wrong way round. We've been seeing the camp's secrecy as something negative, but I don't think that's right.' Elin tries to steady the shaking in her hands as she picks her plate off the tray.

He leans over the table. 'Explain.'

'What he said just then, in the tourist office, about the leaflet being for *people who need it the most*, it tells us that whatever Maggie's doing is something that helps people, right?'

Isaac nods.

'It got me thinking about some things Bridie's said. She was talking about the camp being like a family, said something about Leah understanding her. *Got what it was like.* She mentioned Leah being like a daughter to Maggie too.'

Isaac still looks bemused.

'I took what she was saying about Maggie in a purely

matriarchal way, but seeing this' – Elin lays her hand on the leaflet – 'I think it's more than that. I think the camp . . . I think it's a refuge, and the pira is some kind of . . .' She gropes for the right word. 'Symbol for it.'

Hand still trembling, she waits a moment before continuing, watching as he tries to put the pieces together.

'A *refuge*?' Isaac says finally.

'Yes, and I think Maggie is running it. It explains the secrecy, the hostility to outsiders. We saw how fragile Leah was, her worries about her ex being the one who blew up the van.' She pauses. 'Think about the scars on her arms, Maggie's face too.'

'But that could be explained by something else, surely? It doesn't definitively tell us it's a refuge.'

'You might change your mind after seeing this.' Elin passes him her phone. 'I've just found an article about Leah's ex, Raymond Kenney. He just got out of prison for a serious assault. Look at the name of the victim. Indie *Blake*. It says she was seriously injured by Raymond after Indie came to her sister's defence when she found him attacking her at their home.' She gestures to the screen. 'The sister's name—'

Isaac takes a sharp intake of breath. '*April Blake*. That explains what Leah said to us at the falls. *It should have been me, not her*.'

'Exactly, and all this, the refuge – it would explain why Romy would leave New York like she did and end up here, with a new identity.'

'You said some of the charities Romy was involved with were related to domestic abuse.' His foot is tapping the floor, his eyes flickering from left to right as he thinks it over. 'I'm guessing we got Ned all wrong too.'

She nods. 'Looks that way. He must have been helping Leah down from the falls, like Bridie said, offering Kier support rather than anything romantic.'

Isaac's quiet for a moment. 'All of this,' he says eventually, 'makes sense, bar Kier. I don't get why she'd have joined them.'

'I'm wondering if Kier needed refuge too.' Elin takes a breath, trying to steady herself for what she was about to say next. Something she's still trying to grapple with.

'From whom?'

'Zeph. I've been thinking about the connection between Kier and Romy, the evidence we have about them befriending each other. After we found his passport, I did some digging. One of the photos I found triggered something.' Elin screws up her face, thinking, aware she's probably not going to be able to describe it properly. 'A memory, about the time Kier said she was in contact with me. Only got a flicker, but I remembered seeing Zeph.'

'In Devon?'

'Yes, and just then, sitting here, parts of it came to me. I remembered Zeph leaving a van near the beach. There was someone shouting, slamming a door.' Elin chooses her words carefully. 'Another time, outside a club.' Closing her eyes, she plays it out again in her mind, trying to make sure she does the memory justice. 'Two people, arguing. One of them was Zeph, I'm certain. I saw him push a woman, I'm guessing Kier, against a wall. I remember going closer, but that's it. Nothing else.' She hears the tremor in her voice. 'Maybe that's how Kier and I connected. I approached her outside the club because of what Zeph was doing. It explains why I struggled to remember Kier. My focus was all on Zeph.'

'But what about everything Clio said about Kier's behaviour towards Zeph? That doesn't fit.'

'I think we've got to question that. Most of what we know about Zeph and Kier's relationship is based solely on what Zeph told Steed and Clio. What if it isn't true? What if Zeph planted seeds with them both, probably other people too, about Kier's behaviour?'

'But Clio saw the messages Kier sent him.'

'Well worth the effort to fabricate if your aim was to take control of the narrative. We know what Zeph did to trigger the closure of his restaurant. He's clearly volatile, had anger issues. Steed said he wasn't keen when they first met, before he warmed to him. Maybe his initial instinct was right. Perhaps Zeph's behaviour was the reason they broke up. The same thing that triggered Romy's decision to leave New York.'

'I see what you're getting at, but after everything that happened with her parents, would Kier stay with someone who was abusive towards her?' Isaac's fingers tighten around his cup. 'Surely that's the last thing she'd put up with.'

'I don't think that's always the case. I remember a colleague working on a domestic abuse case telling me that people who've witnessed abuse, experienced it themselves, can sometimes be more vulnerable to it. Maybe Zeph sensed that. Used it against her.'

'Christ.' Isaac bites down on his lip, shaking his head. 'If all this is true, Steed clearly had no idea.'

Elin lowers her voice as an elderly couple take a seat at the table next to them. 'I don't reckon he did.'

'So what are you thinking about why Kier came out here, found Romy?'

'Maybe she wanted to know why Romy dropped off the map. Clio said Kier asked about Romy when she called. Perhaps she was worried because of her own experience with Zeph.'

'Then when Kier came out here, spoke to Romy, she found out that she had good right to be,' Isaac says softly. 'So say Kier discovered the refuge, decided to stay, then what?'

'My guess, from finding Zeph's passport and the leaflet with it, is that he tracked her down.'

'And from there, there's only one way this ends, isn't there?' Isaac pushes his cup away. 'Finding Kier's clothes, burnt up like that, the passport stashed away, both of them missing ...' His expression is set. 'Something happened, didn't it? Between Zeph and Kier.' A loud beep sounds out from his phone. Scanning the screen, he frowns.

'What is it?'

'Steed's just messaged.' His eyes widen. 'Something ... odd. It says ... *you lied.*' Scrolling down, his brow furrows. 'He's attached a photograph.' He tilts the screen towards her. 'It's the fire at the clearing.'

'He found Kier's clothes.' Elin takes a sharp intake of breath. 'Did he say anything else?'

'No, just the photo and message.' Isaac's expression is bleak as he pulls his eyes up to meet hers. 'The tone ... it feels off, doesn't it?'

Elin's throat tightens as she takes in the fear in his eyes. She gets what he's implying. Knowing how close Steed was to the edge, the message is ominous.

This was exactly what she was frightened of when she'd seen him at the clearing: that once he found Kier's clothing, he'd extrapolate from that, draw the worst conclusions.

Once Steed believed Kier was hurt, all bets would be off, and she genuinely has no idea what he's capable of.

89

Elin

Parque Nacional, Portugal,
October 2021

'Call him,' Elin urges.

Fingers fumbling, Isaac dials. 'It's not even ringing. He's switched his phone off.'

Her stomach pitches. 'We need to find him. You want to try his Airstream first?'

Isaac nods, his face grey. 'It's probably the best place to start.'

Grabbing their bags, they leave some money on the table and head out onto the street.

As Isaac weaves through a group clustered outside the shop ahead, Elin's mind is already chasing over possible scenarios. Not one of them sees this ending well.

It takes them over half an hour to reach the plateau where Steed's Airstream is parked.

Elin pounds into the clearing, struggling to catch her breath. They'd barely stopped on the way up the trail from town, and she's feeling it. Total exhaustion. Her legs are heavy, thick with lactic acid, a dull throbbing in her rib.

Waiting a moment for her breathing to come under control, Elin looks around with trepidation. Everything's silent, still. All she can hear is the sound of the wind, ruffling the trees. 'Want to try knocking?'

Isaac nods.

'Steed?' Elin calls, walking closer. 'You there?' She loudly raps on the door, raising her voice. 'Steed?'

No answer.

Elin knocks again, waits, her breathing still ragged.

Nothing.

'Maybe try round the back?'

Together, they move around the perimeter of the van, trying to peer through the windows, but all the curtains are drawn. 'Looks pretty dead,' Isaac murmurs. 'Don't reckon he's in there.'

Elin nods, feeling a rising sense of panic. 'I'll take a look over here.' Walking forwards into the long grass at the back of the van, she scopes out the space around her. It's even wilder than the woodland backing onto their van. Nothing but trees for miles, towering pines and thick underbrush.

'Steed,' she calls, delving deeper into the grass, but nothing comes back in return, only the faint stirring of the breeze.

'We're not going to get any joy out here. Let's try and get inside.'

Elin jogs back around to the front of the van, Isaac behind her. Moving closer to the door, she reaches for the handle. 'It isn't even locked,' she says, pushing it open.

Inside, she's barely taken a step forwards before she stops, frozen in position.

'Shit.' Clamping her hand to her mouth, she's struck by the stale sour smell. The rancid scent of body odour.

Isaac swears under his breath.

It's a mess.

Clothes strewn everywhere. Half-drunk coffees, growing cold on the surface, filthy plates lying unwashed in the sink.

But it isn't that which gets her: it's the paper.

Sheets of it littering every surface inside the van – tacked to the wall, lying scattered on the floor.

A prickle of fear. 'Guessing this is why he didn't want you to come inside when you had that chat . . . '

'Yeah.' His voice wavers. 'What's he been doing in here?'

Grabbing a couple from the counter, Elin starts reading. At first, the notes look similar to the ones she'd made about Kier's disappearance, as if Steed's been trying to make sense of what's going on, but they quickly descend into nonsense, the words scrawled and illegible.

'The same as us from the looks of it,' she says. 'These are notes about Kier.' But as she bends down to pick up a few pieces of paper from the floor, Elin realises she's missed something: the word 'camp' written on some of the pages. The word has been underlined several times, written over to give it more emphasis.

'He's written stuff about the camp on these. None of what he's noted down around it is very readable, but he's clearly been focusing on it. Maybe—' she breaks off, her eyes alighting on a notebook near the sink. Picking it up, she starts flipping through it. It's blank on the first few pages, but then she sees the photographs.

Polaroids.

Different backdrops, but all versions of the same thing.

'These are photos of Ned.' Elin's gut lurches. 'I reckon that's where he is. He's gone down there, to the camp.'

90

Elin

The first thing Elin hears when they get to the clearing is scuffling, grunts, the muffled sound of Etta crying in one of the vans.

Ahead of her, Isaac comes to an abrupt stop and turns, his face stricken. 'Steed's there,' he mouths. 'With Ned.'

As they push past the final line of trees, Elin sees them in front of Ned's van, rolling around on the ground, dust and dirt clouding the air. Blood spatter is everywhere: pocking their clothes and the soil around them.

The scene is frantic. There's no way of seeing who's who among the jumble of limbs thrashing against the ground, the flailing arms, fingers scrabbling to get purchase in the dirt.

It's only as a dull thud sounds out and the movement briefly stops that Elin gets a clear picture: Steed is straddling Ned, who is lying with his back flat on the ground.

A low moan punctures the air.

Elin watches, dizzied, as Steed wrenches his arm back and

362

lands another punch. The sound resonates, and Ned's head jerks back, slamming against the dirt.

No moan from him this time, just shallow, ragged breaths.

You couldn't describe this as a fight, she thinks, looking at Ned, motionless, his eyes half closed. The only one still in the game was Steed, and it looked like he was just getting started.

As Steed rams his fist against Ned's face again, this time hitting his jawbone, Elin can't stop herself from gasping.

For a split-second, Steed turns to look her way, his eyes wild. Every bit of his face is filthy, blood pouring from a gash on his lip.

Fear slips through her.

It looks like Steed's crossed a threshold, lost whatever fragile grip he had on the world.

Watching him, Elin tries to calm the chaos in her mind to think about her next steps. Getting physical won't work, it'll only escalate things, add fuel to what is already a raging fire.

The truth, she thinks.

That's the only thing that will cut through: what he's wanted for months, what he's really here at the camp for. The truth not just about the camp but about Kier.

'Look, we know the truth.' Elin moves closer. 'About what happened to Kier. We got it wrong. The camp were helping Kier. Not hurting her. This, here . . . it's a refuge.'

But it's as if Steed hasn't heard her. He's in his own world.

Without even a passing look in her direction, he clambers off Ned and roughly hauls him to his feet before landing another punch that sends him tumbling sideways to the ground.

Ned makes no move to get up or protect himself, lying motionless in the foetal position, his face pressed against the dirt.

'Please, stop.' A voice sounds out, thin with fear, desperation. Elin turns. *Maggie*.

She hadn't even noticed them – Maggie and Leah – stood on

363

the grass a few metres away, Leah violently trembling in Maggie's arms. *Echoes, for them*, Elin thinks. Everything they'd come here to escape.

'Please,' Maggie says again. 'Stop.'

From behind her, Isaac lunges forwards and tries to pull Steed off Ned, but Steed's too quick. Wrenching his arm back, he elbows him in the jaw.

Isaac cries out, staggering backwards.

'Try that again,' Steed spits, 'and I'll take you out as well.'

Isaac turns to look at her and Elin shakes her head. 'Leave it.' In this state, Steed could be capable of anything. He's drawing not just on his strength and training, but rage. None of them will be a match for him.

'He's a coward. Can't even bring himself to fight back.' Dragging him towards the van, Steed pins him against the metal, his right arm drawn against Ned's chest.

Beside her, Isaac takes a sharp breath as they catch the first proper look at Ned's face.

It's a mess.

Not just dirt and dust, but blood smeared over his cheeks and shirt. Her gaze travels upwards to a deep gouge above his eye. It looks bad, but his demeanour is worse. Ned's head is hanging, his eyes almost fully closed. It looks like only Steed's hand pressed against his torso is keeping him upright.

Elin feels a deep-seated sense of dread. She'd seen the blows Steed had already inflicted, and they're probably only the tip of the iceberg depending on how long they'd been brawling.

If Steed lands another punch like that . . .

Next to her, Isaac's having the same thought. 'You want me to try again?'

'Not while he's like this, it'll only make it worse. I'm going to try to get him to listen. Explain what we've discovered.'

She takes a deep breath and steps forwards. 'Steed, you need to stop,' she says, louder this time, her throat hot, tight. 'Think this through. You're going to do something you regret. We need to talk, so I can explain.' From the corner of her eye, she sees Bridie's panicked face through the window of the van opposite.

Steed cuts her off, his lip curling. 'Do you honestly think we can fix this by *talking*? That's the only thing you've done since you've got here and look what good that's done. These people, they're still out here, living their lives, when *Kier* . . .' His voice trembles. 'They need to tell us the truth, Elin, and if they don't, I'll knock it out of them.' His face is shining with tears, pale lines streaking through the dirt and blood on his face.

Elin takes another slow step forwards. 'Steed, you need to listen to what I'm saying. We know the truth. Ned hasn't hurt Kier. It's the opposite of that.'

'Keep the fuck back.' Steed whips his head around to look at her.

His face is contorted into an expression of pure rage. *I don't recognise him*, she thinks, panicked. Not a single part of him is familiar to her. Although the thought is paralysing, Elin knows she has to keep him talking. If she can get him to listen, there's a chance something will cut through.

'Look, if you'll just let me explain properly, everything we've found out these past few days—'

'And how exactly do you expect me to believe what you "explain"?' Steed replies, a mocking tone to his voice. He keeps his hand pressed against Ned's chest. 'You've been *lying*, Elin, ever since I got out here. Said you had nothing concrete, but I saw Kier's clothes up at the clearing, all burnt up. You saw that days ago, and you've done nothing since then but pussyfoot around, asking me questions about Zeph, when all along, it's *them*. This fucking place. They're the ones who've done something to my sister. You're just feeding me all this bullshit so I'll back off.'

Elin doesn't even get a chance to reply as Steed suddenly turns back to Ned. She knows as soon as he yanks back his arm, what he's about to do. 'Please, don't!'

The sound of her voice throws the blow off course. Steed's fist only grazes Ned's cheek, but she can tell, from how Steed's torso lurches backwards exactly what kind of damage it would have caused had it landed.

He'd kill him, she thinks. *In this state of mind, he'd kill him in a heartbeat.*

Elin's eyes sting, the wave of sadness she'd felt before now a deep sorrow.

How had they got here? To this.

She watches him, unsure of what to do, then she remembers something that until this past week, she's always treasured about their relationship: how comfortable they were with each other. How easy it was to look at one another, hold eye contact. Something that didn't always come naturally with other people.

Slowly, Elin walks around the side of him so she's able to see him properly. Maybe, if he can see her face, read her expression, he'll understand that what she's saying is genuine.

'What I said, it's true.' She holds his gaze. 'We got it wrong. The camp is a refuge and they were protecting Kier, not hurting her.'

Steed's face twitches.

'What do you mean ... *protecting*?'

'Kier came here because of what Zeph was doing to her.' Elin steadies her voice. 'Whatever happened to her, after that, it wasn't because of the camp. All of them here were trying to protect her.'

Steed's face registers different emotions all at once – confusion, shock, relief – and Elin feels the first flicker of hope that she's going to be able to talk him down.

Though it's hard to keep her voice under control, she keeps going, telling him everything they'd discovered. As she speaks, her words eventually finding a rhythm, she feels a sense of peace that's long eluded her. Relief: no more lies and unanswered questions. Everything, at last, out on the table.

When she finishes, an odd noise emerges from the back of Steed's throat. His face crumples, and the arm rammed up against Ned's chest begins to shake.

In one quick movement, Maggie and Leah spring forwards to stop Ned from slipping to the floor.

'Please,' Maggie shouts at Steed, who still has hold of him, 'let go so we can help him.'

Lowering his arm, Steed stands there, frozen, while Maggie and Leah grab Ned and move him towards the van door.

When Elin looks back at Steed, he's still locked in position. The emotion in his eyes has gone, replaced with an emptiness.

'I'll take him back to the Airstream,' Isaac says, walking over to Steed. 'Leave you to help with Ned.'

It's the right call, Elin thinks, glancing at Leah. Though she's helping Maggie with Ned, she looks like she did up at the falls. There, but not there. Detached from the world.

91

Elin

Parque Nacional, Portugal,
October 2021

Bridie steps out of the van, Etta balanced on her hip. The worried expression she'd worn as they'd helped Ned into the van has softened into one of relief, but her face bears witness to the last few hours; still etched with shock.

'Ned's come to,' Bridie says. 'We'll get him checked out later, but Maggie thinks he'll be okay. She's going to sit with him for a bit, with Leah.' Hoisting Etta a little higher up on her hip, she meets Elin's gaze. 'Thanks for the help. I don't think we could have managed on our own. Leah was in shock, I think.'

'That's okay. Glad to be useful.' An awkward silence falls before Elin clears her throat. 'Let me know if it's not the right time, but I reckon you've probably got some questions.'

'You could say that.' Giving a faint smile, Bridie gestures to the bench. 'I'm guessing we sit down for this, huh?'

'Probably a good idea.' Elin follows behind Bridie as she picks her way across to the bench.

'I'm taking it you know him, then?' she says as Elin takes

the seat opposite and raises an eyebrow. 'Should have known when you started sniffing around, you weren't just trying to make friends.'

Elin nods. 'Yes, I know him, but not as Penn. We worked together, back in the UK. It's ... complicated.' Sweat pricks beneath her underarms as she plays out what she's about to say in her head. It feels like so much is riding on how well she delivers it. 'Isaac and I were trying to help him find out what happened to Kier.'

'So he told you that he'd been out here looking for her before?'

'Yes, but we had no idea about this.' Elin gestures around her. 'What you do here.'

'And you do now?' Her face is expressionless. 'You honestly think you know what this is?'

'Not completely,' she says hesitantly. 'But I think we have an idea. You and Kier – you shared an ex-partner, didn't you?'

Bridie still looks guarded. 'And who's that?'

'Zeph. I think he's the reason you came here, gave up the career you loved.' Elin looks around her. 'This camp ... it's a safe space, isn't it? For you and other women?'

Bridie meets the question with more silence.

Time seems to slow as the silence lengthens, the air shimmering with tension, but then Bridie's expression wavers, just for a second, and Elin knows she's hit a nerve.

Eventually, Bridie's face opens a little. Elin glimpses fear, doubt, and something unexpected too: relief. Like she's shed something that's been weighing heavy on her.

'I think I'd better go get Maggie.' Her voice is so quiet Elin has to strain to hear her. 'It's not my call whether ...' Trailing off, she stands up, walking towards the van, Etta loudly chattering in her ear.

Elin watches as Ned's door swings open and Maggie steps

outside. Bridie says something inaudible, and Maggie looks in her direction. The conversation goes back and forth for a few minutes before they start to head her way.

Before they reach the communal area, Bridie lowers Etta to the ground, pointing at the book on the table. Etta picks it up and settles on the rug nearby.

'Bridie says you wanted to talk to us,' Maggie says, stopping beside her.

'If that's okay.' Elin gestures towards Ned's van. 'If it's too much, given everything, we don't have to do it now. It can wait.'

'It's okay,' Maggie says, sitting down. 'Ned needs to rest a while.'

Her gaze shifting awkwardly between them, Elin knows she's going to have to speak first. 'I just want to reiterate that I'm not here to cause any issues.' She swallows, her mouth dry. 'Like I said to Bridie, all Isaac and I wanted to do was help Steed find his sister. You told him the last time he came out here that Kier didn't stay for long, but that wasn't true, was it?' With their faces giving nothing away, she keeps her voice level, steady. She has no idea how Maggie's going to take what she's about to ask. 'Kier . . . she *was* here, with you, wasn't she? A part of the camp.'

Neither reply, their eyes fixed on only each other.

Elin continues. 'I think Kier . . . she came here because of her ex-boyfriend, Zeph. We know what he did to her, and we think she came here to escape him. To find refuge.'

Her voice wavers on the final word, and there's a shift in Maggie's expression. She seems to be considering something before her eyes find Elin's. There's a sense of resignation in them, of letting go of control, of the story, of the guard she's tried so hard to keep in place.

A beat passes before Maggie turns to Bridie. 'If you're okay to, I think it's best if you take it from here. Anything gets too much, I'll step in.'

'You're sure?' Bridie's tone is hesitant. 'You really think it's okay to tell her?'

Looking back at Elin, Maggie nods. 'I think so.'

'Kier came here to find me,' Bridie starts, her foot tapping the floor. 'She thought that Zeph was doing the same to her as he'd done to me.' Her voice wobbles. 'Total destruction. Breaking us down, piece by piece. Gaslighting us, making us believe that what he was doing was our fault. That all we had to do was be better and it would stop.' She's tapping the floor with her foot so hard her leg starts to shake, and Maggie lightly lays a hand on her knee until it passes.

Pausing, Bridie collects herself. 'The last few months they were together, Kier found some photos that Zeph had taken of me and started putting the pieces together about why I'd left the US. She came here to try to figure out whether the doubts she had about him were justified before they gave it another shot.'

'That's what Kier was planning? To get back with him?' Elin can't disguise the surprise in her voice.

Bridie gives a brittle smile, her eyes hollow. 'Yes. Despite everything, Kier was planning on giving it another try.' She takes a breath. 'I went through the same thing before I found Maggie. Wanted to believe that this time, it'd be different, but it never was. Every time I gave him another chance, all it did was let him know exactly where my line was and how far he needed to go to cross it.' Her words suddenly tip into one another, so fast that Elin can't get a grip on them. 'He kept crossing it. Every time he crossed it, I'd tell myself that it would be the last time, but then' – she screws up her eyes, and it seems as if she's in physical pain – 'he'd do it another time and another.'

Elin blinks, finding it hard to look at her. Swallowing hard, she pictures it again: Zeph leaving the van. Outside the club. The rage she'd glimpsed in his eyes. She can't even begin to imagine that sense of fear you'd feel at a moment like that. Someone you love, *turning*.

Maggie puts her hand on top of Bridie's. 'You don't have to carry on.'

'No, I want to.' Slowly exhaling, her eyes find Elin's. 'Kier ended up joining us.' A brief smile flickers on her face. 'By the end, she was a different person, and that's down to Maggie. This ...' She gestures around her. 'Everything here is because of her. Maggie puts people back together. People who've not just reached the bottom, but a place beyond that. A place where no one imagines they'll ever be.'

She looks at Maggie and nods, as if prompting her to say something.

Maggie roughly rubs her eyes. 'All I've ever wanted,' she says quietly, 'was to create a space for people who couldn't find sanctuary anywhere else. Women, from anywhere, can stay with us as long as they need to feel safe again.' She blinks. 'I worked in refuges in the US for a long time, and I saw that some women needed a total escape. Physically. Psychologically. This ... our ability to keep moving, it's provided that.'

'And more,' Bridie says fiercely. 'She makes us feel like we're part of a family. Kier became a part of that,' she says, smiling broadly, the first proper smile Elin's seen from her, her eyes creasing at the corners. 'A part of us. She did so much for us while she was here ... helped me rediscover my love for dance.' She clears her throat. 'Before Kier came, I'd lost that part of me. I associated it with Zeph and everything that happened in New York. I thought I'd never dance again.'

'You dance up at the clearing, don't you?' Elin says softly, imagining it: Bridie up there, dancing like she was in the videos she'd seen online. 'Where the forest fires have burnt the trees.'

Bridie nods. 'Yes, I do.' She hesitates. 'Kier ... she used to watch me.'

'Kier did some artwork for you, too, didn't she? We saw it on the leaflet we found.' Elin continues. 'The pira she drew on ... is it a symbol for the refuge?'

It's Maggie who speaks this time. 'It is, but here we don't call them pira.' She exchanges a glance with Bridie. 'That's what other people call them. Our name for them is the wilds.'

92

Elin

Parque Nacional, Portugal,
October 2021

Maggie's voice catches. 'Because that's what they're built from. The wilds that live inside us after we've hit the very bottom and can't see a way back up.'

'The wilds,' Elin echoes, the hairs rising on the back of her arms.

'Yes, that's what we call the feelings inside us that can't be tamed. Feelings that burn. Feelings that take you to the edge.' Maggie's face constricts. 'All our women have feelings like that after what they've been through, and here, we take those feelings and we build with them.' Encasing Bridie's hand in hers, she smiles. 'Because when you're building up, there's no chance to look down. No time to think about destruction.' Her voice is thick. 'I built my first one when I was a child, the day my daddy went to jail. My mama and I went to the woods at the back of our house, and we built. The first time in our lives that something was being made instead of destroyed.' She pushes a loose strand of hair away from her eyes. 'We let it sit for a few days, and then piece by piece, we took it down. A blank slate.'

Elin's heart is drumming as her thoughts shift to seeing Leah in the woods that day. 'That's what Leah was doing the day we saw her in the forest. She was taking it down.'

'I think so . . .' Maggie falters. 'She wanted that blank slate so badly, but everything got too much. She started thinking that her ex had found her, that he was the one who blew up the van.'

'And was he?'

'We're not sure. Ned saw the spare gas canisters had gone up, in the debris, but it's hard to say if it started there or somewhere else. An electrical fault, maybe.'

'Ned is Maggie's brother,' Bridie says. 'He'd do anything for her. Saved her life after he found her in her apartment, beat up by her ex. He's a big part of what we do here, especially in terms of helping the women feel secure. They obviously need to be ok with him being around, but we make that clear before anyone joins us.'

She continues to talk, but the sound of her voice briefly drops away as Elin catches on something at the very edge of her vision: the clothes hung on the line strung between Maggie's and Ned's vans, flapping in the breeze.

Her thoughts slip back to the very first time they'd entered the camp.

Different clothes, obviously, but the same insistent breeze.

Though she can sense Maggie's and Bridie's eyes on her, Elin watches for a moment, left with the same feeling that she's had every time she's come down here – that she's missed something.

Trying to block out everything else around her, she replays the last few times she was at the clearing, layering the memories one on top of another, and on this moment too.

She's got no idea *what* she's seen or where exactly, but it's something *here*, something in or around Maggie's van, near to where she's strung up the clothes.

It's as the breeze pulls a shirt sideways, wraps the arms around themselves, that she glimpses it.

An anomaly.

Not with the van itself, but the colour.

White, yes, but around the very edges of the window frame, there are glimpses of another colour.

Blue.

It's been painted over, she thinks, staring, and it looks like whoever sprayed it hadn't quite got all of the area around the window frame.

Still examining it, it's as if that idea has opened the door to the fine, fragile thread of another. She looks and then looks again, the idea she's clinging to casting new light and shade on every part of the van.

Not just modern, as she'd first thought when she looked inside that night at the camp, it's all new, she thinks, growing cold all over. *Too new*, at odds not just with Maggie's van in the woods, but the others here.

New and a bit slapdash. Brush marks visible, the lino not quite fitting.

Hastily done.

Again, Elin pictures the photograph Isaac showed her of Kier's van. Maggie's.

It had been staring them in the face the whole time, she thinks. The ending to this.

Kier and Zeph ... they hadn't just disappeared into thin air.

The final part of the story – it played out here.

93

Elin

Parque Nacional, Portugal,
October 2021

When Elin finally looks back at them, Maggie smiles, resigned, a sense of understanding passing between them. 'You've seen it, haven't you?'

Elin nods. 'It's been bothering me ever since I first saw the camp,' she says softly. 'That van.' Her gaze settles on it. 'It's not yours, is it?'

Maggie doesn't reply, and Elin can see from the look on her face that this is a part of the story she either isn't prepared for, or is frightened to tell, and so she keeps talking, keeps moving this story on, because it's important that it has an ending. That after all this time, they know it all.

'That van is Kier's, painted over to look like yours. Someone's made some changes to the interior too. We found your actual van, hidden in the forest. You swapped them out, didn't you?' Still, Maggie says nothing, her fingers playing with a fold in the fabric of her skirt. 'That makes sense on one level, after what you said about Kier going to Italy, that you wouldn't want her van out in the open, but then, why not? It's plausible she might have dumped it, hitched a ride. Why go to all the trouble of swapping the vans unless there's something about Kier's van itself that you didn't want anyone to see?'

Bridie sharply inhales, but Elin continues. 'The inside of your van here ... it's new, a bit slapdash. Fresh paint, new flooring – cheap flooring – that doesn't fit with your old one and the others here. The redecoration has been done to hide something, hasn't it? Something that happened there, in Kier's van.'

A heaviness settles across Maggie's features, and Elin senses that she's going to need to brace herself for whatever's coming next, but when a voice sounds out it isn't Maggie's, but Bridie's.

'You're right, it *is* Kier's van.' Bridie's face is pale as she brings up her eyes to meet Elin's. 'Zeph found us,' she says dully. 'Tracked Kier down, put a camera in her van. We think he was watching her for a while, came and went a few times, stayed in the cabin up at the clearing, then went back to the US. But all the while, because of the camera, he had eyes on her.' Her voice cracks. 'We found the hard drives in his bag. What he'd done – it was deranged. He'd divided the footage up and isolated some of the clips. We think he watched them over and over – got it in his head that Kier was involved with Ned.' She shakes her head. 'It was obsessive. Like the photos he took of me in New York.'

'We saw some of the footage.' Elin swallows, thinking about how they'd interpreted it: in a negative light, but they'd never imagined anything as sinister as this.

Bridie nods. 'I think Kier always knew, deep down, that Zeph wouldn't let it lie. You know, he said the same thing to her that he used to say to me. He used to whisper it when he hurt me. He used to say, without me, there can be no you.' Tears are shining in her eyes. 'I never really believed it until he came here and found us.'

94

Kier

Parque Nacional, Portugal,
Autumn 2020

Shoving the map inside the bench seat, I slam the lid closed and make for the door, a delayed reaction, but it's too late.

It's already opening, and Zeph is coming inside. I smell him first – the usual odours of smoke and spice, but something else too. Alcohol. Sweat.

I force myself to take big breaths, but it feels like someone has a hand around my lungs, is squeezing tight. Shock, part of it, at him being here, in front of me, even though I'd thought of this, of course I had.

A tiny voice whispered in my head: *He'll find you. One day, he'll find you*, but I'd let myself believe it could go on like this forever. That the bubble we'd built around ourselves here would never burst.

'It didn't have to be like this,' Zeph says slowly, conversationally, closing the van door behind him. 'You could have just been honest. Said, *Zeph, I'm unsure about things*, and we could have talked it through. I could have explained—' He's got that odd, frozen look on his face. That calm voice that means something bad.

I blink, knowing what I need to do. *Play for time. Don't rile.*

'What do you mean?' I hitch my voice up a notch, hoping it sounds like confusion. 'I don't understand.'

Zeph shakes his head. '*You don't understand.* Have you forgotten that you told me we were going to have a fresh start, then that's it, you're gone?'

I don't reply. Something in his eyes is making me wary.

'Is that what you do, Kier, to the people you love? You *ghost* them?'

'It wasn't like that.' I dig my nails into my palm, hating the sound of my voice. It's the voice I've always had with him. An appeasing voice. Part of a pattern that would play out in our conversation: He as parent. Me as child.

'But it was, Kier. You left me high and dry, and we both know why, don't we? It's because you came out here, looking for *her.*'

'You're going to have to explain. I don't know what you're talking about.' I keep my voice slow, steady.

'Oh, but you do.' His voice is so calm, so measured, it makes my heart twist. 'You found her. You found Romy.'

'That isn't what happened.'

'That's a lie, Kier, isn't it? I've been watching you. In the van.' He glances up at the shelf, a smile playing on his lips.

I follow his gaze. Something there, between my books.

My heart lurches.

A camera.

The feeling I had ... it was right. He's been watching me. Wormed his way inside my private space.

Zeph shakes his head. 'I have to say, Kier, I'm pretty fucking disappointed, because the last thing I knew, we were meant to give it a go. Become a family. That's what all this was about. You and me. You and me, we were going to fly.'

Agonisingly slowly, he reaches out, cups my face in his hands. They feel the same as they always have. Rough and warm. I can see the bumps and nicks on them, the tiny, silvered scars I know so well, and for a moment, despite everything, my body reacts to him as it always has.

I start to lean in, but then wrench myself backwards.

'We had it all planned out, Kier. We were going to travel, be together properly, but you went dark on me. All I want is to know why. Why you left, came here. To her.'

Seeing the odd twist to his mouth, the strange look clouding his eyes, I know I can't tell him the truth. Can't tell him that although every part of me wanted to believe the relationship would work, that seed of doubt was always there. A thorn pressed deep in my side. 'I needed some time on my own. We talked about that, didn't we?'

'*Time?* I get that.' Zeph shrugs. 'If you were on your own. But not with my daughter, Kier. Not my fucking baby. You don't just get the right to take *her* away from me.'

My stomach drops with a force that makes me put a hand on the counter to steady myself.

No. He can't know.

'I told you, Zeph. I lost the baby.' My voice sounds strange, even to my own ears.

'No, you didn't. You had the baby, and she's here, isn't she? She's with Romy, in her van. You two have been quite the team, haven't you? Looking after her together.'

My palms are slick. *He might be bluffing. You've got to try . . .*

'She's Romy's, Zeph. I promise, she's Romy's.' *Believe me. Believe me.*

The colour drains from his face. 'She's *Romy's*?'

382

I sense him looking at me and I make my mouth into a smile. 'She is. I just help Romy out with her.' My words hang in the air between us, alive and thrumming.

A bob in his throat. He holds my gaze for a moment, then takes a step forwards.

I moisten my lips. My chest is sore, like the breath in there is hard and scratchy, but I reach out a hand, lightly touch his arm and smile.

'Do you honestly think I wouldn't have told you? And I'm probably going to be condemned to eternal damnation for saying this, but what happened, not having the baby, it was probably the right thing in the long run, for both of us. I wasn't ready, you weren't ready, but that doesn't mean we won't be in time.'

For a moment, he starts to smile back, and I think: *I've done it, he believes me, and if this is the point that he's fixed on, then maybe, just maybe, I can walk him back from here.*

But the smile stays frozen in place, stays too long to be real.

'And I thought for a moment there that you were going to be honest, but no.' He blinks. 'I'm going to give you one last shot. Are you going to say it, Kier?' Stepping closer again, he brushes the tip of his finger along my jaw. 'Say it, Kier. Say Etta's mine and we can start this all over again.'

From the corner of my eye, I see a movement, and I glance outside, pulse catching in my throat.

Have they come back early?

'No good looking out there.' Zeph shakes his head. 'No one's coming to help. The rest of your *friends* are in town, and Romy's with Etta. She won't disturb you when you're meant to be head down. I know your patterns. This is the time you work, when Romy looks after Etta.' Finding my gaze, he looks me dead in the eye. 'It's just you and me. You and me and the truth. All you have to do is say it. Tell me that Etta's mine.'

My thoughts scatter.

I need to get out.

If I shout now, Romy won't hear me. If I can get outside, I can raise the alarm.

We have code words for this. Romy will be able to get out the back of her van and into the woods.

I smile, open my mouth as if about to speak and then lunge sideways, slipping past him.

Nearly there . . . I make it one step, two, but I know, even as my hand is closing around the handle, that he's on me.

'Not so fast.' Zeph grabs my arm, yanking me around to face him, his hand locked tight around my wrist. He tugs me closer.

'Zeph, please, you're hurting me.' My heart sounds out an unsteady beat.

He shakes his head, a sorrowful look in his eye.

'Jesus, Kier, you have to make this so difficult, don't you? We could have been happy, the three of us. If you'd have done the right thing just then, when I asked, we could still have been. The three of us could have left here and been *happy*. But we can't do that now. You lied, and I know you lied because she looks like me, doesn't she?' His voice is hoarse. His first real smile. 'Etta looks like her daddy.'

I feel ill. Every breath hurts inside my chest.

'Or maybe the reason you don't want to say she's mine is because you're planning on being a family with someone else? Is that it?'

His words catch me by surprise: a new narrative. 'I don't know what you mean.'

'You and *Ned*.' Zeph's lip curls. 'I've been watching you these past few weeks. Him coming in here, you two talking, late into the night. Do you like him, Kier? Is that what it is? Because if it is, you need to tell me. Be honest.'

So this is why he's come here now to confront me. Jealousy. This is what's pushed him over the edge.

'No, Ned and I are just friends. I don't want to be with anyone right now, I told you that.'

'But that doesn't work, you can see that, can't you?' Zeph is breathing hard now, like he's been running. 'It doesn't work, you being on your own. Because without me, there can be no you.' He says it again, the beginning and end of the words running together. 'Without me there can be no you without me there can be no you.'

He shoots me a look I've never seen before.

All the other times, there's been love there, a sense of self-reprimand, reluctance, swinging in the balance, as if he weren't even sure which way he wanted it to go, but now, there's nothing. A complete detachment, a calm acceptance of what he's about to do next.

Zeph swallows, his hands coming up to my throat. Pressing and squeezing. Almost questioningly, as if he's testing it out, working out if it's really what he wants to do, and then it comes. He shoves his fists against my chest, slams me back against the wall, wedging me in the gap between the kitchen counter and the door.

He thrusts his hands towards my throat again and this time there's no question: he presses hard, so hard I can't catch my breath. I brace myself against the wall, try to push back, try to pull his hands away but my palms are slick and they fall away from his. All he does is dig in deeper, his hands crushing me.

I extend my arm instead, fingers scrabbling out sideways, trying to find something, anything, that I can use to strike back. There's Mum's glass bowl on the counter, but I'm too far away. I can't reach it.

Something flickers on his face as he watches me. For a moment, I think he might be having doubts, but then I feel a burning heat in my side. A searing pain, as if someone's slid a hot poker between my ribs.

He says it again. Just whispers now.

Without me there can be no you without me there can be no you, and the pain comes again, a little higher.

Something warm and wet trickles down my side.

His words are getting faster and faster, so fast I can't even catch the thread of them.

A strange blackness has appeared at the corner of my vision. A deep, inky dark, a gravitational force, pulling me inwards.

The pain comes again, but this time I'm not there. I've already gone, to the places I can reach in my head.

We do this exercise with Maggie when the wilds inside us take over: we travel.

This time, I go to one of the places on my very first map.

I'm at home and the sun is shining. Penn's running towards me holding a spider in his cupped hands. *Look, Kier, look!* My mother is in the chair, a cup of tea on the table in front of her. She is smiling.

The next pain makes this image shudder – like someone's jolted the camera. But I hold on to it fast even though the picture is bleeding at the edges.

I try to hold on because this is what it's about, isn't it? Power. He wants power over me because despite his strength and how he's using it, he feels weak. The only way he feels strong is not from this, when he hurts me, but when he can see my fear.

But I'm not scared. I'm not weak. I'm not a victim. I'm strong. A survivor.

I think of what we say when we make one of the wilds for the first time.

I am not the wilds and the wilds are not me.

I say it over and over in my head, blocking out his words,

because he's still saying it, as if the more he says it, the more it will be true.

Without me there can be no you without me there can be no you.

I look him in the eye and his face constricts, and it's because he no longer sees stars in mine, like he used to. All he can see now is a reflection of him. A reflection of a monster.

Out of everything I've learnt since I've been here, that's the most important.

He's the one with the monster inside him, not me.

'Kier,' he says, but I can't really see any more. The blackness at the corner of my vision has turned to white, the room dissolving into a hazy light.

He lets me go, but I don't have the strength to keep myself upright. I try, but I slip sideways, down.

Kneeling beside me, he starts to talk. More whispered words his breath hot against my cheek, but then I notice him hesitate.

A noise.

My eyes slip past him. The door, opening.

Romy.

95

Kier

Parque Nacional, Portugal,
Autumn 2020

Romy cries out when she sees me, lunges forwards to try to get to me, but Zeph grabs her by her hair.

She screams, an awful, guttural scream and I watch him take her head all tender in his hands like it's something precious and slam it back against the wall.

Her eyes roll back, a thick line of blood trickling down her temple.

I watch as he does it again and again. Thud after thud, and all I can think is: *He'll get away with this.*

He'll kill us both and he'll escape without leaving any trace, because this is what men like Zeph do. They're clever. They manipulate people. They turn their charming face to the world, and even when there's an aberration, they can make excuses for it.

Zeph has his hands on the tops of her arms now, gripping tight, and then he starts to shake her, making her body rattle as he leans forwards and says something in her ear.

I want to move, do something, but my limbs won't move, that haze, hovering at the very edge of my vision.

But as I turn my head a little, I see it; on the shelf, something I hadn't been able to grasp for myself.

The glass bowl, Mum's glass bowl: the only thing I took from our old house.

It looks fragile, delicate, but it's heavy when you weigh it in your hands.

I look back at Romy, try to catch her eye, try to talk with my eyes again like I did the day the policeman came to the door, but she doesn't see me. Zeph's doing to her what he did to me; his hands now clasped around her throat, pressing, squeezing.

I watch her eyelids flicker, then close.

I need to do something else.

Think. Think.

I raise my right hand, try to point, hope she'll catch the sudden movement.

But it doesn't seem to register. Her gaze is cast to the floor.

My stomach drops in despair. *She didn't see. It's over.*

Then I hear it: an odd, dull crack.

Glancing up, I see his hands slip away from her throat in one juddering motion. The glass bowl falls from Romy's hand to the floor. I'm not sure if it's the dizziness I'm feeling, distorting it, but his body seems to pause, as if it's questioning what she's done.

For one terrifying moment, I think it's not enough. That he's going to lunge forwards, come for her again, but all at once he crumples to the floor, his frame sagging as he falls backwards.

A few moments pass, Romy gasping, crying, still locked in the position where he'd left her.

Finally, she looks toward me. I open my mouth to try and speak and it's then I sense something: a twitch from Zeph's body.

A definite movement: his arm.

My stomach dips. *It wasn't enough. He'll come back from this. I know he will.*

Desperate, I look around.

It only takes a split-second before I see it: the glass bowl, still lying on the floor, light from the lamp on the counter bouncing across its surface.

I summon up my last remnants of strength and snatch it from the floor. Clasping it tightly in my hands, I bring it upwards and slam it with all the force I have against his temple.

Once, twice, then the bowl slips from my grasp.

Things start to fade in and out.

The light, again, appears around me, but as it dims, I register Romy next to me.

She's crying.

I want to say something, tell her what these past few months have meant; how watching her dance has set a part of me free, but it hurts inside me, a weird kind of hurt.

More than pain, because it doesn't have a point it starts from – a thread I can clutch on to – or even waves, it's everywhere, across my whole body, as if I am the pain and it is me.

A tide that's sweeping me away.

All at once, there's no demarcation between the here and now and the light that's filling my vision.

I close my eyes, and though I can't see Romy any more, she's there in my head.

She's dancing, Penn and Etta beside her. My mother too.

They are in one place and every place that is precious to me, defying the laws of gravity and nature, making shapes in the sky.

96

Elin

Parque Nacional, Portugal,
October 2021

'I went in too late,' Bridie says, a quiet devastation in her eyes. 'I'd heard the door of Kier's van go earlier, but I thought she'd just gone outside for something. I shouldn't have waited.'

'You didn't know.' Maggie reaches over, takes Bridie's hand in hers. 'How were you to know?'

'But Kier said she thought she was being watched. She told us, didn't she? We should have been on high alert.' Bridie's voice stretches thin, to breaking point. 'Never should have left her alone ...'

Elin watches, silent, as Bridie starts to cry, her chest heaving.

It feels like it's smothering her: not just the palpable weight of Bridie's guilt, but the violence still lingering in the air from the horror she's described. Though she's trying to block it out, she can see in her mind's eye exactly how it all played out – every scream, every ugly moment.

An image of Steed comes to her.

Elin pictures his face as he'd turned to look at her earlier, the raw hurt in his eyes. Although the evidence had been building to this moment, a part of her still longed for a different end to this story. Her heart aches for him, for his loss. Despite her anger at what he'd put her through, she knows what this will do to him, how it will tear him apart.

'So Kier ... she's here, isn't she?' Elin's asking the question, but part of her knows that Kier's here, somewhere in the camp. Zeph too.

It was why the camp hadn't moved on. Hadn't escaped this nightmare.

They couldn't. Couldn't leave either of them behind.

For a long time, she says nothing, then finally, Bridie nods. 'She's here.' Tears fall down her cheeks as she looks first at Maggie, then at Etta chattering to herself as she flicks through the book on the rug. 'She isn't far.'

97

Kier

*Clínica de recuperação, Portugal,
October 2021*

When the nurse walks in, Penn is behind her.

I can't take my eyes off him. His hair, freckles. The lopsided smile that redraws every part of his face.

As the nurse murmurs a few words, *I'll leave you to it. Let me know if you need anything*, he stops short of the chair by the window that's been my lifeline to the outside world these past months. Through it, I watch it all – clouds that swell and drift away, airplane trails that daub a line through the blue and then dissolve to nothing.

Once she's left the room, Penn moves towards me. 'Shit,' he says hoarsely. 'I never thought I'd get the chance to do this again.' All at once his head is against mine, his hands on my shoulders.

I breathe it all in, his skin smell. Aftershave. Soap.

It's almost too much.

My senses have become heightened in here. Not to the clinical smells – it's anything normal that catches me – the damp, sweet scent of Etta's neck, the smell of the ground outside, sunbaked earth, flowers.

'I know,' I say into his hair. 'I know.'

We stay, locked together a while until I'm forced to move, sharp bolts of pain jagging through me.

I hate it. On bad days it feels like I'm running against a strong wind – though I try to move forwards, it keeps pulling me back, physically, mentally.

'Are you going to sit down, then, or aren't you planning on staying?' I gesture to the chair on my left, smile, but the joke doesn't land. My voice doesn't sound right. Like I'm trying too hard.

'Not sure . . . the name on the door isn't yours, so I don't know if you're an impostor. . .' Smiling, he perches on the edge of the chair and puts his bag on the floor beside him. 'So how are you doing? You look—'

'A state?' I interrupt, bringing a hand up to the tangled mess of my hair. 'You don't have to be nice. I look like crap, but I'm on the right track, at last. Still some rehab, physio, but I'm getting there.' *Coming back to life after a long winter.* That's how the doctor described it. *Waking up.*

'Good. Bridie said it's been rough.'

'In parts. This bit's been okay, but the start, I don't remember much. Those first few months, I was in a . . . coma.' I struggle to say the word. Talking about how bad it got – it's hard, something I've been working on, accepting what happened. Understanding it. 'The middle bit was the worst. When I was aware of what was going on, knew I was meant to be better, but it didn't happen.' I blink. 'It's been one complication after another. Infections, more operations . . .'

We're quiet for a few moments, but it isn't real silence. It's never quiet in here. Constant low-level noise: the rattle of the air-conditioning; clatter-shakes of drinks trolleys wheeling past the room.

'And how about you?'

A heavy silence falls. 'Not great,' he says eventually. I get the sense he's holding back, but I don't push. Awkward under my scrutiny, he bends down to rummage in his bag. 'Before I forget, I'm under strict instructions to give you these.' Holding a small bunch of slightly limp wildflowers, he passes them to me. 'They're from Etta. Romy helped her wrap them.'

'Etta.' I can't help but smile.

'She looks like you, you know,' Penn says softly. 'It's the eyes.'

Blinking, I reach for my water glass. Unwrapping the damp tissue around the flowers, I plunge the stems into the water and loosely arrange them.

Penn watches. Both of us are delaying the inevitable, but I want it over with, done.

In the end, it's him who speaks first. 'Kier, I—' His voice splinters. 'Look, we don't have to talk about it, not if you're not ready, but I wanted you to know that I'm sorry for not listening when I should have. For not being there.'

'What do you mean?'

'Back in Devon.' Penn's face is serious. 'I was so consumed in the wedding that I didn't listen when you said someone was watching you. I should have.'

It takes a while for me to digest his words. I've thought about this a lot. *Sliding doors*. Whether this, or another moment, could have stopped what was coming in its tracks.

'I think,' I say carefully, 'that the decision I made, to give it another go with Zeph, would have happened anyway. If not then, then another time. I needed to find out for myself who he was. Nothing you could have done would have changed that.'

Even now, I know I'd make the same decision over and over, because I wanted, so badly, for Zeph to prove to me that he was still the man that I first met. The man who believed we could fly. The man who could conjure food from words, from the very air.

We're both quiet for a minute, and it isn't loaded, I know he's not expecting anything from me in return, but I need to explain. 'Look, I'm sorry too. For not getting in touch sooner, letting you know I was okay.'

He gives me a crooked smile. 'You don't have to apologise. Everything that's happened, you weren't exactly in a fit state to be catching up.'

'Yeah, but the past few months I have been. I've tried, you know, even picked up the phone, but I couldn't . . . get there. All I could think about was your job. Putting you in a shitty position.' I swallow, finding it hard to say the words. 'And I knew that if you called it in, Zeph's family would have had to be told. I couldn't take that risk. Not with—'

'Etta?'

I nod. 'Not while I was still in here and there was a chance of another complication. Knowing I wouldn't be able to advocate for myself. . .' The thought still chills me. Someone from his world, a world that had damaged him so acutely, being able to take her from me.

I hesitate, working out how to say the next point.

Penn's studying me. 'You okay?'

Dragging my gaze up to meet his, I look him properly in the eye for the first time. I feel a sudden tightening in my chest, a strange mixture of emotions rushing to the surface. Love, relief, but also fear.

Despite everything he's said, I'm frightened. I'm frightened that now he knows what happened with Zeph, he's going to think differently of me.

I steel myself, nod. 'Part of the reason I've been worried about getting in touch wasn't just your job. I was scared . . . scared of what you'd think of me. If you'd see me like we used to see Mum.' I search his face, then search again, looking for some kind of echo of what I saw back then, but there's nothing. No judgement.

'I never believed that,' Penn says fiercely. 'With Mum at the beginning maybe, because of how Dad messed with our minds, but not now, never you.'

As he leans across and takes my hand, I feel the hard kernel of fear that's lived inside me for so long start to dissolve. 'There's something I wanted to give you,' I say. 'Ever since I knew you were here.' With his hand still in mine, I rummage in the drawer with the other, pass him a piece of paper. A piece of paper that's been by my side ever since I drew it that night. 'I made this in case anything happened to me. Places I hoped you'd take Etta in the future.'

Letting go of my hand, he unfolds it, takes a sudden pull of breath. 'A map ... It's beautiful, Kier.'

This map is in pencil – black and white – and less finished than the others, but I've tried to put everything on there. Everything that matters. 'It's not a map of one particular place, like the others, it's all of them, combined. All the places that are really special to me.' I run my finger over the paper. 'That's the cove where we learnt to swim. The bonfire field. Some of them are places from other maps I've sent you. Sri Lanka. France.'

Penn doesn't say anything for a minute, then blinks. 'When you're better, we can do these together. Take Etta.'

'We can, but it's my last map, I think, for a while.'

'You're not going to do any more?'

I shake my head. 'Making this one ... it felt ... different. I wanted to do it for you, in case something happened to me, but that urge I've always felt to make them ... it's gone.' I look at him. 'Do you remember you asked me before your wedding why I couldn't settle?'

He nods.

'What I told you . . . it wasn't quite true. I think all the travelling I did was a way of running, you know, running from what I thought I might become.'

'The monster's daughter?' His voice is barely a whisper.

'Yeah, and I think I was looking for something too.' I run a finger across the map. 'I think I was looking for the happiness we had on that first map. The happiness we had because we were with Mum. The Mum before it all happened.'

Penn steeples his fingers, presses the tips together so hard the ends turn white.

'I think every place I've mapped since has been a way of trying to find her again, the Mum before she did what she did.' I struggle to keep my voice steady. 'Part of me thought that if I looked hard enough, she might be out there somewhere, Penn, but I could never find her, never find that happiness again.'

'Kier, we should have talked about it. I didn't realise—'

'I know, but it doesn't matter, because I get it now. Mum . . . she was there all along, wasn't she? I just had to pluck up the courage to see her.'

His eyes slowly trace my face. 'You were . . .' – he hesitates, as if looking for the right word – 'frightened to, before, weren't you?'

'Yeah.' There's a catch in my throat. 'But since I've been out here, I'm not any more. I know the monster wasn't inside Mum any more than it was in me. It was in them, wasn't it? Dad, and Zeph.'

An expression flits across Penn's face that I can't decipher: something like hope and fear, combined. 'I knew you were struggling with that, but it wasn't just the whole monster thing, was it?' he says carefully. 'You blocked Mum out because of what she did, in prison. Taking her own life.'

I know where he's going with those words, and for the first time ever, I don't shut him down. Block him out.

'Yeah, I did. I always thought she chose to leave us, Penn, but it wasn't a choice, I get that now.' I hesitate. 'One of the places I painted on the map Elin found was a waterfall in the park called Suicide Falls. One day, I was chatting to someone there whose brother had committed suicide. They told me they'd read a book describing what it felt like to want to take your own life. It said . . .' I try to keep my voice level. 'It said something like *no one leaps to their death from a burning building by choice. The person jumps because the flames are worse, a terror way beyond falling.*'

He visibly swallows. 'That's a good way of looking at it.'

'And you know, that night, after I spoke to him, I dreamt of Mum for the first time in ages.' I clear my throat. 'I realised then that I can stop looking, Penn. I can stop looking because she's always been there. Everywhere we go.'

His throat bobs again, and he's quiet for a minute before he says, 'Does that mean you're not going to travel any more?'

I nod. 'One day, I want to go with you and Etta to all those places on the map, but for now, I want to stay put for a bit.'

Hope flares, clear now, in his eyes. 'Back in Devon?'

'Yeah,' I say after a beat. 'Back in Devon. You and me and Etta.'

As he puts his hand over mine, I think about what Zeph used to say to me.

We're going to fly, Kier. You and me, we're going to fly.

I don't need to fly, I think, looking at Penn. In fact, it's the last thing I want to do.

I want to settle, feel the soil grow warm beneath my feet. Stay a while.

98

Elin

Clínica de recuperação, Portugal,
October 2021

'Thanks for coming. I wasn't sure you'd make it.'

Elin glances up to see Steed walking down the steps from the clinic towards her.

A cool breeze sends her hair dancing about her face, momentarily obscuring him, but when she pushes it away to get a proper look at him, she senses a change. Though he still looks tired, drawn, the wild skittishness of the past week or so is gone.

There's a softness to him that brings to mind the old Steed. The Steed who was one of her closest friends.

Memories flicker to life in her head – the two of them poring over notes in the office, splayed on the sofa together in her flat. Hours spent in their local café, heads bent close over coffee. Little moments that turned strangers into friends.

Elin finds herself faltering, mouth caught somewhere between a grimace and a smile. 'I wanted to see her, after everything.' She gestures towards the blocky shape of the clinic. 'How is she?'

'Better than I thought.' A brief light appears in Steed's eyes.

'Don't think it's going to be long before she's out. Still got some more rehab, but she's getting there.'

'I'm glad.'

An uneasy silence falls between them, broken only by a motorbike growling past them, the exhaust loudly misfiring as it reaches the end of the road.

'Kier . . .' he starts and then stops, heat creeping up his cheeks.

'I'm not going to tell Kier about what you did, if that's what you're wondering,' Elin says quickly, noticing his awkwardness. 'I'm guessing she probably couldn't cope with any more. Not right now.'

Steed's face constricts as he shifts from foot to foot. 'That's not what I was going to say. It's up to you what you tell her. None of that's my call.' He exhales. 'I just wanted to say a proper thank you. To you and to Isaac. For everything you did. How you helped find her . . . It means everything to have her back, Elin. Etta too.' The light appears in his eyes again as he says Etta's name.

'You don't have to thank me. I wanted to do it, for Kier.' It's the truth. She could now lay that nagging guilt to rest, the sense that she'd somehow failed Kier, in not getting back to her.

'I know, and for what it's worth, I'm sorry, again. Sorry for it all.' Steed's eyes are shining with emotion. 'No excuses this time. No caveats. How I behaved, it was shitty, inexcusable, and I'm sorry.'

Though he's trying to keep his expression neutral, a flicker of it is there – what she'd glimpsed up at the clearing – hope. A part of him is still clinging to the idea that she'll accept his apology. That it will open up a route to them becoming friends again.

In all honesty, Elin can't say that the same route hadn't, however briefly, crossed her mind.

These past few days she'd thought about it a lot, and with the initial raw outrage dulled a little, her feelings weren't quite as clear-cut as before. While she was still struggling with what he'd done, she felt she was starting to understand parts of what may have triggered it.

But now, with him stood just a few feet away from her, it's clear that kind of sentiment is one thing in theory, but very different in practice. Forgiveness is an easier concept to grapple with at a distance. Seeing him is dredging everything back up. Not just what he'd done to her, to Isaac, but how much she'd once cared for him.

The enormity of what they'd lost.

Her cheeks are burning, her mouth dry. Panic flares: she's not ready for this, not for any kind of rapprochement.

'Look, I'd better go. Don't want to miss visiting hours.' Making a fuss of checking her watch, Elin starts to walk past him.

Steed nods, a sadness in his eyes. 'You take care, okay?'

'You too.' Striding towards the clinic, Elin can sense his gaze on her, but she doesn't turn.

Eyes fixed straight ahead, she keeps on walking up the steps, head held high. No looking back.

99

Elin

Lights are coming on one by one in the village on the opposite side of the valley, little pinpricks of glow appearing against the shadow of the hills. The sun is sinking below the mountains beyond, the blue of the sky above just tipping into pastel.

It's Elin's favourite time of day in the park; when the land quietened, drew breath, let go of the day gone by.

It's getting properly cold, though, she thinks, zipping up her jacket. Mornings and evenings now feel sharp-edged, inhospitable. Autumn's bedding in. Making its mark.

It felt like the right time to leave. Not just the park, but the situation with Kier. Resolution, of a kind: Kier had decided to speak to the Portuguese police and cooperate.

To Elin, it was clear that she'd been acting in self-defence, but the onus would be on her to prove it. The justice system worked differently here: Kier would be put up in front of a judge who would assess the evidence and make the final call.

Her thoughts move to the camp. Their situation was more complicated. Getting rid of Zeph's body at the falls would be an unlawful burial in the UK and probably illegal here too. Until the police confirmed it wasn't murder, they'd potentially be seen as accessories as well. Things had been muddied further by Ned and Maggie sending messages from Zeph and Kier's phones – effectively impersonating them. She had no idea how that would be seen here.

Elin wouldn't be surprised if the camp moved on before it went any further. Part of her hoped they did. Despite the job, her moral obligations, cases like this had so many grey areas. No definite rights or wrongs.

'So ... last day.' Isaac squeezes in beside her, breaking her reverie. 'How are you feeling, about going back? All this going on, we haven't really checked in.'

Elin picks up her drink, thinking for a moment. Among the craziness of the past week, it's something she hasn't really considered, not properly.

'Good,' she says finally. 'It feels like I can just ... be, for the first time. You were right, you know, what you said the other day. Just because something's hard, doesn't mean it isn't progress. After all this time, it's like I can actually' – she stops, trying to find the right words – 'like I can actually see myself.'

'And what do you see?' he asks softly.

'Someone I like. Someone human. Flawed.' Elin takes a sip of beer. 'But someone who's always relied on other people for her happiness. That's been the toughest pill to swallow, I think. I thought that by leaving Will, I'd taken a step forwards, but I'd just come to rely on Steed instead.' She shrugs. 'That's the thing I still need to work on. Being happy on my own.'

Isaac takes a long pull of his own beer. 'To be honest, I think that's something most people struggle with.'

'Even you?'

He nods. 'All the time. I reckon it's the hardest thing to wrap your head around – being comfortable in your own company.'

They sit for a minute, lost in their own thoughts.

'And how do you feel about the whole Steed thing?' Isaac asks after a beat. 'Now you've seen him?'

'Still can't stop thinking about how close he got, at the camp, to doing serious damage to Ned.' Elin stares into the distance. 'Makes you wonder if that kind of violence is in everyone given the right circumstances.' She pauses. 'I reckon people probably hold a whole lot more inside than we ever realise. Good, bad, everything in between.'

'You think that's the case with him?'

'Yeah. I think he probably *did* mean what he said, about the friendship being real. That most of the time, who he was with me was genuine, and somehow, that part of him was somehow able to exist quite happily alongside the person who sent those shitty messages.'

Isaac nods, his expression conflicted.

'Are you thinking about your friendship with him?' Elin asks.

'Yeah.' His voice is raw. 'Same as you, just wonder how much of it was real. I keep thinking back about everything I told him. About me ... Laure.'

'I get it,' she says quietly. 'And how's all that going now?'

'I don't know ...' Isaac shrugs. 'Not much has changed, the grief, I mean, but I think *this* has been good, even with everything that's happened. Getting away, with you.'

As the conversation lapses, they sit together in silence, spend a while looking out as the night closes in around them. The sun had dipped completely behind the hills now, casting the valley into deep shadow.

'I'm going to miss this place,' Elin says quietly. 'It's funny, when we first arrived, I saw the park as something dark, malevolent even, but I've done a complete one-eighty. Being out here . . . it feels like I can breathe again.'

He nods. 'I know what you mean. Makes me think about Kier's maps. When Steed first showed me, I didn't get it, not properly, but now I reckon there *are* places that make you really feel something.' He looks out. 'I think it's not just the place, sometimes it's about who you're with when you're there.'

'Probably.' Elin smiles. She hadn't thought about it that way: people and place combined.

Isaac tips his head sideways to look at her. 'So what would you put on your map, if you had to do one? No thinking it over. First place that comes to mind. Right now.'

Tracing the path of a bird swooping low overhead, Elin thinks. 'Here,' she says. 'First place would be here.'

'The park?'

'No . . . well, yes, but a bit more precise than that. I was thinking more about this spot, right here.'

A silence falls, suddenly thick between them. There's so much more she wants to say: about them, their past, her hopes for the future, but she can't quite find the words.

'Me too,' he says finally. 'You and me . . . it's better, isn't it?'

Elin nods, his words summing it up better than hers ever could. It was better.

For the first time in a long time, things felt easy between them. It just *was*, as real and present as the trees and the sky. No sense of something missing or even something found.

Shuffling her chair closer, she lays her head against his shoulder.

His jacket smells like him: like family. Like coming home.

Side by side, they look out over the valley, watching the bird above them doing nothing, going nowhere, turning imperfect circles, wheeling carelessly through the sky.

Acknowledgements

Sometimes, when you are writing, you are lucky enough to have a character come to you almost fully formed, and this was the case with the character of Kier Templer. I couldn't wait to tell her story in *The Wilds* and bring to life the unique maps she creates to make sense of the world, but none of it would have come to pass without my family and my beautiful hometown here in Devon.

Like Kier, there are so many places in Devon where I've left little pieces of my soul, and every one of these are special to me because of the times I've spent with my family there. Thank you so much to all my loved ones for helping to make those memories. I'm looking forward to many more to come.

This book is also the final instalment of this part of Elin's story; she is another character very close to my heart. Weaving Elin's and Kier's story together proved a challenging task and one I don't think would have been possible without an expert team to help refine and shape that story. A huge thank you to my brilliant editors in the UK, Lucy Malagoni and Tilda Key, at Sphere, Little, Brown, for tackling this task with aplomb. Their thoughtful and intelligent editing and their unerring eye for detail at every stage of the process helped to make Elin's and Kier's story the absolute best it could be. Their enthusiasm for the book from the first draft and their ability to see the 'big picture' has made every part of the editing process a pleasure. A special mention also has to go to Jane Cavolina for her immense skill with the copyediting process. How you hone the book and make it shine to perfection is something I'll always be in awe of.

A book goes through so many stages to become what you see on the shelf and I wanted to thank Zoe Carroll and Tom Webster for their amazing work in proofreading and production to ensure the book is refined and presented in the best way possible.

Another huge thank you to Celeste Ward-Best, Stephanie Melrose and Niamh Anderson, whose hard work in marketing and publicity ensures that the book finds its way into as many readers' hands as possible. With so many books being published, it takes such talent and dedication to make sure a book is seen, and I couldn't be more grateful.

The art of designing a cover is something that never fails to astound me, and the cover of *The Wilds* works on so many levels to capture the words inside – a big thank you to Sean Garrehy at Little, Brown for his wonderful interpretation of the book.

Further afield, thanks to my Portuguese publisher, Porto Editora, and Ana Luísa, my Portuguese editor, who were a constant source of information for the novel.

I want to say another thank you to Reese's Book Club for all their continued support – having *The Sanatorium* selected as a Reese's Book Club pick allowed my books to find such a brilliant audience, and I will always be grateful.

Thanks as always to my wonderful agent, Charlotte Seymour, for her support and hard work on all my books – I'm so looking forward to continuing this exciting journey together. Another big thank you has to go to Helene Butler at Johnson & Alcock for her work on foreign rights, helping the book be read in so many countries. Seeing the foreign editions of all my novels always feels like a dream come true and I'm so thankful.

I also want to thank Sue Cade for her invaluable PR assistance locally and Sue Davies for her continued support.

As is always the case, there are a host of people who have helped with the details of the book.

In *The Wilds*, emotional abuse and coercive control is a key theme, and I wanted to say a huge thank you to the charity Refuge in the UK (www.refuge.org.uk) and both Sarah Berry-Valentine and Rebecca Bond. You gave me such invaluable insights into so many aspects of this insidious form of abuse, all of which helped shape *The Wilds*. Thank you for reading an early draft.

During the research, I couldn't have met more helpful people, from the Gerês Police and boat team to the Forest Rangers and Joel Pereira. The park described in the book isn't directly based on any particular national park in Portugal: much of my research and time was spent in and around Gerês and the national park there has fuelled much of my inspiration, but ultimately I have taken some fictional liberties and this isn't meant to be an accurate depiction of any particular park.

Dr Tod Guest, a family friend and local A&E consultant, helped explain the medical side in technicolour and 4K detail: everything now seems dangerous! Thank you to Stuart Gibbon, who has helped me from the start, and again had all the details to hand when asked, especially around extradition. Any factual errors or inaccuracies in police procedure are either my error or to fit the story. A serving officer helped with some of the 'explosive' details – you know who you are and thank you. James Normington, barrister, confidant, and family friend, keeps everything above board, and one day you will rewarded with a curry as promised!

All the booksellers who champion my work are also very

411

close to my heart – thank you especially to Matt at Ivybridge Bookshop, Emily and Tanya at Waterstones Torquay, and the teams at Waterstones Newton Abbot and Waterstones Yeovil. Hearing you talk about the books with such enthusiasm is such a highlight of every publication experience, and I'm so grateful to you for recommending all the books to your customers and readers.

Another massive thank you to my friends and family who see me through thick and thin, my daughters for supplying endless supplies of chocolate and coffee and putting up with my questions on plot, and to my husband, James, for supporting me at every step and being the best sounding board an author could ask for. FTB!

One of the biggest thank yous of all must go to my readers. Places and settings in general are hugely important to me and my writing, and I've always wanted to write a book that explores the emotional hold that certain places have on all our hearts. When I asked my readers to share some of their special places in the early stages of writing, I was lucky enough to discover that I'm not the only one who finds place so important, and I was deeply moved by the responses. A big thank you to everyone who entrusted me with their 'favourite' places and memories; they have guided me, and some have even made it into these pages. I couldn't be more grateful. On publication, I look forward to hearing more of my reader's special places from all over the world.

Author note

Dear Reader,

The books I write are thrillers, but they also have intense relationships at their heart – be it sibling and family relationships, romantic relationships or even those within a workplace. In my novels, I'm always looking to explore not only *how* a crime happens, but *why* people might be driven to commit that crime. The answer is often in the power struggles within these relationships, together with the unsettling idea that we might not always know the people closest to us as well as we think we do.

In *The Sanatorium* and *The Retreat*, one relationship in particular captured reader's imaginations and has become a hotly discussed topic: the relationship between my protagonist, Detective Elin Warner, and her boyfriend, Will.

While some people like their relationship dynamic, others see Will in a negative light: picking up on elements of gaslighting and control within their relationship among other things.

This perception emphasised to me not only how powerful fiction can be in raising issues that readers identify with, but how complex relationships are in general.

Mulling over past relationships of my own and of friends, I realised I could recognise in some of them elements of the control issues people saw between Elin and Will. I never thought about this as a problem at the time because of the general lack of awareness and understanding of coercive control.

I think I, like many women, have experienced moments where something 'crosses the line' but because of your age, the power dynamic within the relationship, or your past vulnerabilities, you either ignore it or make excuses for it.

The more I researched the topic of emotional abuse and coercive control with the help of the charity Refuge, the more I realised how widespread it is and how it is rapidly evolving as a form of abuse. As technology has developed, there are many more ways someone can control someone within a relationship – from geo-location tracking on people's devices through to Internet of Things (IoT) home security systems such as smart doorbells and digitally tracking a partner's expenditure.

To me, that's exactly why this insidious form of abuse is so frightening – it can manifest in so many ways and I think as women, often we are conditioned to 'people please' and not see these red flags for exactly what they are.

I really wanted *The Wilds* to explore a relationship like this, to show how multi-faceted this form of abuse can be, how it can escalate and to highlight how a relationship that seems on the surface to be very 'loving' can actually be anything but.

The crime in *The Wilds* is as much of a 'why dunnit' as a 'who dunnit' and I hope people find it interesting putting the pieces together.

Thank you for reading.

If you have been affected by, or want more information about any of the issues raised in the book regarding emotional abuse or coercive control, please visit Refuge's website: www.refuge.org.uk

A beautiful, eerie hotel in the Swiss Alps, recently
converted from an abandoned sanatorium, is the last
place Detective Elin Warner wants to be. But her estranged
brother has invited her there for his engagement party,
and she feels she has no choice but to accept.

Arriving in the midst of a threatening storm, Elin
immediately feels on edge. And things only get worse
when they wake the next morning to find her brother's
fiancée is missing. With access to the hotel cut off,
the guests begin to panic.

**But this is only the first disappearance. Everyone's
in danger – and anyone could be next . . .**

'Spine-tingling . . . A must-read' **Richard Osman**

'I absolutely loved *The Sanatorium* – it gave me all the
wintry thrills and chills' **Lucy Foley**

'An addictive, creepy and twisting read' ***Stylist***

'A chillingly vivid thriller' **T. M. Logan**

'A menacing, creepy debut [. . .] echoes of Hitchcock
and du Maurier' ***Daily Mail***

An idyllic wellness retreat has opened on an island off the coast of Devon, promising rest and relaxation – but the island itself, known locally as Reaper's Rock, has a dark past. Once the playground of a serial killer, it's rumoured to be cursed.

A woman is found dead below the yoga pavilion in what seems to be a tragic fall. But DS Elin Warner soon learns that the victim wasn't a guest – she wasn't meant to be on the island at all.

The longer Elin stays, the more secrets she uncovers. And when someone else drowns in a diving incident, Elin begins to suspect that the old stories about the island are true.

Because history seems to be repeating itself – and the guests might not make it home alive . . .

'An eerie, atmospheric thriller that will have you looking over your shoulder as you read' **Ashley Audrain**

'Full of foreboding and high-stakes tension, Sarah Pearse's latest is a page-turner. The past doesn't stay buried for long, at sea or on land, and what comes to the surface is both shocking and chilling' **Nita Prose**

'Atmospheric and hold-your-breath tense with cleverly executed twists and a finale that gave me the chills. Brilliant!' **Claire Douglas**